EX LIBRIS

VINTAGE CLASSICS

THE FAR COUNTRY

Nevil Shute Norway was born on 17 January 1899 in Ealing, London. After attending the Dragon School and Shrewsbury School, he studied Engineering Science at Balliol College, Oxford. He worked as an aeronautical engineer and published his first novel, *Marazan*, in 1926. In 1931 he married Frances Mary Heaton and they went on to have two daughters. During the Second World War he joined the Royal Navy Volunteer Reserve where he worked on developing secret weapons. After the war he continued to write and settled in Australia where he lived until his death on 12 January 1960. His most celebrated novels include *Pied Piper* (1942), *No Highway* (1948), *A Town Like Alice* (1950) and *On the Beach* (1957).

OTHER WORKS BY NEVIL SHUTE

Novels

Marazan

So Disdained

Lonely Road

Ruined City

What Happened to the Corbetts

An Old Captivity

Landfall

Pied Piper

Pastoral

Most Secret

The Chequer Board

No Highway

A Town Like Alice

Round the Bend

In the Wet

Requiem for a Wren

Beyond the Black Stump

On the Beach

The Rainbow and the Rose

Trustee from the Toolroom

Stephen Morris and *Pilotage*

Autobiography

Slide Rule

NEVIL SHUTE

The Far Country

VINTAGE BOOKS
London

Published by Vintage 2009

5

First published by William Heinemann in 1952

Vintage
Random House, 20 Vauxhall Bridge Road,
London SW1V 2SA

www.vintage-classics.info

Addresses for companies within The Random House Group Limited can be found at: www.randomhouse.co.uk/offices.htm

The Random House Group Limited Reg. No. 954009

A CIP catalogue record for this book
is available from the British Library

ISBN 9780099530039

The Random House Group Limited supports The Forest Stewardship Council (FSC), the leading international forest certification organisation. All our titles that are printed on Greenpeace approved FSC certified paper carry the FSC logo. Our paper procurement policy can be found at: www.rbooks.co.uk/environment

Printed and bound in Great Britain by
CPI Antony Rowe, Chippenham and Eastbourne

Into my heart an air that kills
From yon far country blows:
What are those blue remembered hills,
What spires, what farms are those?

That is the land of lost content,
I see it shining plain,
The happy highways where I went
And cannot come again.

From The Collected Poems *of A. E. Housman, published by Messrs. Jonathan Cape Ltd., and reproduced by permission of The Society of Authors.*

One

TIM ARCHER got into the utility and drove it from the Banbury Feed and General Supply Pty. Ltd., down the main street of the town. The car was a 1946 Chevrolet, somewhat battered by four years of station use, a sturdy practical vehicle with a coupé front seat and an open truck body behind. In this rear portion he was carrying a forty-four-gallon drum of Diesel oil, four reels of barbed wire, a can of kerosene, a sack of potatoes, a coil of new sisal rope, a carton of groceries, and a miscellaneous assortment of spades and jacks and chains that seldom left the truck. He drove down the long tree-shaded main street, broad as Whitehall and lined with wooden stores and bungalows widely spaced, and stopped at the post office.

He was a lad of twenty-two with a broad, guileless face, with yellow hair and blue eyes, and a fair, bronzed skin. He thought and moved rather slowly; if you disliked the Victorian countryside you would have said that he looked rather like a sheep, one of the sheep he spent his life in tending. His father had escaped from country life to Melbourne at an early age and had become a solicitor; Tim Archer had been sent to Melbourne Grammar School. In turn, he had escaped from city life when he was seventeen, and he had gone to learn the business of sheep upon a station at Wodonga in the north part of the state. Now he was working for Jack Dorman on a property called Leonora, twelve miles out from Banbury, and near a place called Merrijig. Leonora was hardly to be classed as a sheep station, being only eighteen hundred acres, and Merrijig was hardly to be classed as a place, being only a school and a little wooden pub and a bridge over the river. He had been at Leonora for three years, largely because he was in love in a slow, patient manner with the youngest daughter of the house, Angela Dorman. He did not see much of her because she was away at Melbourne University taking Social Studies. He wrote to her from time to time, simple, rather laboured letters about lambing and floods and bush fires and horses. She answered about one in three of these letters, because the country bored her stiff.

He got out of the utility, a big young man dressed in a check shirt open at the neck, a pair of soiled blue canvas working trousers stained and dirty from the saddle, and heavy country boots. He went into the post office and said to the girl at the counter, "I'll take the letters for Leonora." The mail delivery would not reach the station till late afternoon.

1

The girl said, "Morning, Tim." She handed him a bundle from the stacked table behind her. "Going to the dance on Saturday?"

"I dunno," he said. "I haven't got a partner."

"Go on," she chaffed him. "You don't need a partner. There'll be more girls there than men."

"Where have all the girls sprung up from?"

"I don't know," she said idly. "There seem to be a lot of girls about the town just now. Mostly New Australians. They've got two new girls at the hospital—ward-maids. Lithuanians they are, I think."

"I don't speak Lithuanian," the young man said. "Aussie's good enough for me—Aussie or English. Like cartridges for a twenty-two. The continental stuff's no good." He shuffled through the letters, looking for the one that was not there. "That all there are? Nothing for me?"

"Not unless it's there," she said with a touch of sympathy. "That's all there were for Leonora."

"Okay." He stood in silence for a moment while his mind changed topic. "I'll have to see about the dance," he said. "I don't know that I'll be able to get in."

"Come if you can," she said. "There's one or two Aussie girls'll be there, in among the New Australians." He smiled slowly. "They're having favours—paper caps, balloons, and all that."

"I'll have to see what Jack says. He may be using the utility." He turned to go. " 'Bye."

He went out and got into the utility and drove out of the town upon the road to Merrijig that led on to the lumber camps up at Lamirra in the forests of Mount Buller. It was October, and the spring sun was warm as he drove, but the grass was still bright green and the upland pastures were fresh and beautiful. There were wattle trees in flower still, great splashes of yellow colour on the darker background of the gum-tree forests, and the gum trees themselves were touched with the reddish brown of the young shoots, making them look a little like an English wood in autumn. Tim Archer did not fully realise the beauty of the scene, the wide sunny pastures and the woods that merged into the blue mountains to the south and east, because this was where he lived and worked and scenery like that was normal to his life. He only knew that this was where he liked to be, far better than the town.

He was depressed as he drove out of town because he hadn't had a letter from Angela, as he had so often been depressed before. He was sufficiently intelligent to know that his chance of getting Angela was slender, because she liked town life and hated the country, while he was exactly the reverse. He comforted himself with the opinion that all girls were like that when they were young; they talked big about getting a job in Melbourne and doing interior decoration and

2

going on a business trip to England, but in the end most of them came home and married and settled down in the district. He'd have to sit tight and let Angie get it out of her system, but it was going to be a long job, and the thought depressed him.

The property he worked on, Leonora, borders the road for about half a mile at Merrijig. From there the boundary of Leonora runs for a mile up the Delatite River, then up to the wooded foothills of Mount Buller, and then in a great sweep eastwards to the road again. It is a good, well-watered property of eighteen hundred acres carrying two sheep to the acre with some beef cattle. The homestead lies half a mile from the road, a small bungalow built of weatherboard with an iron roof and with verandas on three sides; there is a stockyard near the homestead and a few outbuildings. It is reached from the road by a rough, pot-holed track across the paddocks with three gates to open. Jack Dorman had occupied the property for eighteen years, first as manager and later as the owner by the courtesy of the Bank of New South Wales.

He was sitting on his horse that morning by the road gate waiting for Tim Archer to come out of town in the utility. The horse was a rough pony, an unkempt, long-haired bay that lived out in the paddock and was never under cover, and never groomed, and seldom fed. His property was about three miles long and a mile wide, and though it was possible to drive over most of it in the utility, Jack Dorman preferred to ride over it on horseback every morning. As Tim came over the crest of a small hill he saw his boss sitting waiting for him at the road gate, and he wondered a little; the rider moved the pony up to the road gate and hooked it open for the car to enter. Tim stopped the car just inside the gate, and Dorman reined up alongside.

"Get the letters?" he enquired.

"I got them here, Mr. Dorman," the lad said, and handed up the bundle from the seat beside him.

Dorman took them, and sat on his horse looking through the envelopes. He was fifty-eight years old, but he had never strained his eyes with a great deal of reading, and he could still read small print without glasses. He took one letter from the bundle and put it in the breast pocket of his khaki shirt; on that warm day he wore no coat. He gave the rest of the letters back to Tim Archer, who wondered what the one letter was about.

"Take them into the house," his boss said. "Get all the rest of the stuff?"

"Not the engine oil. They hadn't got any drums, not till next week's delivery. They said I could have quart cans, but it costs more that way. I went along to the garage and had the sump checked, but she only took a pint. She's in good nick."

"Don't ever go buying oil less than five gallons a time," the rider said. "Daylight robbery. There's another thing you want to watch. They'll try to kid you that you want an oil change every thousand

3

miles, and that's a quid or so. Two thousand miles is what it says in the book. My word, you want to watch those jokers."

"I never let them change the oil unless you say."

"That's right. Go down and give Mario a hand out with the crutching. I'm going up to the top end."

The lad drove on, and Jack Dorman walked his pony up-hill across his pastures, heading for the highest part, where the uncleared virgin bush bordered his land on the slope of the mountain. There were no sheep in the paddocks that he crossed because most of them were in the paddocks nearer to the homestead, where Mario Ritti, his Italian man, was skilfully heaving each sheep up on to a waist-high board upon its back, holding it with shoulders and elbow while he sheared the soiled wool from its tail, gave it a dab of disinfectant, and put it on the ground again. It was heavy work, but he could do them at the rate of about one a minute, or more quickly with Tim Archer helping him, but even so it would take a fortnight to work the crutching through.

Dorman rode across the top paddock to where a rocky outcrop and a few gum trees made a place to sit in the shade, a place from which you could look out over the whole valley of the Delatite. He could see most of his property from there, and the winding river with the road bridge over it, and the Hunt Club Hotel, and the track from the road to the homestead through his paddocks, and the homestead itself, small, red-roofed, and insignificant in the great panorama. He sat upon his horse, contented, looking out over all this for a minute; then he dismounted and tethered the pony to the fence by the reins. He crossed to the rocky outcrop and sat down in the shade, and opened his letter.

It was a note of account from his agent in Melbourne, a long typescript sheet covered with figures which itemised the lot numbers of the wool sold for him at auction and the price paid for each lot. A cheque was enclosed in settlement for twenty-two thousand one hundred and seventy-eight pounds, eight shillings and twopence.

He had known beforehand approximately what the sum would be, from watching the sales in the newspaper. Last year's wool cheque had been over ten thousand pounds, and the year before that about seven thousand, figures which had seemed amazing to him in their day. Those cheques, however, had meant little to him in terms of spending money; they had gone straight into the bank in reduction of the loans upon his property and stock. They had purchased his security, but nothing tangible. This time, however, it was different; this twenty-two thousand pounds was his own money, to spend or save exactly as he wished, after the tax was paid.

Jack Dorman had come to Leonora as manager in 1930, when times were bad and wool was less than two shillings a pound. Before that he had been manager of stations in Gippsland and in the Benalla district, and before that again, for six years after the first

4

war, he had been a traveller in agricultural machinery and fertilisers. In 1932 his wife's father had died at his English country home at Sutton Bassett, near Wantage, and with her legacy the Dormans had managed to buy Leonora with the very maximum assistance from the bank. Since then they had been deep in debt, head over ears in it. For the first four years it had been touch and go whether they would not go bankrupt, whether the bank would not have to foreclose on an unprofitable business and sell the land to liquidate the increasing overdraft. The demand for wool for uniforms had saved them as rearmament got under way and wool prices began to rise, and for the last twelve years Jack Dorman had been paying off the debt. On paper he had been gradually becoming a wealthy man, but this was hidden deep in the accountancy. The land and the stock on it had been gradually becoming his and not the bank's, but he still rose at dawn each day and got his two hired hands to work at the same time, and still Jane Dorman worked from dawn to dusk in the old-fashioned kitchen of the homestead, rearing her four children and cooking all the meals for the three men, and eating with them at the long kitchen table. In all those years she had had no help in the house, and she had only been away from Leonora three times for a week's holiday. They had had no electricity till two years previously, when Dorman had put in a little Diesel plant. Now she was tired and old and grey at fifty-three, and the children were all out in the world except Angela, and they were rich.

Jack Dorman sat turning the wool cheque over in his hands, twenty-two thousand one hundred and seventy-eight pounds, eight shillings and twopence. Last year's cheque had virtually cleared the overdraft. His balance fluctuated a good deal, but, broadly speaking, if he had died last year the whole of the money from the sale of land and stock would have gone to his heirs, a matter of eighty or ninety thousand pounds at the inflated prices of the time. It was an academic figure to him, because neither he nor Jane would have wanted to leave Leonora; they had grown into the place and it had become a part of them. The eighty thousand pounds was quite unreal to them; if it was there at all it only concerned the children, and they might not touch a quarter of it if the bad times came again. All that concerned Jack Dorman and his wife was that last year's cheque had made them safe; however much wool slumped they could never be turned out of Leonora. They could sleep without bad dreams of wandering bankrupt with no home, nightmares that had plagued them through their thirty-two years of married life.

Jack Dorman folded the wool cheque and put it in his shirt pocket again; this one was his own. He sat on in the shade for a few minutes looking out over his property, a grey-haired, heavy man of fifty-eight, humming a little tune. He had little musical appreciation but he liked the lighter programmes on the radio; he was normally five years behind the times with the tunes that pleased him and stayed in his memory. If Jane had heard him she would have known that her stout, ageing husband was very happy.

> I don't want her, you can have her,
>   She's too fat for me,
>   She's too fat for me,
>   Oh, she's too fat for me . . .

Twenty-two thousand pounds and a bit, and the fat lambs, and the bullocks—say twenty-six thousand pounds in all. Expenses, and income tax. . . . He drew a stub of pencil from his pocket and began figuring on the back of the wool cheque envelope. He'd whoop up his expenses this year, my word he would! He'd have to see his accountant to find out what he could get away with. He ought to have a new utility, a Mercury or an Armstrong Siddeley even. A station like this needed a Land Rover. He'd keep the Chev for the boys to use. Buildings—Mario ought to have a house and get his girl out from Italy; he'd be more settled then. Could a weatherboard shack go on the one year, or would they make him do it on depreciation? If it went on the one year the tax would pay three-quarters of the cost . . .

> I go dizzy—
>   I go dumbo—
>   When I'm dancing,
>   With my jum—jum—jumbo . . .

Say twenty thousand for tax. He figured with his pencil. He'd have about seven thousand left after paying tax. Seven thousand pounds of his own money to spend or save that year, and the price of wool still holding nicely. He was in the money, for the first time in his life.

There must be something that the station needed, besides a Land Rover, and a new utility and a house for Mario. . . .

Presently he got on to his horse again and rode down to the homestead, humming his little tune. In the yard he unsaddled and hung saddle and bridle on a rail of the hay-barn, gave the pony a slap behind and turned it into the house paddock. Then he went into the kitchen and sat down at the long table. Jane was roasting a saddle of mutton for dinner as she had cooked mutton most days of her married life; they ate a sheep in about ten days.

"Want a cup of tea?" she asked.

"I don't mind," he said, and she poured him one out from the teapot on the table. And then he told her, "Got the wool cheque."

"How much?" she asked idly.

"Little over twenty-two thousand," he told her.

She was only mildly interested. "That's a bit more than last year, isn't it?"

"Aye."

She said, "Like to peel these potatoes for me, if you're doing nothing?"

6

"We don't have to do anything," he told her. "Not with a wool cheque like that." But he got up and began to peel them at the sink. "You ought to have a girl to help you, make her do things like this."

"Where do you think I'd get the girl from?" And then she asked, "How much would we have of that to spend, after paying tax and expenses?"

"About seven thousand, near as I can figure it." He scraped away at the potatoes. "It's all ours this time. What do you want out of it?"

She stared around the kitchen. "I want a Memory Tickler like Bertha Harrison's got, one of those things you hang upon the wall, with a long list of things to get in town, and tabs to turn over to remind you. She got hers in Melbourne, at McEwens."

"That's only about five bob's worth," he complained.

"I know, but I want it. Could we have a new stove, Jack? This one's about worn out, and the top plate's cracked."

"We'd better have an Aga, or an Esse."

"You've got to have coke for those," she said. "A wood stove's best out here, and only about a tenth the money. Another one like this would be all right."

He said, "Aw, look, Jane, we've got money to spend now."

The anxious years had bitten deep into her. "No need to chuck it away, though," she said.

"We wouldn't be chucking it away. It'ld be cooler in the kitchen with a stove like that. It's time we spent a bit of money, anyway; my word, we haven't had a holiday for years. What do you say if we go down to Melbourne for a week and do a bit of shopping, stay at the Windsor and see some theatres? I've got a lot of things I'd like to do down there."

"I've not got any clothes for staying in a place like that," she said.

"We'll get some," he replied. "After all, we've got seven thousand pounds to spend."

"We won't have long, if you go on like this."

"We don't want to have it long. If we hang on to the money it'll only go to the kids after our time, and they'll have enough to spoil them, anyhow. I don't hold with leaving kids a lot of money. We never had any, and we got through."

She poured herself a cup of tea and he left the sink and came and sat at the table with her. "I'd like to go to Melbourne for a week," she said thoughtfully, "if we've really got the money. When was it we went down there last?"

"Two years ago," he said. "When we took Angie to the University."

"Is it as long as that? Well, I suppose it would be. I wouldn't want to go before the Show." The Banbury Show was in the middle of December; she always competed in the Flower section and in the Home-Made Cakes, and usually won a prize in both. "And then

7

there's Christmas," she said. "Everybody's on holiday till the middle of January."

He nodded. "Suppose we booked a room for a week about the middle of January?"

She smiled. "I'd like that, Jack. Give me time to get some clothes made up. I couldn't go to the Windsor with what I've got now."

He pulled a packet of cigarettes out of his pocket and passed it across to her; she took one and he lit it for her, and for a while they sat smoking in silence. "We could do a lot of things," he said. "We could make that trip home."

In their hard early married life a trip home to England had been her great desire, always to be frustrated by their circumstances. She was English, the daughter of an admiral, brought up in all the comfort and security of a small country house before the first war, and sent to a good school. In 1917 she had joined the W.A.A.C.s with a commission as was proper for the daughter of a senior naval officer, and in 1918 she had shocked her parents by falling in love with an Australian, a lieutenant in the first A.I.F. Her family never understood Jack Dorman and did everything they could to dissuade her from marrying him, and succeeded in preventing her from doing so till she was twenty-one, in 1919; she married him on her birthday. He was a ranker officer, for one thing, which in those days damned him from the start; he had been an N.C.O. in Gallipoli and in France for nearly three years, and he had only recently been commissioned. He was an unpleasantly tough young man, addicted to a strange, un-English slang, and he never pulled up men for not saluting him because he didn't believe in saluting, and said so. He used to have meals with private soldiers in cafés and in restaurants, and even drink with them; he had no idea of discipline at all. All he could do, with others like him, was to win battles.

Thirty-two years had passed since those bad months of 1918, but Jane could still remember the unpleasantness as she had rebelled against her family. She was too young, too immature to be able to stand up and state her conviction that there was solid stuff in this young man, the substance for a happy and enduring marriage; she felt that very strongly, but she could never get it out in words. She could remember as if it were yesterday her father's frigid politeness to this uncouth young officer that she had brought into the house, and his blistering contempt for him in their private talks, and her mother's futile assurances that "Daddy knows best". She had married Jack Dorman in February 1919 in Paddington a week before sailing with him to Australia, and her parents had come to the wedding, but only just. Nobody else came except one old school friend, and Aunt Ethel.

Aunt Ethel was her father's sister, Mrs. Trehearn, married to Geoffrey Trehearn, a Commissioner in the Indian Police, at that time stationed in Moulmein. Aunt Ethel had come home with her two children in 1916 to put them to school in England, and she was

8

still in England waiting for a passage back to Burma. Aunt Ethel, alone of all Jane's relations, had stood up for her and had told the family that she was making a wise choice, and she had cut little ice with her brother Tom; indeed, in some ways she had made matters worse. Admiral Sir Thomas Foxley had little regard for the sagacity of women, and to mention the woman's vote to him in those far-off days was as a red rag to a bull.

All these things passed through Jane Dorman's mind as she sat sipping her tea in the kitchen of her homestead thirty-three years later. Seven thousand pounds to spend after paying tax, all earned in one year and earned honestly; more money than her father had ever dreamed of earning, or any of her family. Extraordinary to think of, and extraordinary that after their hard life the money should mean so little to them. Jack didn't quite know what to do with it, so much was evident, and certainly she didn't.

"I don't know about going home," she said at last. "I don't believe I'd know anybody there now except Aunt Ethel, and I don't suppose I'd recognise *her* now. There was a letter from her in the post today, by the way. I'd like to see the old thing again before she dies, but she's about the only one. She must be getting on for eighty now."

"Wouldn't you like to go and see your old home?" he suggested. He knew how much her mind had turned to that small country house when first she had come to Australia.

She shook her head. "Not now that it's a school. It'ld be all different. I'd rather remember it as it used to be." Her father had kept two gardeners and a groom, and three servants in the house; she knew that nothing would now resemble the gracious, easy routine of the home that she had lived in as a child.

He did not press her; if she didn't want to go to England that was all right with him. He had only memories of a cold, unfriendly place himself, where he had been ill at ease and that he secretly disliked. He would have liked very much to go back to Gallipoli again, and to France and Italy—it would be interesting to see those. His mind turned to his Italian hired man. "There's another thing," he said. "About Mario. He's got that girl of his in this town that he comes from. I don't know how much he's got saved up now, but it might be a good thing if we could help him with her fare. It wouldn't be so much, and we might be able to charge it up against the tax. After all, it's all connected with the station."

Mario Ritti was a laughing man of about twenty-eight, tall and well built, with dark curly hair, a swarthy complexion, and a flashing eye; a peril to all the young girls in the neighbourhood. He had been taken prisoner by the Eighth Army at Bardia in 1942, and he had spent two years in England as a prisoner of war, working on a farm in Cumberland where he had learned about sheep. After the war he had got back to his own place, Chieti, a hill town in the Abruzzi mountains near the Adriatic coast where his parents

9

scratched a bare living from a tiny patch of rather barren land. In Italy there were far more people than the land could support, and Mario had put his name down almost at once for a free immigrant passage to Australia. He had worked as a labourer and as a waiter in a hotel in Pescara and as a housepainter till his turn came round upon the quota three years later and he could leave for an emptier country. By the terms of his free passage he had to work for two years as directed by the Department of Immigration in Australia, after which he would be free to choose his work like any other man. Jack Dorman had got him from the Department, and was very pleased with him, and he was anxious not to lose him at the end of the two years.

"I was thinking that we might build on to the shearers' place," he said. "Extend that on a bit towards the windmill and make a little place of three rooms there. Then if we got his girl out for him he'd be settled, and the girl could help you in the house."

Jane laughed shortly. "Fat lot of help she'd be, a girl who couldn't speak a word of English having babies every year. I'd be helping her, not her helping me. Still, if she could cook the dinner now and then, I wouldn't say no." She sat for a moment in thought. "How much is her passage going to cost, and how much has he got saved up?"

"He sends money back to Italy, to his parents," Jack said. "He was sending home five pounds a week at one time, so he can't have very much. I suppose the passage would be about fifty quid. We'd better pay that, and let him spend what he's got saved on furniture."

"Find out how much he's got," his wife said. "He ought to put in everything he's got if we're going to do all that for him."

"That's right." He pushed his chair back from the table." Like to drive into town this afternoon and put this cheque into the bank?"

She smiled; he was still very young at times. "Don't you trust the postman?"

"No," he said. "Not with twenty-two thousand pounds. A thing like that ought to be registered." He paused. "We could take a drive around," he said. "Look in on George and Ann for tea, at Buttercup."

"Giving up work?" she asked.

"That's right," he said. "Just for today."

"Who's going to get tea here for the boys if we go gallivanting off to Buttercup?"

"They can have cold tonight," he said.

"All right." She reached behind her for an envelope upon the table. "Want to read Aunt Ethel's letter?"

"Anything new in it?"

"Not really," she said slowly. "You'd better read it, though."

She tossed it across to him; he unfolded it and began to read. Jane got up and glanced at the clock and put the saucepan of potatoes on to boil, and put a couple more logs into the stove. Then she sat

10

down again and picked up the pages of the letter as Jack laid them down, and read them through again herself.

It was addressed from Maymyo, Ladysmith Avenue, Ealing, a suburb to the west of London that Jane had never seen. Till recently her old aunt had always written by air mail but lately the letters had been coming by sea mail, perhaps because there was now little urgency in any of them. Her handwriting was very bent and crabbed; at one time she had written legibly, but in the last year or two the writing had got worse and worse. The letter ran,

"MY DEAR CHILD,

"Another of your lovely parcels came today all candied peel and currants and sultanas and glacé cherries such lovely things that we do so enjoy getting just like pre-war when you could buy everything like that in the shops without any of these stupid little bits of paper and coupons and things. I get so impatient sometimes when I go to buy the rations which means I must be getting old, seventy-nine next month my dear but I don't feel like it it was rather a blow when Aggie died but I have quite got over that now and settled down again and last Friday I went out to bridge with Mrs. Morrison because it's three months now and I always say three months' mourning is enough for anyone. I'm afraid this is going to be a very long winter I do envy you your winter in our summer because it is quite cold already and now Mr. Attlee says there isn't any coal because he's sold it all to America or Jugoslavia or somewhere so there won't be any for us and now the miners and the railwaymen all want more money if only dear Winston was back at No. 10 but everybody says he will be soon."

Jane turned the pages, glancing over her old aunt's ramblings that she had already deciphered once and that were clearly giving Jack some difficulty. Aggie was Mrs. Agatha Harding who had shared the house at Ealing with her aunt; she was the widow of an army officer. Now she was dead, Jane supposed that her old aunt must be living alone, although she did not say so. The letter rambled on,

"Jennifer came down to spend the day with me one Sunday in August and she is coming again soon she has grown into such a pretty girl reddish hair and our family nose twenty-four this year she ought to have been presented at Court long ago but everything seems to be so different now and she works in an office at Blackheath the Ministry of Pensions I think. I asked her if there was a young man and she said no but I expect there is one all the same my dear I hope he's as nice a one as Jack I often think of that time when you were so naughty and ran off and married him and Tom was so angry and how right you were only I wish you didn't have to live so far away."

Jane wished she didn't live so far away as she read that. It might be worth while to make the long journey back to England just to see this kind old lady again, who still thought of her as a child.

11

"It seems so funny to think of you over fifty and with all your children out in the world and so prosperous with wool my dear I am glad for you. Our Government are so stupid about wool and everything I went the other day to Sayers to buy a warm vest for the winter but my dear the price was shocking even utility grade and the girl said it was all due to bulk buying of wool and the Socialist Government so I told her to tell Mr. Attlee he could keep it and I'd go on with what I've got my dear I do hope things are cheaper with you than they are here but I suppose you can always spin your own wool on the station and weave it can't you my grandmother always did that better than this horrible bulk buying that makes everything so dear. My dear, thank you again for all your lovely parcels and your letters write again soon and all my love.

"Your affectionate Aunt,

"ETHEL."

"Keeps it up, doesn't she?" said Jack Dorman.

"Yes," said Jane, "she keeps it up. I don't like the thought of her living alone though, at her age."

"That's since this Aggie died?"

Jane nodded. "It looks as if she's living by herself now, quite alone. I wish we were nearer."

He turned the pages of the letter back. "Who's this Jennifer she speaks about?"

"That's Jennifer Morton, her granddaughter. Her daughter Lucy married Edward Morton—the one that's a doctor in Leicester."

"Oh." He did not know where Leicester was, nor did he greatly care. "This girl Jennifer works in London, does she?"

Jane nodded. "Just outside London, I think. Blackheath."

"Well, can't she go and live with the old girl?"

"I don't know," said Jane. "I don't suppose there's much that we can do about it, anyway."

Jack Dorman went out to the yard, and Jane began to lay the kitchen table for the midday dinner. She was vaguely unhappy and uneasy; there was a menace in all the news from England now, both in the letters from her old aunt and in the newspapers. The most extraordinary things seemed to be going on there, and for no reason at all. In all her life, and it had been a hard life at times, she had never been short of all the meat that she could eat, or practically any other sort of food or fruit that she desired. As a child she could remember the great joints upon her father's table at Sutton Bassett, the kidneys and bacon for breakfast with the cold ham on the sideboard, the thick cream on the table, the unlimited butter. These things were as normal to her as the sun or the wind; even in the most anxious times of their early married life in Gippsland they had had those things as a matter of course, and never thought about them. If she didn't use them now so much it was because she was older and felt better on a sparing diet, but it was almost inconceivable to her that they should not be there for those who wanted them.

It was the same with coal; in all her life she had never had to think about economising with fuel. From the blazing fireplaces and kitchen range of Sutton Bassett she had gone to the Australian countryside, milder in climate, where everybody cooked and warmed themselves with wood fires. Even in their hardest times there had never been any question of unlimited wood for fuel. Indeed, at Merrijig with the hot sun and the high rainfall the difficulty was to keep the forest from encroaching on the paddocks; if you left a corner ungrazed for three years the bush would be five feet high all over it; in ten it would have merged back into forest. Even in the city you ordered a ton of wood as naturally as a pound of butter or a sirloin of beef.

Whatever sort of way could Aunt Ethel be living in when she could not afford a warm vest for the winter? Why *a* warm vest— why not three or four? She must do something about the washing. Was clothing rationed still? She seemed to remember that clothes rationing had been removed in England. She stopped laying the table and unfolded the letter and read the passage over again, a little frown of perplexity upon her forehead. There wasn't anything about rationing; she hadn't got the vest because it was expensive. How foolish of her; old people had to have warm clothes, especially in England in the winter. It was true that the price of woollen garments was going up even in Australia by leaps and bounds, but Aunt Ethel couldn't possibly be as hard up as that. The Foxleys had always had plenty of money. Perhaps she was going a bit senile.

She went and rang the dinner bell outside the flyscreen door, rather depressed.

The men came back to the homestead for dinner; she heard Tim and Mario washing at the basin under the tank-stand in the yard, and she began to dish up. They came in presently with Jack and sat down at the table; she carved half a pound of meat for each of them and heaped the plates high with vegetables; she gave Jack rather less and herself much less. A suet jam roll followed the meat, and cups of tea. Relaxed and smoking at the end of the meal, Tim Archer said,

"Would you be using the utility Saturday evening, Mr. Dorman? There's the Red Cross dance."

"I dunno." He turned to Jane. "Want to go to the dance on Saturday?"

It was a suggestion that had not been made to her for seven or eight years and it came strangely from Jack now, but everything was strange on this day of the wool cheque. She laughed shortly. "I don't want to go to any dance," she said. "My dancing days are done, but let the boys go if they want to."

"You going, Mario?"

The dark, curly-haired young man looked up with laughing eyes. "Si, Mr. Dorman."

"Go on," his boss grumbled. "Talk English, like a Christian. You can if you want to."

13

The young man grinned more broadly. "Yes," he said. "I like to go ver' much. I like dance much."

"I bet you do. . . ." He turned to Tim. "If you go you've got to look after him," he said. "Don't let him get in any trouble, or get girls in any trouble, either." There was some prejudice against the New Australians in the district, well founded in part, and there had been a row over Mario once before at the first dance that he attended and before he was accustomed to the social climate of Australia.

"I'll keep an eye on him, Mr. Dorman."

"All right, you can take the Chev." He paused. "Did you get the tickets?"

"Not yet. Thought I'd better wait and see about the ute."

"I'll be going down to Banbury after dinner, in about an hour. I'll get them if you give me the money."

"Thanks, Mr. Dorman." Tim hesitated. "Would you be going by the post office?"

"I could."

"Would you look in and tell Elsie Peters I'll be coming to the dance with Mario?"

Jack nodded. "I'll tell her."

Presently they got up from the table, Tim to unload the utility, Jack Dorman to go into his office, and Mario to help Jane to clear the table and wash up. A quarter of an hour later Jack Dorman, going out on the veranda, saw Mario and Tim rolling the drum of Diesel oil down from the truck on timbers to the ground. He waited till the drum was on the ground, and then said, "Hey, Mario—come over here a minute." They crossed to the paddock rail and stood together there in the warm sunlight.

"Say, Mario," he said. "I've been thinking about that girl you've got, back in Italy. You still want to get her out here to Australia?"

"Yes, Mr. Dorman. I wanta ver' much. I love Lucia. We marry when she come here."

"That's her name, is it? Lucia?"

"Yes. Lucia Tereno she is called."

"Lucia Tereno. She lives in this town that you come from, Chieti?"

"She is from Orvieto, close to Chieti, signore."

"Are you saving up to get her out here?"

"Si, signore."

"How much does the ticket cost?"

"Fifty-eight pounds."

"How much have you got saved towards it?"

"Twenty-seven pounds. I send—send money to mio padre."

"Send money to your father, do you?"

"Yes, Mr. Dorman. E vecchio."

"What's that?"

"He—old man. Madre old also."

The grazier stood in silence for a minute, thinking this over. At

14

last he said, "Look, Mario. I was thinking of building a bit of a house for you and Lucia, 'n paying for her ticket. You could spend your twenty-seven quid on furniture for it, 'n make the rest in the evenings. If I do that, will you stay with me two years after your time's up, 'n not go off to someone else for better money?"

Only about half of that got through. They discussed it for a little, the Italian gradually breaking into rapture as the proposal became clear. "I pay her ticket and give you a three-room house on the end of the shearers' quarters. You stay with me till September 1953 at the money you get now, plus the award rises. You get all the meat you want off the station at threepence a pound, and vegetables from the garden. Capito?"

"Si, signore."

"Talk English, you great bastard. You stay with me till September 1953 if I do this for you. Is that okay?"

"Okay, Mr. Dorman. I thank you ver', ver' much."

"You've been working well, Mario. You go on the way you're going and you'll be right. Okay, then—that's a deal. What do you want to do now—send Lucia the money for her passage right away?"

"Yes, Mr. Dorman. Lucia—she very happy when she gets letter."

"Aw, look then, Mario. You go and write her a letter in your own bloody language, 'n tell her to come out 'n marry you, 'n you're sending her the money for the ticket. You go and write that now. I'll take it into town with me this afternoon and put the money order in it, fifty-eight pounds, 'n send it off by air mail." He got that through at the second attempt.

"Thank you ver', ver' much, Mr. Dorman. I go now to write Lucia." He went off urgently to his bunkroom.

Dorman went into the house again to change for his journey into town; he had a dark tweed suit that he wore on these occasions, and a purple tie with black stripes on it. He sat in the kitchen polishing his town shoes while Jane changed, and presently he went out into the yard to get the utility. By the car, Mario came up to him with an envelope in his hand.

"For Lucia," he said. "I no have stamp. Will you fix stamp on for me, please? For air mail?"

"Okay. You've told her in the letter that there's a money order going in it, fifty-eight pounds?"

"I have said that, Mr. Dorman. In Italian I have said that to Lucia, and now she is to come, ver' quick."

"I bet you've said that that she's to come ver' quick, you bastard. Mind and keep your nose clean till she comes. I'll see about the timber for your house when I'm in town."

"I thank you ver', ver' much, Mr. Dorman."

"Okay. Get down and go on with that crutching."

He drove into the town that afternoon with Jane by his side; they parked the utility outside the bank and went in together while she cashed a cheque. She went out first and went on to the dressmaker, and Jack went into the bank manager's office to see about the draft for fifty-eight pounds payable to Lucia Tereno at Chieti, Italy. At the conclusion of that business he produced his wool cheque for the credit of his account.

The manager took it and glanced at it with an expressionless face; for the last week he had been receiving one or two like it every day. "I'll give you the receipt slip outside, Mr. Dorman," he said. "What do you want done with it? All into the current account?"

"That's right."

"If you think of investing any of it, I could write to our investments section at head office and get up a few suggestions. It's a pity to see a sum like that lying idle."

"I'll think it over," said Dorman. "I'm going down to Melbourne in a month or two. A good bit of it'll go in tax, and there's one or two things wanted on the station."

The manager smiled faintly; he knew that one, too. "I expect there are," he said. "Well, let me know if I can do anything."

Dorman left the bank and went to the post office; he bought stamps and an air mail sticker for Mario's letter and handed it to Elsie Peters for the post. "I was to tell you that Tim Archer's coming to the Red Cross dance, with Mario," he said.

"Goody," she replied. "He was in this morning, but he didn't know then if he'd be able to get in to it."

"Aye, they can have the car. If that Mario gets into any trouble they won't have it again. I said I'd get the tickets for them. Where would I do that?"

"Mrs. Hayward, up by Marshall's. She's selling them. I'll get them for you if you like to give me the money, Mr. Dorman, and send them out with the mail."

He handed her a note from his wallet. "Thanks. Anything more happened about you going home?"

She nodded, with eyes shining. "I've got a passage booked on the *Orontes*, fifth of May. It's terribly exciting, I just can't wait. Dad did well out of the wool this year."

"Fine," he said. "What part of England are you going to?"

"Ma's people all live in a place called Nottingham," she said. "That's in the middle somewhere, I think. I'm going to stay with them at first, but after that I want to get a job in London."

"London's all right," he said. "I was in England with the first A.I.F. and I don't suppose it's altered very much. From what I hear they don't get much to eat these days. We'll have to send you food parcels."

She laughed. "That's what Ma says. But I think it's all right. People who've been there say there's a lot of nonsense talked about food being short. It's not as bad as they make out."

"I never heard of anyone send back a food parcel, all the same," he observed.

16

"I don't think they've got as much as all that," she said thoughtfully. "I mean, they do like to get parcels still. I'm going to take a lot of tins with me." She paused. "It's going to be a beaut trip," she said thoughtfully. "I just can't wait till May."

Jack Dorman went out of the post office and got into the car, and went to see the builder. He stayed with him some time talking about the three-roomed house for Mario, and arranged for him to come and measure up for the timber and weatherboarding required. This all took a little time, and by the time he got back to the dressmaker to pick up Jane she was ready for him. They did a little more shopping together, put the parcels on the ledge behind the driving seat, and drove out on the road to Buttercup.

George and Ann Pearson lived on rather a smaller property of about fifteen hundred acres; they had no river and they got the water for their stock from dams bulldozed or scooped out to form catchment pools at strategic points upon the land. They were younger than the Dormans, and they still had a young family. The youngest child was Judith, only eight years old, but old enough to catch and saddle her own pony every morning and ride six miles to school with her satchel on her back. Because this was the normal way of going to school the schoolhouse was provided with a paddock; the children rode in and unsaddled, hung their saddles and bridles on the fence, and went in to their lessons. After school they caught their ponies, the schoolmistress helping them if there were any difficulty, saddled up, and rode six miles home again.

George Pearson had rigged up a diving-board and a pair of steps to turn his largest dam into a swimming-pool, and the children were bathing in it as the Dormans drove by. They had evidently brought friends on their way back from school, because three ponies grazed beside the dam with saddles on their backs. Weeping willows seventy feet high grew around the pool, and half a dozen little bodies flashed and splashed with shrill cries from the diving-board in the bright sun.

"I'd have thought it was too cold for bathing still," Jane observed. "It's only October."

"It's warm in the sun," Jack said. "It was up to eighty, dinnertime."

"It's cold in the water, though," she replied. "George told me that it's twelve feet deep, that dam. It'll be cold just down below the surface."

"They don't mind," he said. He took his eyes from the track and looked again at the dam. "I often wish we'd had a dam," he said. "Those kids, they get a lot of fun out of that."

They drove on to the homestead and parked in the grassy yard. Ann Pearson came out to meet them; she was Australian born and spoke with a marked Australian accent, in contrast to her husband, who had come out as a farmer's son in 1930 and still retained a trace of Somerset in his speech. "Didn't you see George?" she asked after the first greetings. "He went down to the dam, with the children."

"We didn't stop," said Jane. "He's probably down there."

"Just dropped in to see if George had got his wool cheque," Jack Dorman said, grinning.

Ann said, "Oh, my word." There seemed no need for any further comment.

Jack turned to Jane and said, "It's all right. They've got enough money to give us tea."

"Give tea to everybody in the shire," said Ann. "How long's it going on for, Jack? I tell you, we get sort of frightened sometimes. It can't go on like this, can it?"

"It'll be down next year," Jack Dorman said, "Not real low, but down to something reasonable, I'd say. It can blow a blizzard after that, for all I care."

They got out of the car and went with her to the wide veranda, and sat down in deck-chairs. "That's what George thinks, too. I'd be quite glad if it went down a bit. It doesn't seem right, somehow. It's not good for the children, either, to see money come so easy."

She told them that they were sailing for England in April on the P. and O. *Strathmore*; the children were going to stay with their grandmother at Nagambie. "George booked the cabin six months ago," she said, "but I never really thought it'ld come off. Still, now we're going, definitely. His dad and mum, they're still alive at this place Shepton Mallet where he was brought up. I never thought I'd meet them, but now it looks as if I shall."

She turned to Jane with a question that had been worrying her a good deal. "When you go on those P. and O. boats travelling first-class," she said, "what do you wear at night? Is it a low evening dress every night, or is that just for dances?"

George Pearson came back presently with six hungry children, and they all sat down to tea at the long table in the kitchen, eleven of them, counting the hired man, a Pole from Slonim, who spoke little English. They ate the best part of two joints of cold roast mutton with a great dish of potatoes and thought nothing of it, topping up with bread and jam and two plum cakes, and many cups of tea. Then the men went out into the yard and put the three visiting children on their ponies and saw them off so that they would be home by nightfall, which comes early in Australia.

The two graziers talked quietly for a time on the veranda while their wives washed up indoors. "Going home in April, so Ann told us," Dorman said.

"Aye." George smoked for a few minutes in silence. "See the old folks once more, anyway. I don't know what it's going to be like there, now."

"I asked Jane if she'd like to go back home, but she didn't want to. She said it'ld all be different."

"Aye. I want to see my brother, see if he won't come out. There's still land going if you look around a bit."

18

"Ninety pounds an acre." They both smiled. "Forty-five or fifty, if you look around," said George. "He'd get that for the land he's got at home."

"All right while the wool keeps up."

"I want to see what things are like at home," George Pearson said. "They may not be so bad as what you read."

"They don't have to be," said Dorman. "I see where it says in the paper that you can't have a new car if you've had one since the war, and now they're selling squirrels in the butchers' shops. What's a squirrel like to look at? Is it like a possum?"

"Smaller than that," said George. "More the size of a rat. It's a clean feeder, though; I suppose you could eat squirrel. Gypsies used to eat them, where I come from."

There was a slow, bewildered silence. "I'd not know what the world was coming to, if I'd to eat a thing like that. . . ."

Everything foreign in the newspapers was puzzling to them, these days. The murders and the pictures of the bathing girls were solid, homely matters that they could understand, but the implacable hostility of the Russians was an enigma. Fortunately they were seven or eight thousand miles away, and so it didn't matter very much. Korea and the Chinese provided another puzzle; Australian boys were fighting there for no very clear reason except that a meeting of the United Nations nine thousand miles from Buttercup had said they should. Mr. Menzies made a speech sometimes and told them that all this was terribly important to Australians, and failed to convince them. The only thing from all these distant places that really touched the graziers was the food shortage in England; they did not understand why that should be, but they sent food parcels copiously to their relations at home, and puzzled over their predicament. They could not understand why English people would not come to this good country that had treated them so well.

The two wives came out and joined their men on the veranda. Jane said, "Ann's been telling me about Peter Loring falling off his horse, Jack. Did you hear about that?"

Her husband shook his head. "That one of the Loring boys, from Balaclava?"

She nodded. "The little one—eleven or twelve years old. You tell him, Ann."

Ann Pearson said, "It was a funny thing, Jack. I had to go into town early on Friday, about nine o'clock. Well, I got just up to the main road—I was all alone in the utility, and there was a pony, with a saddle on and bridle, grazing by the side of the road, and there was Peter Loring with blood all over him from scratches, sitting on the grass. So of course I stopped and got out and asked him what was the matter, and he said he fell off the pony; he was on his way to school. So I asked him if he was hurt, and he said it hurt him to talk and he felt funny." She paused. "Well, there I was, all alone, and I didn't know what to do, whether to take him home or what.

19

And just then a truck came by, with a couple of those chaps from the lumber camp in it."

Jack Dorman said, "The camp up at Lamirra?"

"That's right. Well, this truck stopped and the men got down, and one of them came and asked what was the matter. New Australian he was, German or something—he spoke very foreign. So I told him and he began feeling the boy all over, and then the other man told me he was a doctor in his own country, but not here in Australia. He was a tall, thin fellow, with rather a dark skin, and black hair. So I asked him, 'Is it concussion, Doctor?' I said. Because, I was going to say we'd bring him back here, because this was closer."

She paused. "Well, he didn't answer at once. He seemed a bit puzzled for the moment, and then he made little Peter open his mouth and took a look down his throat, and then he found some stuff coming out of his ear. And then he said, 'It is not concussion, and the bleeding, that is nothing.' He said, 'He has ear disease, and he has a temperature. He should go at once to hospital in Banbury.' My dear, of all the things to have, and that man finding it out so quick! Well, I felt his forehead myself, and it was awful hot, and so I asked the truck driver to go on to Balaclava and tell his mother, and I drove this doctor and Peter into town to the hospital. And Dr. Jennings was there, and he said it was a sort of mastoid—otitis something, he said."

"Pretty good, that," said Jack Dorman.

George Pearson said, "Dr. Jennings knew all about this chap. He's a Czech, not a German. He works up at the camp there, doing his two years."

"What's his name?"

"He did tell me, but I forgot. One of these oreign names, it was —Cylinder, or something. Not that, but something like it. Ann drove him back to Lamirra."

His wife said, "He was quite a quiet, well-behaved one for a New Australian. I do think it was quick of him to find out what was wrong."

"Lucky he came along just then," said Jack.

"My word," said Ann with feeling. "If he hadn't come I think I'd probably have put Peter into the utility and brought him straight back here, because it's so much closer here than Balaclava. I wouldn't have known what to do with mastoid."

The Dormans left soon after that, and drove back to Leonora. Life went on as usual on the station, and on Saturday evening Tim Archer drove into Banbury with Mario Ritti for the Red Cross dance. He hit it off all right with Mario in spite of their very different backgrounds, but there was always a little difficulty with Mario at a dance. There was a barrier of language and experience between the Italian and the local Australian girls; he was inclined to be too bold with them, and they would not willingly have been

seen with him except at a dance, where social barriers were somewhat broken down. There had been an Italian girl at one of the
hotels till recently, and Mario had done most of his dancing with
her, but now she had left to go to Melbourne to earn eight pounds a
week in a café, and Tim was a little anxious about Mario in
consequence.

There were about eighty thousand pounds' worth of new motor-
cars parked outside the Shire Hall that night, for wool had been
good for a couple of years. They parked the old Chevrolet and went
into the hall, neat in their blue suits, with oiled hair carefully
brushed. For a time they stood with a little crowd of young men
round the door while the girls sat on chairs in long lines on each side
of the floor waiting to be asked to dance; only two or three couples
were yet dancing, and the place was still stone cold. Tim studied the
girls; Elsie Peters was there talking to Joan McFarlane. If he had
been alone he would have gone and asked one or other of them to
dance, but that meant leaving Mario high and dry. He felt an
obligation to the Italian to get him started with at least one partner
before going off to his own friends, and he did not think that either
Elsie or Joan would appreciate it if he landed her with an Eyetie
who spoke poor English and was full of rather obvious sex appeal.

He glanced down the row of girls beside the floor, and saw two
black-haired girls sitting together. They were both rather broad in
the face, and both wore woollen dresses of a sombre hue and rather
an unfashionable cut. They were obviously a pair and strangers to
Banbury; Tim had never seen them before. They were clearly New
Australians.

He nudged Mario. "What about that couple over there?" he
asked. "They'd be Italian, wouldn't they?"

"I do not think," said Mario. "I think Austrian perhaps, or
Polish. I have not seen these girls before."

"Nor have I. Let's go and ask them." Once Mario was launched
with these two, he would be able to go off and dance with his own
sort.

They crossed the floor to the girls, and Tim, taking the nearest
one, said, "May I have this dance? My name's Tim Archer." Mario
bowed from the waist before the other, looking as if he was going
to kiss her hand at any moment, and said, "Mario Ritti."

Both girls smiled and got to their feet. Tim's girl was about
twenty-five years old and pleasant-looking in a broad way; in later
life she would certainly be stout. She danced a quickstep reasonably
well, and as they moved off she said with a strange accent, "Teem
Archer?"

"That's right," he said. "Tim."

She tried again. "Tim?"

"That's right," he said again. "Short for Timothy."

"Ah—I understand. Timothy."

"What's your name?"

21

She smiled. "I am Tamara Perediak."

"How much?"

"Tamara Perediak."

"Tamara? I never heard that name before."

"It is a name of my country," she said. "Where I was born, many girls are called Tamara."

"Are you Polish?" he asked.

She shook her head. "I was born in the Ukraine." He did not know where that was, but didn't like to say so. "Now I am come from Mulheim, in the American zone, to Australia." She called it Owstrahlia. "I am to work here at the hospital."

"Have you just arrived?" he asked.

"In the camp I have been three weeks, but here only three days."

"Three days? Then you're brand-new!" They laughed together. "How do you like Australia?"

"I like it very much, what I have seen."

"Are you a nurse?"

She shook her head. "I think you call it ward-maid. I am to do scrubbing and the carrying trays, and the washing dishes, and the washing clothes."

"Do you know anybody in Australia?"

She said, "I have good friends that I met on the ship, but they have gone to Mildura. But I have here Natasha who came with me, who is dancing with your friend. She comes also from the Ukraine and we were together at Mulheim, working at the same canteen."

"Natasha?"

She laughed. "That is another name of the Ukraine. Natasha Byelev. Are our names very difficult?"

"My word!"

"Tell me," she said presently, "your friend, is he Australian also?"

"No," he replied. "He's Italian. His name's Mario Ritti."

"Ah—an Italian. I did not think he was Australian."

"That's right," Tim said. "He works at Leonora, where I work. He's on top of the world tonight, because he's got a girl in Italy and the boss is going to pay her passage out here so that Mario can get married."

He had to repeat parts of that once or twice before its full import sunk in. "He will pay for her to come from Italy to Australia?" she said in wonder. "He must be a very rich man."

"He's doing all right with the wool," Tim said. "He's not a rich man, really."

"Your friend is very lucky to work for such a man. Is his loved one to come soon?"

"Soon as the boss can get her on a ship. He's scared that Mario will leave when his two years are up. He wants to get him settled on the station in a house of his own, with a wife and family."

She stared at him. "He is to make him a house also?"

"That's right. Just a shack, you know."

She thought about this for a minute as they danced. "I also must work for two years," she said. "I am to work here in the hospital, with Natasha."

"Do you like it?"

She shrugged her shoulders. "I have been working so since five years, in the works canteen at Mulheim. Once I was to be schoolteacher, but with the war that was not possible."

"Where were you in the war?" he asked.

"In Dresden," she said. "When I was little girl my father and my mother left Odessa because they were not members of the Party and the life there was not good, and so they went to live in Dresden. There my father was schoolteacher, to teach the boys Russian. All before the war, and in the war, we lived in Dresden. Then the English bombed Dresden and my father and my mother were killed, both together. Our house was all destroyed. I was not there, because I worked that night in the factory outside the city and that was not bombed. But I went to go home in the morning, our house and the whole street was all destroyed, and my mother and my father were dead, both of them. So then the war came to Dresden very soon after, and I went first to Leipzig and then to Kassel because the Russians were coming, and there I met Natasha and we went to Mulheim in the end to work in the canteen."

Tim Archer said, "You've seen a mighty lot of foreign places. I should think you'd find it a bit slow in Banbury."

"I think it will be better to be in a slow place and live slowly for a time," Tamara said. "So much has happened since I was a little girl."

Presently the dance ended and he took her back to her seat. Mario immediately asked her to dance again, and Tim escaped, and went to dance with Joan McFarlane.

At the same time, at Leonora, Jane sat with Jack before the kitchen stove in wooden arm-chairs with cushions; they generally sat there in the evening rather than in the parlour, a prim, formal room where nothing was to hand. Jack Dorman was reading the *Leader*, a weekly farming paper which was about all he ever read. Jane sat with the open letter from Aunt Ethel in her hand, worrying about it.

"I wrote to Myers with a cheque," she said. "They sent a statement for the parcels, seven pounds eighteen and six. I told them to keep sending them, one every month. . . ."

He grunted without looking up. "What are you sending now?"

"I told them to keep sending the dried fruits," she said. "It's what she seems to like." She turned the letter over in her hand. "It's so difficult, because she never asks for anything, or says what she wants. She does seem to like the dried fruit, though."

"I'd have thought that a meat parcel might be better," he said. "They haven't got much meat, from all I hear."

"An old lady like her doesn't eat a lot of meat," she replied. "She can make cakes with the dried fruit for when she has people in to tea."

She turned the letter over, reading it again for the tenth time. "I can't make out about this vest," she said, troubled. "It almost reads as if she's short of money, doesn't it?"

"Could be," he observed. He laid the *Leader* down, and glanced across at his wife. He could still see in her the girl he had brought out from England, stubborn in her love for him to the point of quarrelling with her parents, supported only by this aunt to whom they now sent parcels.

"Like to send her some?" he asked.

She looked up quickly, and met his eyes. "Send her money? She might take it as an insult."

"She might buy herself a vest," he said.

She sat in silence for a time. "We couldn't send her just a little money, Jack," she said at last. "It would have to be nothing or else quite a lot, as if it was a sort of legacy. Enough to be sure that she wouldn't take it badly. Enough to keep her for a couple of years if she's in real trouble."

"Well, we've got a lot," he said. "We'll do whatever you think right."

There was a pause. "I feel we kind of owe it to her," he said presently. "To see her right if she's in any trouble. We haven't done so bad together, you and I. It might never have come to anything if she hadn't backed us up."

"I know. That's what I feel." She stared down at the letter in her hands. "I'm not a bit happy about this, Jack," she said at last. "I don't like the sound of it at all. If we've got the money, I'd like to send her five hundred pounds."

THE FAR COUNTRY

Two

JENNIFER MORTON went home for the following week-end. She was the daughter of a doctor in Leicester, his only child now, for her two brothers had been killed in the war, one in the North Atlantic and one over Hamburg. She was twenty-four years old and she had worked away from home for some years; she had a clerical job with the Ministry of Pensions at their office in Blackheath, a suburb of London. Most of her life was spent in Blackheath, where she had a bed-sitting-room in a boarding-house, but once a month she went home to Leicester to see her parents, travelling up from London early on the Saturday morning, and returning late on Sunday night.

These were duty visits; she was fond enough of her father and her mother, but she had now no interests and few acquaintances in her own home town. The war and marriage had scattered her school friends. She had no particular fondness for the Ministry of Pensions or for her job in Blackheath; she would have stayed at home and worked in Leicester if there had been any useful purpose to be served by doing so. In fact, her mother and her father were remarkably self-sufficient; her mother never wanted to do anything else but to stay at home and run the house and cook her father's dinner. Her father, an overworked general practitioner, never wanted to go out at night unless, in the winter, to a meeting of the British Medical Association or, in the summer, to a meeting of the Bowls Club. This was a good thing, for the night air made her mother cough, and she seldom went out of the house after midday in the winter. As the years went on, her father and her mother settled firmly into a routine of life moulded by overwork and by poor health, a groove that left little room for the wider interests of a daughter.

Jennifer went to Leicester for her week-end once a month, but there was never very much for her to do there. She could not help her mother very much without breaking through routines that she was not familiar with; unless the water jug was on a certain spot upon the kitchen shelf, unless the saucepans were arrayed in a certain order, her mother became fussed and unable to find things, and very soon made the suggestion that Jennifer should go and sit with her father, who was usually deep in the *British Medical Journal* if he wasn't out upon a case. She came to realise that in her case the barrier of the generations was higher than usual in families because her father and her mother were so complementary; she accepted the situation philosophically, and found the interests of her life away from home.

Those interests were not very startling. She had been mildly in love when she was twenty, soon after the war, but he had gone to a job in Montreal and gradually the correspondence languished; when finally she heard that he was married it was just one of those things. She was friendly with a good many men, for she was an attractive girl, with auburn hair that had been bright red as a child, and the grey eyes that go with it, but she had been inoculated and never fell seriously in love. She knew a good deal about the London theatres, and she saw most of the films worth seeing, including the Continental ones; she could speak a little French, and she had spent two summer holidays in France with a couple of girls from her office. Now she was planning a trip to Italy for her next holiday, but that was nine months ahead, for it was October. She had bought three little books by a gentleman called Hugo, and she was teaching herself Italian out of them.

That week-end was like all the others, only more so. Though it was only October her mother was coughing as if it were January; she had not been out of doors for a week, but she had her household organised so that she could order from the shops by telephone, and what could not be done that way the daily woman did. Her father was more overworked than ever; he seemed to spend most of his time writing certificates for patients of the nationalised Health Service, who stood in queues each morning and afternoon at the surgery door. There was nothing Jennifer could do to help them and no place for her; she left them late on Sunday afternoon and travelled back to London, and so by the electric train from Charing Cross down to her own place at Blackheath. She got back to her room at about ten o'clock, made herself a cup of cocoa, washed a pair of stockings, did an exercise of Hugo, and went to bed.

She worked all next day, as usual, at her office. She left at five in the evening, and walked back through the suburban streets in the October dusk to her boarding-house. Very soon now it would be dark when she came out from work; for two months in the winter she would not walk home in daylight. She was beginning to dread those two months; in mid-winter she got a sense of suffocation, a feeling that she would never see the sun and the fresh air again.

It was raining a little that evening, and she walked back with her blue raincoat buttoned tightly round her neck. She had intended to go out to the pictures with a friend from the boarding-house after tea, but now she thought that she would stay at home and read a magazine and do her Hugo. There wasn't much joy in going to the pictures and then walking home in the rain.

She went up the steps of the shabby old brick house that was her home, spacious with its eight bedrooms, its four reception-rooms, and its range of basement kitchens, and she let herself in at the front door with her latch-key. As she took off her wet coat her landlady climbed up the stairs from the kitchen.

"There was a telephone call for you about an hour ago," she

said. "A personal call. I told them you'd be back about five-thirty."

Jennifer looked up in surprise. "Do you know who it was from?"

The woman shook her head. "They didn't say."

Jennifer went to the telephone booth and told the exchange that she could take the call, and learned that it was a call from Leicester. She hung up, and stood uncertain for a moment, hoping there was nothing wrong at home. Presently she went up to her room on the first floor and changed out of her wet shoes, and then she stood looking out of the window at the glistening lamplight in the wet suburban street, waiting and listening for the call. In the yellow lamplight the plane trees in the street waved a few stray leaves that still held to the twigs.

The call came through at last, and she hurried downstairs to take it. It was her mother, speaking from their home. "Is that Jenny? How are you, dear?"

"I'm all right, Mother."

"Jenny dear, listen to this. We had a telephone call from the district nurse, at Ealing. She said that Granny's ill. She had a fall in the street, apparently, and they took her to the hospital, but they hadn't got a bed so they took her home and put her to bed there. The nurse said somebody would have to go there to look after her. Jenny, could you go to Ealing and see what's the matter, and then telephone us?"

Jennifer thought quickly. Ealing was on the other side of London; an hour up to Charing Cross if she were lucky with the trains, and then an hour down to Ealing Broadway, and a ten minutes' walk. She could get something to eat on the way, perhaps. "I can do that, Mummy," she said. "I've got nothing fixed up for tonight. I could be there by about half-past eight."

"Oh, my dear, I *am* so sorry. I think you'll have to go. She oughtn't to be living alone, of course, but she won't leave the house. We'll have to fix up something better for her, after this. You'll be able to get back to Blackheath tonight, will you?"

The girl hesitated. "I think so, Mummy. If I leave by about half-past nine I should be able to get back here. It sounds as if somebody ought to stay the night with her, though, doesn't it?"

There was a worried silence. "I don't know what to say," her mother said at last. "You've got to be at work tomorrow. Oh dear!"

"Has Daddy heard about this yet?"

"He's out still on his rounds. I couldn't get hold of him."

"Don't worry, Mummy," said the girl. "I'll go over there and give you a ring when I've seen the nurse. We'll fix up something between us."

"What time will you be telephoning, dear?"

"It may be very late, if I've got to hurry to catch trains," the girl said. Her grandmother was not on the telephone. "It may be after midnight when I get back here."

"That'll be all right, Jenny. I always hear the bell."

"All right, Mummy. I'll go over right away and ring you back tonight, probably very late."

She did not wait for supper, but started for the station straight away. She travelled across London to the other side and came to Ealing Broadway station about two hours later. It was raining here in earnest, great driving gusts of rain blown by a high wind down the deserted, shimmering, black streets. Her stockings and her shoes were soaked before she had been walking for three minutes.

Her grandmother lived in a four-bedroomed house called Maymyo, built in the somewhat spacious style of fifty years ago, a house with a large garden and no garage. Her husband had bought it when they had retired from Burma in 1924; he had bought it prudently because he had an idea even then that he would not survive his wife, and so he had avoided an extravagant establishment. In fact he had died in 1930, comfortable in the knowledge that her widow's pension, her small private income, and the house in perpetuity would render her secure until she came to join him.

There she had lived, surrounded by the treasures they had gathered up together in a life spent in the East. A gilded Buddha sat at the hall door, a pair of elephant tusks formed a hanger for a great brass dinner gong. Glass cases housed Indian dolls, and models of sampans and junks, and imitation mangoes out of which a wood and plaster cobra would jump to bite your finger, very terrifying. There were embossed silver and brass Burmese trays and bowls all over the place; on the walls were water-colour paintings of strange landscapes with misty forests of a bluish tinge unknown to Jennifer, with strange coloured buildings called pagodas and strange people in strange clothes. Ethel Trehearn lived on surrounded by these reminders of a more colourful world, more real to her than the world outside her door. Nothing was very interesting to her that had happened since she got on to the ship at Rangoon Strand, twenty-six years before.

Jennifer came to the house in the wet, windy night; it was in total darkness, which seemed most unusual. She pushed open the gate and went up the path through the little front garden, and now she saw a faint glimmer of light through the coloured glass panels let into the front door in a Gothic style. She stood in the porch in her wet shoes and raincoat, and pressed the bell.

She heard nothing but the tinkling of water running from a stackpipe near her feet.

She waited for a minute, and then pressed the bell again. Apparently it wasn't working. She rapped with the knocker and waited for a couple of minutes for something to happen; then she tried the handle of the door. It was open, and she went into the hall.

A candle burned on the hall table, held in a brass candlestick from Benares. Jennifer went forward and pressed the electric switch for the hall light, but no light came. She thought of a power cut, unusual at night, and stood in wonder for a moment. In any case, there was no electricity, and it was no good worrying about the cause.

She stood in the hall, listening to the house. It was dead silent, but for the tinkling of the rain. She raised her head and called, "Granny! It's me—Jennifer. Are you upstairs?"

There was no answer.

She did not like the empty sound of the house; it was full of menace for her. She did not like the lack of light, or the long, moving shadows that the candle cast. She was a level-headed young woman, however, and she took off her coat and laid it on a chair, and picked up the candle, and went into the drawing-room.

There was nothing unusual about that room; it was clean and tidy, though stone-cold. She would have expected on a night like that to see a fire burning in the grate, but the fire was not laid; apparently her grandmother had not used the room that day. Jennifer went quickly through the dining-room and kitchen; everything was quite in order there. A tin of Benger's Food and a half empty bottle of milk stood on the kitchen table.

She turned, and went upstairs to the bedrooms. The door of her grandmother's room was shut; she stood outside with the flickering candle in her hand, and knocked. She said again, "Granny, it's me —Jennifer. Can I come in?" There was no answer, so she turned the handle and went into the room.

Ethel Trehearn lay on her back in the bed, and at the first glance Jennifer thought that she was dead, and her heart leaped up into her throat because she had never seen a dead person. She forced herself to look more closely, and then she saw that the old lady was breathing evenly, very deeply asleep. With the relief, Jennifer staggered a little, and her eyes lost focus for an instant and she felt a little sick; then she recovered herself, and looked around the room.

Everything there seemed to be in order, though her grandmother's day clothes were thrown rather haphazard into a chair. The old lady was evidently quite all right, in bed and asleep; if she had had a fall a sleep would do her good. It looked as if somebody had been in the house looking after her, possibly the district nurse who had telephoned to Jennifer's mother. It seemed unwise to wake the old lady up, and presently Jennifer tiptoed from the room, leaving the door ajar in order that she might hear any movement.

The time was then about nine o'clock, and she had eaten nothing since lunch except a cup of tea and a biscuit at the office. She had a young and healthy appetite, and she had the sense to realise that her momentary faintness in the bedroom had a good deal to do with the fact that she was very, very hungry. She went down to the kitchen, candle in hand, to get herself a meal.

In a few minutes she had made the extraordinary discovery that there was no food in the house at all. The half bottle of milk and the tin of Benger's Food upon the kitchen table seemed to be the only edibles, except for a few condiments in a cupboard. The larder—her grandmother had no refrigerator—was empty but for a small hard rind of cheese upon a plate and three cartons of dried fruits, candied peel and sultanas and glacé cherries, open and evidently in use. There was a flour-bin, but it was empty, a bread-bin that held only crumbs. There were no tinned foods at all, and no vegetables.

Jennifer stood in the middle of the kitchen deeply puzzled, wondering what her grandmother had been eating recently, and where she had been eating it. Had she been having her meals out, or was there something blacker waiting here to be uncovered? She had been down to visit the old lady one Sunday about a month before and her grandmother had given her a very good lunch and tea, a roast duck with apple sauce with roast potatoes and cauliflower, and a mince pie to follow; for tea there had been buttered scones and jam, and a big home-made cake with plenty of fruit in it. She thought of this as she stood there in the kitchen in the flickering candlelight, and her mouth watered; she could have done with a bit of that roast duck.

One thing at least was evident; that she would have to spend the night in the house. She could not possibly go back to Blackheath and leave things as they were. Whoever had lit the candle and left the door open had done it in the expectation that some relation would arrive, and the unknown person would probably come back that night because her grandmother was clearly incapable of looking after herself. If Jennifer was to spend the night there, though, she felt she must have something to eat. Ealing Broadway was only a few hundred yards away and there would probably be a café or a coffee-stall open there; she could leave a note upon the hall table and go out and have a quick meal.

She went upstairs again, and looked in on the old lady, but she was still deeply asleep. Thinking to find a place in which to sleep herself she opened the door of the guest bedroom, but it was empty. Pictures still hung upon the wall, but there was no furniture in the room at all, and no carpet on the bare boards of the floor. Unfaded patches on the wallpaper showed where bed and chest of drawers and wash-hand stand had stood.

This was amazing, because Jennifer had slept in that room less than a year before; it had been prim and neat and old-fashioned and very comfortable. What on earth had the old lady done with all the furniture? The girl went quickly to the other two bedrooms and found them in a similar condition, empty but for the pictures on the wall. There was no bed in the house except the one that her grandmother occupied; if Jennifer were to sleep there that night she would have to sleep on the sofa in the drawing-room. There did not seem to be any bedding, either; the linen cupboard held only a pair of clean sheets, a couple of towels, a table-cloth or two, and a few table-napkins.

The shadows began to close in upon Jennifer as she stood in the empty bedrooms with the flickering candle in her hand. It seemed incredible, but the old lady must have sold her furniture. And there was no food in the house. The darkness crept around her; could it be that Granny had no money? But she had a pension, Jennifer knew that, and she had always been well off. More likely that she was going a bit mental with old age, and that she had deluded herself into the belief that she was poor.

She went downstairs and found a piece of writing paper in her grandmother's desk, and wrote a note to leave on the hall table with the candle; then she put on her raincoat and went out to get a meal. She found a café open in the main street and had a sort of vegetable pie. It was dull and insipid with no meat, but she had two helpings of it and followed it up with stewed plums and coffee. Then she bought a couple of rolls filled with a thin smear of potted meat for her breakfast, and went back to the house in Ladysmith Avenue.

In the house everything was as she had left it; her note lay beneath the candle unread. She took the candle and went up to her grandmother's room, but the old lady was still sleeping deeply; she had not moved at all. The girl came out of the bedroom, and as she did so she heard movement in the hall, and saw the light from an electric torch. She came downstairs with the candle, and in its light she saw a middle-aged woman standing there in a wet raincoat, torch in hand.

The woman said, "Are you one of Mrs. Trehearn's relations?"

Jennifer said, "I'm her granddaughter."

"Oh. Well, I'm the district nurse. You know she had an accident?"

"I don't know very much, except that my mother got a telephone call asking somebody to come here. She rang me."

The nurse nodded. "I rang your mother at Leicester as soon as I could get the number out of the old dear. I'd better tell you what it's all about, and then you can take over."

Jennifer moved towards the door. "We'd better go in here—in case she wakes up."

"*She* won't wake up tonight—not after what the doctor gave her." However, they went into the drawing-room and stood together in the light of the one candle. "She had a fall in the street this morning, just the other side of the bridge, between here and the Broadway. She didn't seem able to get up, so the police got an ambulance and took her to the hospital. Well, they hadn't got a bed, and anyway there didn't seem to be much wrong with her except debility, you know. So as she was conscious and not injured by her fall they rang me up and sent her home here in the ambulance. I put her to bed and got in Dr. Thompson. He saw her about five o'clock."

"What did he say?"

The nurse glanced at her. "When did you see her last?"

"About a month ago."

"How was she then?"

"Very much as usual. She doesn't do much, but she's seventy-nine, I think."

"Was she eating normally?"

"She gave me a very good meal, roast duck and mince pie."

"She ate that, did she?"

"Of course. Why?"

"She doesn't look as if she's eaten anything since," the nurse said shortly. "She's very emaciated, and there's not a scrap of food here in the house except some dried fruits. She vomited at the hospital, and what came up was raisins and sultanas. She couldn't be expected to digest those, at her age."

Jennifer said, "I simply can't understand it. She's got plenty of money."

The nurse glanced at her. "You're sure of that?"

"Well—I think so."

"I rang up the electricity," the nurse said, "and told them that the power had failed and they must send a man to put it right because I'd got a patient in the house. They said they'd disconnected the supply because the bill hadn't been paid. You'd better see about that in the morning if you're going to keep her here."

"I'll go round there first thing."

"I had to go and get a candle of my own," the nurse said. "I brought another one around with me now." She took it from her pocket. "I looked for coal to light a fire, but there's not a scrap. I got a tin of Benger's Food and some milk, and I got the people next door to let me boil up some hot milk for her, and fill the hot-water bottles. I'll take them round there and fill them again before I go." She glanced at Jennifer. "You're staying here tonight?"

"I wasn't going to, but I'd better. Will you be here?"

The nurse laughed shortly. "Me? I've got a baby case tonight, but she's got an hour or two to go so I slipped round here to see if anyone had come. I'll have to get some sleep after that. I'll look round here about midday to see how you're getting on. I said I'd give the doctor a ring after that."

Jennifer nodded. "I'll see you then. Is she in any danger, do you think?"

"I don't think she'll go tonight," the nurse said. "Whether she'll pull round or not depends a lot on her digestion. I couldn't say. When she wakes, give her another cup of the Benger's. She can have as much of that as she'll take—I'll show you how to make it. But don't let her have anything else till the doctor's seen her. And keep the bottles nice and warm—not hot enough to scorch, you know, just nice and warm."

Practical, hard-headed, and efficient, she whisked through her duties, showing Jennifer what to do, and was out of the house in a quarter of an hour. The girl was left alone with all the Indian and

32

Burmese relics, with one candle and no fire and nowhere much to sleep.

She gave up the idea of going out in the rain at ten o'clock at night to find a public telephone to ring up her mother; that would have to wait till morning. She went up to her grandmother's bed-room and took off her wet shoes and stockings and rubbed her feet with a towel; then she found a pair of her grandmother's woollen stockings and put them on, and her grandmother's bedroom slippers, and her grandmother's overcoat. She found a travelling rug and wrapped it around her and settled down to spend the night in an arm-chair by her grandmother's bedside, chilled and uncomfortable, dozing off now and then and waking again with the cold. In the middle of the night she ate her breakfast rolls.

In the grey dawn she woke from one of these uneasy dozes, stiff and chilled to the bone. She looked at the bed and saw that her grandmother was awake; she was lying in exactly the same position but her eyes were open. Jennifer got up and went to the bedside. The old lady turned her head upon the pillow and said in a thin voice, "Jenny, my dear. Whatever are you doing here?"

The girl said, "I've come to look after you, Granny. They tele-phoned and told us that you weren't so well."

"I know, my dear. I fell down in the street—such a stupid thing to do. Is the nurse here still?"

"She'll be back later on this morning, Granny. Is there anything you want?"

She told her, and Jennifer entered on the duties of a sick-room for the first time in her life. Presently she took the hot-water bottles and the remains of the milk and went to the house next door, where a harassed mother was getting breakfast for a husband and three little children. As she warmed the milk and filled the water-bottles the woman asked her, "How is the old lady this morning?"

"She's staying in bed, of course," said Jennifer, "but she's not too bad. I think she's going to be all right."

"I am so sorry," the woman said. "I wish we'd been able to do more for her, but everything's so difficult these days. I'd no idea that she was ill. She's been going out as usual every morning. It was a terrible surprise when she came back in an ambulance yesterday."

Jennifer was interested. "She goes out every morning, does she?"

"That's right. Every morning about ten o'clock. She goes down to the Public Library in the Park to read *The Times*. She told me that one day."

Jennifer thanked her for her help, and went back with the hot milk to make a cup of Benger's, and took it up to the bedroom with the hot-water bottles. She propped her grandmother up in bed with the pillows and helped her while she drank, but she could not get her to take more than half the cup. "I don't want any more, my dear," she said. "I think I'm better without anything."

The hot drink had stimulated her a little. "Jenny," she said, "I've been thinking. Haven't you got to go to work?"

The girl said, "That's all right, Granny. I'm going out presently to ring up Mummy to tell her how you are, and I'll ring up the office then. I'll stay with you for a few days until you're better."

"Oh, my dear, that isn't necessary at all."

"I'd like to, Granny. It'll be a bit of a holiday for me."

"But Jenny, dear, you *can't* stay here. There isn't anywhere for you to sleep. Where did you sleep last night?"

"I'll be all right here, Granny," the girl said. "I'll fix up something in the course of the day."

"But there isn't any electricity. You *can't* stay here." A facile, senile tear escaped and trickled down the old, lined cheek. "Oh, things *are* so troublesome."

"That's all right, Granny," the girl said. "I'll go and see about the electricity this morning, and get them to turn it on."

"But it's seventeen pounds, Jenny—they came and turned it off. Such a nice man, but he had to do his job. I've been getting on quite well without it."

"Well, you're not going to get along without it any longer, Granny," Jennifer said firmly. "You can't when you're in bed." She thought quickly; she had about thirty pounds in her bank, but her cheque-book was at Blackheath on the other side of London. "I'll get them to turn it on again," she said. "Don't worry about it."

"Oh, my dear, I don't know what to do. . . ."

The girl wiped the old cheeks gently with her handkerchief. "Cheer up, Granny," she said. "It'll be all right. Tell me—isn't there any money?"

The old lady said, "None at all. You see, I've lived too long."

"Don't you believe it," Jennifer said. "You've got a good many more years yet. But what about the pension? That goes on until you die, doesn't it?"

"That's what Geoffrey thought, and so did I. But it was an Indian pension, dear, and when the Socialists scuttled out of India there weren't any civil servants left in India to pay into the fund. Only us widows were left drawing out of it, and now the money is all gone."

"But wasn't it a Government pension?"

"Not for widows, dear. Geoffrey's pension was a Government pension, but that stopped when he died. This was a private fund, that we civil servants in India all paid into. They had to halve the pensions a few years ago, and then last year they stopped it altogether and wound up the fund."

The girl said, "Oh Granny! And you gave me such a lovely dinner when I came here last!"

"Of course, my dear. A young girl like you must have proper meals. Although it's so difficult, with all this rationing. Jenny, have you had your breakfast yet?"

"Not yet. I'm going out in a few minutes, and I'll get some then."

"I'm afraid there's nothing in the house, Jenny. I *am* so sorry."

"Don't think about it, Granny. I'll get a few things when I'm out and bring them in."

"Yes, do that, dear." She paused. "Will you bring me the little red morocco case that's on the dressing-table?"

"This one?"

"Yes, that's it. Bring it to me here."

The girl brought the jewel case over to the bed and gave it to her grandmother, who opened it with fingers that trembled so that they could barely serve their function. Inside there was a jumble of souvenirs, the relics of a long life. A gold locket on a gold chain, broken, with a wisp of a baby's hair in it. A painted miniature portrait of a young boy in the clothes of 1880, a faded photograph of a bride and bridgegroom dated 1903, a small gold sovereign purse to hang upon a watch-chain, three small gold and alabaster seals, a string of black jet beads. She rummaged among these things and many others with fingers that were almost useless, and finally produced a gold ring set with five diamonds in a row, unfashionable in these days.

She gave this to Jennifer. "I want you to do a little job for me when you are out, Jenny," she said. "In the New Broadway, two doors on the other side of Paul's patisserie shop, you'll find a jeweller's shop called Evans. Go in and ask to see Mr. Evans himself, and give him this, and tell him that you come from me. He's a very nice man, and he'll understand. He'll give you money for it, whatever it's worth. I'm afraid it may not be enough to pay the electricity, but you can get a joint of beef and some vegetables, and we'll cook a nice dinner for you. Take my ration book with you—it's on the corner of the bureau in the drawing-room—and get some flour and dripping and sugar, and then we'll make a cake; there's plenty of dried fruit downstairs that dear Jane sends me from Australia. So kind of her, after all these years. And if there's enough money, get a little bottle of claret. A young girl like you ought not to look so pale."

"You mustn't sell your ring," the girl said gently. "Look, I've got plenty of money to carry on with—I've got over thirty pounds in the bank. I'll use some of that, and I'll be telephoning Mummy this morning and she'll send us down some more. I expect Daddy will come down to see you tomorrow, when he hears that you're in bed."

Her grandmother shook her head. "Your mother hasn't got any money to spare," she said. "She might have had once, but now with this horrible Health Service and doctors getting less money than dentists . . . Sell the ring, my dear. I can't get it on my finger now, I'm so rheumatic, and I shan't want it any more."

"What is it, Granny?" the girl asked, turning it over in her fingers. "Who gave it to you?"

"Geoffrey," the old lady said. "Geoffrey gave it to me, when we became engaged. We went to the Goldsmiths and Silversmiths in Regent Street together to buy it . . . such a fine, sunny day. And then we went and had lunch at Gatti's; it felt so funny on the fork, because I wasn't used to wearing rings. And then we took a hansom for the afternoon and drove down to Roehampton to see the polo, because Geoffrey's friend Captain Oliver was playing. But I didn't see much of the polo, because I was looking at my new ring, and at Geoffrey. So silly. . . ." The old voice faded off into silence.

"I can't sell that," the girl said gently. "I'm not going to sell your engagement ring."

"My dear, there's nothing else."

"Yes, there is," the girl said. "I've got thirty pounds. I'm going to spend that first. If you don't like it, you can leave me that ring in your will."

"I've done that already, Jenny, with a lot of other things that aren't there now, because I had to sell them. I'm so very, very sorry. There was a little emerald and ruby brooch that Geoffrey got at Mandalay, and a pair of pearl ear-rings that came from Mergui. So pretty; I did want you to have those. But everything has been so troublesome. . . ."

The girl put the ring back into the jewel box. "Leave it there for now," she said. "I promise you I'll come and tell you if we have to sell it. But we shan't have to; we've got plenty of money between us."

She made her grandmother comfortable and promised her that she would be back in an hour and a half; then she went out with a shopping basket. She got a good breakfast at Lyons' of porridge and fish, and as she breakfasted she made her plans. She had only twelve and threepence in her purse, and her breakfast cost her three shillings of that. Before she could lay her hands on any more money she must go to Blackheath to get her cheque-book and cash a cheque, and the fare there would be about four and three. That left her about five shillings; she had to telephone her mother, but perhaps she could reverse the charges for the call to Leicester. She must keep a margin of about two shillings for contingencies; if she could reverse the charges for the call she would have about three shillings to spend on food for her grandmother.

The sense of crisis, and the breakfast, stimulated her; she could beat this thing. She went out and stood in a call-box and rang up her parents; she was early, and the hundred-mile call came through at once. She told her father what had happened.

"She's got no money at all, Daddy," she said. "She's just hasn't been eating—I think that's really all that's the matter with her. She's very weak, and she's in bed, of course." She told him what the district nurse had said about her grandmother's chances. She told him about the pension.

They extended the call. "Can you let me have some money,

Daddy? I've only got a few shillings. I'm going back to Blackheath about midday and I'll get my cheque-book then, but I'm not sure if I'll be in time to cash a cheque. I may be too late. I'll be back here in Ealing this afternoon, anyway, before dark."

He said, "I'll send you a telegraph money order at once for ten pounds. You should get that this afternoon. Either your mother or I will come down tomorrow and be with you some time tomorrow afternoon, and we'll see what's to be done then. It's a bit of a shock, this."

"Don't let Mummy worry over it too much," the girl said. "I think she's probably going to be all right. I'm going now to see if I can talk them into turning on the electricity again. It'll make a lot of difference if we can get a radiator going in her room."

In a quarter of an hour she was talking to the manager in the office of the Electricity Commission, having got past his girl with some difficulty. He said, "I'm sorry, Miss Morton, but we have to work to rules laid down by our head office. Two years ago I might have been able to use my own discretion in a case like this, but—well, things aren't the same as they were then. Nationalisation was bound to make some differences, you know. I'm afraid the account will have to be paid before the supply can be re-connected."

She said, "I'm going over to Blackheath to get my cheque-book today. I can let you have the cheque first thing tomorrow morning."

"Fine," he said, with forced geniality. "Then we shall be able to re-connect the supply."

"Can't you do it today?"

"I'm afraid the account will have to be settled first."

Jennifer said desperately. "She's really terribly ill, and we can't even warm up hot milk in the house, or get hot water for her water-bottles. We *must* have electricity tonight."

He got to his feet; this was too unpleasant, and he had no power to act. "I'm sorry, Miss Morton," he said. "It sounds as though she would be better in the hospital—have you considered that? Perhaps the relieving officer would be the man for you to see. He's at the Town Hall."

The red-haired girl flared into sudden anger. "God blast you and the relieving officer," she said. "I only hope this happens to you one day, that you're old and dying of starvation, and you can't get anyone to help you. And it will, too."

She turned and left the office, white with anger. She shopped carefully with her three shillings, and bought two pints of milk, a few water biscuits, and a little sugar; that finished her money. She thought deeply; she could get some more food for her grandmother and for herself on the way back from Blackheath. It was urgent to get over there at once, before the bank shut, so that she could get her money. She turned and made for Ladysmith Avenue; on the way she stopped and spent fourpence on a copy of *The Times*, thinking that it would give the old lady an interest while she was absent,

37

and give something for her morale to hang on to during the afternoon.

When she got into the house she took *The Times* up to her grandmother's room. The old lady lay in bed exactly as Jennifer had left her; her eyes were shut, and though she was breathing steadily it seemed to the girl that the respiration was now fainter than it had been when she had been lying in the same way on the previous night. Jennifer spoke to her, but she did not answer; however, when she reached in to the bed to get the hot-water bottles the old lady opened her eyes.

"Just getting your hot-water bottles, Granny," the girl said. "I'll make you another cup of Benger's, too. I brought you *The Times.*"

"So sweet of you," her grandmother said. "I had to give up *The Times*, but I always go down every morning to look at the Births, Deaths, and Marriages. It's so easy to miss things, and then you write to somebody and find they're dead."

The girl said, "I'm just going to get these water-bottles filled, and make you another hot drink. I'll be back in about five minutes."

When she got back the old lady was reading the front page of *The Times*. Jennifer packed the hot-water bottles around her and got her to take the best part of the cup of the milk drink, and to eat about half of one biscuit. While she was coaxing her to eat the rest there was a knock, at the front door; she went dowstairs, and it was the postman with a heavy parcel.

She took it from him, and carried it up to show to her grandmother, with an instinct that anything that would stimulate and arouse her interest was good. "Look what the post's brought," she said. "Myer's Emporium. What have you been buying?"

The old lady said, "Oh, that's dear Jane. How sweet of her. It's a parcel from Australia, Jenny. She sends one every month."

"It's got an English postmark, Granny," the girl said.

"I know, my dear. She puts the order in Australia and the food comes from England somehow or other. So funny."

"Shall I open it?"

"Please. I must write and thank her." The parcel contained six cartons of dried fruit and a tin of lard; Jennifer now knew where the cartons she had seen in the larder came from. She asked, "Granny, who is Aunt Jane? She isn't Mother's sister, is she?"

"No, my dear. Your mother never had a sister. She's my niece, my brother Tom's daughter."

"She's the one who quarelled with the family because she married an Australian?"

"Yes, dear. Tom and Margaret were very much upset, but it's turned out very well. I liked him, but Tom found him drinking white port with Jeffries, the butler, in the middle of the morning, and he used to swear dreadfully, and never saluted anybody. So different to our Army."

Jennifer smiled. "What was Aunt Jane like?"

"Such a sweet girl—but very stubborn. Once she decided to do a thing there was no arguing with her; she had to see it through. I sometimes think that you're a little like her, Jenny."

Time was slipping by; if she were to get money that day she could not linger. "I'm going over to Blackheath now," she said. "I'll get a few things for the night, and I'll get some money and some bits of things we need. I'll be back about tea-time, but I'll leave a note explaining everything to the nurse. Will you be all right, do you think?"

"I'll be quite all right, my dear. Don't hurry; I shall get a little sleep, I expect."

Jennifer went downstairs and left a note on the hall table for the nurse, and travelled across London to her rooms at Blackheath. She got there about midday, packed a bag, went to the bank, and rang up her office to say that she would have to take the rest of the week off to look after her grandmother. Then she snatched a quick meal in a café and travelled back to Ealing.

She was lucky in that when she reached the house the doctor and the nurse were both there, with her grandmother. She waited in the hall till they came down from the bedroom; a few letters had arrived, two that seemed to be bills and one air-mailed from Australia. That would be Jane Dorman, Jennifer thought, who had married the Australian who drank port with the butler and never saluted anybody, and who still sent parcels of dried fruit to her aunt after thirty years. They must have been very close at one time for affection to have endured so long.

She looked round for the candle, but she could not find it; perhaps the doctor and the nurse had it upstairs with them. She stood in the dusk of the hall, waiting.

Presently they came out of the room upstairs, and the staircase was suddenly flooded with light as the nurse turned the switch. Jennifer went forward to meet them. "The electricity's come on!" she exclaimed.

"Of course. Didn't you go and see them?"

"They said they wouldn't turn it on until I paid the bill."

"The man came and turned it on this afternoon." They left that for the moment, and the nurse said, "This is Dr. Thompson."

He was a fairly young man, not more than about thirty; he looked tired and overworked. He said, "You're Miss Morton? Let's go into one of these rooms."

They went into the drawing-room; it was as cold as a tomb, but anyway the light was on. Surrounded by the Burmese relics the girl asked, "How is she, Doctor?"

The young man glanced at her, summing her up. "She's very ill," he said. "Very ill indeed. You know what's the matter with her, of course?"

Jennifer said, "She's got no money."

"Yes. Malnutrition. Starvation, if you like." He glanced around the drawing-room, taking in the worn Indian carpet of fine quality, the old-fashioned, comfortable furniture, the sampler as a fire-screen, the multitude of ornaments and bric-à-brac. "She wouldn't sell any of this stuff, I suppose."

"She's very set in her ways," the girl said. "She likes to have her own things round her."

"I know." He glanced at her. "Are you going to keep her here?"

"Could we get her into a hospital?"

He shook his head. "I don't think there's a chance. I don't think any hospital would take her. You see, the beds are all needed for urgent cases; she might be bedridden for years if she gets over the immediate trouble."

"She must have paid a lot of money into hospitals in her time," said Jennifer. "She was always subscribing to things."

"I'm afraid that doesn't count for much in the Health Service. Things are different now, you know."

"My father's coming down from Leicester tomorrow," the girl said. "He's a doctor. I think he'll have to decide what to do. I'll stay with her tonight in any case."

"You'll be alone, here, will you?"

"Yes." She hesitated, and then she said, "Do you think she'll die?"

"I hope not. Would you be very frightened if she did die, and you were alone with her?"

"I've never seen anybody die," the girl said evenly. "I hope that I'd be able to do what was best for her."

"You'll be all right. . . ." He bit his lip. "I don't think she'll die tonight," he said. "She's definitely weaker than when I saw her yesterday, I'm afraid. . . . Nurse here has to get some sleep tonight. I tell you what I'll do. I'll look in again myself about eleven, just before I go to bed. In the meantime, this is what she's got to have."

He gave her her instructions, and went off with the nurse; Jennifer went up to her grandmother's bedroom. It was warm with an electric radiator burning; the old lady lay in bed, but turned her eyes to the girl.

"I see you've got a radiator going, Granny," she said. "That's much better."

"It was that nice man," she said weakly. "I heard somebody moving around downstairs, and I thought it was you, Jenny. And then somebody knocked at my door, and it was him. He said he hoped he wasn't intruding, but he thought I'd like the radiator, and he came in and turned it on and saw that it was burning properly. And then he said he hoped I'd soon be better."

"How nice of him," the girl said.

She made her grandmother comfortable and went out quickly to get to the shops before they shut. She bought the things that the doctor had told her to buy and a little food for her own supper. On

40

her way back to the house she passed the Electricity Department, and saw a light still burning in the office window, though the door was locked. She stopped, and rang the bell; the manager himself came to the door of the shop.

He peered at her in the half light, his eyes dazzled by the strong light at his desk. "It's after hours," he said. "The office is closed now. You'll have to come back in the morning."

"It's me—Jennifer Morton," she said. "I just looked in to thank you for turning on the electricity."

He recognised her then. "Oh, that's all right," he said. "I rang up head office, and they gave permission." In fact he had sat for an hour staring blankly at the calendar, unable to work, and with the girl's words searing in his mind. Then he had rung up his supervisor and had repeated to him what Jennifer had said. He had added a few words of his own, saying that he had checked with the district nurse, and he was going to re-connect the supply. He had said quietly that they could take whatever action seemed best to them; if the job required behaviour of that sort from him, he didn't want the job. He was now waiting for the storm to break, uncertain of his own future, unsettled and reluctant to go home and tell his wife.

"I've got my cheque-book here," she said. "I can pay the bill now, if you like."

It might soothe the supervisor if the cheque were dated on the same day as his own revolt. He showed her into the office and she sat down and wrote out the cheque; in turn he wrote out the receipt, stamped it, and gave it to her. "How is your grandmother tonight?" he asked.

"Not too good," she replied. "She's got a better chance now that we can get some warmth into the house. I'm sorry I said that to you this morning. One gets a bit strung up."

"Oh, that's all right," he said. "Can't you get her into the hospital?"

The girl shook her head. "She's too old," she said a little bitterly. "They don't want people in there who are just dying of old age. She's lost her pension because we've left India and the fund's run dry. She can't get an old age pension under the new scheme because she hasn't contributed to it for fifteen years, or something. She's spent all her capital in trying to live, and sold most of her furniture, and the bank won't give her any more upon the house. There's no place for old ladies in the brave new world."

He tightened his lips, conscious of his own dark fears. "I know," he said. "It's getting worse each year. Sometimes one feels the only thing to do is to break out and get away while you're still young enough. Try it again in Canada, perhaps, or in South Africa."

She looked at him, startled. "Is that what you're thinking of?"

"If I was alone, I'd go, I think," he said. "But it's the children— that's what makes it difficult. They've got to have a home. . . ."

She had no time to stay and talk to him; she cut it short and

41

hurried back to the house. There was a telegram there now from her father saying that he was coming down next day without her mother, who was not so well, and enclosing a telegraphed money order for ten pounds. She put that in her bag and glanced at the two bills, one for groceries and one for milk, each with a politely-worded note at the bottom that was a threat of action. No good worrying her grandmother with those. She took off her coat and hat, and went upstairs with the letter from Australia in her hand.

In the bedroom the old lady was still lying in much the same position. She was awake and she knew Jennifer, but she was breathing now in an irregular manner, with three or four deep breaths and then a pause. There was nothing that Jennifer could do about it; the only thing was to carry on and do what the doctor had told her. It was time for another drink of warm milk, this time with brandy in it.

She gave the air-mail letter to her grandmother. "There's an air-mail letter for you," she said brightly. "Like me to get your glasses?"

"Please, dear. Did you see where it was from?"

"It's from Australia."

The old lady took the spectacle case with trembling hands, fumbling a little and put the glasses on, and looked at the letter. "Yes, that's from dear Jane. So sweet of her to keep on writing, and sending me such lovely parcels. We must make a cake, Jenny. Such lovely things. . . ."

Jennifer went downstairs and warmed the milk up in a saucepan on the stove and made herself a cup of tea at the same time; she mixed the Benger's Food and added the brandy, and carried both cups up to the bedroom. She found her grandmother staring bewildered at a slip of paper in her hand, the envelope and the letter lying on the counterpane that covered her.

"Jenny," she said weakly. "Jenny, come here a minute. What is this?"

The girl took it from her. It clearly had to do with banking; it was like a cheque and yet it was not quite an ordinary cheque. The words were clear enough, however. "It's a sort of cheque, Granny," she said. "It's made payable to you, for five hundred pounds sterling. I'm not quite sure what sterling means. It seems to be signed by the Commonwealth Bank of Australia. It's as if the bank was giving you five hundred pounds."

The old lady said, "It's from Jane. She says so in the letter. Oh, my dear—we'll have to send it back. Such a sweet child, but she can't possibly afford it. She ought not to have done such a thing."

"If she's sent it to you, perhaps she *can* afford it," the girl said.

"Oh, my dear, she's only a farmer's wife, living in quite a poor way, I'm afraid, and with all those children. Wherever would she get five hundred pounds?"

Jennifer said, "May I see her letter, Granny?"

42

"Of course, my dear."

It was written in the round schoolgirl hand that Jane Dorman had never lost. The first four pages dealt with news of the older children, news of Angela at Melbourne University, news of Jack's rheumatism, and news of the spring weather. It went on,

"Jack and I have been a little worried by the part of your letter where you said you hadn't bought a new vest, and we have been wondering if rising prices are making things difficult for you. Out here everything is going up in price, too, but we station people are all making so much money that we hardly notice it. Jack's wool cheque this year was for twenty-two thousand pounds, and though most of that will go in tax of course it means that we shall still have about seven thousand for ourselves after paying all the expenses of the property.

"We don't know what's the right thing to do with so much money. We can't expect it to go on, of course; wool will come down again next year and it's quite right that it should. It could fall to a quarter of the present price and not hurt us; the bank was all paid off last year and we've never spent much on ourselves, and we're too old now to do much gadding about. We're going down to Melbourne for a week or ten days after Christmas to do some shopping and Jack still talks of a trip home, but I don't suppose we'll really get much further than the Windsor Hotel.

"I'm sending with this letter a little bank draft for five hundred pounds, with our dear love. It doesn't mean anything to us now, because we have more than we can ever spend. If you don't need it, will you give it to some charity in England for us? But we've been really worried about you since reading that letter about your vest, and Jack and I owe so much to you for all you did to help us thirty years ago. So if this will make things easier for you, will you take it with our very dearest love?

"Your affectionate niece,

"JANE."

The girl laid the letter down. "It's all right, Granny," she said a little unsteadily. "She's got all the money in the world. They're making twenty-two thousand pounds a year—at least, I think that's what she means."

"Nonsense, my dear," the old lady said weakly. "She's only a farmer's wife. Stations, they call them in Australia, but it's only a big farm and not very good land, I'm told. She's made some mistake."

The girl wrinkled her brows, and glanced at the letter again. "I don't think it's a mistake—honestly. It's what she says, and I was reading something about this in the paper the other day." She laid the letter down. "Look, drink your milk before it gets cold."

She held the old lady upright with one arm, and raised the cup to her lips. She could not get her to drink much, and the effort seemed

43

to tire her, because she lay back on the pillows with her eyes closed, disinclined to talk. Jennifer removed the letter and the envelope to a table at the bedside and put the bankers' draft upon the dressing-table, carefully weighted with an embossed Indian silver hand-mirror.

She went downstairs to get her own supper. Meat and eggs were out of the question, of course, but she had got herself a piece of cod and some potatoes and carrots. She put the cod on to boil because she would not encroach upon her grandmother's fat ration or open the tin of lard, and she peeled some of the potatoes and carrots to boil those. This insipid meal was normal to her life and she thought nothing of it; she had bought a pot of jam and some buns and a piece of cheese to liven it up a bit. She started all this going on the stove, and slipped upstairs to see how her grandmother was getting on.

The old lady had not moved, and she seemed to be asleep. Her breathing, if anything, was worse. To Jennifer as she stood motionless in the door, looking at her, she seemed smaller and more shrunken, further away. The room seemed suddenly a great deal colder; she shivered a little, and went in softly and turned on the second element of the electric stove.

As she ate her supper at the kitchen table she wondered what could best be done for her grandmother in the new situation presented by this five hundred pounds. Her father was coming down next day and he would decide what was the best course; she was rather ignorant about the practical points of illness and of nursing, but she knew that this five hundred pounds would make a difference. Perhaps it would be possible to get the old lady into a nursing home, or clinic. She knew that her parents had no money to spare; it was only with difficulty that they could keep up her father's considerable life insurance and endowment premiums; they had their own old age to think about. It had probably been a real difficulty for her father to send her ten pounds at a moment's notice, as he had that day.

She went up once or twice to look into the bedroom, but she did not speak; better to let her grandmother rest quietly till it was time for her next cup of milk food and brandy. She took that up after a lapse of two hours, and spoke to the old lady. "I've made you some more Benger's, Granny," she said quietly. "Are you awake?"

The old eyes opened. "I'm awake, Jenny. I've been thinking about so many things."

The girl sat down beside her and raised her in the bed with an arm round the old shoulders, and held the cup for her to drink. "What have you been thinking about?" she asked.

Her grandmother said, "About when I was a girl, my dear, and how different things were then."

Jennifer asked, "How were they different, Granny? Drink it up."

44

She took a little sip. "It was all so much easier, dear. My father, your great-grandfather, was in the Foreign Office, but he retired early, when I was about fifteen. Before that we lived in a big house on Putney Hill, near where Swinburne lived, but when he retired, in about 1886, we moved down into the country. My father bought Steep Manor near Petersfield with about thirty acres of land. I don't think his pension and my mother's investments together amounted to more than a thousand pounds a year, but they seemed to be able to do such a lot with it, such a great, great deal."

"Drink a little more," the girl suggested. "What sort of things did you do?"

"Everything that gentlefolk did do in those days, dear. My father kept three maid-servants in the house—everybody did then. And there was a gardener, and a gardener's boy who helped in the stables and a groom. That was before the days of motor-cars, of course. My mother had her carriage with a pair of matched greys, such a pretty pair. My father and Tom and I all had our hacks, or hunters as we liked to call them, because we followed the hunt every week all through the winter."

She sat in silence for a time; the girl held her, motionless. "I had a chestnut mare called Dolly," she said. "Such a sweet little horse. I used to groom her myself, and she always knew when I was coming because I always brought her a lump of sugar or an apple, and she would put her head round, and whinny. Tom rode her sometimes, and she could jump beautifully, but I never jumped her myself except over a ha-ha or a ditch, because I rode side-saddle of course, in a habit. We thought it was very fast when girls began to ride astride in breeches just like men. I think a habit looks much nicer."

The girl held the cup to the old lips again. "Wasn't it dull, just living in the country?" she asked.

"Oh, my dear, it wasn't dull. There was always such a lot to do, with the servants and the gardens and the greenhouses and the horses. We kept pigs and we used to cure all our own hams and bacon. And then we used to give a dance every year and all our friends did the same, and the Hunt Ball, and people coming to stay. And then there were all the people in the village to look after; everybody knew everybody else, and everybody helped each other. There was never a minute to spare, and never a dull moment."

She took a sip of the milk that Jennifer pressed on her. "We always had a week in London, every year," she said. "We used to stay at Brown's Hotel in Dover Street, generally in May or June. It was theatres and dances every night. I was presented at Court in 1892, to the Prince of Wales, and the old Queen came in for a moment and we all curtsied to her, all together. The lights, and all the men in their scarlet and blue dress uniforms, and the women in Court dress, with trains—I don't think I ever saw anything so splendid, except perhaps at the Durbar in nineteen hundred and eleven." She paused. "You haven't been presented, have you, Jenny?"

The girl said "No Granny. I don't think it happens so much now."

"Oh, my dear, how much, how very much you young girls have to miss. We had so much, much more than you when we were young."

Jennifer tried to get her to drink a little more, but the old lady refused it. "Garden parties all through the summer," she murmured, "with tea out on the lawn under the cedar tree. There was tennis on the lawn for those who felt like it, but archery was what everybody went in for. We had a special strip of lawn by the herbaceous border that we kept for archery, and the targets upon metal stands, stuffed with straw, with white and red and blue and gold circles. Such a pretty sport upon a sunny afternoon, dear, with the sun and the scent of mignonette, between the cedar and the monkey-puzzle tree. . . ."

The old eyes closed; it was no good trying to get her to take any more of the Benger's Food. The girl withdrew the cup and put it on the side table, and gently relaxed her arm to lay the old head down upon the pillow. Her grandmother seemed to sleep where she was put; the girl stood for a moment looking down at her as she lay with eyes closed. It didn't look so good, but there was nothing more that she could do for the time being, except to change the hot-water bottles.

When she had done that, she went downstairs again. In spite of the bad night that she had had the night before she was not sleepy; there was a sense of urgency upon her that banished fatigue. She considered for a moment where she was to sleep, and put it out of her mind; the only possible place for sleep was the sofa in the drawing-room and that was much too far from the old lady's bedroom. It was warm up in the bedroom, and she could shade the light; she would spend the night up there in the arm-chair again, within reach of her grandmother.

The doctor came at about eleven o'clock as he had promised; Jennifer was making another cup of the milk drink when he arrived, and she came out of the kitchen to meet him in the hall.

"Good evening," he said. "How is she now?"

"Much the same," the girl replied. "If anything, I think she's a bit weaker."

"Has she taken anything?"

"She takes about half a cup each time. I can't get her to take more than that."

"I'll just go up and see her. You'd better come up, too."

She was with him in the bedroom while he made his examination; the old lady knew him, but said very little. He made it short, bade her good-night cheerfully, and went downstairs again with Jennifer.

46

In the drawing-room he said, "I'm very sorry that there isn't a nurse with you."

She look at him. "You mean, she's going?"

"She's not making any progress," he replied. "She's weaker every time I see her. I'm afraid there's only one end to that, Miss Morton."

"Do you think she'll die tonight?" the girl asked.

"I can't say. She might, quite easily. Or she might rally and go on for days or even weeks. But her heart's getting very bad. I'm afraid you'll have to be prepared for it to happen any time."

He spoke to her about the practical side of death, and he spoke to her about the continued effort to feed the old body. And then he said, "I rang up the relieving officer about her today. I think he'll be coming round to see you tomorrow."

She said, "That's somebody who doles out money, isn't it?"

"In a way," he replied. "He has power to give monetary relief to cases of hardship that aren't covered under any of the existing Acts. He's a municipal officer." He paused. "I wish I'd known about this patient earlier. I could have asked him to come round and see her months ago, but I had no idea."

Jennifer said, "I don't believe my grandmother would have seen him."

"Why not?"

She shrugged her shoulders. "She'd have looked on it as charity money. All her life she's been more accustomed to giving to charities than taking from them."

"He's very tactful, I believe."

"He'd have to be," she said. "My grandmother's a lady—the old-fashioned sort."

There was a pause. "In any case," she said, "that won't be necessary now. Granny got a cheque today for five hundred pounds, from a relation in Australia who was worried about her. There's enough money now to pay for anything she ought to have."

"Five hundred pounds!" he said. "That's a lot of money. Pity it didn't come three months ago."

"I know," she said. "It's just one of those things."

He thought for a moment. "Would you like me to see if I can get a nurse for her tomorrow?"

"My father will be here tomorrow," she said. "He's a doctor. He'll be here about midday. Could we talk it over with you then? I should think a nurse would be a good thing."

He nodded. "I'll see if I can get one for tomorrow night. You'll need some relief by then."

They went out into the hall, and he put on his coat. He paused then, hat in hand. "She's got relations in Australia, has she? Do you know where they live?"

"They keep a sheep farm," the girl said. "Somewhere in Victoria, I think." He nodded slowly. "I still can't quite understand it," she

47

said. "Granny thought they were quite poor, but then this money arrived for her today. They must be very well off to send a sum like that."

"The graziers are doing very well," he said. "Everybody in that country seems to be doing very well." He hesitated. "I'm going to try it out there for a bit, myself."

She looked at him, surprised. "*You* are? Are you leaving England?"

"Just for a bit," he said. "I think it does one good to move around, and there's not much future in the Health Service. I think it'll be better for the children, too, and it's not like going abroad. I've got a passage booked on the *Orion*, sailing on April the eighteenth. It's a bit of a gamble, but I've had it here."

"Where are you going to?" she asked. "What part of Australia?"

"Brisbane," he said. "I was there for a bit in 1944, when I was in the Navy. I liked it all right. I believe you could have a lot of fun in Queensland." He hesitated for a moment, and then said, "Don't talk about this, please, Miss Morton. It's not generally known yet that I'm going."

"I shan't talk," she said. "I don't know anyone in Ealing."

He went away, and she went back into the kitchen and stood thoughtful over the electric stove as she warmed up the milk again. The house was dead silent but for the low noise of wind and a little trickling noise of water from some gutter. She poured the milk into the cup and added the brandy, and took it up to her grandmother.

"How are you feeling now, Granny?" she asked.

The old lady did not answer, but her eyes were open and she was awake. Jennifer sat down on the bedside and lifted her with an arm around her shoulders, and held the cup to her lips. She drank a little, and the brandy may have strengthened her, because presently she said in a thin voice, "Jenny, I'm going to die."

The girl said, "So am I, Granny, but not just yet. Nor are you. Drink a bit more of this."

"Have you ever seen anybody die, Jenny?"

The girl shook her head.

"I wish there was somebody here with you."

The girl held the cup up to the lips. It was stupid to feel frightened, and she must not show it. "Try a little more. It's good for you."

Too weak to argue, the old lady took a tiny sip or two. Then she said, "Jenny." There was a long pause while she gathered strength, and then she said. "My cheque-book. In the small left-hand drawer of the bureau. And my pen."

"Do you want to write a cheque, Granny?" The old eyes signified assent. "Leave it till the morning. Drink a little more of this, and then get some sleep."

The old lady pushed the cup aside. "No. Now."

The girl put the cup down and went downstairs. She knew that the doctor had been right and that her grandmother would die that night. She was not frightened now; her duty was to ease the passing of the old lady and do what she wanted in the last few hours. She was calm and competent and thoughtful as she brought the pen and cheque-book and a blotting-pad to the bedside.

"Are these what you want, Granny?"

The old lady nodded slightly, and the girl put them on the sheet before her, and arranged the pillows, and lifted the old body into a sitting position. She gave her another drink of the hot milk and brandy. Presently the old lady said, "Bring that thing."

The girl was puzzled. "What thing is it?" And then she got up and fetched the draft from the dressing-table, and said, "This?"

Her grandmother nodded weakly and took it from her and looked round, questing, till Jennifer divined what it was that she wanted, and gave her her spectacles. She put them on, and then she said distinctly, "Such a funny sort of cheque. I never saw one like it." And then she endorsed it on the back with a hand that trembled, with a signature that was barely legible.

Jennifer held the cup to her lips, and she drank a little more. Then, with a sudden spurt of energy, she took the cheque-book and wrote quite a legible cheque for four hundred pounds, payable to Jennifer Morton.

The girl, looking on as she wrote, said, "Granny, you mustn't do that. "I don't want it, and you'll need the money when you get well."

The old lady whispered, "I want you to do something for me, Jenny. Write letters now, send this to my bank and this to yours. Then go and post them."

"I'll do that in the morning, Granny. I can't leave you alone tonight."

The old lady gathered her ebbing strength, and said, "Go and write them now, my dear, and bring them up and show me. And then go out and post them."

"All right." She could not disobey so positive and direct a command. She thought as she wrote the letters at her grandmother's bureau in the drawing-room that she could sort the matter out with her father next day and pay the money back; the thing now was to ease the old lady's passing and not disobey her. She brought the letters and the envelopes up to the bedside and showed them; the old lady did not speak, but watched her as she put the letters and the cheques into the envelopes and sealed them down. The girl said, "There they are, Granny, all ready to post. May I post them in the morning?"

The head shook slightly, and the old lips said, "Now."

"All right. I expect I'll be away about ten minutes, Granny; I'll have to go down to the Broadway. I'll be back as quick as ever I can."

The old head nodded slightly, and the girl went down and put her coat on, and ran most of the way to the post office and most of the way back. She came back into the bedroom flushed and breathing quickly, but her grandmother's eyes were closed, and she seemed to be asleep.

The girl went down to the kitchen and made herself a cup of tea, and ate a little meal of toast and jam. Then she went back to the bedroom and settled down in the chair before the electric stove.

At about half-past twelve the old lady opened her eyes and said, "Jenny, did you post the letters?"

"I posted them, Granny."

"There's a dear girl," the voice from the bed said weakly. "I've been so worried for you, but you'll be all right with Jane."

The girl blinked in surprise, but there were more important things to be done than to ask for explanations. "Don't try to talk," she said. "Let me get some more hot water in these bottles."

Her grandmother said, "No. Jenny . . . Jenny . . ."

The girl paused in the act of taking the bottles from the bed. "What is it, Granny?"

The old lady said something that the girl could not catch. And then she said, "It's not as if we were extravagant, Geoffrey and I. It's been a change that nobody could fight against, this going down and down. I've had such terrible thoughts for you, Jenny, that it would go on going down and down, and when you are as old as I am you would look back at your room at Blackheath and your office work, as I look back to my life at Steep Manor, and you'll think how very rich you were when you were young."

It did not make sense to the girl. She said, "I'm just going to take these bottles down and fill them, Granny. I'll be back in a few minutes."

Her grandmother said, "I always took a hot-water bottle with me when we went out on shikar. Geoffrey's bearer, dear old Moung Bah, used to boil up water over the wood fire and fill it for me, while Geoffrey cleaned his gun in front of the tent. Such lovely times we had out in the jungle, dear. Such lovely places . . ." The old voice died away into silence.

The girl took the hot-water bottles and went quickly downstairs to fill them. When she came back with them and put them in the bed around the old lady, her grandmother was lying with closed eyes; she seemed fairly comfortable, but the respiration was much worse. She was breathing in short gasps three or four times in succession; then would come a silence when for a long time she did not seem to breathe at all. It was fairly obvious to the girl that the end was coming. She wondered if she ought to go and fetch the doctor from his bed, and then she thought that there was nothing he could do; better for other and more vital patients that he should be allowed to rest. She sat down by the bedside in the chair to wait, holding her grandmother's hand, filled with deep sadness at the close of life.

The old lady spoke suddenly from the bed. Jennifer missed the

50

first words again; she may have been half asleep. She heard, "—on twenty-two thousand a year, better than we lived at Steep. Give her my very dearest love when you see her, Jenny. I'm so happy for you now. It was so sweet of her to send those lovely fruits. Be sure and tell her how much we enjoyed them."

There was a long, long pause, and then she said, "So glad she sent the money for your fare. I've had so much, much more than you poor girls today."

Jennifer was on her feet now; there was something here that had to be cleared up. She held her grandmother's hand between her own young, warm ones. "What did you give me that money for, Granny? What do you you want me to do with the four hundred pounds? Try and tell me."

The old lips muttered, "Dear Jane. Such lovely fruits."

The girl stood by the bedside, waiting. If she had understood the old lady at all she was making an incredible proposal, but, after all, the doctor was going.

She said, "Try and tell me what you want me to do with the four hundred pounds, Granny."

There were a few faint, jumbled words that Jennifer missed, and then she heard, "—a little horse for you, everything that I had at your age."

There was very little time left now. The girl said, "Granny! Did you give me the four hundred pounds because you want me to go to Australia to visit Aunt Jane? Is that what you're trying to say? Is that what you'd like me to so with the money?"

There was a faint, unmistakable nod. Then the old eyes closed again, as if in sleep. The girl laid the hand carefully beneath the bedclothes and sat down again to wait. There was a terrific mess here that her father must help her to clear up.

At about two o'clock her grandmother spoke again for the last time. Jennifer, bending by the old lips, heard her say, "The dear Queen's statue in Moulmein . . . white marble. So sweet of the Burmese . . ."

About an hour later the old lady died. Jennifer, standing by the bedside, could not say within a quarter of an hour when death occurred.

Three

JENNIFER met her father at the front door of the house early the next afternoon. She had gone out into the wet, windy streets at about four in the morning to stand in a call-box in the Broadway to ring him up in Leicester; the telephone was by his bed and she got through to him without delay, and told him of the death. Then she had walked back to the house. She had expected to be troubled and reluctant to go back there, but in fact she found she was not worried in the least by the thought of her dead grandmother upstairs. She was calm and serious; she felt that she had done a good job and her grandmother was pleased with her; if she had still been alive the old lady would have wanted her to have a little meal and get some sleep. So she made herself a meal of tea and bread and jam in the kitchen of the silent house, turned on the radiator in the living-room, curled herself up on the sofa with a rug over her, and slept. She did not wake until the middle of the morning, when the district nurse came.

Her father came down to Ealing alone. Her mother had made arrangements to come with him, but she was coughing a good deal and far from well, and on the news of her mother's death Jennifer's father had persuaded his wife to stay at home and not risk making herself ill just for the funeral. So he came down alone, and met his daughter at the house at about two o'clock.

"I'm very sorry you had this alone, Jenny," he said. "I'm very sorry indeed."

"That's all right, Daddy," she said. "It's a good thing I was working in London."

He glanced around the drawing-room. "She was very fond of this house," he said. "We tried once or twice to get her to come up to Leicester and live near us, but she insisted on staying here."

The girl nodded. "This was her own house, and she wouldn't have wanted to be a burden upon anybody. She was very independent."

Her father said, "We never dreamed that there was anything wrong with her pension, or her money generally. I suppose I should have come to see her more often, and gone into things a bit more."

"She probably wouldn't have told you," the girl said.

He asked her about the practical business of the doctor and the death certificate and the undertaker, and went out to see about these things himself. Jennifer went out to find somewhere for her father and herself to stay that night, and with some difficulty found a private hotel with a couple of bedrooms empty; then she went back to the house to wait for her father. When he came she made him tea, and they sat in the drawing-room among the Burmese relics before an electric radiator while she told him what had happened the night before.

"She insisted on giving me the cheque," she told her father, "and she made me go out and post it to my bank. What ought I to do, Daddy? I'll have to pay it back to the executor, shan't I?"

He shook his head. "Keep it."

"Is that all right?"

"I think so," he said. "Unless she's changed her will, I'm the executor and the whole of the residuary estate goes to your mother. The four hundred pounds is probably yours, legally. But anyway, it doesn't matter."

"Oughtn't it to go back to Aunt Jane?" She paused. "After all, she sent it for Granny, not for me."

He pondered this. "Did you say there was a letter from Jane Dorman?"

She went and fetched it for him from her grandmother's room, and he read it carefully. "I don't think you need give it back," he said. "The intention is quite clear; she says that if Ethel didn't need it she was to give it to a charity. Well, she doesn't need it, and she's given it to you. It's yours to do what you like with, Jenny."

The girl stared at the hot elements of the fire. "I'm not so sure about that," she said. "I think it's mine to do what Granny liked."

"What do you mean?"

She told him what had passed between them in the last hour of the old life. "She kept saying what a rotten time girls have in England now, compared with when she was young," she said. "I suppose all old people are like that, that everything was better in their day. And then, it seemed quite definite, she wanted me to go and see Aunt Jane with the money. Go to Australia, I mean. It seemed as if she thought that I'd be getting back into the sort of life she knew when she was a girl, if I went out there and stayed with Aunt Jane."

Her father said thoughtfully, "I see. Do you want to go, Jenny?"

The girl said honestly, "I don't know. I've not had time to think about it. I'd love to travel, of course, and see something of the world. But Granny's world . . . that's gone for ever, surely? Huntin' and shootin' and fishin', and about fifteen servants all calling you Madam. . . . If that's what happens in Australia, I don't want to go there."

"I should be sorry to see you go to Australia, Jenny. You're the only one we've got."

She smiled at him. "Don't worry, Daddy. I can't see myself going."

There was one job that had to be done before they left for the hotel, and that was to gather up all the papers in the house for examination. Edward Morton decided to start on that that evening at the hotel, but when they came to investigate the papers they found a formidable mass of stuff. The drawers of the old lady's bureau, and a sort of tallboy, were crammed full of letters and papers, the relics of a long life thrust into drawers and there forgotten. Insurance policies of 1907 were mixed up with leases of furnished houses rented on some leaves in the dim past, and personal letters, and receipts, and cheque-book stubs were everywhere among the mass. They found three suitcases in the house and filled them full of all this paper, and at that there was enough left over to fill another two. Her father said, "I'll go through these tonight, Jenny, and chuck away what it's not necessary to keep. Then perhaps I'll be able to look through the rest of it tomorrow here."

Jennifer hoped that The Poplars private hotel would be complacent about a hundredweight of waste paper, in the morning.

They got a taxi from the station and drove to The Poplars and dined together meagrely. Jenny had had two virtually sleepless nights and she could hardly keep her eyes open during the meal. As soon as it was over, she said, "Daddy, do you mind if I go up now? I'm practically asleep." He kissed her and wished her goodnight. Then he went up to his own room and put a shilling in the slot of the gas meter and lit the stove, and pulled a chair up to the little radiants, and opened the first suitcase.

In the white-painted, rather bleak and functional bedroom the pageant of a long life gradually unrolled before him as the heap of torn papers on the floor beside him grew. It was about twenty minutes after he had started that he came upon the cookery book.

It was a small manuscript book. It began in a hand that was feminine and strange to him, and about half the recipes in the book were written in that hand; thereafter it had been written on by Ethel Trehearn, first in an unformed, almost childish hand, later maturing into the writing that he knew. On the fly-leaf was the inscription,

> For my dear daughter, Ethel, on the happy occasion
> of her marriage to Geoffrey Trehearn, from her
> mother. June 16th, 1893.

It had been a pleasant and a practical thought of the mother to give the bride a personal cookery book as one of her wedding presents; fifty-seven years later Edward Morton smiled a little sympathetically, as he turned the leaves. How unformed the writing of the bride was in the first entry . . .

Aunt Hester's cake (*very good*).
Take two pounds of Jersey butter, two pounds best castor sugar, ½ gill of caramel, 2½ lb of flour, 18 eggs, 3 lb of

currants, 3 lbs of sultanas, 1½ lbs of mixed peel, ½ lb of blanched sweet almonds, the grated rind of two lemons, a small nutmeg, 1 oz mixed spice, and ½ a pint of brandy.

He ran his eye down the recipe with the tolerant amusement of a doctor to the final,

—cover with almond icing and coat with royal and transparent icing. Then pipe the cake with royal icing according to taste.

What a world to live in, and how ill they must have been! His eye ran back to the ingredients. Two pounds of Jersey butter . . . eight weeks' ration for one person. The egg ration for one person for four months. . . . Currants and sultanas in those quantities; mixed peel, that he had not seen for years. Half a pint of brandy, so plentiful that you could put half a pint into a cake, and think nothing of it.

He laid the book down on his knee and stared at the stove. Funny the way that things worked out sometimes. This bride had died of starvation, with nothing to eat but currants and sultanas and candied peel in the end. He wondered, had she thought in those days of "Aunt Hester's cake (very good)"?

Things had changed, and people no longer lived as they had done in 1893. He had eaten such cakes when he was a young man before the war of 1914, but now he could hardly remember what a cake like that would taste like. Jennifer had never eaten anything like that at all, of course, and so she couldn't miss it. Funny how the standards of living had changed, at any rate in England.

He thumbed the book through idly, glancing here and there at a page. Her mother had had little confidence in the memory or interest of her daughter before marriage, for she had written out the simplest recipes in full. "For breakfast, bacon and eggs. For four people, take eight eggs or more if the men will want them and about a pound of streaky bacon cut in rashers . . ." He could remember breakfasts like that when he was a boy—how long it seemed since he had eaten like that! He turned the pages idly. "Steak and Onions. Take three pounds of steak . . ."

He had not eaten a grilled steak and onions for twelve years; perhaps Jennifer at twenty-four had never eaten it at all. People seemed to keep healthy enough on the English rationed food. He was approaching sixty years of age himself and he knew well, perhaps too well, that men of his years think everything was better organised when they were young. It was an old man's fancy, doubtless, that the young men were more virile in England, and the girls prettier, in 1914 than they were today. People kept healthy enough, but they had not the zest for life that they had had when he was young. Jennifer with her auburn hair looked pale and sallow most of the time, but at twenty-four she should be in her prime.

He laid the cookery book aside, too precious to destroy; though it might only be of academic interest in England now it was a pity to throw away a little book that had been prized for so many years. He turned over and tore up masses of old letters, only glancing at the signatures in case they were autographs of famous people, and he retained one or two. Then he shook out the contents of a card-board box that once held envelopes, and out fell dance programmes, dozens and dozens of them.

It was years since he had seen the little cards, heavily embossed with gilt and coloured lettering, with little pencils attached by a thread of silk. How thick and fine the paper was, how generous! Dance programmes with little pencils attached seemed to have gone out in England, perhaps because of fashion or perhaps because of paper rationing; if they were used, however, cards like that would cost two or three shillings each, with printing, pencils, purchase tax, and everything. Things had been cheaper, easier, and more gracious when Ethel had been young. And how many of the cards there were, how many dances she had been to! There were thirty-five or forty of them; assuming she had kept the programme of every dance that she had ever been to, which seemed unlikely, even so it was a con-siderable number of formal dances for a young girl to attend. She had been married at twenty-two, younger than Jennifer. He was quite sure that Jennifer had not been to thirty-five or forty formal dances. People didn't seem to give them so much now as they had in his young days; perhaps it had grown too expensive.

There were photographs almost by the hundred. He discarded the faded, sepia snapshots, hardly looking at them; there could be nothing worth keeping in those. He paused longer over the pro-fessional portraits. One was a very grand affair, hand-tinted by a photographer in Dover Street; it showed a mother and daughter in Court dress, the long trains sweeping from behind each side of the standing pair. He could see the Ethel he had first met as a middle-aged woman in the features of the girl. But what a dress, and what a train! White silk with delicate lines of a pale rose pink, showy and ornate by modern standards, it might be, but very lovely all the same. And what jewellery for a young girl to wear! That necklace, carefully worked up by the tinter, apparently of gold and rubies. Jennifer had never worn a dress or jewellery like that, and yet she came of the same family. He put the photograph aside, thinking that Jennifer might like to see her grandmother as a young woman.

There was a little bundle of letters tied with ribbon, perhaps love letters. He hesitated for a moment, thinking to throw them away unread; then he undid them and glanced at the signatures. They were all signed "Jane". He picked one for its embossed letterhead and glanced it through. It was dated March 5th, 1919, and it read,

"MY DARLING AUNT,

"I would have written to post at Gibraltar but I've been terribly seasick ever since we left England just like being in a funny story only I didn't think it funny at all. Jack was only sick one day but I was in my bunk for five days, all through the Bay, in a cabin with five other girls all married to Australians and going out like us, all sick together except one. I felt awfully silly and very glad in a way that Jack and I couldn't have a cabin together because it would have been horrid for him with me being sick all the time. However, it seems to be over now and I've been sitting out on deck in the hot sun for two days and going into the saloon for every meal, and eating like a horse.

"I wanted to write to you before now to thank you for all you have done for us over the last year. I believe you were the only one of the whole family who didn't faint at the idea of me marrying an Australian soldier and who really tried to make Jack feel at home and one of us. I'm sorry in a way that I'm leaving England and going out to live so far away, sorry that I shan't see Father and Mother again for years and years, or perhaps at all. But these last few months haven't been a very happy time as I suppose you know, and though I'm sorry to be leaving everyone and everything I know, I'm glad at the same time, if you know what I mean. I'm glad to be out of all the complications and unpleasantness and able to start fresh in a new place with Jack.

"We're going to have a hard time for the first few years, much harder than if I'd been a good girl and stayed at home and married one of Father's officers, solid bone from the chin upwards. I might have done that if it hadn't been for the war, but two years in the W.A.A.C.s make one different. Jack has been promised a job with a firm called Dalgety which means going round the cattle and sheep stations selling machinery and stuff like that to the farmers in a place called Gippsland; we shan't have much money but he's got a house for us through his uncle in a little market town called Korrumburra somewhere in the depths of the country. I'll write and give you the address as soon as ever I know it; write to me sometimes, because although I'm glad to be going I expect I shall be lonely sometimes, and longing for letters.

"I don't know how to thank you for being so sweet to Jack. It meant an awful lot to him to find one of my family who really liked him for himself—besides me, of course. I don't suppose I'll ever be able to do anything for you like you've done for us, like the elephant and the mouse. Only I'd like to call one of our children Ethel if there is a girl. I think I'm in the family way already but I'm not quite sure, so don't tell anybody yet.

"Our very, very dearest love to you and Uncle Geoffrey.

"Your affectionate niece,

"JANE."

Morton was tired now. He had barely sorted one of the three suitcases, but he was too tired to go on that night; the white bed beckoned him in invitation. He folded the letter carefully and put it with the others of the bundle and retied the ribbon. Better to keep that lot, or send them back, perhaps, to Jane Dorman in Australia.

He had never met Jane Dorman and he knew little of her but that she had made an unfortunate marriage with an Australian soldier after the first war, and had left the country with him, and had never been home since. That was all that he had known about her twelve hours ago; in those hours she had come alive for him, and now she was a real person. She had formed her own life and battled through, and now she had attained a point where she could send five hundred pounds to her old aunt to quell a fear for her that he had never felt. Jane Dorman, twelve thousand miles away, in her enduring affection had sensed that Ethel Trehearn was ill and short of money. Her daughter, who was his wife, and he, living no more than a hundred miles away from the old lady, had had no idea that anything was wrong.

Jane and Jack Dorman, from her recent letter, had become wealthy people now, far better off than he himself. He could hardly have found five hundred shillings for the old lady without selling something. It wasn't that he was extravagant, or Mary, either. In these days, in England and in general practice, the money just wasn't there, and that was all about it.

He got into bed and turned off the light, but sleep did not come easily. How well Ethel Trehearn had lived when she was a young woman; how incredible it all seemed now! And yet, thinking back over his own youth, perhaps not quite so incredible. The standard of living had slipped imperceptibly in England as year succeeded year, as war succeeded war. His own father had been a doctor before him but in York. He could remember how he lived as a boy in the big house in Clifton now used as part of the municipal offices of York and full of draughtsman. They had kept a coachman and a groom before the days of motor-cars, and a horse for his father's dog-cart, and a horse for the brougham. There had been a whole-time gardener, and always two servants in the house, and sometimes three. It was unthinkable in his father's household that there should be any shortage of any food for family or servants; there always seemed to be plenty of money for anything they wanted to do, nor did his father have to work particularly hard. Only the most urgent cases ever called him out on Sunday, and all through the winter one day in each week was sacred to the shooting. It was a good life, that, that Ethel Trehearn had known as a young woman, and his father. It might some day come again in England, but not in his own time.

He turned restlessly in his bed, unable to sleep. It was easy to say that good times would come again in England, but was it true?

In each year of the peace food had got shorter and shorter, more and more expensive, and taxation had risen higher and higher. He was now living on a lower scale than in the war-time years; the decline had gone on steadily, if anything increasing in momentum, and there seemed no end to it. Where would it all end, and what lay ahead of the young people of today in England? What lay ahead of Jennifer?

He lay uneasily all night, a worried and an anxious man. He got up at dawn and went out for a short walk before breakfast, as was his habit. He met Jennifer at the breakfast table and they talked of the work that lay before them, the undertaker coming at ten o'clock, the search for a second-hand furniture dealer to make an offer for the furniture left in the house, the estate agent to be found who would sell the house itself. These were easy and straightforward matters that had to be attended to before Morton went back to his practice in Leicester; more difficult was the personal matter that he must talk over with his daughter.

He broached it as they walked through the suburban streets. "I've been thinking about you going to Australia, Jenny," he said. "There's a lot to be said, for and against. I don't think we want to decide anything too hastily."

She glanced at him in surprise. "You don't think I ought to go, Daddy?"

"I don't know," he said. "I don't know what to think. There's this four hundred pounds dumped right into your lap, so to speak, and that's what she wanted you to do with it. It might not be a bad idea to go out for a few months and see if you like it. There should be plenty of money to pay your passage out and home."

"I wouldn't want to stay out there, Daddy. I couldn't leave you and Mummy."

"We wouldn't want to lose you, Jenny. But I must say, I get worried sometimes thinking of the way things are going here."

The girl was silent. Even in her own memory the stringencies in her parents' home had increased; her own wage packet bought a good deal less than it had bought two years before. With the optimism of youth she said, "We'll get an election and a change of Government before long. Then everything will get cheap again, won't it?"

He shook his head. "I wish I could think so. I don't think it's anything to do with Socialism. It's been going on for thirty years, this has, this getting poorer and poorer. Too many people to feed here in England, out of too few fields. It's the food-producing countries that'll be the ones to live in in the future. You can see it now. Look at Jane Dorman!"

"That's wool, Daddy. They didn't make their money out of food. They made it out of wool."

"Well, we've got to have wool, and we don't grow enough of our own. I'm dressed in it almost entirely. So are you."

59

Jennifer thought of her winter clothes. "Mostly, in this weather," she agreed. They walked on for a time in silence. "If I went out to Australia I'd have to get a job," she said. "I couldn't just go out and live upon Aunt Jane."

He nodded. "You could do that all right. I expect they want secretaries in Victoria."

"What's the capital of Victoria, Daddy? Is it Adelaide?"

He shook his head. "I don't know. I think that's over on the west coast somewhere. I'd have to look at an atlas."

Later in the day, when they were having tea in the kitchen of her grandmother's house before going back to the hotel, Jennifer said, "Of course, I'd like to go out to Australia for the trip. The only thing is, I wouldn't want to stay there."

"You've never been out of England, have you, Jenny?"

"I've been to France," she said. "I'd love to go like that, if one could look on it as just a holiday. Six months or so. But I'd never want to go and live out there."

"Why not?"

She struggled to express herself. "This is our place; this is where we belong. We're English, not Australian."

He thought for a minute. "I suppose that's right. But that's not the way the British Empire was created."

"You don't want me to stay out there for good, do you, Daddy?"

"I want you to do what's best for you," he said. "I'm worried, Jenny, and I don't mind telling you. If this decline goes on, I'm worried over what may happen to you before you die."

"That's what Granny said," the girl replied uncertainly. "She said that she was worried for me. Everybody seems to be worrying about me. I can look after myself."

Her father smiled. "All the same," he said, "no harm in going on a six months' trip out to Australia if it gets dropped into your lap."

"It seems such a waste of money."

"It's what she gave it to you for," he said. "But it's your money to do what you like with. Think it over."

The funeral was on Saturday, and after it was over Jennifer went with her father to St. Pancras to see him off. Then she travelled down by train to Blackheath through the drab suburbs of New Cross and Lewisham. As she went the blazing Australian deserts, the wide cattle stations, the blue seas and coral islands that she had read about in novels danced before her eyes; it seemed incredible that these things could be within her grasp, these places could be hers to go to if she wished. Only the inertia of giving up her job and going, of getting out of her rut, now stood between her and these places.

She had a duty to perform on the Sunday, the duty of writing to Jane Dorman at this queer address, "Leonora, Merrijig, Victoria" to tell her of the death of Ethel Trehearn, and to tell her about the disposition of her five hundred pounds. She sat down on Sunday morning to write this letter; when she had finished, it was a straight, factual account of what had happened, with the unpleasant fact glossed over that the old lady's death had been virtually from starvation. She could not bring herself to tell anyone in another country that such things could happen in England. At the end she wrote,

"As it stands now, I've got four hundred of your five hundred pounds, and I'm not too happy about it. She gave it me because she wanted me to go out to Australia and see if I would like to make my life out there, and to visit you. I should like to see you, of course, but as for living in Australia I think it's very unlikely that I'd like it; I suppose I'm incurably English. If I did come I'd have to get a job, of course; I'm a qualified shorthand typist with four years' experience since I got my diploma. Do you think I could get a job in Melbourne, or would that be difficult?

"Do tell me if you would like to have the money back and I'll send it at once, because honestly I don't feel as though it's mine at all.

"Yours sincerely,

"JENNIFER MORTON."

She got this off by air mail at midday on Sunday, and relaxed.

That was a time of strain and gloom in England, with the bad news of the war in Korea superimposed upon the increasing shortages of food and fuel and the prospect of heavy increases in taxation to pay for rearmament. In the week that followed Jennifer's return to work the meat ration was cut again, and now reached a point when it was only sufficient for one meagre meal of meat a week. When shortages are shared equally they are nothing like so painful as they would be in a free economy; if the Smiths can afford to buy meat and the Jones not, the strain may be intolerable, but if nobody can have the meat the lack of meat soon ceases to annoy. Nevertheless the present cut produced some serious and heated discussion at the lunch table between the men, which Jennifer listened to with interest. There were about three hundred clerical staff in that office of the Ministry of Pensions, and they mostly lunched together in one large canteen.

Forsyth, head of Department D.3. in Rehabilitation, said, "The plain fact of it is that these Argentinos have got us where they want us. They've got the food and we've got to have it or go under."

Morrison, in the Accounts Branch, said, "We can't pay the prices that they're asking. The economy won't stand it."

"We'll have to do without something, then. Free spectacles and false teeth. We've got to eat *something*."

Somebody said something about the Minister of Food, "—that ——fool. Getting the Argentinos' back up."

Sanders, from the Assessment Branch, said, "I don't agree at all. It's easy to sling mud at him, but he's done a marvellous job."

"In what way?"

Sanders said, "Well, the country's never been so healthy as it is now. Everybody gets enough to eat. The only thing that you can say against the food is that it's a bit dull sometimes. But everybody gets enough of it. Nobody dies of starvation in this country, like they do in France. That's the difference between a controlled economy and *laissez faire*."

Jennifer thought of one old lady who had died of starvation, but she said nothing. Her grandmother could have applied to the relieving officer, of course. . . . She could not speak without showing indignation, and it was better not to make a row before the men.

Morrison said, "There's one big difference between this country and France." He spoke with the deliberation of an accountant, and with a slight North Country accent.

"What's that?" asked Sanders.

"You take a successful professional man," said Morrison slowly. "A leading surgeon, maybe, or a barrister. With taxes and costs the way they are, he really hasn't got a chance of saving for his old age, not like he could before the war. He'll save something, of course, but a man like that, he doesn't get into the big money much before he's forty-five or fifty, and in the few good years that he's got left he can't save enough to retire on in the way of life that he's accustomed to. He just can't do it, with the tax and surtax as it is. You've only got to look at the figures to see that it's impossible."

Forsyth said, "That's right."

"Well, if a man like a first-class surgeon can't save properly for his old age, nobody can," said Morrison. "That means that nobody in England can feel safe. Everybody in this country today is worried sick for what may happen to him and to his wife when they get old, except the very lowest paid classes, who can get by on the retirement pension."

"Well, how do you make out that things are any better in France?" asked Sanders.

"This way," said the accountant. "In France the man like the surgeon or the barrister is taxed much less than he is here, and the working man pays proportionately more. I don't say that's a good thing—it may be, or it may not be. The fact is that it's different. In France, the leading surgeon or the leading barrister *can* save for his old age, and save enough to give him security in the way of life he's used to. He's not worried sick for what may happen to him. In France, if you're successful enough, you're all right. That means that in France you've got *some* happy and contented people. Here you've got none."

"Yes, but hell!" said Sanders. "That's at the expense of the under-dogs."

"I don't say it's not," said the accountant equably. "I'm just saying that the French system does produce *some* happy people, and ours doesn't."

The argument drifted inconclusively along till it was time to get back to the offices.

A day or two later, to Jennifer's interest, the subject of emigration came up. None of the older men seemed particularly interested in it. "My nephew, he went out to Canada," one said. "He's an engineer; got a job in a tractor factory in Montreal. He was out there in the war with the R.A.F., so he knows the country. He's doing all right, but he says the winter's terrible."

"It's not right, the way these young chaps go abroad," said Sanders. "If it goes on, the Government will have to put a stop to it."

Jennifer spoke up with suppressed indignation. "Why should they do that?" she asked. "Why shouldn't people go abroad if they want to?"

Sanders was about to answer, but the accountant intervened. "Because the country can't afford it."

The girl said, "They pay their own passages, don't they?"

"I'm not speaking about that, Miss Morton," said the accountant. "Look, suppose it was you who wanted to go to Canada." It was uncomfortably near home, but the girl nodded. "How much do you think you cost?"

"Me? In money?"

"That's right," said Morrison.

"I don't quite know what you mean," she said.

"I'll tell you, very roughly," he said. "When did you start working?"

"I got my first job when I was eighteen," she told him.

"Right. For eighteen years somebody in this country fed you and clothed you and educated you before you made any money, before you started earning. Say you cost an average two quid a week for that eighteen years. You've cost England close on two thousand pounds to produce."

Somebody said, "Like a machine tool."

"That's right," the accountant said. "A human dictaphone and typewriter combined, all electronic and maintains itself and does its own repairs, that's cost two thousand quid. Suppose you go off to Canada. You're an asset worth two thousand quid that England gives to Canada as a free gift. If a hundred thousand like you were to go each year, it'ld be like England giving Canada a subsidy of two hundred million pounds a year. It's got to be thought about, this emigration. We can't afford to go chucking money away like that."

She said puzzled, "It's not really like that, is it?"

"It is and all," said Morrison. "That's what built up the United States. Half a million emigrants a year went from Central Europe to America for fifty years or so. Say they were worth a thousand quid apiece. Right—that was a subsidy from Central Europe to America of five hundred million quid a year, and it went on for fifty years or so. Human bulldozers."

He leaned forward on the table. "Believe it or not," he said, "Central Europe got very poor and the U.S.A. got very rich."

There was laughter at the table. "It's a fact, I'm telling you," said the accountant. "Central Europe got very poor. If all that man-power had stayed at home in Poland and in Czechoslovakia we might have had a good deal less trouble from Hitler. We want to watch the same thing doesn't happen here. It could do, easily, if too many people start emigrating." He paused. "It could be the ruin of this country."

"I don't see how you can keep people here if they want to go," the girl said. "After all, what's the Commonwealth or Empire or whatever they call it these days—what's it for? You can to go Australia if you want to, can't you?"

Sanders said, "You can at present, but it's got to be controlled. People can't always do the things they want to."

"I'm sick of the word control," said Jennifer. "We didn't have to have all these controls before the war."

"No," said Sanders. "We had three million unemployed instead." He leaned across the table. "I'll give you a better reason than the money why people ought to stay here."

"What's that?" asked Forsyth.

"To do a good job for the world," said Sanders. "I'll tell you. Here in England we've got the most advanced form of government of any country in the world. It's experimental, and I know there've been mistakes. Some things that have been tried out aren't so hot, like ground nuts in Tanganyika, and they've had to be written off. But what this country has tried to do, and what it's doing, is to plan a new form of government and put it into practice, a new form of democracy where everyone will get a square deal. When we've shown it can be done, the world will copy it, all right. You see. But it can't be worked out if people are allowed to run away to other countries. It's their job to stay here and get this one right."

Jennifer said, "You mean, one ought to stay here because there's an experiment in Socialism going on, and if we go away we'll spoil it?"

"That's right."

Forsyth said, "Too bad when the guinea-pig escapes from the laboratory before the research is finished. It kind of spoils the experiment, Miss Morton."

There was laughter, and Sanders flushed angrily. "It's not like that at all. It's for the good of everyone to stay in England. This is the most advanced country in the world."

Forsyth said, "Maybe. I'd trade the brave new world for an old-fashioned capitalistic porterhouse steak."

Jennifer said, "If there's one thing that would make me want to go and emigrate it's what you've just said—that one's got to stay here for the sake of an experiment."

Morrison laughed. "She's got a bourgeois ideology," he said. "She's nothing but a ruddy Kulak, Sanders."

Jennifer went back to her work that afternoon, but the incident stayed in her mind, and rankled. She had no particular aversion to Mr. Sanders; indeed he was a healthy, youngish man who had been an officer in the R.N.V.R. during the war and had commanded an L.C.T. in the invasion of Normandy. What irked her was the display of Socialist enthusiasm that pervaded her office, which seemed to her slightly phoney. It was manifestly impossible for anyone who derided the Socialistic ideal to progress very far in the public service; if a young man aimed at promotion in her office he felt it necessary to declare a firm, almost a religious, belief in the principles of Socialism. Jennifer felt instinctively that Mr. Sanders was less concerned with the Brave New World than the progress of Mr. Sanders in the Ministry of Pensions, and she wondered what would happen to his views if an election should bring in a Conservative Government.

In the meantime she felt constrained and restricted by bureaucracy; it could not seriously be true that she would have to stay in England if she wanted to go. Abruptly the thought of going to Australia for a time became attractive to her; if they said she couldn't go, she'd darned well go.

On Monday she got a cable at her boarding-house. It read,

"Deeply grieved Aunt Ethel but so glad you were with her of course keep money and do come out here and visit us plenty of jobs Melbourne about ten pounds weekly writing air mail.

"JANE DORMAN."

She stared at this in amazement that she could have got an answer to the letter she had written only a week before; it made Australia seem very near. Frequently when she wrote on Sunday to her parents in Leicester and missed the evening post she did not get an answer till Thursday; true, Jane Dorman had cabled, but even so . . . Jennifer felt as if Jane Dorman lived in the next county, and Australia no longer seemed to be upon the far side of the world.

It wouldn't do any harm to find out about it, anyway. She made a few discreet enquiries and took Tuesday afternoon off on a pretext that she had to help her father clear up Ethel Trehearn's estate, which was totally untrue. She went up to London and visited the P. and O. office and the Orient Line next door, and Australia House, and Victoria House. She returned with a great mass of literature to study, fascinating windows opening upon a strange new world.

On the Thursday she wrote to the Orient Line and put her name down for a tourist-class passage to Australia five months ahead, the earliest date that she could get a berth. She sent ten pounds deposit, on the assurance of the company that this would be returnable if she changed her mind and didn't go. She wouldn't really go, of course, but it was nice to know she could go if she wanted to. . . .

On the Friday she got a bulky air-mail letter from Jane Dorman in Australia, twelve days after she had written. Enclosed with it were four pages of advertisements in newspapers of situations vacant in Melbourne for secretaries and "typistes", at salaries that made her blink. Jane Dorman wrote six pages, ending,

"As regards the money, do keep it as I said in the cable. Aunt Ethel was terribly kind to us a long time ago when we first got married, and I am only so deeply grieved that I didn't realise before that she was in need of help, because now we've got so much with the wool sales as they are. Of course, we all know that it can't go on, but the debt upon the land and stock is all paid off now so everything is ours, and even if wool fell to half its present price or less we should still be all right, and safe for the remainder of our lives.

"I need hardly say how much we should like to see you out here with us. We live in a country district a hundred and fifty miles from Melbourne. I don't suppose you'd want to live the sort of life we do, because it's very quiet here, rather like living in the depths of the Welsh mountains, perhaps, or in Cumberland. There's not a great deal for young people here unless they're keen on the land, and my children are all living now in the cities, Ethel and Jane in Sydney and Jack in Newcastle, about a hundred miles north of Sydney. I expect if you came here you'd want to work in Melbourne, and I am sending you some pages from the *Age* and the *Argus* to show you the sort of jobs available. Everybody is just crying out for secretaries, it seems, and you'd have no trouble at all in getting work.

"I do hope that you will decide to come, and that before you take up work you will come and stay with us for as long as you like, or as long as you can stand the country. I do so want to hear about Aunt Ethel from somebody who knew her. I had not met her for over thirty years, of course, but we wrote to each other every two or three months. I can't really think of her as old, even now.

"Do come and see us out here, even if it's only for the trip.
"Yours affectionately,
"JANE DORMAN."

Jennifer had no very close friends in Blackheath, but she sometimes went to the pictures with a girl called Shirley Hyman who lived in the room below her. Shirley worked in the City and was engaged to a young man in a solicitor's office; she was with him every week-end but seldom saw him in the week. That Friday evening she was washing her hair for his benefit next day, and Jennifer went down to see her, papers in hand.

She said, "Shirley. Have you ever thought of going to Australia?"

Miss Hyman, sitting on the floor before the gas stove drying her hair, said, "For the Lord's sake. Whatever made you ask that?"

"I've got a relation there," said Jennifer. "She wants me to go out and stay."

"What part of Australia?"

"She's outside Melbourne," Jennifer said. "I'd get a job in Melbourne if I went."

"Perth's the only place I know about."

"Have you been there?"

Miss Hyman shook her head. "Dick's always going on about it," she said. "He wants us to go there when we're married. He thinks he knows a chap out there who'll take him on, as soon as he's got his articles."

"Are you keen on it?"

"I don't quite know," the girl said. "It's an awful long way away. When I'm with Dick it all seems reasonable. There's not much future here and if we're going, well, it's better to go before we start a family. But . . . it's an awful long way."

"I've been finding out about it," Jennifer said. "I got a letter back from my relation in twelve days. It doesn't seem so far now as it did before."

"Is that all it took?"

"That's right." She squatted down before the stove with Shirley and produced her papers and pamphlets. "There's ever so many jobs, according to these advertisements."

They turned over the brightly-coloured emigration pamphlets she had gleaned in Australia House. "Dick's got that one—and that," said Shirley. "It looks all right in these things, doesn't it? But then they wouldn't tell you the bad parts, like half the houses in Brisbane having no sewage system."

"Is that right?" asked Jennifer with interest.

"So somebody was telling Dick. He says it's all right in Perth, but I don't believe it is."

"What do people do?" asked Jennifer. "Go out in the woods or something?"

They laughed together. "They've cut down all the woods," said Shirley. "I was reading somewhere about Australia becoming a dust bowl because they've cut down all the woods."

"I don't think that can be right," said Jennifer. "They've got *some* woods left, or they couldn't have taken these pictures." They bent together over the pictures in the pamphlet about Tasmania, showing wooded mountain ranges stretching as far as the eye could see.

"They probably kept those just to make these pictures to show mutts like us," said Shirley sceptically. "It's probably all desert and black people round behind the camera."

They laughed, and sat in silence for a time.

"What do you really think about it?" Jennifer asked at last. "Do you think it's a good thing to do?"

The girl sat playing with her hair-brush on the floor beside the stove, thoughtful and serious. "Dick expects to be successful," she said presently, "and I think he will. He'd have more opportunity

67

out there, with new things starting all the time as more people get into the country." She raised her head, and looked at Jennifer. "And, anyway, what's the good of being successful in England? They only take it all away from you, with tax and supertax. The way he looks at it, if we stay in England he'd do best in some Government office and get a pension at the end. He wants to be on his own, though."

There was a pause. "I don't know what to think," Shirley said at last. "I'd never thought of leaving England, up until the last couple of months. It seems a horrid thing to do, as if one ought to stay and help to get things right. Dick says there's too many of us in the country. I don't know. If somebody's got to get out, I wish it wasn't me."

"Do you think it would feel strange?" asked Jennifer. "Would people like you in Australia?"

"I don't know. There's such a lot of English people there already, I think one would find friends. People who hadn't been out there so long themselves. I think it'ld be like going to live in Scotland for a job. They talk with a funny accent, some of them, you know."

"I don't think it could be as bad as the Scotch accent," Jennifer said. "I went to Edinburgh once, and I couldn't understand what some of the people were saying—porters and cab drivers, you know. I don't believe Australians are as difficult as that."

"You're all right, of course," said Shirley. "You could come back if you didn't like it. You could save the cost of the passage home. It's different for us. If we went out, we'd have to go for good."

"I know," Jennifer said slowly. "The trouble is, I believe I might like it, and stay there for good. I don't want to do that. . . ."

The little ties that held her to her own land were still strong, ties of friendships, of places that she knew, of things she had grown up with. She went on with her work and life in Blackheath for another three days, uncertain and irresolute. On the following Tuesday she got a telegram from the Orient Line,

> "Can offer returned single tourist passage Melbourne in *Orion* sailing December 3rd holding open for you till midday November 23rd."

November the twenty-third was in two days' time, and if she took this she would have to sail within a fortnight. Her first reaction was that she couldn't possibly go. It was too soon; she hadn't made up her mind. She got the telegram on her return from work; Shirley Hyman was out that evening, and there was nobody else with whom she could discuss the matter.

It was impossible for Jennifer to stay in her room that evening; she was too worried and restless. She had her tea in an abstracted daze, and walked across the heath and took a train for Charing Cross, knowing that it was in her power to have done with that heath and with that train. It was not raining but the night was cold and windy; the chilly draughts whipped round her on the platform in the darkness. In Australia it would be high summer. . . .

The train was unheated owing to fuel shortages, and she was very cold by the time she got to Charing Cross. She went out of the station and turned eastwards up the Strand, and there she met a disappointment. She had hoped that the bright lights and the traffic would be stimulating and cheerful, and that England would hold out a hand for her to hang on to. But the shop windows were all dark because of fuel rationing, and the Strand seemed sombre and deserted, with little life. She was there now, however, and very cold; she walked eastwards quickly for the exercise. She stopped now and then to look into a shop window in the light of an arc lamp, but there was no joy in it.

Warmth and feeling were coming back into her feet as she passed Waterloo Bridge. She went on past the Law Courts, down Fleet Street, empty and dark but for the street lamps and the lights and clamour from the newspaper offices. By the time she reached the bottom of Ludgate Hill she was warm and comfortable again and beginning to wonder why she had come there, and where she was heading for. There was no point in walking on into the City. She moved up the hill at a slower pace, looking for a bus-stop, and so she came to St. Paul's Cathedral, an immense black mass towering up into the darkness from the blitz desolation that surrounded it.

She moved towards it, and stood staring at the mass of masonry. This was the sort of thing that Australia would never have to show her, this masterpiece of Wren. If she left England she would be leaving this for ever, and a hundred other beauties of the same kind that the new country could never show her. She stood there thinking of these things, and two devastating little words came into her mind—so what?

She had been taken inside St. Paul's once as a schoolgirl. She remembered it as the biggest building that she had ever been in, and for that alone. She knew that she was probably foolish and ignorant, because there must be much more to St. Paul's than that, but she stepped back till she could see the whole bulk in the fleeting moonlight as the swift clouds passed and re-passed. She would be leaving this for ever, and she must be honest with herself about it.

Would she miss it very much? She tried to examine her own feelings, and she said to herself, "Well, there it is. Now am I getting a great thrill out of it?" She had to confess within her own mind that she wasn't. The enormous, inert mass of masonry meant little to her; there was nothing in those great columns of stone to affect her decision one way or the other.

She turned back towards the West End, rather thoughtful. A bus came rattlingly by and stopped near her; she ran and got on to it, and rode back up Fleet Street. She got off at Charing Cross and walked on to Trafalgar Square. She stood by St. Martin-in-the-Fields for a time looking round her, at the National Gallery, the Nelson Column, the Admiralty Arch, the long broad way that was Whitehall. Here was the very centre of her country, the very essence of it. Here were the irreplaceable things that she would have to do without if she left England. Surely, that would be unbearable?

She felt that there must be something wrong with her, because she knew that it wouldn't be unbearable at all. In fact, she didn't much care if she never saw any of them again.

She had a queer feeling now that she was becoming a stranger in her own country, that she no longer fitted in. She had to consult her parents in Leicester about this matter of the passage, and there was so little time. She thought for a few minutes and then went diffidently into the Charing Cross Hotel and spoke to the girl at the desk, and ordered coffee and biscuits in the writing-room, and sat down to write a letter to her father and mother.

She put the matter very simply to them, and asked them to telegraph her to advise her what to do.

Then she went by Underground to St. Pancras station and posted her letter in the special box upon the platform, so that it would get to them next morning.

She got a telegram from them in answer when she returned from work next day. It read,

"Think you had better go but come home for a few days first our dearest love.

"DADDY AND MUMMY."

She sailed a fortnight later for Australia in the *Orion*.

Four

THE man with the crushed fingers got down awkwardly from the cab of the rickety, dust-covered truck into the timber road; his mate climbed over the tailboard and dropped down into the road beside him. He raised a hand to the driver. "Thanks, Jack. We'll be all right." The door of the cab slammed to, the engine roared, and the truck moved on, swaying and lurching down the unmetalled road in a great cloud of dust.

The two men stood together at the entrance to the timber camp. The wooden hutments stood in a forest in a valley. A little river ran beyond the buildings and a mountain climbed up steeply beyond that, covered in eucalyptus gum trees, full of brilliantly-coloured parrots. The buildings stood among the trees for shade from the hot Victorian sunlight, blazing down out of a cloudless sky. "This way," the well man said. "Down here, fourth hut along."

They turned into the camp; the hand of the injured man was wrapped in a blood-stained rag, and he walked with it thrust into his open shirt as in a sling. He asked, "What's the bastard's name?"

"Splinter," said his mate. "He'll fix you up."

"What's the bastard's real name?"

"Splinter—that's all the name he's got. He's right, as good as any doctor."

"Company ought to keep a mucking doctor here," the injured man said. "They've got no mucking right to carry on with just a first-aid box. One day some bastard's going to cop it proper, and I hope it's Mr. Mucking Forrest."

"Hurting bad?"

"Like bloody hell. I'll go down to the Jig tonight; get mucking well pissed."

They went into the fourth hut by the door in its end, and into a central corridor of bare, unpainted, rather dirty wood. The uninjured man opened a door at random and said to a man inside, "Say Jack—which is Splinter's room?"

"Last on the left, down by the wash-room. Someone hurt?"

"Too right. Fred here got his hand under a log."

"Aw, look—he may be in the canteen. See if he's in the room— if not, I'll go find him."

The two men went down the passage to the last room and opened the door. There was a man inside sitting on the bed reading an old

71

newspaper, a lean, swarthy, black-haired man about thirty-five years old. He looked up as they entered.

"Aw, Splinter," said the uninjured man, "this is Fred." The dark man smiled, and nodded slightly. "He got his hand mucked up."

The man got up from the bed. "Let me see." He spoke with a pronounced Central European accent.

The other turned to go. "I'll get along Fred. You'll be right."

The injured man withdrew his hand from his shirt and began to unwrap the bloodstained rags carefully, with fingers that trembled a little. The man called Splinter noted that, and stopped him. "Wait, and sit down—on the bed." He switched on the current to a china electric jug and dropped a few instruments into it to boil. Then he rolled up his sleeves and took a white enamelled bowl and a bottle of disinfectant from the cupboard and went out to the bathroom; he came back with his hands washed and sterile and with warm water in the bowl. He moved the bare wooden table to a convenient position in front of the man and waited till the water in the jug boiled, opening a packet of lint while he waited, and adding a little disinfectant to the water in the bowl. Then he sat down facing his patient with the table between them, arranged the hand in a relaxed position, and began his work.

Presently, "This is a bad injury," he said softly. "It must hurt you a great deal. Now, let me see if it possible that you can move the fingers. Just bend a little, to show that you can move them. This one . . . so. And now this one . . . so. And this one . . . so. That is good. It hurts very much now, but a fortnight's holiday and it will soon be well."

"Cripes," said the man, "is it going to hurt like this a mucking fortnight?"

"It will not hurt when I have done with it," the dark man said. "Not unless you make a hit—unless you hit it. You must wear it in a sling till it is well, and keep it carefully. I must now hurt you a little more. Will you like whisky?"

"Thanks, chum."

The dark man produced a bottle of Australian whisky from the cupboard and poured out half a tumbler-full. The patient took it and sat drinking it neat in little gulps while the other worked.

"What is your name?"

"Fred. Fred Carter."

"Where did you do this, Fred?"

"Up on the shoulder."

"And how did it happen?"

"Loading two-foot sticks on a ten-wheeler." He meant, treetrunks two feet in diameter on to a trailer truck. "The mucking chain broke and the stick rolled back. Whipped me crowbar back 'n pinched me mucking hand on to the next stick down."

The dark man nodded gravely. "Now, this will hurt you. I am sorry, but it must be done."

72

Presently it was all over, the hand bandaged and in a sling. The injured man sat white-faced, the shock gradually subsiding as he smoked a cigarette given to him by the doctor and finished the whisky. "Say, chum," he asked, "what's your name?"

"Zlinter," the dark man said, "Carl Zlinter. Most people call me Splinter here."

"Where do you come from?"

"I am from Czechoslovakia. In Pilsen I was born."

"How long have you been here?"

"It is fifteen months that I have come to Australia."

"Where did you learn doctoring?"

"I was doctor in my own country, at home."

"A real doctor?"

The dark man nodded. "In Prague I qualified, in 1936. After that I was in hospital appointment, in Pilsen, my own town. And after that, I was doctor in the army." He did not say which army.

"Cripes. Then you know all about it."

The Czech smiled. "I am not doctor any longer. I am timberman. In Australia I may not be a doctor, unless to go back to medical school for three years. So I am timberman."

He stubbed out his cigarette and got up, and went to the cupboard and shook out some white tablets into the palm of his hand. "Go back to your camp and go to bed," he said. "I will tell Mr. Forrest for you, that you cannot work. Go to bed, and take three of these tablets, and the pain will go away. If it comes back in the night, take these other three. Come back and see me after tea on Sunday, and I will change the dressings for you."

"Aw, look," the man said. "I was going down to the Jig tonight to get pissed."

Carl Zlinter smiled. "It is your hand. It will hurt very bad if you go down to the Jig, because you will hit it without knowing, and it will hurt very bad. If you go to bed it will not hurt."

He turned to the cupboard; the bottle of whisky was about one-third full. He gave it to the man. "Take this," he said, "and get pissed in bed. But go to bed."

"Aw, look, chum, I can't take your grog. And say, how much is it?"

"There is nothing to be paid," the Czech said. "Mr. Forrest, he pays for the dressings and the disinfectant. The whisky—you can shout for me down at the Jig one day, but not tonight." He smiled. "See you Sunday."

Fred Carter went away with the bottle, and Zlinter wondered if he would go to bed, or whether he would drink the bottle and go down to the pub at Merrijig just the same. The labour camps were by the sawmills at Lamirra, four miles from Merrijig and seventeen miles from Banbury, the nearest town. By Victorian law the hotel was supposed to close its bar at six o'clock in the evening; in fact, it stayed wide open day and night, and the police connived at it.

They knew that few of the timbermen would pass an open bar to go twelve miles further on to Banbury; driving past in the dark night the police would see the blazing lights, and hear the songs, and see the trucks parked outside the solitary wooden building, and they would smile as they drove past, congratulating themselves upon the simple stratagem that kept the drunks out of town.

It was a Friday evening; the timbermen worked a forty-hour week on five days, and Saturday and Sunday were holidays. Carl Zlinter was a fisherman, and December was the finest month in the year for trout-fishing in the deserted mountain streams. When Fred Carter had gone away, he set to work to prepare for the week-end; he had a spinning rod and a fly rod, but the rivers were too shallow and too swift for spinning, and he preferred to fish wet fly. He cleared away the litter of his dressings, sterilised his instruments again in the electric jug, and washed out the basin, and then set to work to make up a cast of flies, and to pack his rucksack.

The Delatite River flowed past Lamirra near his camp, but it was too small and too overgrown to fish just there, and down by Merrijig it was fished by many others. Zlinter had developed a week-end of fishing which took him into very wild, almost untrodden forest country, which he loved. His rucksack was a big, shabby thing with a light alloy frame which he had picked up in Germany in 1945 and had carried every since; it held everything that he required for a week-end in the bush. His habit was to start out from the lumber camp early on Saturday morning and walk eight miles or so on half obliterated paths through the forest over a dividing range down into the valley of the Howqua River, untouched by any road. Here the fishing was first-class.

There was a forest ranger living in the Howqua valley, a man called Billy Slim, rather over forty years of age, who lived alone with a few horses and was glad of any company; when the solitude became oppressive he would ride out to the hotel at Merrijig and spend the evening there. Billy had a bed for anyone who came his way, and Carl Zlinter was in the habit of fishing down the Howqua to Billy's place on Saturday, staying the night with him, fishing up the river again on the Sunday, and so back to the camp by the way that he had come.

So far, he was delighted with Australia. He had to work for two years in the woods in return for his free passage from the Displaced Persons' camp in Germany, and he was enjoying every minute of it. He had nobody to consider but himself. His father and mother had been killed in the Russian advance that surged through Pilsen late in 1944. He had heard nothing of his brother since 1943, and he believed him to be dead. He had never married; the war had begun soon after he was qualified, and he was not a man to marry unless he could see, at any rate a little way, into the future. He had remained unattached throughout his service in the German Army and through the long ignominy of the peace, when he had worked as a doctor in various Displaced Persons' camps. When finally the reduction of the D.P. camps gave him the chance to go to Australia with one of the last batches of emigrants, he was almost glad of the condition that he should not practise as a doctor; he would have to work for two years as a labourer wherever he might be directed, and then if he still wished to be a doctor in Victoria he would have to repeat the last three years of his medical student's course. Medicine had brought him nothing but the most intimate contact with the squalor and distress of unsuccessful war; when the time came to choose his labour he elected to be a lumberman because he loved the deep woods and the mountains, and he put medicine behind him.

On landing he had been sent to a reception camp for a few days, but as he was unattached and spoke tolerable English he had been sent on quickly to Lamirra, and he had been there ever since. He knew a good deal about camps and how to be comfortable in them, and he settled down quite happily to work out his two years in the woods he loved.

He had little regret for the loss of his medical profession. After his two years in the woods were over he would have to do something else; he did not quite know what, but in this prosperous country he was confident that he could earn a living somehow or other. In the meantime he was well clothed and fed, paid highly by the European standard, and given so much leisure that he could get in two days' trout fishing every week. Better than lying dead and putrefying in the Pripet marshes or the fields round Caen, where he had left so many of his friends. That was the old world; he was glad to put it all behind him and enjoy the new.

He left the camp at about seven o'clock that Saturday morning before the day grew hot, with his rucksack on his back and his fly rod in his hand in its cloth case. He got to the river soon after ten and put up his rod and began to fish down-stream, wading in the cool water in his normal working boots and trousers.

He caught a rainbow trout after ten minutes' fishing, a good fish about two pounds in weight that leaped into the air repeatedly to shake the fly out of its mouth. He kept his line taut and played the fish out, and landed it upon a little shoal with one hand in its gills; he never burdened himself with a net. He caught a brown trout a few minutes later; then, as the day warmed up, the fish went off the feed, and he caught nothing more.

He got to Billy's place about midday. The forest ranger lived in a clearing by the river, in a long, single-storeyed building with a veranda, built, of course, of timber with an iron roof. There was a living-room which was the kitchen, with a harness room opening out of it, which in turn communicated with the stable; in winter when the snow was lying in the valley Billy Slim could feed his horses without going out into the snow. His own bedroom opened out of the living-room, and there were two bunkrooms off the veranda. He kept his house very neat and clean, having little else to do.

In one corner of the living-room there was a radio telephone set run off a large battery, with which the ranger could communicate with his headquarters in case of forest fires or similar disasters. When Carl Zlinter walked in, Billy was seated talking to the microphone, he raised a hand in greeting, then knitted his brows and bent again to his work. Giving his weekly time sheet to the girl operator on Saturday mornings was always a trouble and a perplexity to him.

"Aw, look, Florence," he was saying. "Tuesday . . . Oh, yes—look—Tuesday I went upstream to Little Bend and then over the spur to the Sickle, that's down on the Jamieson River. There was a party went in there last week from Lamirra."

"Know who they were, Billy?"

"Naw—I didn't see them. There was four of them on horses, and two pack horses, and one of the horses was Ted Sloan's blue roan, so Ted must have been there. One of the horses dropped a shoe and went lame on the way out. They shot a few wallabies and camped three nights. They lit fires which they didn't ought to; I'll see Ted about that." He paused. "Wednesday I had to go into the Jig to pick up a couple of sacks of horse feed. Thursday I stayed home; I wasn't feeling too good. Got that, Florence? Over."

The loudspeaker said, "Thursday's a working day, Billy. What'll I tell Mr. Bennett? I don't like to put down you got sick again. Why can't you do your drinking at the week-end? Over."

"Aw, look, Florence," the ranger said, "I didn't drink nothing down at the Jig. You know me—I wouldn't of a Wednesday. I got one of my bad goes on the Thursday, in the stomach, terrible griping pains. Real bad I was. Over."

"I don't like to put it down, Billy. Didn't you do anything about the house that we could say? Over."

"Aw, right . . . look, Florence. I did a bit on the paddock fence in the afternoon. Put down, Repairs to homestead and stockyards, for Thursday. Yesterday, that's Friday, I was out all day. I went up around Mount Buller as far as the Youth Hostel hut and then down to the King River and along by Mount Cobbler and the Rose River; I didn't get back till after nine last night. Today Jack Dorman's coming out with Alec Fisher from Banbury, and there's Carl Zlinter here, one of the lumbermen from Lamirra. Over."

The loudspeaker said, "That'll be right, Billy—I can make it up from that. That's all I have for you. Over."

"Bye-bye, Florence," said the ranger. "Closing down now. Out."

He shut the set off with a sigh of relief, and turned to Carl Zlinter. "Come fishing?"

"If I may, I would like to spend the night."

"You'll be right. Put your stuff in the end room; I got Jack Dorman coming over, with Alec Fisher. Know them?"

Zlinter shook his head. "I do not know them."

"Aw, well, Jack Dorman, he's got a property just by the Jig. Thought maybe you might know him. Alec Fisher, he's agent for the Australian Mercantile in Banbury. They're coming out to do a bit of fishing."

Zlinter smiled. "We shall crowd you out tonight with a large party."

"Too right. Makes a change to have a bit of company now and then."

"Will they come on horses?"

"Might do. Alec Fisher's got a Land Rover; they can get over the track with that. I'd never sit astride a bloody horse if I'd got a Land Rover to ride in. I'd have thought that they'd be here by now."

Carl Zlinter left his rucksack in the end room and went down to the river, cleaned the two fish, and left them in Billy's larder for the evening. He had brought a sandwich lunch with him from the camp canteen; he went down to the river again and fished on downstream for a little. No fish were moving in the heat of the day; he gave it up after half an hour, and found a shade tree standing in the middle of a grassy sward by the river, and sat down under it to eat his lunch.

It was very quiet in the forest; a hot, windless day. A cockatoo screamed once or twice in the distance, and near at hand there was a rippling noise of water from a little fall in the river. Presently the quiet was broken by the low grinding of a vehicle coming down the horse track into the valley in low gear; he guessed that it would be the Land Rover. It passed along the track a few hundred yards upstream from him and he heard the water as it went splashing through the ford; he heard it breast the rise up from the river to the ranger's house, and then the engine stopped, and there was quiet again.

He went down to the river and drank from it after his meal, cupping up the water in his hands; then he went back and sat down under the tree again, and lit a cigerette. What a good country this was! It had all the charm of the Bohemian forests that he had loved as a young man, plus the advantage of being English. He had not learned to differentiate between English people and Australians; to him this was an English country, and England had the knack of being on the winning side in all her wars. He dislike and distrusted Russians, and his own land was gone for ever into the Russian grip. He liked south Germans and got on well with them and spoke the language fluently, more fluently than he spoke English. The Germans, however, had an unfortunate record for starting wars and losing them, which made Germany a bad country to live in, Australia had everything for Carl Zlinter; the type of country that he loved, freedom, good wages, and no war; he would willingly forgo his medical career for those good things. He revelled in the country, like a man enjoying a warm bath.

He stubbed his cigarette out on a stone, or what he took to be a stone, in the meadow beneath the tree. He looked at the stone curiously, and it was not a stone at all, but a piece of brick.

He looked about him with interest. Half buried in the grass was a low rubble of brick. Beside it, on the level grassy sward, was a series of rectangular patterns, hardly to be described as mounds, more like discolourations of the pasture. He studied these for a minute while his mind, accustomed to the solitude of the Howqua, refused to accept the evidence. Then he woke up to the realisation of the fact that there had been a house there at one time.

Even when he appreciated the evidence, it still seemed incredible, and for a very definite reason. He knew that this part of Australia had been first explored barely a hundred years before; he had found out sufficient of the history of the country to have become aware that it was most unlikely that the Howqua valley had seen any white man before 1850. If the evidence upon the ground before him were to be believed, a house built wholly or partly of brick had been built and lived in, and deserted, and so entirely ruined that only a bare trace upon the sward remained, all in less than a hundred years.

It did not seem possible. He stood looking at the grass for a time, deeply puzzled; then he put it out of his mind for the time being, and walked over to the stream, and stepped out into the shallows and began to cast his fly. He would ask Billy Slim about it that evening.

He fished on down the river; he caught no fish and hardly expected to until the sun began to drop. He stopped presently and smoked a cigarette, and lay on his back under the gum trees, and slept for a little. When he woke up it was about five o'clock; he began to fish back up the river towards the forest ranger's house, and at once he began to catch fish, mostly small undersized brown trout that he tired as little as possible and put them back into the river. Then he caught a couple of takeable fish, each about a pound and a quarter, and with that he gave up, and took down his rod, and walked back along the forest path in the gloaming.

When he got to the shack the two newcomers were there, a heavy man of fifty-five or sixty that was Jack Dorman, and a younger man, perhaps of forty-five, Alec Fisher. They greeted him shortly; they were not unfriendly, but waiting for this New Australian from the lumber camp to disclose himself before showing themselves particularly cordial. They represented the permanent population of the countryside, the men with an enduring stake in the land. The lumbermen were here today and gone tomorrow, frequently drunk and a nuisance to the station people; many of them were New Australians who came for their two years' sentence on arrival from Europe and fled to the towns as soon as they got their release, and anyway the camps themselves were transient affairs, to be moved on to some other district as soon as all the ripe timber from that forest had been taken out.

Carl Zlinter raised the matter of his discovery with the forest ranger over supper. "I have found what seems to have been formerly a house," he said. "In a pasture, where two horses are. There is a big tree, and under there are bricks, all in grass and very old. Was there a house at one time?"

The ranger said, "You mean, where the river makes a turn under a big granite bluff? About a quarter of a mile down?"

"That is the place. There is a fast, dark pool."

"Too right, there was a house," the ranger said. "That was the hotel. My dad kept it, but that was before I was born."

Jack Dorman said, "Your dad kept the hotel, did he? I never knew that."

"One of them," the ranger said. "There was three hotels. He kept the best one, the Buller Arms. Two storeys, it was, with bedrooms. Used day and night, those bedrooms were, from what I've heard."

"Like that, was it?" said Alec Fisher.

"My word," the ranger said, "these gold towns were all the same. Booze and dancing girls and all sorts."

Carl Zlinter said, "Was there a town then?"

"My word," the ranger said again. "It was a big place at one time, over three hundred people. You'll find the adit to the mine up in the trees there, back of the house paddock. It's blocked now; it only goes in a few feet. The battery is still there down by the dam, in that clump of peppermint gums. There was houses all over in this valley flat."

"I knew there was a town here," Alec Fisher said. "What happened? Did the gold run out?"

"Aw, look," the ranger said. "I don't think there was ever much gold there. In 1893 it started, when they found a trace of gold in the conglomerate. The Rand mine in South Africa, that was conglomerate, so they called this one the Rand and floated a company in Melbourne," He paused, and ate a mouthful of trout. "They got a little gold out, just enough to make it look a good bet. But it never really paid. It ran on for ten years and then it bust, in 1903."

"That's right," said Fisher. "Everyone was gold mad at that time."

"My old dad," the ranger said, "he came out from home when he was just a kid, back in the 'eighties some time. He came from a place called Northallerton in England, 'n got a job in the police. Well, then when they found gold here he gave the police away and came and started the hotel. He was a fine, big chap 'n handy with his fists, which you needed running a hotel in these parts in those days. He sold out in '98 or '99 and went to Jamieson 'n got married. I was born in Jamieson."

"How did they get all the stuff in?" asked Jack Dorman. "The track's not so good."

"Aw, it was better then," said Slim. "They had a regular road up from the Jig, and brought it in bullock wagons. I remember the

79

road in here when I was a boy; you could have driven a car in down it, easy. But trees grow up pretty quick, 'n nobody came in here when the mine shut down."

"People all went away," said Fisher.

"That's right. There wouldn't have been many left here after that. There's not enough flat land to make a station, and it's a long way from the town."

Carl Zlinter asked, "What happened to the houses?"

"Aw, look," said the ranger. "There's been a fire through the valley twice at least, in 1910 and 1939. I come here first when I was just a nipper, in the first war some time. I don't remember seeing any houses. There's not much left of houses after a fire's been through," he said. "Only just the brick chimneys, and they soon fall down. Most of the places would have had a wooden chimney, too."

"I remember the fire here in 1939" said Dorman. "A bit too close to home it was, for my liking."

"My word," the ranger said thoughtfully. "A fair cow, that one. Just after I joined the Forest Service, that one was. The house was on the other side of the river then; we rebuilt it after on this side, because the land was flatter, 'n better for the paddock." He turned to Fisher. "Days 'n days of hot sun, 'n not a breath of wind down in the valley here. It got so that you couldn't hardly breathe for the scent from the gum leaves; it made your eyes smart, sort of distilling out in the hot sun, 'n no wind to carry it away. And then one morning I was out in the paddock lighting my pipe although I didn't really want it for the way the air made you choke, and when I lit the match the flame burned blue. There wasn't any yellow in the flame, just kind of blue, out in the open air, dead still, in the middle of the paddock."

The men stared at him. "My word," said Dorman softly.

"We hadn't got no radio in those days," the ranger said. "I put that match out quick and saddled up, 'n rode out to the Jig. Mr. Considine, he was superintendent then, 'n I got on the telephone and told him that my match burned blue, out in the open air, 'n he as good as said that I was drunk. And then he said the fire on Buller was heading down my way, 'n I'd better get anybody in the Howqua out, 'n get my own stuff out."

He paused. "Well, there was nobody else in, that I knew about, and nothing in the house I thought a lot of but my gun, that I got from my Dad. An English gun it was, a good one that some toff had give my dad, a twelve-bore made by a firm called Cogswell and Harrison. Well, I rode back towards the Howqua, and when I got up on the ridge I could see the fire on Buller, and it was a whole lot closer now, not more'n seven or eight miles away. I sat on the horse and thought about the air down in the valley where the match went blue; it was hot as hell, 'n not a breath of wind. I didn't like to go down there a bit, my word I didn't."

"Not worth it for a gun," said Alec Fisher.

"I tell you," said the ranger, "I wouldn't have gone down for the gun. I'd have given it away. But I'd got three horses down there in the paddock, 'n I'd got to get them out. So down I went, and by the river here the air was worse than ever, sort of choking. I just grabbed the gun and left everything else, 'n let the fence rail down and drove the horses out ahead of me and up the track. I never been so frightened, oh my word."

"Lucky to get away with it," Jack Dorman said.

"Too right. Well, I got back on to the ridge in Jock McDougall's pasture with my horses and the gun, and there I stayed a while. I wasn't going to stay down in the valley, but I'd a right to stay as near as I could to where I ought to be. So I stayed there on the ridge for a while. And about three in the afternoon, that fire on Buller, she began to jump. She come down this valley in leaps about two mile each time. She'd be blazing way off up the valley, 'n then there'd be a sort of flash and you'd see everything alight and burning two miles closer on. Then she'd rest a while, and then she'd leap on another mile or two mile down the valley. In a sort of flash."

Alec Fisher said in wonder, "The whole air was exploding?"

"That's right," the ranger said. "The whole air was exploding. That's how the old house come to be burned down. After that we built this one, next year."

Carl Zlinter said, "Let me understand. It was hot, so hot that the sun evaporate the eucalyptus oil out of the trees, and that explodes?"

"That's right," said Jack Dorman. "I've heard of that happening over in East Gippsland, by Buchan in the Cave Country."

"But that is terrifying!"

"Too right," said the ranger. "It terrified me."

"You can't do anything about a thing like that," said Fisher. "You can't stop a fire from spreading when it jumps two miles."

The forest ranger said, "Folks down in the city think you can stop a forest fire by spitting on it. They come along after and ask why you didn't put it out. Maybe you can do a bit to stop one starting, like getting campers not to light a fire in January. But only God can put it out when it gets hold."

"We do not have fires like that in my country," said Zlinter. "Perhaps it is too cold, and too much rain. We have fires sometimes, but not to jump two miles."

"Which is your country?" asked Jack Dorman. "Where do you come from?"

"From Czechoslovakia," the other said, "In Pilsen I was born."

The names meant nothing to the Australian. "Working up at Lamirra?"

"That is right. I work there for two years."

"Like it?"

"I like it very much. It is like Czechoslovakia, with the forests and the mountains. I would rather be working here than in the city."

Billy Slim said, "You don't have gum trees in your forests over there, do you?"

"No, we do not have the gum tree. There all is pines and larches, and oak trees a few, and sometimes the silver birch."

"Get much snow in winter?" asked the ranger.

"Oh, we get much, much snow. Three feet, four feet deep from November until March. It is much, much colder in Czechoslovakia than it is here."

"I wouldn't want four feet," the forest ranger said. "Four inches is enough for me."

Carl Zlinter said, "I am from Europe, where villages remain for many hundred years. I do not know of any village in Bohemia that has vanished with no sign left, as this one has."

The ranger said, "Aw, well, there's plenty left here if you look for it. Only there aren't no people living here any longer. There's the mine adit, and the battery, and down the river, 'bout a mile, there's the cemetery with all the stone headstones still standing up. The fire couldn't burn up those."

"Where's that?" asked Alec Fisher.

"You know where there's a red stone bluff on the right side going down? Well, on past that there's a big tree-trunk lying along the bank, where I pulled it with three horses when it fell across the river. The cemetery's in behind that, on the north side."

"Many graves there?"

"Aw, no—just a few. Just a few headstones, that's to say. Might have been more one time, with a wood cross perhaps; there wouldn't be nothing left to show those."

Jack Dorman sat puzzled, hardly hearing what was going on, a vague memory of little Peter Loring and Ann Pearson stirring in his mind. "Say," he said to the Czech, "is your name Cylinder by any chance? Are you a doctor?"

"My name is Zlinter—Carl Zlinter," said the other. "I am a doctor in my own country, but not here in Australia. Here I work at the timber camp."

"That's right," said Dorman. "I heard about you one time. Didn't you pick up a boy that had fallen off his pony?"

Zlinter smiled. "He had a very high temperature," he said. "The lady was helping him when I arrived. It was not that he fell off because he could not ride. He was ill, that little boy, with a bad ear."

"That's right. You took him into hospital."

The Czech nodded. "I think his mother was a stupid woman not to see that he was ill when he left from his home to go to school. It could have been a serious accident, but he was scratched a little, only."

"You speak pretty good English," said Jack Dorman, curiously. "D'you learn it since you came out here?"

The other shook his head. "I learned English at school, and then for nearly five years I was in Germany, where many people now speak English, in the camps and with the officers. Also, I have been here now for fifteen months, and perhaps I have improved."

"What's it like, coming to Australia from Europe, now?"

"It is good," the Czech said. "It is a good country, plenty to eat and to drink, and plenty of freedom."

"You've not got plenty of freedom, working for two years in the woods."

The other shrugged his shoulders. "I like the woods and the mountains. It is not cruel to me, to send me here."

Alec Fisher said, "Lot of people coming out here to this country now."

"My word," said Jack Dorman. "My wife's got a niece, an English girl, arriving in about a fortnight's time. Seems like it's better out here now than it is in England."

"An English migrant, like your wife's niece," asked Zlinter, "—she will not have to work for two years, like a New Australian?"

The grazier shook his head. "I don't think so. This girl, she's coming out just on a visit, though—paying her own passage. She says she's going back again in six months' time."

"It must be very expensive, to do that."

"She got a little legacy," the grazier said. "She's spending it in coming out here for the trip, to see what Australia's like."

They settled down to an evening of local gossip, with the assistance of a bottle of Scotch whisky produced by Alec Fisher.

They were all up soon after dawn, to take advantage of the cool of the day when fish feed well. They had a quick breakfast of eggs and bacon, and split up for the day's fishing. They tossed a coin for who should go alone, and Alec Fisher won; he started off up-stream. Carl Zlinter and Jack Dorman went down-stream, having arranged to fish alternate pools, leap-frogging each other.

They fished on down-stream for an hour or so, catching a few fish and exchanging a word or two when they overtook each other. Presently Carl Zlinter, going on ahead, came to a red stone bluff upon the right side of the river, and a memory of the conversation of the night before came to his mind.

Jack Dorman was not far behind him. He sat down and waited for the grazier by a little rapid; when he came, Carl said, "There is the red bluff that Billy spoke about. Somewhere here is the cemetery of the old town of Howqua."

The Australian grunted. "Want to go and look for it?"

"It is a pity to be here and not to see it," the Czech said.

"He said it was behind a tree-trunk lying along the bank, didn't he?"

"There is a tree-trunk, there. Perhaps that is the one."

They laid the rods down on a boulder by the rapid, and pushed their way through the scrub that lined the river. Away from the water there were wattle trees in bloom among the gum trees of the forest, vivid splashes of a bright mimosa colour in the dappled sunlight. For a time they saw nothing of the cemetery; they moved down the bank in the forest, keeping near the river. Presently Jack Dorman spied a leaning headstone, and they were there.

There was not very much to see; three leaning headstones, and four or five lying on their faces on the ground, partly covered in creepers and trash. If there had been a fence at any time it had gone the way of the houses in the forest fires; if there had been wooden crosses marking graves, fire and the ants had taken them. Jack Dorman bent to read the lichened names carved on the three headstones still erect. Peter Quilliam, of Tralee, Ireland. Samuel Tregarren of St. Colomb, Cornwall.

He came to the third headstone and stood staring at it, amazed. "Hey, Zlinter!" he said. "This some relation of yours?"

They stooped together at the stone. It read:

Here lies
CHARLIE ZLINTER and his dog.
Born at Pilsen, Bohemia, 1869.
Died August 18th, 1902.

The Czech read it carefully, in silence. Then he looked up at the grazier, smiling a little. "That is my name," he said, "—Carl Zlinter, and I was born at Pilsen in Bohemia. Of all the things that have happened in my life, this is the most strange."

Five

THE Dormans left Leonora for their holiday in Melbourne on New Year's Day. They drove down in the old Chevrolet utility, leaving Mario in charge of the station and taking Tim Archer with them, sitting all three in the front seat and with four suitcases in the truck body. Mario had had letters from Lucia; her passage was booked on the *Neptunia* for April, and he was busy with the builder working on the shack extension of the stable that they were to live in. Tim Archer came to Melbourne with them to drive the old utility back to Leonora and to see his parents; Jack Dorman had already arranged to buy another near-new Ford utility at an inflated price in Melbourne, and to drive it home.

They went with an air of festival excitement. Thinking back over their long married life, Jack and Jane had been unable to remember when they had last gone away together for a real holiday; there had been trips to Melbourne for various business reasons, always cramped and curtailed by the need for rigorous economy and by the need to get back quickly to the station. Certainly, they had not had a genuine holiday for at least ten years. Now, with two men to help them and with what was, for them, unlimited money, they were able to relax and to enjoy the fruits of thirty years' hard, grinding work.

Jane Dorman had heard from Jennifer that she was coming to Australia and that she proposed to take a job at once in Melbourne and would like to come out to Merryjig to see them as soon as she could get a holiday. Jane thought this a bad idea; the *Orion* was due to dock in Melbourne on January 3rd and they had put forward the date of their holiday to meet the ship. There had been no time to write to Jennifer before she sailed, but Jane had written to her at Port Said and at Colombo urging her to come back with them to Leonora for a short visit before taking a job in the city; she was arriving at the hottest time of the year, Jane said, and office work in Melbourne might be trying till the end of February for anybody just arrived from England, especially if the summer was a hot one.

It was hot the day that they drove down from Merrijig; at midday the shade temperature in the country was in the nineties. Before long they stopped by the roadside for Jack Dorman to take off his coat and undo his collar; Tim Archer got out of the front seat and into the back with the luggage; the dust swirled round him there

85

and made sweat streaks of mud upon his temples, but it was cooler so for all of them, and better travelling.

They stopped at Bonnie Doon for the cold, light Australian beer, and at Buxton for lunch. By four o'clock they were running into Melbourne, perhaps the pleasantest city in the Commonwealth, and at four-twenty they drew up in front of the Windsor Hotel.

Tim took the utility away and the Dormans went up to their bedroom, a fine, lofty room with plenty of cupboards and a bath. After the constrictions of their rather mediocre station homestead it seemed like a palace to them; the hard years fell behind them, and for the moment they were young again. "Jack," said Jane, "don't let's see anyone tonight. Let's just have a very, very good dinner and go to a theatre. Any theatre."

"Don't you want to see Angie?"

"Angie can wait till tomorrow," said her mother. "I want to see a theatre. Angie's probably seen them all. Let's go out alone."

"All right," he said. "I'll go down and see what we can get seats for."

She said, "And I want a bottle of champagne with dinner."

"My word," he said. "What'll I order for dinner—mutton?"

"You dare! Oysters and roast duck, or as near as you can get to it."

They went out presently and walked slowly in the heat down the tree-shaded slope of Collins Street, tacking from side to side to look at the shops. Jane said presently, "I know what I want to buy."

"What's that?"

"A picture."

He stared at her. "What sort of picture?"

"An oil painting. A very, very nice oil painting."

"What of?"

"I don't mind. I just want a very nice picture."

"You mean, in a frame, to hang on the wall?"

"That's right. We had lots of them at home, when I was a girl. I didn't think anything of them then, but now I want one of my own."

He thought about it, trying to absorb this new idea, to visualise what it was that she wanted. "I thought you might like a bracelet, or a ring," he said. With so much money in their pockets, after so long, she should have something really good.

She squeezed his arm. "That's sweet of you, but I don't want jewellery, I'd never be anywhere where I could wear it. No, I want a picture."

He tried to measure her desire by yardstick. "Any idea what it'll cost?"

"I don't know till I see it," she said. "It might cost a hundred pounds."

"A hundred pounds!" he said. "My word!"

"Well, what's the Ford going to cost you?"

"Aw, look," he said. "That's different. That's for the station."

"No, it's not," she said. "The Chev'll do the station work for years to come. It's for you to run about in and cut a dash, and it's costing fourteen hundred pounds."

"It's for both of us," he said weakly, "and it comes off the tax."

"Not all of it," she said. "If you're having your Ford Custom I'm going to have my picture."

He realised that she was set on having this picture; it was a strange idea to him, but he acquiesced. "There's a shop down here somewhere," he said. "Maybe there'd be something there you like."

When they came to the shop it was closed, but the windows were full of pictures, religious and secular. He knew better than to offer her a picture of the infant Christ in her present mood, although he rather admired it himself. He said, "That's a nice one, that one of the harbour. The one where it says 'St. Ives'."

It was colourful and blue, with fishing vessels. "It's not bad," she said, "but it's a reproduction. I want a real picture, an original."

He studied the harbour scene. "Where would that be?" he asked. "Is it in England?"

"That's right," she said. "It's a little place in Cornwall."

"Funny the way people want to buy a picture of a place so far away," he said.

"I suppose it's because so many of us come from home."

There was nothing in the shop window that she cared for, nor did it seem to her that there was likely to be what she wanted deeper in the shop. "I'd like to go to picture galleries," she said. "They have a lot of galleries where artists show their pictures and have them for sale. Could we see some of those tomorrow, Jack?"

"Course we can," he said, "I've got to pick up the Custom in the morning, but we'll have all day after that."

She smiled. "No, we won't—you'll be wanting to drive round in the Custom. We'll go to the picture galleries in the morning and pick up the Custom in the afternoon."

They went back to the hotel, and rested for a time in the lounge with glasses of cold beer, and dined, and went out to see *Worm's Eye View*, and laughed themselves silly. They got up late by their standards next day, and early by those of the hotel, and went down to their breakfast in the dining-room. As country folk they were accustomed to a cooked breakfast and the hotel was accustomed to station people; half a pound of steak with two fried eggs on top of it was just far enough removed from normal to provide a pleasant commencement for the day for Jack. Jane ate more modestly, three kidneys on toast and a quarter of a pound of bacon. Fortified for their day's work they set out to look at pictures with a view to buying one.

The first gallery they went to was full of pictures of the central Australian desert. The artist had modelled his style upon that of a short-sighted and eccentric old gentlemen called Cezanne, who had been able to draw once but had got tired of it; this smoothed the path of his disciples a good deal. The Dormans wandered, nonplussed, from mountain after mountain picture, glowing in rosy tints, all quite flat upon the canvas, with queer childish brown scrawls in the foreground that might be construed into aboriginals. A few newspaper clippings, pinned to the wall, hailed the artist as one of the outstanding landscape painters of the century.

Jack Dorman, deep in gloom at the impending waste of money, said, "Which do you like best? That's a nice one, over there."

Jane said, "I don't like any of them. I think they're horrible."

"Thank God for that," her husband replied. The middle-aged woman seated at the desk looked at them with stern disapproval.

They went out into the street. "It's this modern stuff," Jane said. "That's not what I want at all."

"What is it you want?" he asked. "What's it got to be like?"

She could not explain to him exactly what she wanted, because she did not know herself. "It's got to be pretty," she said, "and in bright colours, in oils, so that when it's raining or snowing in the winter you can look at it and like it. And it's got to be *like* something, not like those awful daubs in there."

The next gallery that they went into had thirty-five oil paintings hung around the walls. Each picture depicted a vase of flowers standing on a polished table that reflected the flowers and a curtain draped behind; thirty-five oil paintings all carefully executed, all with the same motif. A few newspaper cuttings pinned up announced the artist as the outstanding flower painter of the century.

Jane whispered, "Do you think she can do anything else?"

"I dunno," her husband said. "Don't look like it. Do you like any of these?"

"Some of them are quite nice," Jane said slowly. "That one over there . . . and that. But they aren't what I want." She paused. "I'd never be able to forget that there were thirty-four others just like it, if I bought one of these."

The last exhibition that they visited that morning was of paintings and sculpture by the same artist; at the door a newspaper cutting informed them that the artist was a genius at the interpretation of Australia. The centre of the floor was occupied by a large block of polished mulga wood with a hole in it, of no recognisable shape or form, poised at eye-level on a stand that you might admire it better. Beneath it was the title, "Design for Life".

"Like that one to take home?" asked Jack. He glanced at the catalogue. "It's only seventy-five guineas. . . ."

The paintings were a little odd, because this artist was a primitive, unable to paint or to draw, and hailed as a genius by people who ought to have known better. Purple houses that might have been drawn by a five-year-old child straggled drunkenly across vermilion streets that led to nowhere and meant nothing; men with green faces struggled mysteriously and perhaps discreditably with ladies who had square blue breasts. "That's a nice one . . ." said Jack thoughtfully.

Jane said, "Let's get out of here. People must be mad if they like things like that."

Out in the street he said, "There's another gallery in Bourke Street, up by William Street or somewhere."

Jane said, "I want a cup of tea."

They turned into a café; over the tea she said that she was through with picture galleries. "I know what I want," she said, but it's not here. I want a picture that an ordinary person can enjoy, not someone who's half mad. I'll find it some day."

He said tentatively, "There might be time to go down and pick up the Ford before dinner. . . ."

"Let's do that," she said. "Take the taste of those foul paintings out of our mouths."

The new utility was a very lovely motor-car, a low, flowing dark-green thing with more art in it than anything that they had seen that day. Twenty minutes before lunch-time it became their property, and they got into it, thrilled by the new possession, and drove it very carefully and slowly to park it in the Treasury Gardens. Jack Dorman locked it up, whistling softly between his teeth,

"I don't want her, you can have her,
She's too fat for me . . ."

His wife caught the air, and smiled a little. "We must ring Angie," she said. "See her this afternoon." Their daughter was staying for a few days with a college friend in Toorak, the most fashionable suburb of the city.

Her father said, "Maybe we could run her out into the country somewhere. She might like a drive. . . ."

She was in fact driving in their utility at that moment, with Tim Archer. He had picked her up in the old Chevrolet that morning and was driving her southwards to bathe in Port Phillip Bay, thirty miles from the city. He had collected a lunch of sandwiches and soft drinks and they had set off at about twelve o'clock; they were now coming to the beach that was their destination.

Angela Dorman was twenty years old; she was taking Social Studies at Melbourne University and was just about to start upon her third and last year. She was a well-built blonde girl, superbly healthy. Like many Australian girls, a country life in her early years with an abundance of good food, plenty of riding, plenty of swimming, and the good Australian climate had made her a magnificent physical specimen; she would have graced a magazine cover in any country of the world. Now she was going through that phase of youth that can find nothing good in its own country; in Australia the only places that could satisfy her were Melbourne or Sydney, and her one ambition was to escape altogether from Australia to a rose-tinted and a glamorous England.

She had known Tim Archer for three years, since he had come to work for her father at Leonora. She knew that he was devoted to her in the inarticulate, dumb manner of a dog. She found him slow and unenterprising, without much interest in the world outside Victoria; a typical country boy. For all her restlessness she had enough of her father's shrewd common sense not to throw away lightly something that she might want later on; she was sufficiently realist to know that she might not find so steady an affection easily again. She left most of his letters unanswered but she was kind to him when they met, and when he had rung her up and asked her to come swimming down past Mornington she had put off another engagement to go out with him.

They parked the old utility beside the road, took their lunch and bathing gear, and walked down through the tea trees to the beach. They had it practically to themselves, that little beach; they went back into the tea trees to change and came out in their bathers wearing dark glasses to sit and sun themselves a little before going in. Then they swam in the hot sunshine, keeping an eye open for the possible shark; although they were both strong swimmers, like most Australians they did not venture very far from the shore. Sharks in Port Phillip Bay were a rarity, but then you only meet one once. . . .

They came out presently, and sat drying in the sun on the hot sand till they began to burn; then they moved into the shade of the tea trees and got out their lunch. Over the cigarettes he broached the subject that was foremost in his mind.

"Coming up to Leonora soon?" he asked.

"I suppose so," she said reluctantly. "I'm going to spend a week or so in Sydney with Susie Martin at the end of the month. I suppose I'll have to go home for a bit before that."

"It's nice up there now," he offered. "Cooler than the city."

"There's nothing to do there," she replied. "It's different for you. You've got a job to do. When I come home there's nothing to do but help Mummy with the cooking and washing up. There's nobody to talk to."

"I know," he said patiently. "It must seem a bit slow."

She turned towards him. "Don't you ever get tired of sheep—seeing the same sheep every day?"

"There's the beef cattle," he said slowly and quite seriously. "They make a bit of a change."

"But don't you get *bored* up there?"

"I dunno," he said. "There's always something that wants doing —fences or rabbits or spreading the super. We're going to plough about eighty acres of the middle paddock in March and sow it down to rye-grass and clovers."

"Will that make it better?"

"My word," he said. "If we did that all over we could carry twice the stock. Costs a lot of money, though."

She was silent. She knew that she ought to be able to take an interest in the property that had given her the university, and pretty clothes, and leisure; she knew that the fault lay in her. "I can't stand the country," she said quietly.

He knew that what she said was true, and it was painful to hear her say it. "What are you going to do when you leave the university?" he asked. "Get a job down here in the city?"

She said, "I want to go to England."

"What's the matter with Australia?" he asked in his slow way.

"It's so small, so petty, and so new," she said. "Everything we think about or talk about—everything that's worth while—comes from England. We're such second-raters here. I want to go home and work in London and be in the centre of things and meet some first-class people. I want to be where things really happen, things that are important in the world."

"Australia's all right," he said. "We've got some pretty good people here."

"But not like England," she said. "It's not like things are at home."

"You don't get enough to eat in England."

"That's all nonsense. The children's health at home is as good as it is here." She paused. "The trouble is we eat too much here. Be a good thing if we all ate a bit less and sent more home."

"What'ld you do in London?" he asked presently.

"I'd like to get a job with a hospital," she said. "An almoner or social work of some kind, with one of the big London hospitals. If I could get that, it'ld be a job worth doing."

"Down in the slums?" he asked. "With very poor people?"

She nodded. "I want to get a job where one could help—help people who need helping."

"Couldn't you do that in Australia?"

"There's not the scope," she said. "There aren't any poor people here—not like there are at home."

He knew that to be true, and he thought it was a very good thing. "Too many people in England," he said. "That's the trouble. Do you know this girl Jennifer Morton that your ma's come down to meet?"

She shook her head. "I've never seen her, nor has Ma. I don't think any of us know much about her."

"She worked in London, so you ma was saying. She might be able to give you a few tips."

"I want to meet her," the girl said. "Be somebody to talk to up at Leonora, anyway."

He lay propped on one elbow on the warm sand, staring out at the sunlit beach and the blue sea. He was trying not to keep looking at her, but it was difficult to keep his eyes under control. "When do you suppose you'll be going?" he asked at last.

"About this time next year," she said. "I've not told the parents yet, but it's what I want to do. I think they'll let me—if the wool keeps up."

"How long do you think you'll be gone for?"

She stared down at the sand and traced a little pattern on it with one finger. "I don't know," she said. "I'd rather work in London than work here. I might never come back."

"Bit hard on your dad and ma," he said.

"I know. That's what makes it difficult." She paused. "I ought to be home by five, Tim," she said. "I must see Dad and Ma this evening."

"Too right. Your dad won't worry because he was taking over the new Ford today. Your ma will want to see you, though. Like me to run you straight to the hotel, or do you want to go back to Toorak first?"

She thought for a moment. "I'd better go back to Toorak. I can't go to the Windsor straight from here, like this."

"I'll run you back and wait while you change and take you on to the hotel."

"Will you, Tim? That's terribly sweet of you."

He coloured a little, and she noticed it, and knew that she had been a shade too kind. "That's all right," he said gruffly. "We'd better get changed and get upon the road, if you want to be at the hotel by five."

They changed back into their clothes in the tea trees and got into the utility, and drove back to the city with hardly a word spoken all the way.

The *Orion* docked at eight o'clock next morning, with Jennifer on board. Jane Dorman had written to her again at Fremantle, and Jennifer had replied agreeing to go to Leonora for a few days before she came back to the city to take a job. Now as the vessel docked she was uncertain if she had been wise; she knew little of the Dormans and nothing of Australia; she would have preferred to go to a hotel for a few days, and find a lodging in the suburbs, and settle down in her own way. It was impossible to refuse the evident kindness, however, and it would be interesting to see a bit of the country before starting on a city job. Moreover, it was to visit Jane Dorman that her grandmother had given her the money; but for that she would not have been there at all.

When she met the Dormans in the tourist-class saloon, in response to a loudspeaker call, she was surprised in one or two respects. For one thing, they were far smarter than she had expected them to be. Jack Dorman in a new grey suit, heavy though he might be, was better dressed than her father, and Jane Dorman, though her hands were old and worn, was very smart in a new black and white coat and skirt. Their daughter, Angela, was with them, rather younger than Jennifer, but even better turned out than her parents; Jennifer felt pale and shabby in comparison with this glorious young woman.

As she came into the saloon Jane Dorman got up to meet her; in the crowd of passengers and friends she came straight to Jennifer. "It's Jennifer Morton, isn't it?" she said. "I'm Jane Dorman."

Jennifer said, "How did you know me, Mrs. Dorman?"

Jane said, "You've got a look of your grandmother about you, my Aunt Ethel. I knew you right away."

Then there were introductions, and enquiries about the passage, and business of the luggage. The Dormans had brought both utilities to the pier-head and Tim Archer was sitting in the Chevrolet below. Presently Jennifer was passing through the Customs, and then her suitcases and trunk were down in the new Ford utility, and she was free into Australia.

She drove to the hotel with Jack and Jane Dorman, Angela following behind in the old Chevrolet with Tim. In a blur of first impressions the width of the streets and the great number of motor-cars impressed Jennifer most; whatever else Melbourne might be, it was a beautifully laid-out city, and obviously a very prosperous one. The Dormans had engaged a room for her at the Windsor for a couple of nights; she found herself whisked up into this, and then they all had lunch together, except for Tim Archer, who had started back for Merrijig in the old utility.

Jennifer decided that it was easier to submit until the hospitality of these kind strangers had exhausted its first impetus; she felt that it would be rude and ungenerous to battle against it now. Angela disappeared after lunch upon her own affairs, and Jane and Jack Dorman took Jennifer out to the new Ford utility. They all sat together in the wide seat and started out on a long drive up into the Dandenong mountains, clothed in trees finer and taller than any that Jennifer had seen in England. At the outset she protested diffidently at the waste of their time in making this outing for her, but she was quickly told about the newness of the car and made to realise that her host would certainly have done that anyway that afternoon for his own pleasure. Indeed, the fun that Jack Dorman was getting out of his new possession was so evident that Jennifer relaxed, content to enjoy herself.

By the time they got back to Melbourne she was dazed with new impressions. By common consent they spent the evening quietly in the hotel. Jennifer was tired, and at Leonora the Dormans were in the habit of getting up at six in the morning and going to bed soon after nine each night. So for a while after dinner Jennifer sat talking quietly with Jane Dorman in a corner of the lounge of the hotel, while Jack smoked a cigar and read the *Herald*.

The girl said presently, "I'd like to take a little time tomorrow looking for a room or a small flat to live in here. It's terribly nice of you to ask me up to Leonora, and I'd love to go back with you for a week, but after that I'll have to come back here and take a job. I thought I'd better see about that tomorrow."

Jane said, "I know just how you feel. We'll get you fixed up with somewhere nice to live before we go back home. I don't think you ought to be in too much of a hurry to start work, though. The temperature was over a hundred the day before yesterday, in the city here. It's the worst time of the year for anybody coming out from England, and you're bound to feel it more than we do. You'd be much more comfortable if you stay with us at Leonora for a month, and start work in the autumn. It's much cooler out there."

The girl said awkwardly, "I think I ought to start earning something sooner than that, even if it is a bit hot." The austerities of England were still strong in her; to relax and rest was somehow vaguely disgraceful. "I'm living on your money as it is," she said.

The older woman said evenly, "You're doing nothing of the sort, my dear. When we sent that money to Aunt Ethel we gave it to her. That was the end of it, so far as we were concerned."

The girl said, "I'm sorry—I oughtn't to have said that. But I would rather start earning my own living fairly soon. I don't want you to think I'm ungrateful, when you've been so very kind. But I've got to paddle my own canoe sometime, and the sooner I start the better."

"I know," said Jane. "So long as you know that we should love to have you for as long as you can stay with us. None of our children are home now; Angie will be coming up at the end of the week, but she won't stay longer than ten days. It's dull for young people up at Merrijig, of course—nothing ever happens there."

"I think I'd find it rather interesting," said Jennifer. "If I stayed up there too long with you, I might not want to come back to the city at all."

Jane glanced at her curiously. "Have you ever lived in the country, at home?"

The girl laughed. "No," she said frankly. "I've always lived in towns—in Leicester, and then in London. I don't really know what living in the country's like. I suppose that's why I'm interested in it."

"It can be very dull in the country," Jane said. "Long periods of doing nothing but the daily work a woman has to do, cooking and washing and cleaning the house. No one but your husband and the men to talk to, and only the radio to listen to. But . . . I don't know. I wouldn't like to live anywhere else."

Jennifer thought about this for a minute. Then she asked, "How many sheep have you got?"

Jane looked up in surprise. "I don't quite know—about three thousand, I think. Jack, how many sheep are there on Leonora?"

He looked up from his paper. "Three thousand five hundred and sixty, unless someone's been along and pinched some of 'em."

"Then there's the beef cattle," Jane Dorman said. "About two hundred Herefords."

"Two hundred and six," said Mr. Dorman, and returned to his paper.

"I suppose you sell a lot of them for meat," said Jennifer.

"Sell about six or seven hundred fat lambs every year," Jane replied, "and a good few ewes. But most of the money comes from the wool clip, of course."

"I wasn't thinking so much about the money," the girl replied. "It must be rather fun raising so much food."

"Fun?"

"Don't you feel pleased at being able to turn out such a lot of meat?"

Jane smiled. "I never thought about it. Send them to market and that's the end, so far as we're concerned, except to bank the cheque when it comes in."

"It seems such a good thing to be doing," said the girl.

Jane Dorman glanced at her curiously. It was the first time that she had heard it suggested that there was any ethical value in the work that she and Jack had spent their lives in. In the early years they had been looked down upon as country hicks, unable to make a living in the city and so compelled to live upon the land; in those hard days between the wars when wool was one and six a pound nobody had cared whether they lived or starved. In recent years with wool ten times the price, they had been abused as profiteers. In neither time had anyone suggested in her hearing that their work had any social value. Jennifer, she thought, came to Australia with a fresh outlook; it would be interesting to find out what it was.

She asked, "How are things at home now, in regard to food? What's it really like, for ordinary people?"

Jennifer said, "It's quite all right—there's really heaps of food. Of course, it's not like it is here, or on the ship. But there's heaps to eat in England."

"Not meat, is there?"

"No. Meat *is* a bit scarce."

"When you say scarce, Jenny, what does that mean? One hears such different stories. One day you see a picture of a week's ration of meat in England about the size of a matchbox, and then someone like you comes along and says it's quite all right. Can you get a steak?"

"Oh, no—not what *you'd* call a steak."

"What about restaurants? You can't go in and order a grilled steak?"

The girl shook her head. "I don't think so. You might at the Dorchester or some hotel like that that ordinary people can't afford to go to. I'd never tasted a grilled steak till I got on the ship."

"Never tasted a grilled steak?"

"No. Even if you could get the steak, I don't think you'd cook it that way, because of wasting the fat."

Jane asked, "But what do you cook when you go out on a picnic?"

95

The question rather stumped the English girl. "I don't know," she said, and laughed. "Not that, anyway."

"You eat a lot of fish, don't you?"

Jennifer nodded. "A lot. Do you get much fish here?"

"Not much fresh fish. I don't think we've got the fishing fleets that you've got at home. We get a lot of kippers and things like that."

"Like the English kippers? Herrings?"

"They *are* the English kippers," Jane said. "Scotch, rather. They all seem to come from Aberdeen."

"Do you get those out here?"

"Why, yes. You can buy kippers all over Australia."

"They're getting very scarce at home," the girl said. "I remember when I was a schoolgirl, in the war, the kippers were awfully good. But it's very difficult to get a kipper now at home."

"Funny," Jane said, "We've had lots of them out here for the last two or three years. It always makes me feel very near home when we have kippers for breakfast."

The girl asked, "Have you ever been home since you came out here?"

Jane shook her head. "Jack suggested we should go home on a trip a few months ago," she said. "But I don't know. All the people that I'd want to see are dead or gone away—it's over thirty years since I left home. And everything seems to have changed so much— I don't know that I'd want to see it now. Our old house is a school. It used to be so lovely; I don't want to see it as a school."

"That's what everybody says," the girl replied, "that England used to be so much nicer. Of course, I only know it as it is now."

"Old people have always talked like that, I suppose," said Jane. "And yet, I think there's something in it this time."

There was a silence, and then Jennifer said, "Have you been doing a lot of shopping since you came down here?"

"Oh, my dear. Do you know anything about pictures?"

Jennifer knew absolutely nothing about pictures, but she listened with interest to the results of the picture hunt to date. She went to bed early with the Dormans, thinking that these were simple and unaffected people that she was beginning to like rather well.

She went shopping with them next day, feeling rather shabby as she walked with them on a round of the best shops. Jane wanted to buy a wrist-watch for Jack Dorman to commemorate their holiday, and they all went into a shop that Jennifer alone would never have dreamed of entering, and looked at watches; finally Jane bought a gold self-winding wrist-watch for her husband for ninety-two guineas, and never turned a hair. Clothes did not appeal to Jane very much—"I so seldom go anywhere, Jenny"—but shoes were another matter, and she bought thirty-eight pounds' worth in half an hour. Jack left them while this was going on, and they went on to Myer's and bought a new refrigerator for a hundred and twenty pounds and a mass of miscellaneous kitchen gadgets and equipment for fifty-three pounds eighteen shillings and sixpence. "We get down to Melbourne so seldom," Jane said happily.

Jennifer wandered after her relation in a daze; she had never spent a morning like that before. Jack caught up with them as they were having morning coffee and said that he'd sometimes thought that Jane should have a car of her own and not use the station utilities, and he'd found a Morris Minor that had only done a thousand miles and was a bargain at a hundred quid above list price, and would Jane like to come and look at it? They went and looked at it and bought it, and then they had lunch and started on the curtain materials and carpets. "The homestead *is* so shabby," Jane remarked. "I don't know what you'll think of it, coming from England. I must brighten it up a little."

By tea-time they were all dead tired and they had spent about thirteen hundred and sixty pounds. Jennifer felt with all her instincts that the Dormans must be crazy, and then she reminded herself of the letter to Aunt Ethel and the statement that the wool cheque had been twenty-two thousand pounds, and thought perhaps that goings-on like this were normal to Australia. After all, Australia was on the other side of the world and so all Australians, and she herself, must now be walking upside down relative to England, so it was reasonable that all their standards should be upside down as well.

"We don't always go on like this," said Jane. "In fact, I don't think we've ever done it before." Later that evening she showed Jennifer a gold and blue enamel dressing-table set that Jack had bought for her all by himself, and had presented to her rather sheepishly.

Jennifer felt that surely there must be something wrong in spending so much money; her upbringing in the austerities of England insisted that this must be so. The queer thing was that here it all seemed natural and right. The Dormans had worked for thirty years without much recompense and now had won through to their reward; in spite of the violation of all her traditions Jennifer was pleased for them, and pleased with a country that allowed rewards like that. She had been brought up in the belief that money spent by the rich came out of the pockets of the poor, and she had never seriously questioned that. But in Australia, it seemed, there were very few poor people, if any. In her two days in the country she had seen great placards at the railway stations appealing for boys of nineteen to work as railway porters at twelve pounds a week, and she had seen sufficient of the prices in the cheaper shops to realise that such boys would be much better off than she had been when working for the Ministry of Pensions in England. It was all very difficult and very puzzling, and she fell asleep that night with a queer feeling of guilty enjoyment in Australia.

They took things a little more easily next day, and bought

nothing but an English grandfather clock for one hundred and eighty guineas, because it was just like one that Jane remembered in her English home, thirty years before. They took delivery of the little Morris before lunch and Jane drove it to Toorak to show it to Angela, and after lunch they all drove out in the two cars, Jane driving the Morris with Angela beside her and Jack Dorman following with Jennifer in the new Ford utility to pick up the pieces if Jane hit anything. They followed the shore of Port Phillip Bay in the hot sunshine nearly to Mornington, and had tea in a café, a Devonshire tea with splits and jam and a great bowl of clotted cream with a yellow crust. They were back in the city in time for drinks before dinner, and then to the theatre to see Sonia Dresdel in *A Message for Margaret*.

Next morning Jane and Jennifer went out early in the little car to look for a boarding-house, and found one that they had had recommended in a suburb called St. Kilda, not far from the sea and about twenty minutes from the centre of the city in the tram. There was no room vacant for three weeks, which Jane Dorman considered to be a very good thing. Jennifer liked the look of the woman who kept it and bowed to the inevitable, and paid a deposit, and engaged the room. Jane and Jennifer drove back to the city and had their hair set, rather expensively.

"I'll have to watch out how I spend my money," the girl said a little ruefully. "You're getting me into bad habits."

"We don't go on like this at home," said Jane. "I think we must be a bit touched, the amount of money that we've spent in these few days. We've never done it before. Do your father and mother ever go mad like this?"

Jennifer shook her head, thinking of the hard economies her parents had to make. "I don't think you could do it in England, even if you had the money," she said. "There wouldn't be the things to buy—not the cars, anyway."

They went to the pictures that night and saw Gary Cooper; next day they left for Leonora. By a last-minute decision Angela came with them. The virtues of a utility became clear then to Jennifer, because Jack Dorman went out in the morning and loaded up the refrigerator and the grandfather clock and about a hundredweight of kitchen gear, and came back and took on board five suitcases and Jennifer's trunk. At about eleven o'clock they were ready to start.

Jane Dorman was not a fast driver, and the Morris was new to her; it was evening when they came to Leonora after a slow drive through magnificent mountain and pastoral country. Jennifer learned a good deal of Victoria as they drove; she was amazed at the brilliance of the birds. The robin was more brightly coloured than a bird had any right to be, and the red and blue parrots in the woods amazed her. Here birds, apparently, had few enemies and so no need of a protective colouring, and freed from that restraint they had let themselves go. Only the lyre bird, a sombre being with a long tail like a peacock, appeared to exercise a British discretion in colours. The rest of them, thought Jennifer, were frankly gaudy.

They saw wallabies at one point, hopping across a paddock at a distance from the road, and at another place a black and silver animal about the size of a large cat, with a bushy tail like a silver fox fur, ran across the road in front of them; she learned that this was a possum. She saw a good many rabbits, exactly like the English rabbit, and was told about their depredations and the methods that were used to keep their numbers down. The style of the small towns and villages through which they passed reminded her of movie pictures of the Middle West of the United States; the same wooden houses with wide verandas and tin roofs, the same wide streets, at one time cattle tracks. It was a gracious, pleasant country that they passed through on that drive, the grass becoming yellow in the midsummer sun, but a well-watered and a friendly country, all the same.

In the evening they came to Leonora homestead on the slopes of the Buller range above the bridge and school and hotel that was Merrijig. Jennifer was driving with Jane Dorman for the last part of the journey; she closed the last paddock gate and got back into the car, and Jane drove into the yard behind the homestead where the new Ford was already parked with Mario and Tim admiring it. They got out of the Morris, and stretched after the long journey. "Well, this is it," said Jane. "Is it like what you thought it was going to be?"

Jennifer looked around her. All the buildings were severely practical, the walls of white-painted weatherboard, the roofs of corrugated iron painted with red oxide. There were numbers of great corrugated iron water tanks, cylindrical in form, disposed to catch the rain that fell upon the roofs, and there was another such tank high up on a wooden stand from which the house was supplied. The house itself had deep verandas on two sides and fly-wire doors, and screens on all the windows. Standing in the yard she had a wide view out over the basin of the Delatite, pastures and occasional woods, and behind that again the sun was setting behind a wooded mountain. It was very quiet and secure and peaceful in the evening light.

"I think it's simply lovely," said the girl from London. "I don't think I've ever been in such a beautiful place."

They turned to the homestead and started on the business of getting themselves and the luggage indoors, and the refrigerator, and the grandfather clock, and began the business of preparing supper. Mario had killed a sheep and butchered it and there was cold roast mutton in the larder; salad and tinned peaches with cream and plum cake completed the impromptu meal, which they ate in the big kitchen that was the central room of the homestead.

Leonora homestead had several bedrooms, but, with Tim Archer and Mario both living in, Angela Dorman and Jennifer shared a room. Jennifer soon found that Angela was frankly curious about England; the barrage of questions began as soon as they retired.

"Have you ever seen Westminster Abbey?" Angela asked.

Jennifer was taken by surprise. "Why—yes."

"It's very beautiful, isn't it?"

The girl from London had to think a bit. "It's all right," she said at last. "I don't know that I ever noticed it particularly."

"It's where they have the Coronation, isn't it? Where the King and Queen get crowned?"

Jennifer wasn't quite sure if the Coronation took place there or at St. Paul's; neither of them meant a great deal in her life. "I think it is," she said, and laughed. "You know, it must sound awfully silly, but I'm not quite sure."

"I'm sure it's Westminster Abbey," said the Australian girl. "I was reading a book about the Coronation of the King and Queen in 1937. It had a lot of pictures taken in the Abbey. It must be marvellous to see a thing like that."

"I should think it would be," Jennifer agreed. "I haven't seen it, of course. I was a kid at school, in Leicester. I remember that we got a whole holiday."

"We got a holiday here, of course," said Angela. "I was only little, but I remember Banbury was all decorated with flags and bunting everywhere."

Jennifer tried to visualise the little country town that they had passed through all decorated and rejoicing over an event that happened twelve thousand miles away, and failed. "Really?"

"Why, of course. And then when the film came to the picture house Daddy and Mummy took me to it. It was the first film I ever saw; I think I was about five. It came back during the war, and I saw it again then. I've seen it three times altogether."

"I remember it was a good film," said Jennifer. "I saw it in England." She reflected as she brushed her hair that Angela Dorman, then a little country schoolgirl at Merrijig, probably knew a good deal more about the Coronation ceremonies and Westminster Abbey than she did.

"Have you ever seen the King and Queen?" asked Angela.

Jennifer tried to remember if she had or not; surely she must have seen them some time, other than at the cinema. Surely she must have? In any case, she couldn't possibly say she hadn't. Recollection came to her just in time, and saved her from having to tell a lie. "I saw them in the procession when Princess Elizabeth got married," she said. "I was standing in the Mall; they passed quite close."

"How marvellous! The Mall—that's the avenue between Buckingham Palace and the Admiralty Arch, isn't it?"

"That's right." It was incredible how much Angela knew about London.

"Did you see Princess Elizabeth, too?"

Jennifer nodded.

"And the Duke of Edinburgh?"

"Yes. I've seen them several times."

"Tell me—do they look like their pictures?"

"Yes, I think so—as much as anyone looks like their picture. They look very good sorts."

"It must be wonderful to see them close to, like that," Angela said. "I suppose you've seen everything there is to see in London?"

"I don't know about that," said Jennifer. "I lived in London for two years, but I was outside in one of the suburbs, at a place called Blackheath. I worked in an office there. I didn't see an awful lot of London, really."

"I'm going to London next year, if the wool holds up," said Angela. "I want to get a job in one of the big hospitals. Have you ever seen Winston Churchill?"

"I'm not sure," said Jennifer. "I've seen him on the pictures so many times, one gets muddled up." She searched for a palliative for her disgrace. "I've seen Bob Hope."

"Have you really? Have you seen any other film stars?"

"One or two. I saw Dennis Price once, at a dance."

"You *are* lucky. Have you seen Ingrid Bergman? I think she's beaut."

It went on and on, long after they were both in bed and growing sleepy. To Angela the English girl was a visitor from another planet, a beautiful rose-coloured place where everything that happened was important to the world. "I should think you'll find it awfully dull in Melbourne, after living in London," she said once. "Nothing interesting ever happens here."

Jennifer could have answered that nothing interesting ever happened in Blackheath, but she forbore to; she had not known Angela for long enough to damp such a guileless enthusiasm for England and everything English. She herself, so far, had found Australia far more interesting than England. She liked the prosperous dignity of Melbourne better than the shabby austerity of London; she was deeply and inarticulately pleased with the good country she had seen that day, with the brilliant birds and the novel beasts that roamed the woods and pastures where there were so few people to disturb them. She could do without the sight and the propinquity of famous or of interesting people in return for these good things, for a time anyway.

She slept well, and woke with the first light of dawn to the sound of people moving about in the homestead; she looked at her watch and found that it was half-past five. Outside was sunshine and a man's step in the yard; she rolled sleepily out of bed and sat on the edge. Angela opened an eye and said, "What's the time?"

"Half-past five."

"We don't get up till eight. I never do."

"People seem to be moving about."

"It's only Mummy. She gets up in the middle of the night all the year round." Angela rolled over firmly and went to sleep again.

Jennifer got up and dressed in jumper and slacks, and found Jane Dorman drinking a cup of tea at the table in the kitchen; the fire was already lit in the new stove. She poured Jennifer a cup. "You didn't have to get up," she said. "Angela isn't, is she? I thought not. I often get a bit of cooking done before breakfast, in the hot weather. It's better than having the stove going in the middle of the day."

Jennifer went out presently into the yard in the fresh morning, and found Tim Archer lifting a couple of dogs into the back of the old Chevrolet utility. They were nondescript dogs, one a sort of mongrel collie and the other a blue roan, a kind of dog that Jennifer had never seen before. She asked Tim what it was, and he said it was a "heeler", but when she pressed him to say if that was a breed or not, he could not tell her. It was a heeler because it went for the heels of the cattle and not their heads, apparently.

"Do you use them for the sheep as well?" she asked.

"My word," he said. "I'm going down to get the mob out of the river paddock 'n put them down the road. Want to come along?"

She got into the utility with him, and they started off across-country in it, driving over the short pastures. They went about a mile, passing through three gates, and drove round behind the sheep; here Tim stopped the utility and put the dogs out. He shouted a few orders to the dogs and got one out on one flank and one the other and got the sheep moving, seven or eight hundred of them, in the direction of the gate. They got back into the utility and drove about the paddock for a time rounding up the stragglers with the dogs; then when the mob was compact in one bunch they drove along behind them in the centre, one dog at each side. They went very slowly, at the walking pace of a sheep.

Jennifer stretched in the warm sun. "I suppose this is the modern way of herding sheep," she said. "By motor-car."

"Too right," he said. "It's a sight quicker and easier that messing about with a horse. The boss, he likes a horse and he'd ride if he was on this job. But to my way of thinking, by the time you've caught the horse and saddled up, you could have done the job in a utility."

He turned to her. "Don't they use utilities in the paddocks in England?"

She was nonplussed. "I don't think so," she said. "They don't have utilities at all. Most of the farms in England are quite small, much smaller than these. It's all different here."

"I know," he said. "The properties are bigger here, but you've got better land. Or else, perhaps you improve it more than we do. How do you like it here, after England?"

"I like it so far," she said. "It's a very, very pretty bit of country, this."

He stared at her in surprise. "Prettier than England?"

"It's different," she said. "You'd have to go a long way to find such unspoilt country in England. England might have been like this once."

He digested this in silence for a time. Then he said, "Angie doesn't like it here. She wants to go to England."

"I know. She was telling me last night."

"Do you think she'll like it there?"

"She'll like it all right," said Jennifer. "She's determined to. She's expecting an awful lot, and she'll have some disappointments, I should think. But—yes, she'll like it."

They drove on for a time in silence while he digested this unpalatable opinion. The sheep baa-ed and scuffled in front of them, the dogs whimpering on either side. "What I can't make out," he said at last, "is why anybody leaves England, if it's such a bonza place as that. Is it because they don't get enough to eat?"

"I don't think it's that," said Jennifer. "England can be difficult at times." She paused. "I think Angie may find that, when the glamour wears off. I shouldn't think she'd want to spend her life in England, after living here."

"You think she'll come back here?" he asked quickly.

She laughed. "I don't know. She might marry somebody in England and settle down there."

"Too right," he said quietly. "She might do that."

It seemed to be a difficult conversation, and Jennifer changed it, and asked him what sort of sheep they were. He told her that they were Corriedales, and described to her the points that made them so. From that they passed to discussing the Hereford cattle in an adjacent paddock, and the difference between those and Shorthorns.

"I wish I knew more about all this," she said presently. "About the land, and how to make it grow more grass. That's important, isn't it it?"

He said, "Well, stands to reason if you grow more grass you can feed more beasts. There's a lot to be done in this part of the country to improve the pastures."

"Aren't people doing all they can?"

"Aw, look," he protested, "it costs money, you know. Mr. Dorman, he's ploughing up eighty acres of the river paddocks we've just come from this autumn, and sowing it down to clovers and rye-grass. He'll have to spend three hundred pounds on seed alone, let alone the labour and the tractor and that, and then the paddock will be out of grazing for six months. I'd like to see him doing a lot more than that, but it's a big thing to close a paddock for six months, with wool the price it is."

"I see. You'd get more meat and wool later on, but not this year. You'd get less."

"That's right. And next year the prices might not be so good. The time to close the paddocks for reseeding is when prices are low, and then you generally can't afford to do it."

"It's terribly important to turn out more meat," said Jennifer. "I should have thought people would have taken a chance."

"It's just a matter of pounds, shillings, and pence," he said.

"It's a good thing to do as well," she retorted. "That ought to count for something."

He stared at her. "How do you mean?"

"The food's so badly needed," she said. "It's important to turn out as much as possible, isn't it?"

"Well, I dunno." All his life Tim Archer had lived in communities that had a surfeit of food; it was a condition of his employment on a sheep station in Victoria that he should be entitled to buy as much mutton as he wanted at threepence a pound, and this for a family meant half a sheep a week. It was hard for him to realise what this English girl was getting at. "We don't need any more food here," he said. "You mean, because of people at home?"

She nodded. "It'ld make a difference at home if people could live like you live here. It isn't till one comes away that one realises how bad things have got in England. If anybody here wants to do something for England they can just set to and grow a bit more food."

"I wish you'd tell Angie that," he said with a faint smile. He could not keep from talking about Angie to this girl; every topic seemed to work round to her in the end. "She's wanting to do something for England by going home to take a job in a London hospital."

"She wants to see England," Jennifer said. "That's what she wants to go for. She'd do a better job for England by staying here at home, on Leonora, and driving the tractor to help make more food."

"Well, you just tell her that." He was grinning now.

"I don't mind, but it won't cut any ice. She wants to see England. But it's true, all the same. If there was a bit more food we mightn't want so many hospitals."

Jennifer spent the morning in housework with Jane; Angela did a little bit about the house and then borrowed her mother's Morris and disappeared for the day to look up old school friends in the district, and to bring back a few vegetables and stores from Banbury. Jennifer refused an invitation to go with her, preferring on this first day to stay around the homestead and help Jane to get the lunch. It was hot in the kitchen and they let the wood stove out at about ten o'clock, and served a cold saddle of lamb for dinner with a great dish of potatoes cooked upon a Primus, and a cold jam tart.

They sat out, after washing-up, in deck-chairs on the veranda; Jack and the two men were away in one of the paddocks cutting up a dead tree for firewood. There was a little breeze from off the mountain, cool and refreshing; they sat drowsing and gossiping, looking out over the wide valley in the blazing sunshine.

Presently Jane said, "Tell me about Aunt Ethel. What did she die of? I didn't gather that from your letters."

It was an awkward question, and one that Jennifer was not prepared to answer directly. Ealing and the suburban house in the dark November rain seemed very far away. "She was an old dear," she said at last, "but in some ways she was rather stupid. She ran out of money, and she wouldn't tell anybody about it. You see, her pension came to an end."

She explained the matter of the pension to Jane. "She had another old lady living with her," Jennifer explained, "a Mrs. Harding, widow of an Army officer."

"Is that the one she called Aggie, who died?"

"That's right," said Jennifer. "Aggie died last May, and that probably made things difficult because, of course, they shared expenses. My mother wrote and asked her, but she said that she'd be quite all right. Well, she wasn't all right at all. It was about that time her pension came to an end, but she never told anybody about that. She hadn't got anything to live on then, so she began selling things. Furniture that she hadn't any use for—and little bits of jewellery."

"My dear . . ."

"We didn't know a thing about it," the girl said. "I went and saw her one Sunday only a month before she died, and she gave me a marvellous lunch—roast duck with all the trimmings, and a mince pie made out of some of the dried fruit parcels that you sent her. . . ." It was incredible, sitting here on the veranda in the warm breeze, that those cartons had come from here. "She had buttered scones for tea, and a great big cake. She never let on for a moment that there was anything wrong. And all the time she was—well, starving. That's what it amounted to. When she got ill, it came out that she hadn't eaten anything for days, except a few of your dried fruits."

"My dear, I am so very, very sorry."

"I know," the girl said. "She was very proud, and she wouldn't tell a soul. She needn't have let things get to such a pitch. If she didn't want to tell us, she could have got help from the Town Hall. There's an official called the relieving officer who's there to deal with cases like that, and help with money. She could have gone to him. But she wouldn't do that."

"She didn't want to take charity, I suppose."

The girl said, "I think that was it. She'd have thought that was an awful thing to do."

"I can't imagine Aunt Ethel ever taking charity. She—she was different."

"I don't think it a very good thing to be different in England," Jennifer said. "It's better if you go along like everybody else."

They talked about the details of what had happened in Ealing for a time. Presently Jane asked, "Tell me, Jenny—is this sort of thing common now? Do old people, people of Aunt Ethel's sort—do many of them die in poverty?"

The girl said cautiously, "I think a good many of them have a pretty bad time. It's difficult to tell, because one doesn't hear a lot about them. Old ladies who die quietly and make no fuss don't get into the newspapers. Granny didn't have to die like that. She was too proud to let anyone know that she was hard up. She could have died like that anywhere—it wasn't anything to do with England. It could have happened in Australia."

"It could, but it doesn't," said Jane.

"Why not?"

"I think this country's too prosperous for that to happen. An old lady who was as old-fashioned and as proud as that would almost certainly have some relation, some son or grandson or nephew, who was making a whole heap of money, to whom the little assistance that she'd need would be a flea-bite. It *could* happen here, as you say, but I can't imagine it doing so."

"She had some odd ideas," Jennifer said presently. "It all happened within twenty-four hours of her death, so I suppose she would be a bit funny."

"What sort of ideas?"

The girl said, "She was thinking of the time when she was young, and how easy and how prosperous everything was then, in England. She kept talking about that, saying what a much better time she'd had when she was a girl than I was having. I let her talk, of course; one couldn't argue." She sat staring out across the sunlit valley to the blue hills. "And then your letter came with the five hundred pounds, and you said that you were sending it because the wool cheque had been twenty-two thousand. I suppose you said that to make it easy for her to accept."

Jane said, "I thought it was best to tell her. She'd known that we were hard up for so many years."

"I thought that was it. I think she thought a lot about your wool cheque, although she didn't say. She was lying there so still. . . . I think she got to feeling that if you had twenty-two thousand a year, you'd be living in the way that she lived in when she was young—a great big house with three servants and a butler, and grooms, and hunters, and being presented at Court—all that sort of thing. I think she thought that if I came out here to see you, I'd be getting back into the world she knew when she was young. . . ."

"Poor old dear," Jane said softly. "You mean, she was a bit confused."

"I think she was," said Jennifer. "I don't think she could realise all that sort of thing has gone for ever."

"I wonder if it has!" said Jane.

Jennifer turned and stared at her. "People don't live like that out here, do they?"

There was a short silence. "No . . ." Jane said slowly. "Only a very, very few—big station owners in the Western District. They

106

have big homes, and play a lot of polo, and they hunt, and give dances, and get presented to the Governor-General. They *do* live rather in the way Aunt Ethel lived when she was young, but there aren't very many of them. Ninety-five per cent of graziers are people like ourselves, people who've always been hard up until the last few years. Since the beginning of the war the price we get for meat and wool has gone up steadily, and now we've got so much money that we don't know what to do with it. So far we've all been paying off our debts and mortgages. What happens next is anybody's guess."

Jennifer asked, "But will these high prices go on?"

"I don't know," said Jane. "We'd still be well off if they fell to half what they are now."

"They're bound to fall, aren't they?"

"Wool's bound to fall," she said. "Wool will go down when the rearmament stops, but meat has been going up steadily for years. The world seems to want more and more food, and each year more and more gets eaten in Australia as our population rises, and so there's less each year to export. It's the same in the Argentine, and everywhere. That seems to mean higher and higher prices for meat. . . ."

She laid her darning in the basket, and got out her cigarette-case, and gave Jennifer one; they sat smoking in silence for a little. "I don't know what's going to be the end of it," she said. "This property would fetch about ninety thousand pounds at present-day prices, and it's all free of debt. That's heaps to leave the children when we die. We want them to work, not to live on money that we leave them. We want to go on working here ourselves; it's what we like doing. And these enormous sums of money keep coming in. I don't know what we'll do with it, I'm sure."

"Make a trip home," suggested Jennifer.

"We've thought of that," said Jane. "I don't know that I really want to go to England now. I don't think I'd know anybody there at all. Jack sometimes says he'd like to make a trip to Europe and go to Gallipoli, but he doesn't really want to, I don't think." She sat smoking in silence for a minute. "If Angie goes next year, we might go home the year after to see her. But that wouldn't take much money, not compared with what we're making. . . ."

Jennifer smiled. "You'll have to buy another grandfather clock."

Jane laughed. "I know it was stupid, Jenny, but I *did* like buy-ing it. Made in Chester in 1806, before this country was even explored. It's a lovely thing to have." She spoke more seriously. "No, if things go on like this, some day I'd like to rebuild the homestead."

"Rebuild this house?"

Jane shook her head. "I'd like to build another house down by the river, and turn this over to a foreman. I'll show you where I want to have it. A new brick house designed by a good architect, rather like an English house, but single storey; a house with English trees and an English lawn and a garden all around it, like we used to have at home. Leave the stables and the stockyards all up here, and let the men have their meals up here with the fore-man's family. I want a gracious sort of house, where Jack and I can slack off as we get older and not have to cook for the men. A house where one can have good furniture, and good pictures, and good china and glass, like we used to have at home when I was a girl."

"An English country house," said Jennifer thoughtfully.

"Like that in a way, but adapted to the country and the station." She paused. "I believe a good many people'll start doing that, if the money goes on like this."

"So you'll get a lot of English country houses here?"

"We might," said Jane. "After all, the English country houses came when agriculture was doing well, and agriculture's doing well here now. We all came out from England, and we've got the English way of doing things. I don't see why we shouldn't have the same sort of houses—adapted to the times and to the labour shortage."

"Cut out the butler," Jennifer suggested.

Jane smiled. "And the second parlourmaid. It'll be different, of course. More cars and travel, and no servants. But it might be something just as good."

"You mean, there's something in what Granny was trying to say?"

"There might well be. Old people have a knack of being right, sometimes."

Jennifer settled down at Leonora very happily. In recent years she had worked in an office, first in Leicester and then in London, and working so she had done little serious cooking or housework. It was no burden to her to take some of the cooking and cleaning off Jane for a few days; she rather enjoyed it, having nothing else to do and as a means of learning new techniques. She went out in the paddocks and the stockyards with Jack Dorman and the men whenever she got asked, and she found the management and care of stock and pastures interesting after her office life. She found a very great deal to occupy her at Leonora.

She would have found it even pleasanter if the weather had been cooler, and she came to realise the value of Jane's insistence that she should avoid the city at the height of the hot weather till she was acclimatised. It was an exceptionally hot January. Each day the sun rose in a cloudless sky at dawn and set in a cloudless evening sky at dusk; each night Angela and Jennifer lay with few coverings in the somewhat stuffy little bedroom of the homestead, unable to sleep till midnight for the heat. Each day thin wreaths of smoke behind the mountains told of forest fires in the high country to the south of them; each day Jack Dorman listened to the wireless weather forecasts, worried, for some news of rain.

"Don't like the look of it at all," he said more than once. "It's a fair cow."

He was too worried and preoccupied for Jennifer to bother him with questions, and Angela knew little about the station, and cared less. She asked Tim Archer to tell her what the trouble was, and he said that the boss was worried over the condition of the top paddock, bordering on the forest. The spring up there which usually ran all through the summer had dried up some weeks before and the paddock had got very dry; on account of lack of water they had moved the stock out. The paddock, in consequence, had been little grazed for some time and the grass was far too long for safety; if a fire should run through the forest to the Leonora boundary it would sweep across that paddock in a flash. The homestead would probably be safe enough, but fences would be destroyed; the dry wood of the posts would burn like tinder.

"The trouble is with these darn fires you don't know where they'll stop," said Tim. "You can't do much about it, either."

It was on one of these cloudless days that Jane went into town with Angela in the Morris; to make a break for her Jennifer had volunteered to get the dinner so that Jane could dine at the hotel with Angela. She served the inevitable hot roast mutton with potatoes and vegetables competently, though she was dripping with sweat; Tim and Mario finished the meal, and helped her with the washing-up. Then they went out to their work, and Jack Dorman stood with her on the veranda looking at the wreaths of smoke rising almost straight up into the sky behind Buller.

He said anxiously, "I believe that's nearer. Think I'll run up the road a bit in the Ford, 'n see if I can find out where she's burning. Like to come?"

She got into the car with him and they started up the road towards the mountain. They passed the Merrijig hotel and went on towards Lamirra and the timber camps. At Lamirra Jack Dorman stopped the car and went with Jennifer into the store, kept by an English couple who had recently come out from Portsmouth, but they knew little of the local conditions and were ignorant about the fires; they did not think that they were very near.

"Run up the road a bit to where they're cutting," Jack said when they got outside. "We'll get a view over the ridge up there, and see for ourselves."

They drove on up a broad, smooth, well-engineered road winding up the mountain-side; he told her that this was a timber road made for the passage of the timber lorries getting the wood out; it was designed eventually for use as a main highway. They went on winding up the hillside, and it was cool in the forest; the great trees met high over their heads and practically the whole road was in shade. From time to time they passed a trailer truck loaded with tree-trunks coming down, sighing with air brakes; from time to time they passed a track leading off into the forest on one side or the other, and saw groups of men handling the fallen timber, who paused in their work to stare curiously at the new utility.

They stopped to ask the ganger of a group of road-makers what the fire position was. He was reassuring; he said that it had not crossed the King River and he did not think it would; the forest fire patrol were there and they had cleared a fire break three miles long to save the forest timber. Jennifer sat in the car while the men gossiped, understanding only about half of what they said; the names of mountains, rivers, people, and official bodies meant nothing to her and she did not fully understand what it was all about.

It was lovely sitting there in the car. They were at an altitude of about four thousand feet and in the speckled shade of the forest; for the first time that day she was cool and dry from sweat. She stretched luxuriously in her clothes. It was quiet in the forest, or it would have been, but for the distant and rhythmic rumbling of a bulldozer at work.

She sat listening to the bulldozer as the men talked. The noises repeated in a regular cycle; a roaring acceleration of the motor followed by a few seconds of steady running, then a period of idling, and then a few seconds of light running as the thing reversed, another idling period, and the cycle began again. It varied very little; she sat listening to it dreamily, half asleep in the coolness of the forest.

The cycle was disturbed, and woke her from her doze. A rumbling of heavy timber broke in and the roaring of the engine mounted suddenly to a climax, and then stopped dead. There was a noise of tumbling machinery and a continued rumbling of rolling logs; a few men shouted in the distance, their voices puny and lost among the greater noises. Then everything was quiet again.

Then men broke off their discussion of the fire and looked in the direction of the row. "What's going on down there?" asked Jack.

"Bulldozer at work, shifting logs," the ganger said. "Sounds like he's got into trouble. Those bloody things are always getting into trouble. We had one bogged up to the seat last winter; took a winch and a day's work to pull him out."

They went on with their talk; down in the forest everything was quiet. Presently the ganger went on and Jack Dorman let the clutch in and the car moved on up-hill. "Sounds a bit better," he said to the girl beside him. "We'll go up to the top of the road and have a look. He says we can see the fire from there."

A quarter of a mile further on, a track led down the hill to the right. As they approached they saw a man running up this track towards the road, a man in lumber jacket and dirty canvas trousers,

110

a rough man, running clumsily up-hill, half-foundered. He waved at the car when he saw it; they stopped and waited for him to come up to them.

"Aw look," he panted. "Give us a run down the road to Lamirra. There's been an accident in there, and two blokes got hurt bad. I got to telephone the doctor and the ambulance at Banbury, 'n find a bloke called Splinter."

Six

JENNIFER opened the door of the utility and slid across the seat towards Jack Dorman; the man tumbled in beside her and slammed the door. He was panting and streaming sweat. Jack Dorman began to turn the car. "It's a proper muck-up," the man said urgently. "I got to get Splinter quick."

The car swung round and headed down the road. "Where d'you want to go?"

"You know the office building, other side the bridge? They'll telephone the ambulance from there. Maybe they'll know where Splinter's working."

"Where it says the name of the company, on a big board?"

"That's right. They'll telephone from there, and then I'll have to find Splinter."

They did not speak again; Jack Dorman devoted his attention to the road as they went flying round the curves down into the valley. Once as they swung violently round a corner with a scream of tyres the man was flung heavily against Jennifer; he wrenched himself off her and said, "Sorry, lady."

"That's all right," she said. "Who is this man you've got to find?"

"Who? Splinter? He's the doctor here."

Jack Dorman, eyes glued to the road, said, "Is that the chap that goes fishing at the week-ends?"

"That's right," the man said, "he's just one of these D.P.s, working in the timber with the rest of us. He's a doctor in his own country, like. He's not allowed to be a doctor here."

They came to the office building at the bottom of the stream, a small weatherboard shack of three rooms; the man flung himself from the car. "I'll wait here a bit," Jack Dorman called after him. "'Case you want to go back."

They sat in the car for a few minutes, waiting. "Where is the nearest proper doctor?" the girl asked.

"Banbury," he said. "There's a hospital there with an ambulance, and there's a doctor—Dr. Jennings."

"How far is that from here?"

"About seventeen miles."

She was a little shocked; accustomed as she was to city life it was difficult to realise that there could be no doctor close at hand. "How long will it take him to get here?"

112

He hesitated. "That depends. If he's in Banbury and he's free, he might be out here in an hour. But I believe this is his Woods Point day."

"What's that?"

"He goes to Woods Point once a week," he said. "They haven't got a doctor there. I think this is the day he goes there—Tuesday. I'm pretty sure it is."

"How far is that from Banbury?"

"About forty miles."

She said, "You mean, it could be hours before he could get here?"

"Too right."

"But what happens, in a case like this?"

"Just got to do the best you can," he said. "Most doctoring for accidents is common sense."

They sat together in the car, waiting. Then the man that they had brought down from the woods came to the door of the office with the manager, a man called Forrest. Jack Dorman knew him slightly as an acquaintance in various local bars.

"Eh Jim," he said. "Got a bit of trouble."

Jim Forrest glanced at him in recognition, and then at the new Custom utility. He crossed the road to Dorman. "Aw, look, Jack," he said. "Are you busy?"

"Not particularly."

"Joe here, he says there's two men got hurt bad, up where you picked him up upon the road. They'll have to be fetched down and taken into hospital, unless we can get the ambulance to come out for them. Could you stand by a few minutes while we get through to Banbury? If we've got to send them in, they'll travel easier in this utility than in one of my trucks."

"Do anything I can. I'll run them into Banbury if you want it."

"Thanks a lot. I've got the call in now. Say, while you're waiting, could you run Joe up to Camp Four, fetch a man called Zlinter?"

"I know him. That's the chap that fishes?"

"That's right. He's a D.P. doctor, been working here for quite a while. I got him on the telephone and he's gone down to his camp by truck, pick up his stuff. I'd appreciate it if you'd slip down there 'n pick him up. Joe can show you. By the time you've got back here I'll have spoken to Banbury."

The utility went sliding off with Joe in it again; a mile down the road it turned into the camp and ran between the rows of hutments under the gum trees, and stopped outside the fourth on the right. Joe got out and called to a man at the door. "Hey!" he said. "Seen Splinter anywhere about?"

The man said, "He's inside."

Joe vanished into the hut and Jack Dorman got out of the utility with Jennifer; together they unfastened the black twill cover of the truck-like body. Joe came out carrying in his arms a very large first-aid box. "Put it in the back," said Dorman.

A tall, dark man came to the door of the hut and glanced at the utility and then at Dorman; recognition came to him. "So," he said, "we have already met, upon the Howqua. It is your car, this?"

"That's right."

Carl Zlinter paused in thought. "I have much to take," he said. "It will be all right to drive this car into the woods, up to the accident?"

"I should think so. The ground's pretty hard."

"I will take everything, then, in the car."

He went back into the hut, and reappeared with Joe, carrying five cartons roughly packed with packages of cotton-wool, dressings, splints, bandages, bottles of antiseptic; these with a worn leather case completed his equipment. It only took three or four minutes. "Now we are ready to go," he said.

Joe got up into the back with the stores, and Zlinter got into the front of the utility with Jennifer and Dorman. "It is better to bring everything," he said. "Much will be not needed, but for the one thing left behind—it is better to take everything."

Dorman said, "Go back first to the office?"

"I think so. Perhaps the ambulance and doctor are already on the way. In any case, we must pass by that place."

They slid off up the road again to the weatherboard office. The manager came out to meet them. "Can't get through yet," he said. "You go on up, and I'll be along soon as the call comes through."

Jack Dorman said, "The doctor's day in Woods Point, isn't it?"

"I don't know."

"Tuesday. I've an idea it is."

Jim Forrest made a grimace. "It would be. Will you take Zlinter up there, Jack? I'll be up there myself soon as this call comes through." He turned to the Czech. "Do what you can, Carl, till the doctor gets here."

"Okay, Mr. Forrest," said Carl Zlinter. "I will do the best that I can."

The utility moved off and up the hill. Carl Zlinter sat in silence, mentally conning over the stores that he had brought with him, the information of the accident that he had got from Joe. A man called Bertie Hanson with a crushed leg trapped beneath the upturned bulldozer; a man called Harry Peters, the bulldozer driver, unconscious with a head injury. He was not troubled by the injuries; his long experience in the medical service of the German Army had accustomed him to front-line casualties in Russia and in Normandy. It was the lack of stores that worried him most; there was no blood plasma and no equipment for transfusion, and no dressing station. Still, he had worked and saved men's lives with less than he had now. What a clumsy fool that bulldozer driver must have been!

Jennifer sat silent between the men as the utility sped up the hill. She was somewhat at a loss; only half understanding what was going on. The tall, dark foreigner beside her had medical experience

114

though he was not a doctor; apparently he was a lumberman, for he was dressed like one, yet in this emergency Joe, and even the manager, seemed to defer to him. She did not clearly understand what it was that had happened in the forest and nobody had enlightened her; indeed, perhaps Joe was the only one who really understood the accident, and he was inarticulate, unable to communicate exactly what he knew.

They passed the road gang and reached the track that led down off the road; Jack Dorman headed the Ford down this timber lane in low gear, and they went lurching and swaying down the hill between the trees. Directed by Joe they turned presently and traversed the hillside to the right and came out into a sloping open space, where all the timber had been felled. Down at the bottom of this sloping space, upon the edge of the unfelled forest, there was a bulldozer lying on its side and forepart, lying across a log about two feet in diameter. Two more tree-trunks lay above the bulldozer, one caught upon the spade, the other poised in the air above it, perilously, apparently about to fall. There were men with ropes working carefully around this game of spillikins, attempting to guy back the log poised in mid-air.

"My word," Jack Dorman breathed. "You wouldn't think a bulldozer could get like that. . . ." The girl from London sat silent. These things which had happened in the forest were outside all her experience.

Dorman drove the Ford slowly forward till its way was barred by scrub and timber; then he stopped it, and the dark foreigner with them got out and made his way quickly to the accident. He was wearing soiled khaki drill trousers and a grey cotton shirt open at the neck; his arms were bare to the elbow and very tanned, yet he had unmistakably the air of a doctor. Dorman followed after him with Joe, and the girl came along behind them, uncertain what she was going to see.

She saw a man pinned beneath the bulldozer by one leg bent below the knee in an unnatural attitude; he lay upon the ground beneath the log that rested one end on the bulldozer spade, most insecurely. His face was badly lacerated on one side, and there was blood congealed upon the coat that had been thrust as a pillow beneath his head. He was conscious, and the eyes looked up with recognition at Carl Zlinter.

The lips moved. "Good old Splinter," he muttered. "Better than any mucking doctor in the mucking State. Get me out of this."

The dark man dropped down on his knees beside him. "Lie very quiet now," he said. "I am giving an injection which will make you sleep. Lie very quiet now, and sleep." He opened his case, fitted up the hypodermic with quick, accurate movements, sterilised it with alcohol, broke the neck of a capsule and filled it, and sterilised the forearm of the man upon the ground, all in about thirty seconds. He drove the needle in and pressed the plunger down. "Lie very quiet now, and go to sleep," he said softly. "Everything now will be all right. When you wake up you will be in hospital, in bed."

The man's lips moved. "Mucking German bastard," he said faintly. "Good old Splinter. Good old . . . mucking German bastard . . ."

Carl Zlinter got up from beside the man and crossed to the other casualty. Men parted as he came, and Jennifer saw lying on the ground the second man. He lay upon his face, or nearly so, apparently unconscious. He had been bleeding from the ears and the nose and the mouth; he lay still, breathing with a snoring sound, irregularly. Great gaping wounds were on his scalp, the fair hair matted with blood, with white bone splinters showing here and there. Jennifer bit her lip; she must not show fear or horror before these men.

"We didn't like to move him till you came, Splinter," said somebody. "The poor mugger's got his skull all cracked. We reckoned it was best to leave him as he was."

The dark man did not answer, but dropped down on his knees beside the casualty and began preparing his injection. Gently he bared an arm and sterilised it, and thrust the needle in it. He withdrew it and sat back on his heels, his fingers on the pulse, studying the patient. He did not touch the head at all.

Presently he got to his feet. "We will need stretchers," he said. "Two bed-frames, each with a mattress. I will not wait for the ambulance. Mr. Dorman, please. Will you fetch bed-frames and mattresses for us, in the utility?"

"Sure. One of you chaps come along with me 'n show me where to go."

The utility went off up the cleared glade, and Jennifer was left with the lumbermen and the casualties. The dark foreigner went back to the first man with the trapped foot and dropped on one knee beside him; gently he lifted one eyelid, and felt the wrist. He bent to an examination of the leg beneath the bulldozer.

"Is it possible to lift this thing?" he asked.

"Aw, look," said one, "it's a crook job. We got to take the top stick out backwards first, 'n when we get the weight from off the butt of this one it'll roll off on the top of him. We got to shore up this one first, 'n then take the top one off backwards, 'n rig a sheer-legs 'n a tackle, 'n try and get this one off backwards too. After that we might roll the dozer over, or jack it up maybe. But it's a long job, Splinter, 'n the stick'll roll off on him if we don't watch out."

"How long will it take?"

The man said, "It'll be dark by eight. If we can get the stuff up here, 'n lamps and that, we might get the dozer shifted about midnight."

"Can you safely move these sticks, working in the dark, so that there can be no further accident for him?"

The man said uneasily, "We got to get the poor mugger out of

116

it, Splinter. But it's a crook job, working in the dark. I'd a sight rather do it in the day."

The dark man stood in silence for a minute. The men stood round him waiting for a lead, and Jennifer could sense the trust they had in him. "I do not think that we can save the foot, in any case," he said. "It is practically severed now. If we should lift the dozer by midnight and get him out of it, the leg must then come off in hospital. I think the risk now is too great to move these sticks, for nothing to be gained, but to risk injuring him more. I think it will be better if I take the leg off now and get him to the hospital. We will wait for a message first, to find out if the doctor comes."

Somebody said softly, "Poor old sod." Another spat, and said, "I wouldn't guarantee to shift them mucking sticks without one slipping." There was a long silence after that.

Presently Carl Zlinter crossed to the other man and knelt down by him again, and very gently began to run his fingers over the skull, exploring the unnatural depressions of the scars. He lifted his head after a time, and said, "Is there water, water in a clean billy? There is an enamel bowl in one of the cartons—use that. And a clean piece of cloth, of lint from the blue square package in the big carton. Somebody with very clean hands open it, and give me a piece of the lint."

Water was brought in a billy and a man found the package of lint. He glanced at his hands, and then at Jennifer. "You do it," he said. "You got cleaner hands than any of us here."

She tore open the wrappings and bared the lint. She said to the dark man, "Do you want disinfectant in the water?"

"Please. The big blue bottle, just a little. About one tablespoonful." He glanced at her. "Not that—the other bottle. That is good. Now give it to me here, and a small piece of the lint."

She took the bowl and the lint to him; he dipped his hands in the solution and wiped them with the lint, and threw the lot away. She got him more lint and disinfectant while the men stood round them in a circle watching, and he began very carefully to wipe the dirt from the wounds on the man's head.

"Scissors," he said. "In the leather case, the middle one of the three pairs, And the forceps, also. Put them in the water, in the bowl."

She brought them to him, and stood with the men watching as he worked. The glade was very still; the sun was sinking towards the mountain and it was not now so hot as it had been. The air was fragrant with the odour of the gum trees, and from far away a faint whiff of the forest fire scented the air. In the distance a white cockatoo was screeching in some tree.

The dark foreigner worked on upon his knees, oblivious of the audience. Jennifer stood with the lumbermen looking down upon him as he worked. It was impossible for her not to share their confidence; with every movement the man showed that he knew

117

exactly what he was doing, what the result of every tiny movement of his hand upon the scalp would be. She could feel the confidence that the men standing with her had in Splinter, and watching him at work she shared their trust. This man was good.

Presently there was a faint noise on the road above them. A man by Jennifer raised his head. "Truck coming down," he said. "That'll be Mr. Forrest, come to say about the ambulance."

They listened to the approaching truck till it emerged into the glade and stopped near the wrecked bulldozer. The manager got out and came to them, and Zlinter got to his feet and went to meet him. The men crowded round, Jennifer with them.

"There's no ambulance, Zlinter," he said. "It's gone to Woods Point with the doctor for an appendicitis case. They don't know if it's coming back tonight or not."

One of the men said disgustedly, "No mucking doctor, either?" One of his mates nudged him, indicating Jennifer.

"No doctor," said Jim Forrest. "I'm sorry, cobber, but that's the way it is."

"Aw look," said one, "we've *got* a doctor. Old Splinter, he's a doctor, isn't he?"

"What about it, Zlinter?" asked the manager. "What's the damage?"

"It is not good," the dark man said. "This man, I think we should take off the foot and take him into hospital, not to leave him here for hours while we lift the dozer." The manager pulled him to one side. "It is all right, he cannot hear. He is now well doped. We cannot save the foot in any case, and we must try now to control the shock, or he will die. If he is left here for many hours, I think he will die."

"Take the foot off now, and get him out of it?"

"That is the right thing to do. He must be in a warm bed, soon, with many blankets and hot bottles; he is already very cold. I think that he is very bad, that one. I do not think that he has been a healthy man; perhaps he drinks too much."

"What about the other one?"

They crossed to the man with the fractured skull. "This one," the dark man said, "he seems more badly, but I do not think so. His skull is broken in three places, but he is a healthy man and there is yet no damage that is not repairable. I have seen men as bad as this recover, and be very good—quite well men. With him, it will be necessary to move him very carefully to where he can be operated on, to lift the pressure of the bones upon the brain. If we can so arrange that he is dealt with quickly, then I think he will have a good chance to recover and be well."

Jim Forrest bit his lip. "Have you done operations of that sort, Zlinter?"

"I have done such operations many times," the man said. "But not since the war ended."

"Where did you do them?"

"In the war with Russia," the man said. "I was surgeon in the army. In France also, at the battle of Falaise. Many times I have done emergency trephine. It is not difficult, if you are very careful, and very, very clean. The danger will lie in moving him to where an operation can be done. I could not do that here."

The manager stood in silence for a minute. "Jack Dorman will be back in a few minutes," he said at last. "He's bringing bed-frames and mattresses. They'll ride softer in that utility than in the truck."

He walked a little way away from the men, deep in thought. He knew that he was in a delicate position here, and he wanted a few moments to think it over. Zlinter had no qualifications as a doctor in the State of Victoria, but he was probably competent to do a trephine operation and it seemed logical that he should be allowed to do it. Indeed, he was the only man within reach who could attempt it; without his ministrations the man might well die. The obvious place to do the operation was in Banbury hospital, but would the matron agree to a lumberman who claimed to be an unregistered practitioner doing such an operation in her hospital? Almost certainly she would not. It might well be that while everyone was arguing the man would die. He might die anyway, upon the road to Banbury.

He went back to Carl Zlinter, "What will you do, Zlinter?" he asked. "Will you take them into Banbury? What's the best thing to do?"

"Will the doctor come to Banbury tonight?"

"He's operating at Woods Point on the appendicitis case this evening. If he comes back, it will be very late. We can get him on the telephone at the hotel at about six o'clock."

"He will not be back at Banbury before ten or eleven?"

"I don't think so."

Carl Zlinter stood in silence for a minute. He was very well aware of his position; if he operated on this fractured skull and the man died, there would be trouble and he might end up in prison, a bad start to his new life in Australia. He said at last, "I will take off the foot of the man at the dozer now—we cannot save that foot. For the other one, we must take him very carefully down to Lamirra as he is, and you must telephone again from there. I will decide then what is best to do."

"Okay, Zlinter. What help do you want?"

"Somebody who knows, to hand me things from the case, and to keep clean and sterile as possible. The young lady was good just now." He looked round, and saw Jennifer standing a little aside. "Please," he said. "Come here." She came towards him. "I am going to take off that man's foot," he said. "Have you ever seen an operation?"

She shook her head. "Never."

He looked her in the eyes. "Would you be afraid to help me? If you cannot do it, you must say so now. Can you help this man, and not faint or do any foolish thing?"

"I shouldn't faint," she replied. "I might do something stupid, because I've never done anything like this before. But I'll do my best."

He smiled at her, and she was suddenly confident. "It will be nothing difficult," he said. "Just to keep giving me the things I shall want. I will show you the things before we begin. Just to do what I shall tell you quietly, and to keep a calm head."

He took her to the utility, and began rummaging through his cartons for the dishes and appliances that he would need. He picked up a white rubber sheet and carried it over to the bulldozer, and laid it on the ground beside the trapped man, immediately beneath the menace of the hanging log. She helped him to arrange it neatly on the fragrant, leaf-covered ground beside the man. "Now, come with me," he said.

She became oblivious of the men who stood around and watched them. Her whole attention became concentrated on the job she had to do, and on this foreigner in dirty clothes who wielded so much power. He made her swab her hands and arms in disinfectant at the tailboard of the utility, and then she helped him put the instruments into the bowl and to arrange the ligatures, the dressings and the bandages neatly on the white rubber sheet. Then she went with him and knelt down beside the man, and for a time she listened while he instructed her, naming each article after him. Both became utterly immersed in the work that lay ahead.

The professional detachment of the doctor communicated itself to her, as he intended that it should, and robbed the business of all horror. She saw no sympathy and no emotion in his work upon the injured man, only a great technical care and skill, that noted impersonally every sign of feeling, every change in respiration and pulse as the work went on, and made adjustment for it. He took the leg off about eight inches below the knee with a local anæsthetic injected in several places around the leg, waited ten minutes for this to take effect, and then did the job. From the time they knelt down together by the rubber blanket till the bandaging was complete, about twenty-five minutes elapsed, and in that time Jennifer was completely oblivious of what was going on around her, concentrated only on the work in hand.

Carl Zlinter sat back on his heels. "So," he said. "Now we must get him to the utility." He raised his head. "The mattress, please. Bring it and lay it down here."

He got to his feet and Jennifer got up stiffly with him from her knees; she felt exhausted, drained of all energy. She was surprised to see Jack Dorman there among the men, and to see the utility parked immediately behind the bulldozer; she had not seen or heard it arrive. Carl Zlinter spoke to her. "It was very well done, the help that you gave me," he said. "You have been a nurse at some time?"

She shook her head. "No," she said. "I've never done anything like that before."

He raised his eyebrows. "So?" he exclaimed softly. "It was well done, very well. You have a gift for this." He glanced at her kindly. "And now you are very tired."

She forced a smile. "I don't know why one should be."

"It is the close attending," he said. "I also, I get tired, every time. It would be wrong if one did not grow tired, I think, for that would mean I had not done the best I could."

She smiled at him. "I suppose that's right. I suppose that's what it is." And then somebody said, "Where will they put the mattress, Splinter?"

He moved aside. "Here. Lay it down here, like this."

She turned towards the utility, and Jack Dorman was there. "Good show, Jenny," he said with genuine respect. "How're you feeling? Get into the car and sit a bit."

"I'm all right," she said. "It takes it out of you, though." She got into the car and sat with the door open, talking to him.

"I brought up a bottle of whisky from the store, 'case it was needed," he said. He produced it. "Let me pour you out a nip."

"I don't want that," she said. "I'm all right."

"Sure?"

"Honestly." He slipped the bottle back into the door pocket of the car. "I couldn't have done what you did," he said. "I'd have turned sick." That wasn't true, because when it comes to the point men and women are far stronger than they think, but he thought that it was true. He had seen death and wounds in plenty thirty years before, but time had wiped the details from his mind, and this had come as a fresh shock to him. He was genuinely surprised at the strength of this girl from London.

Under the direction of the Czech the men lifted the unconscious man carefully on to the mattress and carried it to the utility, and laid it in the back, assisted by Jack Dorman and the manager. Jennifer got out while this was going on and stood and watched, but there was nothing she could do to help. The evening sun was now sinking to the tops of the gum trees, flooding the glade with golden light; in the midst of her fatigue and these strange happenings she could wonder at the beauty and the fragrance of the place.

Carl Zlinter came to her by the car. "We have now to put the other man on the mattress," he said. "Do you feel able to help me? It is more delicate, because of the head injuries."

"Of course," she said. "What do you want me to do?"

She crossed with him to the other man while the mattress was brought and laid adjacent to him. They knelt down while Zlinter carefully examined the head again, and felt the pulse, and tested the degree of unconsciousness. He made her fetch a triangular

121

bandage and he raised the injured head while she slipped the bandage beneath it. Then very carefully they manœuvred the rubber sheet beneath the body and head, Zlinter and Forrest lifting each part an inch or so from the ground while the girl slipped the sheet under, straightening the folds as she progressed; in ten minutes the man was lying on the sheet. With three men lifting the sheet on each side of the body and Zlinter tending the head at the same time, they slipped the mattress under and carried it to the utility, and laid it in the back beside the other. Then they were ready to go.

Jack Dorman got into the utility with Zlinter and Jennifer; Forrest followed on behind them with the truck full of men, leaving the bulldozer to be sorted out and put upon its feet in the morning. Dorman drove the utility over the rough ground of the glade at no more than a walking pace, with Zlinter continually observing the effect of the motion on the wounded men through the back window; once or twice he stopped the car and got out to examine them more closely. Presently the truck drew up beside them, and it was arranged that Forrest should go on ahead and telephone the doctor at Woods Point.

The utility moved very slowly up the track towards the road. Jennifer sat silent between the men, Dorman giving the whole of his attention to getting the car over the rough road with as little motion as possible, Zlinter silent and preoccupied with the condition of the head injury. But presently he roused himself, and said, "Please, Mr. Dorman. This young lady that has been of so great help—I do not know her name. Will you make an introduction please?"

The Australian said, "Why—sure. Jennifer Morton, my wife's niece or something."

The girl laughed. "Jennifer's the name," she said. "Jenny, if you like." She hesitated. "You might as well complete it," she observed. "Your name isn't really Splinter, is it?"

"Zlinter," he said. "Carl Zlinter, Miss Jennifer." He achieved as near to a bow as he could manage in the cab of the utility, pressed up against the girl. "They call me Splinter when it is not something ruder. I am from Czechoslovakia. You are Australian, of course?"

"I'm nothing of the sort," the girl said. "I'm a Pommie, from London. I've only been in the country a few days."

"So? A few days only? I have been here for fifteen months."

"Do you like it?"

He nodded. "It is ver' beautiful, almost like my own country, in Bohemia, in the mountains. I would rather live there, in my own country, but I do not like Communists. If I may not live there, then I would rather live here, I think, than any other place in the world."

"You like it so much as that?"

He smiled. "I have been happy since coming here from Germany. I like the country, and the working in the trees."

The utility emerged on to the made road with a lurch. Zlinter made Jack Dorman stop the car and got out to inspect his patients; what he saw was evidently not very satisfactory, because he got up on to the mattresses and crouched over the man with the fractured skull. He got down presently on to the road, and came to the window at the driver's side.

"I will ride in the back," he said. "The motion is not good, but if I kneel down there I can keep the head still, I think. Go very, very carefully. Very slow."

Jennifer said, "Can I help if I get in behind, Doctor?"

"You must not call me 'Doctor'," he said. "Not in Australia." She did not understand that. "There is not room for more than one person," he said. "I can manage alone, but please, go very, very slow. I am afraid for splinters of the bone."

He got back into the rear portion and knelt down between his patients; Jack Dorman let the clutch in and the car moved off at walking pace. It took them half an hour to cover the three miles down to the lumber camp in the valley; they stopped twice on the way for Zlinter to adjust the folded blanket that served as a pillow. It was sunset when the utility crept up to the office building.

Jim Forrest came out into the road to meet them. "The doctor's still at Woods Point," he said. "I got through to the hotel but he's not there; the place he's operating in isn't on the telephone. I left a message asking him to ring us here, soon as he could. I rang the hospital and asked if they could send a nurse out here. They can't do that; they've got one nurse sick and another off on holiday. As far as I can make out they've only got the sister and a couple of Ukrainian ward-maids there. The sister said we'd have to bring them into Banbury."

There was a silence. Everybody seemed to be expecting Zlinter to say something, and Carl Zlinter apparently had nothing to say. At last he got down from the back of the utility. "Please," he said, "may I come into your office, Mr. Forrest?"

"Sure." The manager led the way inside.

In the bare, rather squalid room that was the office of the lumber camp the Czech turned and faced the manager. "This man is now very bad," he said quietly. "This man with the fractured skull. Mr. Dorman, he drives very carefully and very slow, but I have not been able to prevent the head from moving. There are broken bones, you understand, pieces of the skull that are broken, like the shell of an egg. With every movement of the car there is a—a movement of these pieces of the skull against each other, and a rubbing on the matter of the brain."

Jim Forrest made a grimace.

"The pulse is now worse," Zlinter said dispassionately, "and the colour of the face is worse also. The total condition is now seriously worse than when you saw him in the woods, by the

123

accident. I do not think it is wise to take him into Banbury, another twelve miles, till he has had some attention."

"You'll think he'll die upon the way?"

Zlinter shrugged his shoulders. "I do not know. It is seventeen miles and the road is not good until the last part, so we must go very slow. It will take two hours; if we go faster there may be much damage to the brain. I cannot say if he will die or not if he is treated so. I can tell you only that I would not advise for him to go further than here till he has had attention."

"What sort of attention, Zlinter?"

"I think the head should be examined carefully, in clean and antiseptic surroundings, with good light. I think that we shall find a portion of the bone is pressing on the brain. If that is so, that portion must be lifted or removed entirely to relieve the pressure—the operation that we call trephine. When that is done, if it needs to be done, the matter is less urgent; he must then be put into some cast or splint for the movement of the head, and taken to a hospital."

"Could you do that—lift that bit of bone you think wants lifting?"

"I have done that operation many times. In this country, I am not allowed to practise because I am not qualified. If the man should die in the end, there would be trouble, perhaps. I think it is for you to say what is to be done."

"If I said, 'Have a go at it', would you be willing?"

"I would be willing to do what I can for him," the Czech said.

"Even though it might mean trouble if the thing goes wrong?"

Zlinter smiled. "I have crossed that river already," he said. "I am in trouble now with the other man if things go wrong, for I have taken off his leg, and that I am not allowed to do, I think. I am in one trouble now already, and another of the same kind will not matter much."

Jim Forrest nodded. "May as well be hung for a sheep as a lamb." He stood in silence for a minute, looking out of the dirty window at the golden lights outside as the sun went down. It would be dark before they could get this man to Banbury, which would not make the journey any easier for him. There was no guarantee that when they got him there he would receive attention before morning; the matron certainly would not undertake an operation for trephine herself, and she would almost certainly prevent Carl Zlinter from doing anything of the sort in her hospital, even though the patient were in a dying state. Until he could get some news of when the doctor was expected back at Banbury, it might be adverse to this man in every way to take him there.

Too few doctors in the bloody country, he thought, and they tried to stop you using the ones you'd got. He was Australian to the core, bred in the country with only a few years of school in town, an individualist to the bone, a foe of all regimentation and control. He turned suddenly from the window. "My bloody oath," he said. "We've got to do something, and it's no good taking him to Banbury unless the bloody doctor's going to be there. You tell me what's the best to do, Splinter, and I'll tell you to do it."

The dark foreigner laughed. "I think we take them to Hut Five," he said; that was a new hut, recently constructed and so reasonably clean, and there were empty rooms. "Two rooms we shall want, one for the amputation to lie in bed. The other with a bed and a long table from the messroom, very clean, on which I can lay this man with the injured head while I examine him. When I have done that, I will tell you if I should go further with trephine, or if we can wait till the doctor comes. In that room I shall need a very bright light, with a long cord of flex from the lamp fitting." The camp was lit by electricity from a Diesel generator.

"Right," said Forrest. "We'll get on with that, and give the bloody hospital away." He stepped briskly out of the office to the utility and started giving orders to the men. Carl Zlinter went to the door of the utility and spoke to Jennifer.

"Mr. Forrest has decided to make here a little hospital for the night," he said. "We shall clear two rooms, and make all as sterile as we can. I am to make an examination of the man with the broken head, and then we will decide what is the best thing to be done." He hesitated. "Will you be able to stay and help me?"

She said, "Of course I'll stay if I can help at all." She turned to Jack Dorman. "That's all right, isn't it?"

"Sure," he said. "Stay as long as you like. I'll probably go back and tell Jane, and then come back here. If you're going to work long you'd better have some tea."

Zlinter said, "It will be a help if Miss Jennifer can stay while I examine the head. She understands more quickly than the men, the things I want. I will see she gets a meal if it is necessary to work long."

Jennifer got out of the car. "What have we got to do?"

Two hours later, in a little hot room that was roughly hung with sheets and that stank of carbolic, Zlinter straightened up above the patient on the table. It had taken them most of that time to rig up their little hospital and make the surroundings roughly sterile. For the last half-hour Jennifer had held the electric light bulb in the positions that he told her, and had handed him the swabs and bowls and scissors that he needed from the office table behind her. It was airless and stuffy in the little room, for they had closed the window to keep out the dust and the bugs that flew in the Australian night. The girl from London was sweating freely and her clothes were clinging to her body; she was growing very tired.

"It is not good," said Zlinter. "No, it is not good at all." She could see that much, even with the untrained eye; now that the hair was cut away the huge, unnatural depression in the skull was an appalling sight.

"It is ver' hot," the man said. "Hang the lamp upon that nail,

125

and we will go outside where it is cool. Perhaps there is now some news of the doctor."

It was fresh outside the hut, and she felt better in the velvety black night. Zlinter asked the darkness if Jim Forrest was there, and from the darkness somebody said that he would go and get him. Another voice asked, "How's he going on, Miss?"

She strained her eyes, but they were still dazzled by the light she had been holding and she could only see a dark blur of a figure. She could not give a reassuring report; she temporised, and asked, "Which one?"

"Harry Peters," the voice said. "The one what got his head cracked."

"He's going on all right," she said. It was all that she could say.

"Bert Hanson, he's awake," another voice said. "I just been talking to him."

In their preoccupation with the head injury they had rather forgotten the amputation lying in the next room where they had laid him in bed with blankets and hot bottles an hour before. Jennifer plucked Zlinter by the arm. "Did you hear that, Mr. Zlinter? They say the other man's awake!"

"Awake?" He turned back to the hut, and she followed him in. In the little room next to the head case the light was shaded with a towel roughly draped across the fixture. In the half-light the man lay on his back as they had left him, but the eyes were open now, and looked at them with recognition.

"So," said Zlinter, "how are we now?" He took the hand and laid his finger on the pulse, and stood counting, looking at his wrist-watch.

The man's lips moved, and he said feebly, "Good old Splinter. Mucking German bastard."

The Czech stood silent, smiling a little as he watched the second hand move round. Then he laid the hand down. "Do you feel any pain?" he asked.

"Kind of numb all up my leg," the man muttered.

"No sharp pain anywhere?"

The man said something that they could not hear; Zlinter bent to him and made him repeat it. Then he straightened up. "He's thirsty," he said to Jennifer. "Fetch a glass of water. There is a glass in the wash-room." From the darkness outside a voice said audibly, "That'll be the first time Bert's tasted bloody water in ten years."

"Tomorrow," Zlinter said, "the ambulance will come to take you into hospital at Banbury, but for tonight you will stay here. Lie very quiet now, and sleep again. If there is pain, call out; I shall be in the next room and I will come at once and give you something that will stop the pain, but I do not think you will have pain again tonight." Behind him Jennifer came with the water; he knelt and raised the head and gave the man a drink, but he took only a few sips. "Now rest, and go to sleep again," he said. "It is all right now."

There was a knock at the door, and Zlinter went out into the corridor with Jennifer; Jim Forrest was there. "This one is doing well," he said softly, "—the amputation. He is now conscious and resting. The other one, the head case, is not good. Will the doctor come tonight?"

The manager said, "His appendicitis case has turned out bad, Zlinter. Peritonitis, or something. I told him what you said about not taking the head case any further before examining him, and he said to do the best you can. I asked if I should get you to ring him, but he's going back to his appendicitis. He'll be back at the hotel about ten or eleven. He said to do the best you can, and he'll be out here in the morning."

"Did you tell him I may have to lift the bone to ease the pressure on the brain?"

"I told him that you thought an operation might be necessary tonight."

"What did he answer, when you told him that?"

"He said, he couldn't be in two places at once, and you'd have to do the best you could. It was a crook line, and I had to make him repeat a good many times, but that's what it amounted to."

The Czech stood silent for a minute. Then he said, "I would like you to come in and look at him, with me. You do not mind the sight of a bad wound?"

"That'll be right." They went into the room and Jennifer followed. The manager, in spite of his assurance, drew his breath in sharply when he saw the extent of the injury. Zlinter moved his hand above the great depression. "The bone here is much depressed, as you will see," he said. "There is hæmorrhage in the brain cavity, also." He motioned to Jennifer to move the light; she held it above the face, putty coloured and with a bluish tinge. "He is a bad colour," said Zlinter softly, "and the breathing is bad also, and the pulse is weak. I do not think this man will live until the morning in his present state. What do you think, Mr. Forrest?"

The manager said, "I don't know. I've never seen a thing like this before, Splinter. I should think you're right. He's dying now, isn't he?"

The Czech said, "I think he will be much improved if we can lift the bone and ease the pressure on the brain." He motioned Jennifer to put the light back on the nail, and took them out into the corridor. When the door was shut, he said, "I have wanted you to see him now, Mr. Forrest, so that if he should not recover from the operation you can say how he was."

"You're going to operate, Splinter?"

The Czech nodded. "I am going to lift the bone, and perhaps take some of it away completely."

"Right. What do you want?"

Carl Zlinter turned to Jennifer. "Are you too tired to go on again?"

She said, "I'm all right."

"It will be long, perhaps two hours."

"I'll be all right," she said again.

He smiled at her. "That is good." He turned to the manager. "We must eat before we start again," he said, "especially this lady. We shall need a small meal, very quickly now, because we must not wait. Some tea, and boiled eggs, perhaps—something that will be ready soon, in a few minutes. After that we will begin the work. We shall need much boiling water."

They went into the little room again at about a quarter to nine, freshened by a meal in the canteen and a cigarette. Heat, and not horror, was the enemy that Jennifer had to battle against in the next two hours. There was no fly-screen on the window and it was impossible to open it because of the moths and the flying beetles that crashed against the pane, attracted by the light. It was impossible to have the door open without sacrificing sterility. Both worked in a steady drip of sweat, made more intense by the heat from the high-power lamp that Jennifer held most of the time in the positions that the surgeon told her. From time to time they rested and drank lukewarm water from a pitcher before going on.

Thinking it over afterwards, Jennifer came to the conclusion that the heat made the experience easy for her. She was so miserably hot and uncomfortable that it was all that she could do to keep her wits about her, to keep on handing him the things he wanted at the time he wanted them; she had no nervous energy left with which to be upset at what she saw. She needed all her energy for what she had to do.

It was a quarter past eleven by the time the head was finally bandaged. Zlinter went out into the corridor to get some help and with Forrest and Dorman and two other men they lifted the patient in a sheet from the operating table to the bed, and laid him there. The men stood looking on while Zlinter felt the pulse.

Forrest said, "Looking better, isn't he, Splinter?"

The Czech said, "I think so too. It is now a question of the operation shock. If he can live through that, I think he will recover and be a well man."

He turned to the door. "We will leave him for a little now. I shall come back later." He moved them out of the room and shut the door carefully behind them, and leaned for a moment limply against the wall. He said to Jennifer, "You must be very tired."

She was drenched with sweat, her clothes sticking to her body at every movement. "It was so hot in there," she said. She felt now as though she might be going to faint. "Let's get out into the air."

Jack Dorman took her arm, and they moved towards the door of the hut. Zlinter stopped at the room of the other man, and went in softly to look at his amputation case. The man was lying on his back and breathing deeply, sound asleep; he did not seem to have moved since Zlinter had seen him last. He lifted the sheet and glanced at the bandaged leg, and lowered the sheet again. "Good," he said softly to Forrest. "This one is all right." He moved to the door, and then stopped for a moment. "Do you smell anything?"

"Carbolic," said the manager.

"I thought I could smell whisky."

Jim Forrest laughed. "Too right, Splinter. Jack Dorman's got a bottle in his car—it's me you're smelling. Come on and have one."

It was cool and fresh out in the forest night after the close stuffiness of the small room, and the air smelt wonderful after the stenches of the operating table. Jennifer felt better when they got outside; Jim Forrest fetched glasses from the canteen and she drank a small, weak whisky and water with the men, and felt better still. They stood smoking together and relaxing in the cool night air, letting the freshness cool and dry their bodies and their clothes, talking in short, desultory sentences about the operation.

Once Jennifer asked, "Will he really recover, like an ordinary man?"

The Czech said, "He may. Not to do bulldozing again, perhaps, but for light work he may recover very well. There will be danger of paralysis, on the right side. We will see," He turned to the manager. "It is this man who is the student, is he not?"

"That's right," said Jim Forrest. "He's trying to save up to do a university course." He paused. "Should be able to, the money that one has to pay a bulldozer driver."

Jennifer asked, "What's he going to do at the university?"

"Metallurgy, I think." He turned to the Czech. "What about tonight, Splinter? Will he wake up?"

"I think he may, in two or three hours' time. I shall stay with him all night, myself."

Jennifer asked, "Will you want me again?"

He looked down at her. "Not again tonight," he said. "I could not have done very much for these men without your help. I find it wonderful that you have never been a nurse."

She smiled. "My father's a doctor," she said. "Perhaps that makes a difference."

"So?" he said. "A doctor in England?"

"That's right," she replied. "He practises in Leicester."

"And you have helped him in his practice?"

She shook her head. "I know a little bit from living in the house, of course. One can't help learning little bits of things."

"You have learned more than little bits of things," he said. "Now you must be very tired. You should go home and get some sleep."

129

"You're sure you won't want me any more?"

"No," he said. "Nothing will happen now that will be urgent, till the doctor comes in the morning."

She said, "I'd like to know what happens to them."

"Sure," he said. "Perhaps I may come in and tell you, at the homestead."

Jack Dorman said, "That's right. Come in for tea tomorrow or the next day."

"If I can, I will do that," he said. "When the doctor comes, he may wish that I go to Banbury with him, to the hospital, to show what I have done and to hand over the cases in the proper way. I do not know. I will come and tell you tomorrow or the day after."

She said simply, "I'll look forward to you coming."

She got into the utility, and Jack Dorman drove her home. Jane and Angela were waiting up for her with a small meal of cold meat and salad and cheese; she was hungry, but before she ate she had to rid herself of her clothes, that stank of sweat and chemicals. She went and stood under the shower, and put on clean pyjamas and a house-coat, and came back to the kitchen and ate a little cold mutton and drank a cup of tea while telling them about it.

Jack Dorman told Jane, "It was that fellow Zlinter that Ann Pearson told us about, when Peter Loring got his mastoid. He's quite a surgeon, so it seems."

She said, "The one that you met over on the Howqua, who found his own grave?"

"That's right. They all call him Splinter up at the camp."

Jennifer said sleepily. "Found his own grave?"

"That's right," said Dorman. "Get him to tell you about it. It's quite a story."

She was too tired to go into that at the moment. "He's very sure of himself," she said reflectively. "He knew exactly what he wanted to do, right from first to last."

Angela asked, "Is he good-looking?"

"Rather like Boris Karloff," Jennifer told her. "But he's got a nice smile." She paused. "I should think he's a very good doctor."

"He wouldn't be as good as an English doctor, though, would he?" asked Angela.

Jennifer smiled at the rose-coloured dream of England. "I don't know," she said. "All English doctors aren't supermen."

"I thought the English medical schools were the best in the world," said Angela. "Every Aussie doctor who wants to do post-graduate work goes to England."

"Maybe that's because they can't get dollars to go to America," Jane said dryly.

Jennifer got up from the table. "I think I'll go to bed," she said. "I should think we'd all better go to bed. I'm sorry you've had to stay up like this for me."

"Makes a bit of a change, a thing like this. We've not had so

130

much excitement since the cow calved," Jane remarked. "Don't get up tomorrow, Jenny. Sleep in late."

"That's a damn good idea," said Angela.

"I didn't mean you," said her mother.

At the lumber camp after the utility had gone, Carl Zlinter sat on the steps of the hut in the cool, velvety night talking to the manager. Jack Dorman had left the remains of his bottle of whisky with them to finish off; the Czech had a second but refused a third. "I should sleep if I drink more," he told Jim Forrest, "and I must stay awake tonight. Presently this man, he will wake up and I must be with him then."

"Look," said the manager, "is there anything I can do? I'll stay up with you, if you like."

"It is not necessary. There are men sleeping in the hut. If it should be needed, I will send for you. But I think it will not be needed. Everything I think will now be all right."

Presently Jim Forrest went back to his house to bed; Carl Zlinter finished his cigarette and went back to the hut. He looked in on his amputation case; the man was still in the same position, apparently asleep; from the door Zlinter could hear the even, regular breathing. He did not go in or make any close examination; better to let him sleep. He went into his trephine case and began cleaning and tidying the room, clearing away the debris of the operation and cleaning and drying his instruments.

An hour later, at about one in the morning, the man began to come to. He became conscious; once or twice the eyes opened and closed. The colour and the breathing were now much better. Presently the lips moved; the man was trying to say something.

Carl Zlinter bent beside him. "Don't talk, Harry," he said. "Don't move about. You got a blow upon your head, but you're right now. Don't try and talk or move about. Just lie quietly as you are, and rest. You're right now."

He could not make out if the man had understood or not; the lips moved again and he bent to try and hear what he was saying. But now there was a humming in the air, unmelodious but recognisable as a tune. In one of the cubicles of the hut somebody was humming, or chanting to himself in a low tone, "God Save the King".

It was impossible for the Czech to hear if his patient was speaking, or if the lips were merely moving by some reflex originating from the damaged brain. He got to his feet in annoyance; the men in the hut were all good types and they knew very well that there were critically ill men in the hut with them. They should know better than to make a row like that in the middle of the night. He went out into the corridor to find out where the noise was coming from and stop it.

It was coming from the next-door cubicle, that housed his amputation case.

He opened the door. In the dim, shaded light Bert Hanson was

131

lying on his back awake, maundering through "God Save the King" in low, alcoholic tones, and beating time with one hand. The air was heavy with the aroma of whisky. He took no notice of the doctor, but continued beating time and singing, his eyes half closed, the voice getting stronger and the tune louder with every minute.

> Thy choicess gifs insore
> On him beplea stupore . . .

Zlinter went into the room and plucked the towel from the lamp; the room was flooded with light. He saw a lump under the bed-clothes, turned them back, and there was the bottle, uncorked and practically empty. He dropped it on the floor with tightened lips, wondering if his patient had drunk the whole of it. From the look of him, he probably had.

The man said genially in a strong voice, "Good old Splinter. Good old mucking bastard!" He burst into laughter in an access of *bonhomie*. "Come on, le's sing 'God Save the King' together, and muck the mucking Germans!"

A man appeared in the corridor dressed in pyjama trousers and no top. "Want any help, Splinter?"

"This verdamt stupid bloody fool," said the Czech, angrily, "somebody has given him a bottle of whisky. We must try and keep him quiet, for his own sake and for the man next door."

The next two hours were a nightmare. At an early stage Zlinter sent a man to fetch Forrest from his house; by the time he came running the pandemonium was terrific, with three men fighting to keep Bert Hanson in his bed, with Zlinter himself attempting to keep his trephine case quiet and tranquil in the next room behind a beaverboard wall. The man was frantically, fighting drunk; at one stage he got hold of the bottle and used it as a club till it broke, mercifully upon the wall beside him. It was with the greatest diffi-culty that they got the jagged, broken neck out of his hand.

Jim Forrest said to Zlinter at the height of it, "You'll have to give him something. Morphia."

The Czech said, "I do not think that will be good. When this is over, there will be reaction, and he will be very weak. I do not think that any drug will work while there is so much alcohol, unless to give it in a great dose as would kill him later."

"What the hell are we going to do with him?"

"Hold him, until the thing passes. If these men grow tired, get other men."

"How's Harry going on?"

"He is going on ver' well. It would be better for him if there was less noise."

"I'll do the best I can. But if he can't have any dope, he'll have to work it out, and he's got some way to go."

At about three o'clock, and almost suddenly, the man stopped struggling and shouting, and entered on a stage of collapse. Carl

Zlinter left his trephine case and gave his whole attention to his amputation drunk. The heart was now very weak. The man lay in a stupor of weakness, gradually sinking. At about four o'clock Zlinter gave an injection of strychnine, which only had a very temporary, slight effect.

At about half-past five, in the first light of dawn, Bert Hanson died.

Seven

IT is the duty of the police to take note of all serious accidents occurring in their district, and Sister Fellowes at the hospital in Banbury had rung up Sergeant Russell the previous evening to tell him there had been an accident at Lamirra, and that the doctor was away at Woods Point on an operation case. The police got to the lumber camp at about half-past seven in the morning, inspired more by a genuine desire to assist than with any thought of invoking the processes of law. It was unfortunate, however, that they got there before Dr. Jennings, who would probably have extended Bert Hanson's life a little upon paper and signed a death certificate which the police sergeant would have honoured; in a country chronically short of doctors it was no business of the police to go round making trouble.

As it was, they came upon the scene before the stage was set for them. They found a Czech lumberman utterly exhausted, who had conducted two major operations without any valid medical qualifications whatsoever, and they found one of the patients dead and in a shocking state of death, for there had been little time or energy to clean the body up. The other patient, on whom a major head operation had been performed, was clearly very ill and, in the view of the police sergeant, probably dying too. The whole thing was irregular and possibly criminal. In any case the coroner would have to be informed, and there must be an inquest.

Dr. Jennings arrived direct from Woods Point half an hour after the police. He found them taking statements from Jim Forrest and Carl Zlinter in the canteen hut, Zlinter having refused point-blank to go to the office of the lumber company, half a mile from his patient. When the doctor came in he got up from the table. "This can wait," he said to the police sergeant, with small courtesy, for he was very tired. "There are now more important things that must be done."

He walked out of the canteen, and took the doctor over to the trephine case at once. Jim Forrest turned to the sergeant. "He's right, Sarge. He's got to hand over his case to the doctor. Maybe I can go on telling you what happened."

The sergeant thumbed his note-book. "How long have you employed this man?"

"Aw, look—I couldn't say for certain. September or October, a year back, I think. Fifteen or sixteen months, maybe."

"Has he acted as a doctor before?"

"Well, what do *you* think?" said the manager. "If you had a doctor working as a lumberman, you'd use him if a chap got hurt, wouldn't you? Cuts and sprains and bruises and that? Anything serious gets sent into the hospital. We haven't had a real accident before this one."

The sergeant wrote in his book. "Did you know this man wasn't registered as a doctor in Victoria?" he asked presently.

"Sure," said the manager. "I got him as a labourer through the Immigration Office. If he was a doctor, he'd have been doctoring."

"When did you start using him as a doctor?"

"Aw, look—I forget. He's been a labourer all along. The men started going to him for cuts and sprains and that—things it wouldn't be worth going into Banbury for, or getting Dr. Jennings out here. He started coming to me for bandages and stuff, so I made over the first-aid box to him and got a lot more stuff he said we ought to have. It just grew up, you might say."

"But he's been working as a labourer all along?"

"That's right."

"Did you ever make any enquiry into his medical qualifications?"

"Only what he told me, Sarge. He said he'd been a doctor in his own country, in Prague or Pilsen or some place like that. And in the German Army. He told me from the first he wasn't allowed to practise in Australia. I knew that, anyway."

"Did you authorise him to do this operation?"

"Which one?"

"Well—both. Let's say the man who died—the amputation—first."

"He asked me, and I told him that he'd better go ahead and take the foot off. We couldn't get a doctor. We couldn't even get a nurse out from the hospital. Look, Sarge, it was like this . . ."

Sergeant Russell said presently, "I don't want you to think I'm making trouble, Jim. I got to get the facts right for the coroner, because there'll have to be an inquest. There's no doctor that can sign a death certificate. I got to get the facts." He thumbed over his book and sat in silence for a minute or two, reading through his notes. "These operations," he said. "The one where he took the foot off, and the one on the other fellow's head. How long did they take?"

The manager thought for a moment. "Aw, look—I couldn't say. The foot was pretty quick—twenty minutes, maybe not so long as that. The other one was much longer—two hours, I'd say, or longer than that."

The sergeant wrote it down. "Did you help him?"

"No."

Sergeant Russell raised his head and looked the manager in the eyes, sensing prevarication. "Who did help him? He didn't do operations of that sort all on his own?"

"There was a girl there," the manager said. "An English girl staying with Jack Dorman. She was in the utility with him. She gave a hand."

"That's Jack Dorman of Leonora?"

"That's right."

"What's her name?"

"I don't know. Jack called her Jenny, I think. She was English."

"Is she here?"

"She went back to Leonora last night, with Jack, about midnight. She's probably there now."

"I'll look in and see her," the sergeant said, "on my way back." He glanced over his notes. "I'll have to see this man Zlinter again," he said. "I'll have to know the medical degrees he's got in his own country—that'll come into it. I think that's all the questions."

"There's one you haven't asked, Sarge," said Jim Forrest, getting up, "and I'd like to know the answer."

"What's that?"

"Who gave Bert the bloody booze?" the manager said. "I'd like to know the answer to that one."

In the hut Dr. Jennings and Carl Zlinter were debating the same point, standing and looking dispassionately at the body of Bert Hanson. "Too bad this had to happen," said the doctor. "He's been an alcoholic for some time, I'd say. We'll probably find an enlarged liver at the post-mortem. Have you any idea how he got the stuff?"

The Czech shrugged his shoulders. "There were his cobbers all around, all night, here in the corridor," he said. "I was operating in the next room, and I could not see. It must have been in that time. When I had finished the trephine I came in to see this one, and I then smelt whisky, and I asked Mr. Forrest, and he said he had been drinking, himself, so I did not think more about it. And afterwards when I came in, I had had a drink of whisky also, so I did not notice."

The doctor looked at the broken bottle still lying on the floor. "He probably drank a whole bottle."

"I think so, too. We found the lead that is around the cork of a new bottle."

"And there's no saying who gave it to him?"

"Mr. Forrest asked this morning, but nobody would say. I do not think we shall be able to discover that."

"I don't suppose we shall. . . ." He stood in silence for a minute, and then pulled the sheet over the body. "There'll have to be an inquest, Zlinter," he said at last. "It's a pity I couldn't have got here before the police. I think I'll see the coroner before the inquest, and tell him how it all came about."

The Czech nodded. "They will be angry because I have done operations, I suppose."

"It's going to have to be explained, and put in the proper light.

You don't have to worry about anything, though you'll probably have to give evidence."

"One does the best one can," the other said. "It is not possible to do more than that. If I had waited till you could arrive and not done anything, both men would have been dead today. We have now one alive, and we would have the other but for some verdamt fool who gave the whisky."

"I'll go and telephone for the ambulance," the doctor said. "You'd better come down with me to the hospital and we'll have a look at what you did to that chap's head together. Take an X-ray first, perhaps."

Jennifer was still in bed when the police car drove up to the homestead at about half-past eight. Jack Dorman was out on his horse in one of the paddocks, but Mario was in the shearing shed, and Jane sent him to fetch her husband. She made Sergeant Russell comfortable with a cup of tea in the kitchen, and went to call Jennifer, who was awake. "Jenny," she said, "you'll have to get up, my dear. You'll be sorry to hear that one of those men died, the one with the amputated foot. The police sergeant's here, and he wants to ask you a few questions about what happened."

Jennifer sat up, dumbfounded. "He *couldn't* have died," she exclaimed. "He was getting on splendidly. It was the other one who was so bad."

"That's what he says, my dear. You'd better get up and put some clothes on and come out and see him. I've sent Mario to find Jack, to come along as well."

Ten minutes later Jennifer was sitting at the table with a cup of tea, facing the sergeant, who told her about the whisky. "It's just a matter of form, Miss," he said. "I've got to make out a report for the coroner on all this." He asked her name and her address, which Jane told her to give as Leonora. Then he said, "I understand you helped this man Carl Zlinter to do both operations?"

She nodded. "That's right."

"Had you ever helped him to do an operation before?"

She stared at him. "Of course not. I only met him yesterday, for the first time. I've only been in this country about ten days."

He wrote in his book. "That's right," he said equably. "It's just these questions that I have to ask. Now, what made you help him this time?"

She hesitated, not knowing quite where to begin. "Well—I suppose because my hands were cleaner than anybody else's. Look, Sergeant—this is what happened."

Jack Dorman came into the kitchen while she was telling her story; Jane briefed him in a whisper with what was going on. He pulled up a chair and sat down to listen. Jennifer came to an end of her story, and the sergeant made a note or two, and looked back at his notes of what Jim Forrest had said. There was no real discrepancy, which was satisfactory. He said, "That's all clear enough, Miss Morton. Now there's just one or two things arising out of that. Did this man tell you at any time that he wasn't a registered doctor?"

She wrinkled her forehead. "I remember he told me that I mustn't call him a doctor . . . some time or other." She sat in thought for a moment. "I'm afraid I just can't remember," she said. "Such a lot happened last night, and I was so tired, I can't remember who said what. I certainly knew that he wasn't supposed to do operations, but whether he told me or someone else, I couldn't say."

"You did know that, Miss? You knew he wasn't supposed to do operations?"

"Yes," she said. "I knew that."

He made a note in his book. "Then why did you help him to do the operations?" he asked.

She stared at him. "Well—*someone* had to help him."

Jack Dorman broke in, "Aw, look, Sergeant. There wasn't any other doctor—someone had to do something. Jim Forrest tried all ends up to get Dr. Jennings. In the end we just had to do the best we could without a proper doctor. Jenny here gave him a hand. I'd have given him a hand myself, but she could do it so much better. You don't think we should have let 'em lie until the doctor came this morning, do you?"

The sergeant closed his book. "It doesn't matter what I think, Jack," he said. "I'm just the copper. It's what the coroner thinks that matters, and he's got to have the facts. I'm not saying that in Jim Forrest's shoes I wouldn't have done the same as he did, or in this young lady's shoes, either. But if the coroner thinks different when he hears the facts of this man's death, there could be a charge of manslaughter against Carl Zlinter, oh my word. Now that's the truth of it."

He went away, leaving them dumbfounded. Jennifer said, as they watched the car departing through the gates, "It *can't* be like he said. They couldn't be so stupid."

Jack Dorman scratched his head. "What does he think we ought to have done—left 'em lying till the doctor came? It won't go any further, Jenny."

She said, "I'm so sorry for Carl Zlinter if they're going on like this. It must be beastly for him, and he's not deserved it."

The fire that had burned in Lieutenant Dorman thirty years before flared up again. "If they start anything against that chap I'll raise the bloody roof," he said evenly. "Pack of bloody wowsers. I never heard of such a thing."

Jennifer said, "If it should come to manslaughter—I can't see how it could, but if it should—I'd be in it too, wouldn't I? I mean, I helped him do the operations."

Jane said, "Oh no, they'd never bring you into it, dear. You only helped—you didn't do anything yourself. I'm sure we could keep you out of it."

"I don't want to be kept out of it," the girl said. "I was glad to be in it last night, and I'm glad to be in it still. I think it was the right thing to do." She turned to Jack Dorman. "I would like to have a talk with him about what's going to happen—with Carl Zlinter. He said he'd come round here today but if there's a row on he may not come."

Jack Dorman said, "I might take a run up the road and have a talk with Jim Forrest. If Zlinter's there, I'll tell him we're expecting him."

He got into his utility presently and went up to Lamirra; he found Jim Forrest in his office. "Morning, Jim," he said. "We've had the police sergeant at our place, asking Jenny all about last night."

"Pack of bloody nonsense," the manager said. "He hasn't got enough to do. I've been trying to find the bloody fool that gave Bert Hanson the whisky, but I'll never do it."

"He had a bottle, did he?" Mr. Dorman asked with interest. "A whole bottle?"

"I don't know how full it was when he got hold of it. Probably full—we found the tinsel paper that goes round the cork. He had most of what there was, except what got spilt into the bed."

"He took a lot, did he? In the ordinary way?"

"Oh aye—he was a pretty fair soak. A lot of them are, of course. There's nothing else to do, in barracks, in a place like this." He paused. "The New Australians are the sober ones here. All saving their money for when their two years are up, to buy a house or start a business or something. But for the language trouble, they're the best men that I've got."

"This chap Zlinter—what's he like?"

"He's right," said the manager. "Doesn't drink a lot—not more 'n you or I. Goes fishing all of his spare time."

"I know. I met him on the Howqua one time, down at Billy Slim's place." He paused. "The sergeant was saying that if this goes wrong at the inquest, he could be up for manslaughter."

"I know. I don't know what in hell they expect one to do. But anyway, it won't go wrong. We've got Doc Jennings on our side."

"He's satisfied that what was done was right, is he?"

"I think so. They've gone into Banbury now with Harry in the ambulance, him and Zlinter. They took Bert Hanson in the bottom bunk; he's going to do a post-mortem on him after he's got Harry fixed up right. I said that I'd go in tomorrow afternoon and get the news."

"I'd like to come in with you," Dorman said. "My girl Jenny's all mixed up in this, if it should come to manslaughter."

The manager stared at him. "Oh my word," he said. "It couldn't go that far."

"It could if we don't watch it," said Jack Dorman. "Zlinter's in Banbury now with the doctor?"

"That's right. They went in the ambulance."

"Jenny wants to see him. "I'd like to see him myself, 'n have a talk about all this."

"I've got a truck coming out this afternoon with Diesel oil, leaving the Shell depot after dinner. I told him to get a ride out on that."

"I'll ring the hospital and tell him to drop off at our place, and I'll bring him on here later."

Carl Zlinter walked up from the road to Leonora homestead at about three o'clock that afternoon, dressed in a shabby grey suit of continental cut; it was hot coming across the paddocks from the road in the blazing sun, and he carried his coat over his arm. Jennifer, sitting in a deck-chair on the veranda, saw him coming, and went to the last gate to meet him. "Come and sit in the shade," she said. "You look very hot."

She was wearing a clean summer frock and her legs were bare; she looked cool and pretty; the sun lit up the auburn colours in her hair. It was many years since Carl Zlinter had talked to a well-dressed girl and he was rather shy of her; in the camps that he had lived in for so long in Europe women had not dressed like that. He took courage from the memory of the sweating girl who had helped him a few hours before, and went with her to the veranda, where Jennifer introduced him to Jane. They sat down together in the deck-chairs, and talked for a little about the hot road out from Banbury.

He wiped his forehead with a handkerchief. "It is ver' beautiful here," he said. "For me, this is a very lovely piece of country, just this part around here, between Mount Buller and the town of Banbury, with the rivers, the Howqua and the Delatite. I would be happy if I were to stay here all my life."

Jane was pleased. "You like it so much as that?" She paused. "We came here twenty years ago, and we've sometimes talked of getting another station, nearer in to Melbourne. But, well, I don't know. We've never been in the habit of going to the city much, and I wouldn't want to live anywhere else than here. If we went it would only be to see more of the children."

"I would never want to live in any better place than here," he said.

Jennifer smiled. "But not as a lumberman."

He looked at her, smiling also. "There are worse things than to be a lumberman," he said. "It is not what I was educated for. But if I may not be a doctor in this country, I would rather be a lumbermen, in beautiful country such as this, than work in the city."

The girl said, "It's such a waste for a man like you to have to work in the woods. How long will it be, after your two years are up, before you can be a doctor again?"

He said, "I do not think that I shall ever be a doctor in Australia."

"Why not?"

140

"It costs too much," he said. "It is necessary for a foreign doctor to do three years of medical training again, in a Melbourne hospital, before he may practise in this country. That would cost fifteen hundred pounds, and that I have not got, and I shall never have. If I should have the money, it would then be very difficult to get a place in a hospital, because the hospitals are full with your Australian doctors." He paused. "I do not think that I shall be a doctor again," he said.

"But what an idiotic regulation!" the girl said.

He looked at her, smiling at her indignation for him. "It is not so idiotic," he said. "There must be some rule. The doctors from some countries are ver' bad. I would not like you to be treated by a Rumanian doctor, or a doctor from Albania."

Jane asked, "What do you think you'll do when your two years are up?"

He shrugged his shoulders. "I do not know. Perhaps I shall stay on and be a lumberman for ever."

"It seems a frightful waste," the girl repeated.

Jane changed the subject. "Tell me," she said, "how's your patient getting on—the one with the fractured skull?"

"I think he will recover," he said. "We took an X-ray at the hospital and then we took off the dressings, that Dr. Jennings could see what had been done, and he was happy; he did not want to do anything else. We made all clean and more sterile with the better equipment at the hospital. If that one does not drink a bottle of whisky I think he will be well."

"He wouldn't want to, would he?" Jennifer asked. "You said that he was a better type than the man with the foot."

"Did I say that? I think that is true. Dr. Jennings is to do a post-mortem on the man who died this afternoon. I think that he expects to find cirrhosis of the liver."

"It'll be rather a good thing if he does find that, won't it?" she asked. "If it proves he was a bad life, anyway?"

He shrugged his shoulders. "I do not think it matters a great deal. He died because he drank a bottle of whisky after amputation."

There was a little silence. "The police sergeant was here today," she said. "He wanted me to answer a lot of questions."

He looked up. "I am ver' sorry. Is that because you helped me in the operating?"

She nodded. "I'm not sorry a bit. If there's going to be a row I'm quite willing to be in it."

"There is no reason for you to be in it," he said. "You did nothing but to hand things to me when I wanted them, and hold the light. I shall say to the police that you had nothing to do with the operation."

"Don't do that," she said. "Just let things take their course and see what happens."

"There is no reason for you to get into trouble with the police."

"I don't mind getting into trouble with the police a bit," she said. "I think I'd rather like to. It was a good thing to have helped in, and I'm glad I did it. I'd rather like to have the chance of getting up in court, or somewhere, to say that."

"It's her red hair, Mr. Zlinter," Jane remarked. "Quarrelsome young person, isn't she? She might be an Australian."

There was a step on the veranda behind them, and Jack Dorman appeared. "How do, Zlinter," he said. "Go on—sit down—you don't have to get up. You're just the same as Mario." He dropped down into a chair beside them, and laid his hat on the floor by him. "Warming up," he said. "Been down to the Howqua again?"

"I was there last Saturday and Sunday," the Czech said, "but it is now too hot. I only caught two little fishes, and those I set free to grow bigger."

The grazier glanced at Jennifer. "Has he been telling you how he found his own grave?"

"Found his own grave?" she exclaimed. "You said something about that last night."

"You don't know nothing yet," Jack Dorman said. "Go on and tell her about it, Carl."

The Czech laughed, a little embarrassed. "It is nothing."

The girl said "Do tell me."

"It is a stupid thing," he said. "Have you been into the valley of the Howqua River, Miss Morton?"

"The name's Jenny," she said. "I've not been there yet. That's the next valley, isn't it—over those hills?"

"That is the one," he said. "It is very wild because there is no road to it, and very few people have been there. But once there was a town, a town for the gold miners, because there was a mine there, you understand, but now all that is finished. And the town also is finished, because the forest fires, they burnt it, so that now there is nothing of the town left to see at all, only a little machinery by the entrance to the old mine, and nothing else at all. Only the stones in the old cemetery are there still, because those the fire would not burn."

"When did this happen, Carl?" she asked. "When was the town there?"

"Fifty years ago," he said. "It was nearly fifty years since all the people went away, because the gold was finished. And after that the fires came, and there was no one living there to protect the town, and so it was all burnt."

"All except the headstones?"

"That is right. I met Mr. Dorman fishing in the Howqua a month ago, and we went together to find the stones that are on the graves. And on one stone, there is an inscription with my own name, and my town in Czechoslovakia."

He reached for his coat on the floor beside his chair, and took a wallet from the inside pocket. "I have copied the inscription." He

142

took a paper, unfolded it, and handed it to her. "That is what is written on the stone."

Jane Dorman leaned over, and they read it together. The girl said, "What an extraordinary thing! Is your name Charlie?"

"Carl," he replied, "and I was born in Pilsen, but not in 1869." He paused. "It is not so very extraordinary," he said. "We were a large family with many branches in Pilsen, and many people from Pilsen emigrated in this last century, when times were hard. The extraordinary thing is that I should have found the grave, I myself, with the same name." He paused, and turned to the grazier. "I wondered if you have ever heard the name in this country, so that I could find out who this Charlie Zlinter was. He was certainly a relation of some kind."

Jack Dorman shook his head. "I've never heard the name," he said. "I don't suppose anybody in this country could tell you anything about him now. I should think you'd find out something more easily in Pilsen. Get the names of people who left for Australia at the end of the last century."

The Czech shook his head. "It is not possible to find out anything from Pilsen now," he said. "I do not even know who I could write to there, to ask. And if I did write, any letter might make trouble from the Russians. They do not like people who get letters from the West."

"Why did it say, Charlie Zlinter and his dog?" asked Jennifer. "Was the dog buried with him?"

"I do not know. I would like to know, ver' much."

Jack Dorman said, "I think you'll have a job to find out much now, after fifty years."

"There would not be a record of deaths in the shire?"

"What about the parish register?" the girl asked.

"I doubt it," Dorman said slowly. "I never heard there was a church in Howqua. The nearest church would be in Banbury—if there was one there then. I shouldn't think that they'd have taken much account of what went on at Howqua. There *might* have been a shire officer there, but I rather doubt it. These gold-mining towns were pretty free and easy in those days."

"Would there have been a policeman living in the town?" asked Zlinter.

"I shouldn't think so—not in 1902. They'd send police out from Banbury if there was any trouble."

"It is not likely, then, that there would be any record of Charlie Zlinter anywhere?"

"It's just a chance," said Dorman. "If he belonged in Banbury, if he lived there, you might find something about him at the Shire Hall. It's just possible there may be descendants in the district—people of the same name, sons or grandsons, though I never heard the name before. Apart from that, the only thing would be to find somebody who was living in the Howqua at the time. They might remember something about this Charlie Zlinter, some old person."

"Would it be easy to find such an old person?"

"I shouldn't think it would. Those gold-mining towns, they weren't settled places, if you know what I mean. People went there to take up claims and work the gold; if it didn't work out right for them, they went off to some other place—West Australia or South Africa, maybe, where there was gold to be found. They didn't stay around where there wasn't any gold. I think you'll have a job to find anybody who was living at Howqua then."

The Czech said quietly, "That is very bad luck."

He seemed so disappointed that Jennifer asked, "Is it very important?"

He smiled at her. "It is not important at all," he said. "Only, if a member of my family had been here before me, I would have liked to know."

Presently Jane went to the kitchen door and rang the hand-bell on the veranda to warn Tim and Mario that it was five o'clock and time to knock off for tea. Jack Dorman took the Czech off for a wash, he came back to the veranda presently and found Jennifer there alone.

He said, laughing, "I must try to remember the way to behave. This will be the first time that I have eaten in a private house since I left Germany, nearly two years."

She was appalled at the casual statement. "Is that really true?"

"But, yes. I do not think that I know anybody in Australia yet, although I have been here for fifteen months. Hotels and bars and cinemas—I know those. This is the first time that I have entered a person's home."

She did not know what to say. "I suppose you don't meet many people, living up there in the camp?"

He smiled. "Ordinary people keep away from camps, and sometimes for good reason. And I have spent much of my life in camps. Since 1939 I have lived always in camps, with practically no break, twelve years. I really do not know how ordinary people live." He laughed.

Over the meal they talked of small, casual matters of the countryside and afterwards, in the cool of the evening, they sat on the veranda, smoking. When in the dusk he took his leave Jack Dorman offered to run him back to Lamirra. He refused that, saying that Jim Forrest was coming out of town and would pick him up upon the road; they did not press it, thinking that perhaps he meant to stop at the hotel and have a drink. On his part, he was unwilling to extend their hospitality, and preferred the four-mile walk back to Lamirra. Jennifer strolled across the paddocks with him to the road.

She knew that the matter of Charlie Zlinter and his dog was still upon his mind, and she raised the subject for him, in case he wanted to talk about it. "It's funny about that headstone," she said. "Charlie Zlinter."

144

"I would like to find out something about Charlie Zlinter," he said. "I think he must have been related to me in some way. All of the Zlinters in Pilsen are uncles or cousins of each other."

He turned to her. "When you leave your own place and you start again in a new country, with nobody that you know, it is wonderful to find that someone of your family has been there before," he said. "Even fifty years before. It makes a tie with your own home. And however good the new country may be, unless you know somebody in it you are not a part of it."

They walked on in silence for a time. She had not met such loneliness before. "You know some real people now, anyway," she said. "You know the Dormans, and me. More substantial than Charlie Zlinter. I hope you'll come and see us again some time."

"I would like to do that," he said. "But also, I would like to find out about Charlie Zlinter and his dog."

She laughed. "I believe you've been making it all up. I don't believe there's any such person, really."

He laughed with her. "I promise you that it is true. I would say that I would take you there and show you the stone, but it is ten miles to walk and ten miles back. Some day when Mr. Dorman goes with Mr. Fisher in the Land Rover to fish in the Howqua you must come with him, and I will show you the stone."

"That's a bargain," she said. "I'd like to do that some day."

"I should be much honoured if you would," he said.

They walked across the last paddock to the road in silence. It was nearly dark.

At the gate on to the road he turned to her. "Now I must say good-bye. I am afraid that I have been awkward in company this evening, and I ask if you will forgive me."

"You've not been awkward a bit," she said. "You've been very interesting, and very charming, Mr. Zlinter. I hope you'll come again."

He laughed diffidently. "It is many years since I have been in company with people of good family, like you. You must forgive the awkward things I must have done. But I would like to come again, and some day I would like to take you to the Howqua to see the stone."

"We'll fix that somehow or other," she said. "Good-night, Carl. Don't get run over on the way back, and don't stop at the pub too long."

"Good-night, Miss Jennifer," he said formally. "Thank you again for all that you have done for me. I shall not stop at the pub tonight at all."

"I bet," she laughed. "Good-night. Come and see us again."

She walked back across the paddocks deep in thought. She found Jane sitting on the veranda with Jack Dorman; Angela was away with friends in Banbury, driving her mother's Morris. Jane said, "I rather like Carl Zlinter."

Jennifer dropped down into a chair, "It's extraordinary," she said. "He's been in the country fifteen months, and this is the first time that he's been inside a private house."

"Is that right?" asked Jack Dorman.

"That's what he said."

Jane said slowly, "Well, I can understand that in a way, although it sounds rather awful. They're a pretty rough lot up at Lamirra. Before that camp started up, Jack and I used to go down sometimes to the hotel and have a glass of beer and chat with Mrs. Hawkey, the landlady, but we haven't been for a long time. Too many drunks."

"From the lumber camp?"

"Yes—from Lamirra."

"Of course, he's different to the ordinary lumberman," Jack Dorman explained. "He's an educated man."

There was a little silence. "I don't suppose he thinks much of Australia and Australians," Jane said.

"He thinks it's a lovely country," Jennifer told her. "He doesn't want to live anywhere else. Only, he'd like to know some people. That's why he's so keen to find out something about Charlie Zlinter and his dog."

In the dim light Jane stared at her. "But Charlie Zlinter's dead!"

"I know. All the same, he's the only person in Australia that Dr. Zlinter knows, outside the lumber camp."

"My dear. I think that's rather touching."

"I thought that, too," the girl said. "I told him he must come and see us here again—I hope you don't mind. It seemed such rotten luck."

"Of course, Jenny, I liked him. Makes a change to talk to somebody who's lived outside the Shire of Banbury."

"He wants to take me over to the Howqua some time, to see his tombstone," she said. "I'd like to see it, and I'd like to see the Howqua, but I'm not going to walk ten miles there and ten miles back in this hot weather."

Jane said, "You don't have to walk ten miles to get into the Howqua, surely? You can ride over on a horse."

"I can't," said Jennifer. "I'd fall off."

Jack Dorman said, "You could probably get into the Howqua in a utility, in this dry weather. You can get in in a Land Rover any time of year. It's easy going on the track this side; the other side's a bit steep. You could leave the utility parked up in Jock McDougall's paddock on the top of the ridge, and walk down to the river. That'd only be about two miles. Zlinter can drive, I suppose?"

"I really don't know," Jennifer said. "I should think he could."

"I never met a doctor yet who couldn't drive a car," said Jane.

"He wouldn't be used to driving on our side of the road, anyway," said Jennifer.

"Aw, look," Jack Dorman said, "there's only a mile and a half of road before you turn off on the track across the paddocks up into the timber. He won't hit anything in that distance. If you want to get into the Howqua, make him drive you up to Jock McDougall's paddock and then walk. You can take the Chev."

"That's awfully good of you," the girl said. "We'll ask if he can drive, if he turns up again. I'd be afraid he might smash the Chev. up."

"It's worn out, anyway. I've been thinking we should get a Land Rover to replace it."

"That's enough of that," said Jane. "We've got too many cars already. I'm going to have my painting before we get another car."

"I thought you'd forgotten about that," he said.

"Indeed I haven't. It's just that I don't know how to get the sort of painting that I want. I'm not going to have one of those modern things we saw in Melbourne."

Jennifer went to bed that night unreasonably happy. She was deeply grateful to Jack Dorman for his casual offer of the old utility; she had wanted to do something to ease the loneliness of Carl Zlinter, but she had been powerless to do much about it by herself. She was still happy next morning till the postman came by just before dinner, and Mario went down to pick up the mail from their box on the main road. There was a letter from her father, air-mailed from England; the happiness went from her face, and was succeeded by a troubled frown. Jane saw it, and said casually, "Everything all right at home?"

"Not absolutely," the girl said. "Mummy's been in bed with bronchitis. They seem to have had terrible weather in England. Of course, it's January."

"Not serious, is it?"

"Oh, no. The thing is that when Mummy's ill it makes things hard for Daddy. They've only got a woman who comes in in the mornings." She paused, "It happened last winter, and I took ten days of my holiday and went up there and ran the house. I didn't bargain on it happening again this winter."

She said no more, but she was troubled at the thought of difficulties in the snow and rain of the Midlands, so far away. It needed a strong mental effort to picture the conditions of an English winter in the Australian summer heat, though she had left so recently.

At dinner Jack Dorman said, "I'm going in this afternoon to meet Jim Forrest at the hospital. Anyone got anything for the post?"

"I shall have," Jennifer said. "I want to write an air-mail to my mother. I'll let you have it after dinner. What time are you going?"

"Not till about three."

"I'll write it as soon as we've cleared away."

Jack Dorman drove into Banbury in the new utility, posted Jennifer's letter before he forgot it, and drove round to the hospital. Jim Forrest's car was parked in the street; he parked behind it and went in. A New Australian ward-maid told him that Mr. Forrest was with Dr. Jennings in the office; he put his head in at the door.

"Come in, Mr. Dorman," said the doctor. "I was just telling Jim here about these men."

He was a small, brown-haired man with a sandy little moustache and blue eyes; he had been an officer in the Royal Australian Army Medical Corps in the war, and he still had the appearance of an officer in civvies. Jack Dorman went in and sat down. "What's the news, Doctor?"

"I was telling Jim," the doctor repeated. "I've just finished the post-mortem. The man was an alcoholic all right. You never saw such a liver. I'm preserving part of it in spirit until after the inquest, just in case anybody wants to see it. He was full of whisky too."

Jim Forrest said with feeling, "He must have been."

"He certainly was. Matter of fact, I should have thought there was more than a bottle in him, but I suppose I'm wrong. There was certainly a lot." He paused. "I had a look at the amputations, while I was at it. It was carefully done. One of the ligatures was damaged a little, probably while he was struggling. But the job was done all right."

Jim Forrest said, "He'd have been right, but for the whisky?"

"I wouldn't say that. Sepsis might easily have set in. As I understand it, the amputation was done out in the open, to free him from the bulldozer. All I can say is that the job was well done from a surgical point of view."

Jack Dorman said, "It wasn't a botched job?"

"No. It wasn't a botched job. The damaged ligature was clearly the result of a blow. He probably kicked it against something in the struggle, while you were trying to keep him in bed."

Jim Forrest nodded. "He was thrashing about all over the place."

There was a pause. "As regards the other one," the doctor said, "the fractured skull, it's much the same story. I took an X-ray this morning. If I had been doing the job here I'd have taken an X-ray before operating, of course. If I had done so, I should probably have removed one more small piece of bone that Zlinter has left in. Working without the X-ray, as he did, I should very likely have left it, as he did. Considering the X-ray this morning, I decided to leave well alone. I don't really think that it'll make much difference, and one doesn't want to submit the patient to a further operational shock."

He paused. "There again, infection is the danger. Zlinter showed me what he did, and I don't think anybody could have done much more. But there's no denying that the conditions were bad for any cranial surgery."

Jack Dorman said, "Taking it by and large, though, he didn't do a bad job?"

"I think that's a fair statement. Taking it by and large, he didn't do at all a bad job, considering the difficulties."

"You'll tell them that at the inquest, Doctor, will you?" asked Jim Forrest.

"That's right. That's what I shall say at the inquest."

Jack Dorman said, "If he can do a job like that, why can't he be a doctor properly? Get a licence, or whatever you call it?"

"There's a ruling about these immigrant doctors. In this State they've got to do the last three years of their training over again. It varies according to the State, I think. I know it's easier in West Australia."

"Pack of bloody nonsense," said the grazier. "We could do with another doctor here, and now we've got one and we're not allowed to use him."

"You've got to have a rule," Jennings said. "Most of these D.P. doctors are crook doctors, oh my word. You'd be the first to raise a scream if some of them got loose upon your family."

"That's right, is it?" asked Jim Forrest. "They're very bad?"

"I don't really know," the doctor said. "You'd have to ask somebody who knows about these things. I believe the truth of it is this: when they're first qualified their standard is much lower than ours. What they pick up from experience in practice may bring them up to our standard, but who's to say? Take this Zlinter, for example. He seems to be a careful sort of chap, and since he qualified he's had a very wide experience of surgery in front-line conditions with the German Army. You've seen him at his best. He certainly knows a lot about these sort of accidents. But's that not general practice. Ninety per cent. of the general practitioner's job is trying to decide if an old lady's pain is heart trouble or wind, or whether a kiddy's got scarlet fever or a sore throat. Zlinter may be useless at that sort of thing—probably is."

He paused. "I don't want you to think I'm against Zlinter," he said. "I think he's a good man. If he was qualified I'd like to see him practise in this district and take some of the work off me. But not until he's been checked over at the hospital and been passed out as competent."

"And that takes three years?"

"I don't know if that would apply to Zlinter. I don't know if they make any exceptions. Probably not. I think he probably *would* have to do three years again."

"It seems the hell of a long time," the grazier said.

The doctor got up from the desk; he had still a lot of work ahead of him. "It's better to be safe than sorry."

The grazier went out into the street with the timber manager. "What about a beer?" They got into their cars and drove down to the main street, and parked under the shade of the trees in front of the Queen's Head Hotel.

It had been market day in Banbury, but the market was over before dinner, and now in the late afternoon only the dregs of the crowd remained in town. The bars, which had been hot and crowded most of the day, were thinning out; the tired barmen were relaxing, watching the clock for closing time at six. Jack Dorman and Jim Forrest went into the saloon bar and ordered beers, and stood discussing what they had learned from the doctor about Zlinter.

It was still warm and the beer was very cold; they had a glass of beer, and then another, and another in the space of twenty minutes. As they stood their talk was mostly about Zlinter, how he would be situated at the end of his two years of lumber work, whether he would have a chance to qualify as a doctor, how much it would cost, whether he could raise the money on a loan from any bank, whether if he had the money he could get admission to a hospital.

The bar that they were standing in was merely a partitioned part of the long bar-room, but it was select and mostly frequented by graziers and those with money to spare. Drinks at this portion of the bar cost a trifle more, and there were little plates of onions, cheese, and other snacks, all highly spiced to induce a pleasant thirst. A yard away from Jack Dorman and Jim Forrest as they discussed Carl Zlinter was an old man sitting hunched upon a stool, a red-haired old man, now turning grey but still fiery on top; a broad-shouldered old man who must have been a very strong man in his time. He had a comical twist to his mouth and a general appearance of good humour, and he was drinking whisky, evidently determined to sit it out until the bar closed. From his appearance he had been there all the afternoon.

Presently the barman said, "Last drinks," and the clock stood at two minutes to six. Jim Forrest hurriedly ordered four more beers and the barman pushed the dripping glasses across the counter; the old man by their side sat sunk in reflection or in slumber, a half glass of whisky before him. They drank two beers apiece, and then, at ten past six, the barman said, "We're closing now," and it was time to go. He said to the old man, "Come on, Pop. Closing now."

The old man did not stir, but mumbled something incoherent.

Jack Dorman smiled, and put his hand on the old man's shoulder. "Come on, Pat," he said. "Time to go home now. Finish up your drink. Got your jinker here?"

The old man raised his head, and very slowly lifted his glass and drank it off, with the utmost deliberation. Jim Forrest smiled, "Who is he?"

"Pat Halloran. He's got a place five miles out on the Benalla road." Jack knew the old man fairly well. He had come out from Southern Ireland as a stable-boy at the end of the last century, and he had been about the district ever since but for one trip home to Limerick between the wars. He was a widower and his two sons ran the property and did most of the work; he enjoyed coming into market and meeting his cronies and getting drunk, a simple pleasure that he could afford on his five-figure income. His sons drove large and powerful utilities rather too fast, but the old man had never learned to drive a car and came to town each market day in a jinker, a two-wheeled trap drawn by an old horse.

Jack Dorman smiled again, waited till the old man had drained his glass, and said, "Come on, Pat. It's closing time; we're getting thrown out of here. Where did you leave your jinker?"

"It's in the yard out at the back," the barman said. "Take him out through this way, if you like."

"Take the other arm, Jim," said Jack Dorman. "We'll put him in the jinker, and he'll be right."

The old man got down from the stool, and they steadied him, one on each side. "That's right," he said with a marked Irish accent. "Sure, put me up in the jinker, and I'll be right." He paused for reflection, and they began walking him to the back premises and the yard. "I know you," he said. "You're Jack Dorman, up to Leonora."

"That's right."

The old man turned and stared at the timber manager with bleary eyes. "I don't know you."

"Jim Forrest's the name. From Lamirra."

"Oh. D'you know my name? It's Pat Halloran, from Limerick."

"That's right," said Jack Dorman. "I know you and you know me. Watch these steps, now—three steps down. That's fine."

"I'm right," the old man said. "Only I'm drunk. I know you. You're Jack Dorman, up to Leonora." He swayed wildly, and they steered him into the passage, the barman holding the door open for them. "It's a shameful thing I'm telling you," he said seriously, "but I'm drunk, drunk as Charlie Zlinter."

The grazier started. "What's that, Pat? Who am I as drunk as?"

"Drunk as Charlie Zlinter," the old man repeated. "I know you. You're Jack Dorman, up to Leonora. You know me, Pat Halloran, from Limerick. You know me, I know you, and you know Charlie Zlinter. Good old Charlie!"

"I don't know Charlie Zlinter, Pat," the other said. "Who was Charlie Zlinter?" It was quite possible that this old man could have been in the district when Howqua was a thriving township.

Pat Halloran turned bellicose. He checked in the passage; he was still a powerful man, and brought them to a standstill. "What was that you would be saying? Who was Charlie Zlinter? Haven't I heard with my own ears you two talking all the while of Charlie Zlinter? Is it a fool that ye'd be making of me, just because I'm having drink taken? Will ye fight me, now?"

"Nobody's making a fool of you, Pat, and I won't fight you," said the grazier. "Come on—let's find the jinker. Tell us about Charlie Zlinter when you knew him, and I'll tell you what I know about him, and there'll be a pair of us. What did Charlie Zlinter do?"

"He got bloody drunk," the old man said. "I got bloody drunk. You got bloody drunk. Sure, we're all bloody drunk."

They came into the stable yard and there was the jinker, the horse patiently waiting to take his master home. Jim Forrest untied the reins from the tethering ring, tried the girth, and looked the harness over while Jack Dorman steadied the old man. "She's right," he said.

The grazier said, "The jinker's right, Pat. Can you get up in it?"

The old man grabbed the splashboard and the seat-rail, put one foot upon the step, and swung himself up into the seat, the habit of fifty years undefeated by alcohol. He took the reins, and lifted the whip from the socket. "I'll be right, boys," he said. "Sure, an' I'll be wishing you a very good evening." Now that he was in his vehicle he seemed to be at home, indeed, he looked almost sober.

The grazier stood for a moment at the wheel, looking up at the old man. "What else did Charlie Zlinter do, Pat, besides getting drunk?"

The old man stared down at him. "Charlie Zlinter . . ." And then he stood up in the jinker and recited, with dramatic flourishes of the whip that made the grazier retreat hurriedly,

"Charlie Zlinter and his heeler hound
    Fell into the Howqua and got bloody well drowned.
  Be warned, fellow sinners, and never forget
    If he hadn't been drunk he'd have been living yet."

He touched the horse skilfully with the whip and drove out of the yard; the grazier was left facing Jim Forrest, who was laughing. "What the hell was all that about, Jack?"

The grazier scratched his head. "Charlie Zlinter," he replied. "But I reckon it's a different Charlie Zlinter to the one we know.'

Eight

CARL ZLINTER arrived in Banbury at about nine o'clock on Saturday morning, riding in the back of a utility that had picked him up upon the road. In that sparsely-populated district where trucks and utilities were the normal transport it was not difficult to get a ride into town in something or other; he had never had to walk more than half an hour in the direction of the town without getting picked up. He had not breakfasted, and he went and had it in a café, bacon and two eggs and coffee. They gave him a Melbourne paper two days old to read, and he sat smoking a cigarette after it, enjoying the leisure.

When he paid his bill, he said to the girl who had served him, "Do you know a family called Shulkin? They are New Australian. The man works on the railway."

She looked at him blankly; she came of a family of Australians that had been casual labourers for generation after generation, bad stock and mentally subnormal. She and her family were bitterly hostile to all immigrants, especially the European ones who worked too hard and were guilty of the social crime of saving money, thereby threatening the Australian Way of Life. "Never heard of them," she said scornfully.

He looked at her with clinical interest as he paid his bill, wondering if she were tubercular; in spite of his decision to abandon medicine he could not rid himself of interest in symptoms. A Wasserman test would be interesting, and probably positive. He smiled at her, and went out and walked down the long, wide tree-lined avenue of the main street towards the railway station.

The booking office was closed because upon this single-track line there were only two trains a day, but the stationmaster lived beside the station in a weatherboard house, and he asked there for Mr. Shulkin. The stationmaster said, "Aw, look, Stan Shulkin, he's not working today. There's a green-painted shack, the third house down this road, with an old railway coach they use for sleeping in alongside. You'll find Stan there, unless he's in the town."

He found the shack and railway coach, a poor sort of habitation. There was a man digging in the garden, a man of about forty-five or fifty, with black hair going bald on top. Behind the railway coach he saw a fresh-faced woman with a dumpy, peasant figure hanging out some washing, and there were a couple of children playing in the background. He opened the gate and went in, and spoke to the man. "Are you Stan Shulkin?"

The man straightened up, and said with an equally marked accent, "I am Stanislaus Shulkin."

The Czech said in German, "My name is Carl Zlinter, and I work in the timber camp at Lamirra. Do you prefer to speak English?"

"Always," the man said. "Always I speak English. It is better for the children. The wife, she speaks it very bad. She does not try."

Carl Zlinter said, "You must excuse, but I have heard that you can paint very good pictures."

The man smiled shyly across his broad face. "I paint pictures only now one or two each year," he said. "There is not time and people here do not want pictures. When I came first to this place three years ago, I said, Now I will paint pictures and we shall make much money. But it did not happen in that way. Now I paint only a little."

"You work upon the railway?"

"In the platelaying gang. It is very hard work, and not good for the hands, for painting. I do not think that I shall paint many more pictures."

"You are Esthonian?"

"Lithuanian," the man said. "I am from Kaunas."

"I am from Pilsen," Zlinter said. "In my country I was a doctor, but now I am a labourer." The man nodded in comprehension. "I have friends who want a picture. They are not artistic, but they have much land and plenty of money. They are more educated than some, and they have bought all the motor-cars that they can use, and now they want an oil painting."

"So?" said the Lithuanian. "I would have thought it would have been a radio or a washing machine."

"They will have those also," said Zlinter, "but the woman wants an oil painting. She has seen exhibitions of ugly pictures in Melbourne, and those she does not want. She is simple, and she wants a beautiful picture that will give pleasure to those who do not understand about pictures. There is a man called Spiegel in the camp who told me you can paint such pictures."

"I can paint such pictures," Shulkin said. "I can paint any sort of picture."

"May I see?"

Shulkin led the way into the railway coach. It had been an open coach without compartments at one time; now it had been roughly converted into three rooms with match-boarding partitions. Much of the seating still remained unchanged, and each of the three rooms still had two doors upon each side. The end room that they went into was furnished with a bed, an easel, and a great litter of old canvases and frames stacked along one side. "I buy old canvases and frames at the sale," the artist said. "It is cheaper so."

He pulled out a canvas from the heap, a beautifully executed still life of two herrings on a plate, a loaf of bread, a pat of butter, and a glass of beer, laid out in strong light on a soiled table-cloth with a dark background. "This I did in the camp. I call it, Lithuanian Fisherman's Breakfast."

He plucked another canvas from the heap and set it on the easel in place of the still life. "This—a portrait of my mother." The stern old face glowered at them from the canvas, a powerful picture finely executed. He whisked it away, and planted another canvas on the easel. "This, the Delatite River."

It was a bright river scene with a fine blue sky and white clouds, and a riot of golden wattles on the bank, making a delicate harmony of colour. "So . . ." said Carl Zlinter. "This you should show her. The others, they are beautiful in a different way, but this, or something like this, is what she wants."

"I can paint anything she wants," the artist remarked, "but usually they cannot say."

The Czech stood back, and looked critically at the river scene. "I do not know pictures," he said at last. "But I would think that this is very good." He paused. "You must have had a great deal of experience."

"I studied in Paris and in Rome," the platelayer replied. "I was Professor of Artistic Studies in the University of Kaunas."

There did not seem to be anything to say to that. Zlinter stayed a little while and had a cup of tea. "I will tell Mrs. Dorman about you," he said. "If she wants a beautiful picture, she does not need to go to Melbourne for it. She can find it here, in Banbury. I will tell her this evening."

He went off presently, and caught a bus out on the Benalla road. Twenty minutes later he was walking up to the Halloran homestead. A small girl came to the kitchen door and he asked for Mr. Pat Halloran. She turned and called into the house, "Ma, there's a fella asking for grandpa."

"In the wood shed."

"He's in the wood shed," she said. "Round there."

In the wood shed Zlinter found a red-haired old man splitting sawn logs with a sledge-hammer and wedges, doing the work with the skill of a lifetime rather than with any great muscular effort. "Please," he said. "May I speak to you?"

The old man rested on his sledge. "An' who might you be?"

"My name is Zlinter, Charlie Zlinter," the Czech said. "I work in the timber camp, up at Lamirra."

"Sure, an' you *can't* be Charlie Zlinter. Charlie Zlinter's dead these fifty years."

"I am another one with the same name. I am trying to find out about the one who died."

"An' what made you come here, may I ask?"

"Mr. Jack Dorman, he said you were talking about Charlie Zlinter in the Queen's Head, on Thursday."

"Who's this Jack Dorman? Jack Dorman at Leonora? Sure, an' I haven't set eyes on the man these last six months."

"Perhaps you do not remember," the Czech said diplomatically. "He helped you up into the jinker on Thursday."

"Would that be so! Well, Glory be to God, I didn't know a thing about it! Would you believe that, now?"

He evaded the rhetorical question. "Jack Dorman said that you were speaking of this Charlie Zlinter. I have seen the grave."

"Ye have not. Charlie Zlinter was buried in the Howqua, and the fire went through. There's nothing left there now."

"The headstones are left," the other said. "They are stone, and so they did not burn. The headstones are there now, all of them, in the forest by the river, where there was the cemetery."

"Do ye tell me that!"

He had gained the old man's interest, and he held it while he explained the position to him. "This Charlie Zlinter, he was from Pilsen in Bohemia," he said at last. "That is on the stone. I am another Charlie Zlinter, also from Pilsen in Bohemia. I am trying to find out what I can about him."

The old man leaned on his sledge. "He was a bullocky," he said at last. "I wouldn't be able to say at this distance of time if he worked for himself or if he worked for Murphy. He drove a wagon with a team of bullocks, six bullocks, or eight would it have been? Holy Saints above, I'm losing all my memory. I couldn't say at all if it was six or eight. I was just a bit of a boy myself. I came out to this country in 1895 while the old Queen was on the throne, God rest her soul. I worked two years in the stables for Jim Pratt that had the Queen's Head in those days, and then I joined the police. There was work for a policeman in this country then."

"Do you remember Charlie Zlinter?" the Czech asked.

"Sure, I do that. He was a German and he drove a bullock team in and out of the Howqua, from the railway here to Howqua and back again. There wasn't a fine broad highway then, with the motor-cars all racing along at sixty miles an hour. There wasn't hair nor hide of a made road at all, at all. Bullocks were the only teams to get a wagon up over the spur and down into the Howqua, passengers and machinery and food and drink and everything, all went by bullock team. Will ye believe what I tell you, the bullock drivers were the boys that made the money! The miners, they never did much in the Howqua, and in the end the company went broke. What gold there was went into the pockets of the bullock drivers. Not a breath of it did the shareholders ever see."

"What was Charlie Zlinter like?"

"Ah, he was a fine, big fellow with dark curly hair, and he spoke English in the way you speak it. He was one for the booze, and he was one for the girls, Holy Saints above! He had a cabin in the town at Howqua, for he went there as a miner first of all, and then he had the wit to see he'd make more money with a wagon and a team. By the Mother of God, I'd think shame to repeat all that went on in that cabin. He was a big, lusty man, and drink and women were his downfall. That's the truth I'm telling you."

He paused. "Drink and women, drink and women," he said. "It's a sad, sad thing." He shot a humorous glance at Zlinter. "He used to drive in here the one day and back the next, twenty-two miles each day; he'd come in here the one evening and then he'd be away up to the Howqua the next day. Ten hours or so it might take him, and he had two teams, one resting and one working. He used to come to the Queen's Head Hotel, and hobble the bullocks on the green outside and feed them hay, and then he'd come into the hotel and get drunk, and he'd sleep in the wagon and away off out of it next morning, back to the Howqua. And as like as not there'd be a young girl going to the Howqua for a barmaid in Peter Slim's hotel, a girl no better than she should be, or she wouldn't be going to the Howqua . . ." He thought for a minute. "They were fine, noble days, those times, when we were all young."

"What did he die of?"

"Drink and drowning," the old man said, "drink and drowning, and his dog with him, only the dog wasn't drunk, though it might have been at that, the company it kept. It was August, and the river was running full with the melting snows. There was a girl living in the Howqua by the name of Mary Nolan, oh, a wicked girl, I'd think shame to tell you all that that girl did, and she so soft and well spoken, and pretty, too. She lodged on the other side of the river from the Buller Arms Hotel that Peter Slim kept, Billy's father, him that's the forest ranger in the Howqua now. And Charlie Zlinter, he stayed in the hotel till close on midnight, and then he made to go across the river to see this girl. Well, most parts of the year ye'd cross the Howqua and never wet your feet by stepping on the stones, but in August and September, with the melting of the snows on the high mountains, it runs five or six feet deep. There was a cable bridge, a bridge of two wire ropes with planks across the way you'd walk on them, and a third one to hold on to, and Charlie Zlinter, drunk the way he was, must go across this bridge to see this girl. Ye'd think, now, for a man as drunk as Charlie to go on a bridge like that at midnight would have been enough, but he must take the dog with him. He had this heeler dog he kept for rounding up the bullocks and to guard the wagon when he was in Banbury, and he must take it with him over the river. And when he came up to the bridge the dog wouldn't go upon it, and so Charlie picked it up in his arms and started off across the bridge in the dark night, with the dog in his arms and the bridge swaying and going up and down with every step he took, and he as drunk as a lord. And that was the end of it."

"He fell off the bridge into the water?"

"He did that. They found him half a mile down-stream come the morning, him and the dog together. There was never a priest there to say a mass for him, and they buried him and the dog in the

157

one grave, which the priest would never have allowed." He paused. "Aye, it was a sad thing; he was a fine, noble boy. It made a great wonder in the countryside, for he was well known on account of coming in and out of Banbury and people riding with him. And they put a poem in the paper about him, ah, a lovely, lovely poem. Did ye never hear it?"

The Czech shook his head.

The old man declaimed,

"Charlie Zlinter and his heeler hound
Fell into the Howqua and unhappily drowned.
Be warned, fellow sinners, and never forget
If he hadn't been drunk he'd have been living yet."

"Ah," he said, "it was a lovely, lovely poem."

"This Charlie Zlinter was almost certainly some relation of my own," said the Czech, "because he came from my own town. Did you ever hear anything about him—who his relations were, or who he wrote to? Did he leave any papers to say that?"

"Sure, an' I wouldn't know a think like that at all," the old man said. "I was a policeman in those days, and on other duties; I only knew about him from the gossip of the time. I wouldn't know what happened to his gear. It was soon after that the mine closed down and Howqua came to an end; within the year there were only a few people living in the place. I wouldn't say that anyone took on the bullock team after he passed away. I wouldn't know. The Howqua was going down, and there wasn't the work there had been in the beginning."

Carl Zlinter asked, "You do not know what happened to his papers?"

"Ah, I wouldn't know at all. There's only one person left might know about a thing like that."

"Who is that?"

"Sure, Mary Nolan herself."

"Mary Nolan! Is she still alive?"

"Ah, she's alive. She was a wicked girl, and Father Geoghegan, he was the priest here then, he would have nothing to do with her until she came to the confession, and that she would not do, and Holy Mother of God, it's not to be wondered at. And so when the mine closed down and everybody left the Howqua what must she do but go for a barmaid at Woods Point in the hotel there, and very strict she came to be, so that there was no loose talk or dirty jokes in Mary Nolan's bar. I did hear that she made her peace with Father O'Brian from Warburton who went to Woods Point in those days, and like enough he didn't know the whole of it. And then she married a man called Williams who lived on an allotment out by Jamieson, and they lived there until he died at the beginning of the second war. And then she sold the place, and went to live at Woods Point with her brother-in-law's family; I'd say she'd be living there yet. I haven't heard she died."

"She must be old now," said the Czech.

"Seventy-five, maybe," the old man said indignantly. "She'd not be a day older than seventy-five. That's not so old at all. Sure, there's many a man fit and hearty at the age of seventy-five."

"Do you think that Mary Nolan might have kept Charlie Zlinter's papers, or know what happened to them when he was drowned?"

"Ah, I wouldn't be saying that at all. She's the only person living in the district now that might know something, though it's a long while ago. I'll say this now, she knew Charlie Zlinter better than anyone else, and better than she had any right to as a single woman."

Carl Zlinter left him presently, and walked back into the town and got there in time for dinner. He went to a different café for his meal where they were kinder to the New Australian and got a lift out halfway to Merrijig in a truck driven by George Pearson on his way to Buttercup. He walked for two miles then, for it was Saturday afternoon and there were few people on the road, and finally got picked up by the storekeeper from Lamirra driving out of town in his utility. He got down at the gate of Leonora and walked across the paddocks to the homestead.

He was just in time for tea, and they made him welcome. He said to Jack Dorman, "It is quite correct, what you have told me about Mr. Pat Halloran and Charlie Zlinter. I have learned a great deal of my relative this morning."

"What did you find out?" asked Jennifer.

He cocked an eye at her. "I found out that he was a very bad man. I do not think that I can say all that he did with ladies in the room."

Jane and Jennifer laughed. "You can keep the juicy bits to tell Jack afterwards," Jane said. "Tell us the rest."

Jennifer asked, "What did he do for a living?"

"He was a bullock team driver," said the Czech. "He drove a wagon and a team from the railway at Banbury to the town at the Howqua River."

"Is that what he did!" Jack Dorman exclaimed. The pieces of the puzzle were beginning to fall together now; a bullocky driver would have been well known in Banbury and his death would be remembered longer than if he were a transient miner. The verse that Pat Halloran had declaimed would not have been composed except for a man of some local reputation, good or bad. "Did you find out anything else about him?"

Zlinter told them the story as they sat at tea. "Mrs. Williams," Jane said thoughtfully. "Old Mrs. Joshua Williams, would that be? Used to live at Sharon, out past Jamieson?"

"I do not know," he said. "I did not hear the name of the station. Only that she married a man called Williams."

"I think that must be the one." She turned to Jack. "You

remember old Mrs. Williams, the one who used to breed geese when we came here first. You remember—we got six goslings from her, and they all died but one, the first year we were here. Didn't her husband die, and she went to Woods Point?"

"I remember those bloody goslings," Jack Dorman said emphatically. "They were no good when we bought them, and she knew it. I'd have made a row and got my money back, but we were new here then and I didn't want to start off with a row."

"She went to live at Woods Point, didn't she?"

"I don't remember. Easily find out."

"I'm sure she was the one."

They finished tea and washed the dishes, and went out on the veranda and sat down. Jack Dorman gave his guest a cigarette. "Inquest's on Monday morning," he said. "You'll be there, I suppose?"

Carl Zlinter smiled, a little wryly. "I shall be going with Mr. Forrest," he said. "I think he will come back without me, because I shall be in prison."

"That's not going to happen. The doctor's on your side, and it's what he says that counts."

He shrugged his shoulders. "I would not care a great deal if I went to prison," he said, "so long as it should stop at that. But in my state, if I should do a crime in this two years, I think they can send me back to Germany, into a camp. That would be very bad."

Jennifer said, "They'd never do that, Carl. It's not going to be like that at all."

He shrugged his shoulders gloomily. "It could happen."

She laughed. "They'd have to send me too, because I helped."

He turned to her. "Will you be at the inquest?"

"I'll be there. The police rang up this morning and said they wanted me."

"It would be different for you, if this went badly," he said. "The worst that they could do for you would be to send you back to England, and that is your home. This place is now the home for me, and this is where I want to stay."

"Nothing like that's going to happen," Jack Dorman said shortly. "They've got more sense."

"I hope that that is true . . ."

It seemed to Jennifer that he was taking this very badly, but in his position that might be inevitable. She did not like to think of him brooding all the week-end over possible deportation back into the displaced persons' camps of Europe. "You promised that you'd take me to see Charlie Zlinter's grave some time," she said. "I want to see the Howqua. What about tomorrow?"

He glanced at her, smiling; it seemed too good to be true. "I would like to take you there, ver' much," he said. "But I think it is too far for you to walk."

"Jack said he'd lend us the utility—the Chev. Could we go tomorrow, Mr. Dorman?"

"Sure," he said. "Sunday's the best day to take the Chev." He turned to Zlinter. "Say, can you drive a car?"

The Czech smiled. "I can drive. Before the war I had a little car, an Opel, in my own country, and in the war I drove many cars and trucks. I have not driven in Australia, and I have not got a licence."

"Ah, look—it don't matter about the licence, not up here. You can take the Chev tomorrow, if you want it."

The dark man beamed, "It is very, very kind. I will be ver' careful of it, Mr. Dorman."

"You won't be able to be careful of it, not up on that Howqua track. But it'll take you there all right, up on to the top, that is, by Jock McDougall's paddock, I wouldn't take it down the other side, not down into the Howqua valley—I was telling Jenny. But that cuts it down to a two-mile walk instead of ten."

He said again, "It is very, very kind . . ."

Presently he said, "There is one other thing, Mrs. Dorman. This morning, I visited a New Australian who can paint pictures, a man called Stan Shulkin. Do you know about him?"

"No?"

"I know about him," said her husband. "Chap who works on the railway."

"That is the man. Have you seen his pictures?"

Jack Dorman shook his head. "I remember someone saying in the pub one day there was a New Australian who can paint."

Carl Zlinter turned to Jane. "I think it might be interesting to you to go down to his small house and see what he can paint," he said. "I went there this morning. I think perhaps that he could make the sort of picture that you want."

She laid her sewing down. "I want a really good picture, Carl, done by a proper artist. I don't want anything done by an amateur. I want a good picture."

"I do not know very much about pictures," he replied. "I saw some very fine oil paintings this morning that this man had done. I think that he could make a picture that you would enjoy."

She wrinkled her forehead. "Has he ever studied anywhere? I mean, it might be difficult if I went there and his pictures were too bad for what I want. You do see what I mean?"

"I understand," he said. "He has studied in Paris and in Rome; before the war he was Professor of Art Studies in the University of Kaunas. I think he is a very good artist."

"But what's he doing here?"

"He works as a labourer upon the railway."

She stared at him. "Is that the only thing that he can find to do?"

He shrugged his shoulders. "I do not know. He came to Australia three years ago, as a displaced person, and he was sent for his two years to work upon the railway, here in Banbury. He has

161

stayed here since, and what else can he do? Here he has a house and easy work and a quiet life after the camps in Germany. He has tried to sell paintings a little, but not many people buy an oil painting in Banbury. I think he could paint a picture that is what you like."

"Are his pictures pretty? Are the colours nice?"

"I saw a very beautiful picture of the Delatite River in the spring, all blue and golden, with the wattles. It looked like the river, and the colours were ver' beautiful."

"That sounds the sort of thing," she said. "I'd better go and see him." She laughed. "It would be funny if I found the sort of picture that I want in Banbury, after searching all over Melbourne for it."

Jennifer walked down to the road with Carl Zlinter when he went away. Jane watched them disappear across the paddocks. "Are you going with them tomorrow?" she asked.

He grinned. "Give 'em a break."

"I don't know that it's a good thing," she said. "I don't know that her father and mother would be very pleased."

"They shouldn't have let her come twelve thousand miles away from home by herself, then," he said. "Far as I remember, your father and mother weren't too pleased, either."

"I rather like him," she said, "once you get used to the foreign way."

"He's right," he said.

As they were walking across the paddocks, Jennifer was saying, "I don't think there's anything to be afraid of in this inquest, Carl. Honestly, I don't."

"I do not think there is a need to be afraid," he said, "but I shall be happy when it is over."

"They can't possibly make any trouble."

He looked around him. The moon was coming up, and the bowl of the Delatite Valley was touched with a silvery light; it was very quiet. "There is only one trouble that I would be afraid of," he said quietly. "That is to be sent away from this country and back to Europe."

"Are you so fond of it as that, Carl?"

He was silent for a minute. "Here is a beautiful, empty country," he said, "with freedom, and opportunity, and more than that, a King to whom every man may appeal if there is injustice. It is a great thing to have a King, a Leader, to prevent the politicians and the bureaucrats from growing stupid. The Germans had the same idea in seeking for a Führer, only they had the wrong man. The English have managed so much better. The Americans also have discovered great men for their Presidents, in some way that is difficult to understand." He paused. "I should be very unhappy if it happened that I had to leave this country," he said.

"I think I should, too," said Jennifer. "I'm English of course, but this is very lovely. In many ways it's like what England must have been a hundred years ago."

162

"From what part of England do you come?" he asked.

"From Leicester," she said. "That's where my home is. I worked just outside London for a time, before I came out here."

"Leicester," he said. "I have heard the name, but I do not know where it is."

"It's in the Midlands," she told him. "Right in the middle of England, a hundred miles or so from London."

"What is it like there?" he asked. "Is it beautiful?"

She shook her head. "It's a manufacturing town," she told him. "One always likes the town that one was born in, I suppose, and I like Leicester well enough. But—no, I couldn't say it's beautiful. I think it's rather ugly."

"And when you worked in London, what was that like? I have never been to London."

"I worked outside, in one of the suburbs," she said. "I was in an office there. It wasn't very different from Leicester, really."

"Why did you come to Australia?" he asked. "Have you come here to live?"

"I'm not sure about that, Carl," she said. "I had a grandmother, who died and left me a little money. She didn't want me to save it; she wanted me to spend it in coming out here on a visit. I think she thought that if I came out here I'd want to stay, and that I'd have a happier life than if I lived in England. England's very different now from what it was when Granny was a girl, and she'd seen things decaying all her life. I think she had an idea that if I came out here I might be getting back into the England that she knew seventy years ago, when everything was prosperous and secure."

"So . . ." he said. "And how do you find it?"

"I've been here such a little time, it's hard to say. I really haven't seen anything—only a couple of days in Melbourne and this little bit of country here."

"From what you have seen, what do you say?"

"It's a lovely country," the girl said. "Prosperous—yes, it's very prosperous. Secure—I suppose it is. Nobody seems to be afraid an atom bomb is going to land next door tomorrow, like we are in England."

"No," he said. "All that seems very far away from here. Here we are very far from enemies, and a great distance between you and your enemy is still the best defence." He turned to her. "I cannot tell you how I love this country, for that reason perhaps best of all. Since I was a young man there has been this threat of war, or war itself, and death, and marching, and defeat, and camps of homeless people, and the threat of war again, and of more marching, of more death, of more parting from one's home—unending. Here in this place all that is put behind; here is a country where a man can build a home without the feeling that all will be useless and destroyed next year. Here is a country where a man can live a sane and proper life, even if it is only one little log hut in the middle of the

163

woods for a home. I love this country for those things, because here one can gather a few toys around oneself, a fishing rod or two, some books, a little hut, a place to call one's own—and all is safe. If then a war must come in Europe, it may be my duty to go to fight again upon the side that Australia will be on, and that I do not mind, because after the war is over, if I live, I can come back to my little place here in Australia, my hut, my fishing rods, and my books, and all will be quite safe, and I can be at peace again."

He turned to her. "I am so sorry. I have spoken too much."

"I'm glad you did," she said. "I wondered what made you so fond of this country. Now I think I understand a bit."

"I think it is how all we homeless people feel," he said. "People who have lost their own country want more than anything to find a place where they can build a new home round themselves without the fear that they will ever lose it again."

"What'll you do when your time at the camp is up?" she asked. "Where will you make your home?"

"I do not know that," he said. "I think that it will be not very far from here." They came to the road gate. "I have a strange idea in my head," he said, "but I will not tell you now."

"Oh, Carl! What is it?"

He laughed. "Perhaps I will tell you tomorrow. Are you sure that it will be all right if we go to the Howqua?"

"I'd love to, if you're free. I'm not doing anything."

"I will come here for you at about ten o'clock."

"I'll be ready, and I'll have the lunch packed."

He made a stiff little bow. "Till then. Good-night, Miss Jennifer."

"If we're going out tomorrow, Carl, cut out the Miss Jennifer. Everybody calls me Jenny here."

"All right. Good-night, Jenny."

"Good-night, Carl."

On Sunday mornings the Dorman family slept late, but Jennifer was up by seven in the kitchen, with which she was now tolerably familiar. She was a fair cook in an unpractised way, capable of interpreting and following a recipe with a reasonable chance of an acceptable result. She made some pastry and cooked half a dozen sausages and made sausage rolls in the oven, and having the oven hot she made a few jam tarts. Surveying the results of her efforts, she came to the conclusion that it looked a bit light for a lumberman; in the larder she found cold mutton and some cold potatoes, and an onion, and so set to work again and made a couple of enormous Cornish pasties. There were plenty of bananas and grapes and passion fruit in the house so she took some of those, and then, because the basket still looked empty, she cut a pile of honey sandwiches.

Jack Dorman came out in his dressing-gown and found her pondering. "My word," he said. "He's not going home hungry."

She said anxiously, "Do you think it's enough?"

"He won't starve if he gets outside that lot. What are you taking to drink?"

She smiled. "I was wondering if you could let us have some beer." Beer was in short supply in that hot weather; the expanding population had beaten the expanding beer output, as it had beaten the output of everything else in Australia.

"I'll let you have two bottles," he grumbled. "I'm not going to give him any more."

"That's awfully sweet of you." He fetched the bottles and put them on the table.

"How's he getting down here from the camp?" he asked.

"He'll get a lift down, probably," she said. "He said he'd be here at ten o'clock."

"He may not find it easy on a Sunday morning," he said. "He'll have to start off walking about nine or so. I'll take a run up the road in the Chev after breakfast and pick him up, if you'll get breakfast for me before then. Jane's sleeping in."

She glanced at the clock; it was about half-past eight. "I'll have it on the table in a quarter of an hour."

Breakfast was a running meal that day; she fed Jack Dorman and then Tim Archer and Mario, and finally Jane came out and sat down with a cup of tea. It was still on the table when Jack Dorman came back with Carl Zlinter, who he had picked up on the road half a mile outside the camp.

"Morning, Carl," said Jennifer. "Have you had any breakfast?"

He said, "Thank you, I have had some coffee."

"Coffee? Is that all you've had?"

He smiled. "In my country we do not eat a cooked breakfast."

"But you eat a proper breakfast here, don't you, before going out in the woods?"

Jane said, laughing, "Go on, Carl, sit down and let her cook you bacon and eggs. She wants to do it."

He laughed with her. "All right."

"That's better," said Jennifer, breaking a couple of eggs into the pan. "I wouldn't like you to faint by the way, especially if you're driving me in the Chev."

"He's been driving it this morning, down from the camp," said Jack Dorman. "You have to keep on telling him which side to drive on."

Carl Zlinter laughed. "It is the first time I have driven on the left side of the road, and with the steering so."

In spite of that, he proved himself to be quite a reasonable driver when they started off in the utility half an hour later. It was still sunny and cloudless, with the promise of another hot day. Jennifer opened the last paddock gate on to the main road at Merrijig, let the Chev pass through, and closed it carefully behind. As she got back into the car she said, "Did you bring your rod?"

He shook his head. "I would not want to fish today. It would not be sociable."

She laughed. "I've never seen anybody fly-fishing. I'd like to know how it's done."

"So?" he said. "It is very delicate, and always one is learning something new. That is why I like it, because never do you come to the end of learning some new thing. Also, it makes you go to beautiful, deserted country, and that also I like. I will show you how to do it one day, if you like. But now, the water is too warm; the fish will not take a fly until the water grows more cold, in March."

He drove across the bridge over the Delatite and on up the road towards the lumber camp, till after a mile or so he turned off into a paddock, and they drove on a rough track across pastures for a time, heading for the hills. Their passage stirred a great flight of white cockatoos from the trees; they wheeled above the car, brilliant against the deep blue sky before settling in the next paddock.

Presently the track left the pastures and entered the woods, and began to wind up-hill through a forest of gum trees. It was quiet in the dim aisles of the woods, and scented; fantastic parrots with brilliant red bodies and equally brilliant blue wings flew before them up the track and vanished in the glades. "It's amazing, the colours," the girl from London said quietly. "Don't birds have to camouflage themselves in this country?"

He said, "I do not think that there are any beasts of prey to worry them, such as leopards or wild cats. I do not think that birds or koala bears have many enemies in this country."

She said, "I never thought I'd see such lovely birds flying about wild . . ."

He smiled. "There are many lovely things in this country that one would not see in any other place."

The track wound up through the forest, utterly deserted. Once or twice a wallaby started at their approach and went bounding away among the trees, and once a red English fox with a great bushy tail crossed the track in front of them and vanished in the undergrowth, perhaps hunting the occasional rabbit that appeared, and looked at them, and scuttled away with flashing scut. And once Carl Zlinter said, "You have seen a koala bear?"

"Never," she said. "They're little creatures, aren't they?"

He did not answer, but drove on for a few yards, stopped the car and got out quickly, and ran into the bush. He was in time to catch the koala under the armpits as it clambered unhurried up a tree to get away from him; he disengaged it gently and carried it to her on the track, a tubby little brown animal with tattered fur that struggled feebly but did not seem particularly distressed by capture.

"Oh, Carl!" she said, "what a lovely little beast. He's just like a teddy bear."

He did not understand the allusion. "I think he is a very old bear, this," he said. "His fur is bad. You can stroke him if you like; he will not hurt you. But do not let him scratch you, because his claws will be dirty and poisonous, and a small wound may go bad."

He held the bear from behind, gently controlling it while she stroked it. "It's a wild one, isn't it?" she asked, puzzled.

"He is a wild bear," he told her. "He lives here in the forest."

"But he seems so tame. He doesn't mind being handled or stroked bit!"

"He has no enemies in the woods," he said. "No animal hunts koala bears to kill them, only men, and now that is forbidden, very strongly. Because he has no enemies, he has no fear."

"What will happen if you let him go, Carl? Let him go, and see."

He released the bear, and they crouched beside him; he looked from one to the other, looked around, then walked deliberately to a tree and began to climb up it, holding on with the great claws upon each foot. Jennifer walked after him and stroked him as he went till he was out of reach; he paid no attention to her. They stood watching him as he slowly made his way up the trunk above their heads.

"He is going up there for his dinner," Carl said. "He eats only the fresh shoots of the gum trees, and he needs several different sorts of gum tree for good health. That is why you cannot keep them in a cage as captives."

"How did you get to know all that, Carl? Have you handled them before?"

"Many times," he told her. "In the woods, felling the timber, we come on them many times, sometimes one in each day, or more. It is forbidden to kill them, and they are so harmless nobody would kill them if he could help it. Sometimes as we fell the timber we find a tree with a bear in it, and that we leave, if possible, till the next day when he has gone away. Sometimes it is necessary to fell that tree with the bear in it, and usually he is only shaken and frightened a little, so then we pick him up and put him in a smaller tree, that we shall not fell, in a part where we have been to and we shall not come again. It is easy to handle them, but you must not let them scratch."

They got back into the utility and went on up the track, winding around the contours of the hills between the trees; a rough, rutted track, more of a watercourse than a road. Presently they came out on top of the ridge; there was a cleared pasture here, or perhaps a natural clearing due to some geological formation that checked the growth of trees. Zlinter drove into it and stopped the car. "This is Jock McDougall's paddock," he said. "Here we must leave the car and walk for the rest of the way, down to the Howqua."

The paddock stood upon the summit of the ridge, with a wide view across the wooded, mountainous country to the south. In the brilliant sunlight line after line of blue hills stretched to the horizon, with here and there a thin wisp of smoke showing a fire. "Oh Carl," she said, "what a marvellous place. Are there farms and people living in this country?"

He shook his head. "Here is nobody," he said. "Nobody at all." He thought for a minute. "There, where you see the smoke, there is a forest fire, a little one, and there there may be men trying to control it and to put it out. It could be also that somewhere in this country there would be another lumber camp, as at Lamirra, where there would be men. But, except those, there would only be the forest rangers; there would not be more than three or five people in the whole of the country that you see."

She stared entranced. "How far does it go?"

He shrugged his shoulders. "The sun is behind us; we are looking to the south. Seventy or eighty miles, perhaps, the forest goes; not more. Then comes the coastal plain, I think, of farms and pastures that they call Gippsland, and then the sea."

He stood looking over the wide, blue expanse of forest with her. "This is another reason why I love this country," he said quietly. "It is a little like my own home, in Bohemia."

She turned to him. "Do you get homesick, Carl?"

He shook his head. "Not now. I would not ever want to go back there to live. So much is changed, and I have changed so much myself, also. But I remember how it was at home when I was a schoolboy, and this is like the forests are at home a little, and so I am happy to be here."

He glanced down at her. "Do you have big forests such as this in England? You do not have them, do you?"

She shook her head. "Not now. It might have been like this in England two hundred years ago, but it's not now. If this was England it would all be cut up into farms, with roads and filling-stations and villages and towns, and people everywhere. There's nothing like this at home."

"Is it too big for you?" he asked. "Does it frighten you?"

"It's strange," she said. "It's very, very lovely, but it's strange. If I lived here I should have to get to know what you do in a big forest, if you should be lost. Once I knew that, I don't think I'd be afraid of it." She paused. "It's not as if it was full of lions and tigers."

He smiled. "Only flies and mosquitoes, very many of those, and a few snakes. But you are right; in these forests there is nothing much to fear but your own ignorance."

He turned back with her to the utility to take her basket, and she saw that he had put a flabby newspaper parcel on top of her basket of food, and that he had brought a grill with him. "What's that?" she asked. "Meat?"

He said, "I brought some steaks with me, to make a fire and grill them in the way of this country. Have you done that? They are very good."

She said, "I've never done that, Carl. But we're going to have far too much food."

He smiled. "If there is too much, we can take it home, or give it to Billy Slim."

"Can we make a fire in the forest, Carl, without setting everything alight, at this time of year?"

"It is necessary to be very careful," he said. "At the Howqua, by the river, there are stones built up to make a fireplace, and there Billy Slim allows a fire to be made. The fishermen cook steaks there sometimes; I have done that myself."

He would not let her carry anything, and they set off down the track through the woods into the valley. As they went he told her Billy Slim's story of the match that had burned blue down in the open paddock in the valley, and the fire that jumped. "I have not seen that in the two summers I have been here," he said. "One might work in the woods for fifty years, and never see that thing. Yet, I think that it is true."

"That was the fire that burned the town that was here?" she asked.

He nodded. "One of them. I will show you where the town was."

Presently through the green aisles ahead of them, and below, they saw a turn of the river, and then another. They dropped down into the valley flat and came out on an open sward beside the river where no trees were growing, a meadow of perhaps five acres along the river bank. On the other side of the river, in among the trees, there was the iron roof of a weatherboard house. "That is where Billy Slim lives," he told her, "the forest ranger."

He put the basket and the grill down under a tree that stood alone in the meadow, not far from the river. "This is where the town was," he said.

She looked round, startled. "Where? Here?"

"Here where we are standing, in this flat," he said. "There were many houses here fifty years ago, and in the trees up the hill, where we have come."

There was aboslutely nothing to distinguish the place from any other natural glade in the forest, no sign of any habitation but the forest ranger's house. "It seems incredible that it has gone so completely," she said, "and so soon. How many houses were there here?"

He shrugged his shoulders. "A hundred—perhaps more. There were three hotels." He moved a little way from the tree. "Can you see the line here, the rectangle? And here, another room, and here, these bricks? This was the Buller Arms Hotel, that Billy Slim's father kept. Here came the girls to serve as barmaids to the miners, the naughty girls, if that old Irishman was right." He paused. "Only fifty years ago, and now all is gone."

She had great difficulty in believing it. She said, "Carl, how have the trees recovered so quickly? These trees are very big, some of them. Have they all grown up since the last fire?"

"Fire does not kill the gum trees," he told her. "All other trees die in the forest fire, but not the eucalypts. After the fire when everything is burned to blackened stumps, you think the forest will be spoiled for ever. But next spring the gum trees shoot again, and in a very few years all is as it was before." He turned and showed her the blackened streaks upon the bark of the tree they stood under. "You can see—this one has lived through the fire. Only the gum tree can live through the fire like that; all other trees are killed. I think that that is why these forests are all eucalypts."

"Where is the cemetery?" she asked.

"It is a mile down the river, perhaps a mile and a half," he said. "There is a path that leads to it, but it is very overgrown. Also, it crosses the river three or four times, and it is necessary to walk through the water. Would you like for me to ask Billy Slim if he can lend a horse for you? It will be easier for you so."

She laughed. "I'd fall off a horse, Carl. I can't ride. How deep is the water that we've got to walk through?"

"I do not think it will be deeper than your knees."

"Well, that's all right. I don't mind getting these shoes wet. It'll be rather nice to paddle on a day like this." The sun blazed down upon them as they stood; it was unthinkable that wading in the river could be anything but pleasant.

They left the basket of food hung up on a branch of the tree, and started off along the meadow by the river, a clear trout stream running rippling over water-worn stones with alternate runs and pools. Presently the path led them down to the water, and was seen emerging from the river on the far side, among the bushes. "Here is the ford," Zlinter said. "I will go first; I do not think it will be deep."

He walked into the water and turned to look back at her; she followed him gingerly. The water was cool and refreshing about her ankles, plucking at her slacks; she stooped and rolled them up above the knee. Her blouse sagged open and he saw the soft curve of her breasts, because in that hot weather she had little on; he let his eyes rest for a moment in enjoyment, and then quickly averted them in case she should see him looking. She finished with her slacks and stood erect, and found him studiously looking up the river, betraying himself; she knew what he had seen and coloured slightly, but she did not mind; her own eyes had rested once or twice on his brown chest and arms with secret pleasure. She followed him across the river; as it grew deep she reached out and took his hand, and he guided her across. In the thicket on the other side he said, "It would be better to put down your trousers now, or you will get your legs scratched," and she did so, slightly turned away from him.

He went ahead of her on the narrow path, forcing the bushes aside where they grew thickly and holding them back for her to pass. The path wound along through the forest by the river, a narrow track used only by the forest ranger on his horse and by an occasional fisherman on foot. Presently they crossed the river again, and then a third time, and a fourth, as the path changed from side to side to avoid spurs and rocky outcrops.

It was very quiet in the forest. The sunlight fell in dappled patches on the undergrowth through the sparse foliage of the gum trees; an occasional parrot squawked and flew away ahead of them, but they saw no animals. They went on till they came to a red stone bluff on the north side of the river; the path wound round this, and Carl Zlinter stopped. "It is somewhere here," he said. "There must have been a road here at one time, from the town, but there is nothing to see now. I think the stones are over there somewhere."

Jennifer said, "What's that—over there, by the white tree?"

"That is right. That is one of them." He guided her through the undergrowth of bracken and tea tree scrub, and they came to the three stones that were still standing. He stooped beside the furthest one, and rubbed the surface of it. "This is the one."

She stooped beside him, and read the inscription. She had never doubted his story, but it was a satisfaction to her to see the carved letters with her own eyes. "Charlie Zlinter and his dog," she said quietly. "It was nice of them to bury the dog with him."

He looked at her and smiled. "That old Irishman, he said the priest would not have allowed it, but he did not know."

"Do you think he was a relation of yours, Carl?"

"Perhaps," he said. "I would like to think he was. I would like to think that someone of my family had been here before me, and had liked this place as I like it. I think he must have liked it here, because he had his cabin here somewhere, not in Banbury. You would think a bullock team driver who drove every day between this place and Banbury would have had his home in Banbury where there was a railway and more life, but it was not so. He had his home here."

She looked up at him, smiling. "Would you like to have a home here?"

He nodded soberly. "I would like that very much. For many years I have now lived in camps, always with other men, and for at least another nine months I must still live so. I would like very much to have a little cabin in the woods by a trout river, like this one, where I could come and live at the week-end and keep some books and be alone a little. I would like that very much indeed."

"You wouldn't be lonely?"

He shook his head. "I have seen so much of other men, all the time, in all the camps."

"You won't want a cabin in the woods in nine months time," she said. "You'll be off somewhere qualifying to be a doctor."

He shook his head. "I do not think that I shall be a doctor again. It costs too much, and three years of study is too long. I do not think that I shall be a doctor."

"What will you do when you leave the camp, then Carl?"

He smiled. "Perhaps I shall not leave the camp. Perhaps I shall go on as a lumberman."

"That'ld be an awful waste," she said. "You ought to do something better than that."

"It is a good life," he replied. "I like living in the woods, I like that very much. If I had a cabin on the Howqua here as Charlie Zlinter had, that I could come to at the week-ends, I could be very happy as a lumberman."

"Until the lumber camp moved on, and it was too far for you to come here for the week-ends," she said.

"That is the danger," he said. "I have already thought about that. I think we shall be at Lamirra for another two years, but after that the camp may move." He got to his feet and helped her up. "I have shown you what we came to see," he said. "Charlie Zlinter and his dog, who fell into the water and got drowned. Only fifty years ago, and practically forgotten now. I wonder if anybody in Pilsen ever got to hear about it?"

"Somebody would have written, surely?"

"Perhaps. I do not know. Now, I have shown you what we came to see. Let us go back to the centre of the town, and I will take you to the restaurant, and we will see our steak cooked on the grill."

She laughed with him. "A silver grill."

"No," he said. "In this place it would be a gold grill."

They walked back by the way that they had come. At the meadow by the river he showed her the rough fireplace of a few stones heaped together, remote from any inflammable scrub. He gathered a few dry fallen branches from the gum trees and a handful of bark, and laid the fire and put a match to it; she was amazed to see how quickly and how easily a fire was made in that hot summer weather. He laid the grill across the stones, sprinkled the steaks with a little salt and laid them over the fire; in ten minutes from the time that the fire was lit they were ready to be eaten.

"It's awfully quick this way," she said. "And they're delicious."

"It is the best way to cook meat," he said, "especially in this country. The fire is easily made, and the smoke of the gum tree adds a little to the flavour, also. We cook many steaks like this in the forest when we are at work."

They ate in silence, sitting on the grass in the shade of the big tree where Billy Slim's father had kept his hotel, where the naughty girls came to work as barmaids, where the bedrooms worked day and night and where small bags of water-worn gold once passed across the bar in payment for drinks and other recreations. In the tree above their heads a ring-tailed possum peeped down at them shyly, wondering if these two intruders into his domain meant danger to his nest.

They lay smoking on the grass when they had finished eating.

"Carl," the girl said at last. "You promised last night that you'd tell me about your strange idea."

He raised himself on one elbow, laughing, noting the soft curve of her neck with quiet delight. "I have nearly told you that already."

"What have you nearly told me?"

"That I want to build a cabin for myself, here in the Howqua valley."

"I know that. But what's the strange idea?"

"You will say that it is sentimental."

She raised herself and looked at him, wondering what was coming. "Of course I shall, if it is. It may not be any the worse for that. What is it?"

He looked down at the grass. "It was a stupid little fancy," he said. "It was nothing."

"Tell me?"

He raised his head, laughing a little in embarrassment. "It was just this. Here have been many houses, a hundred perhaps, and three hotels at least. I would like if I can to find where Charlie Zlinter had his house, and build mine there on the same place."

She smiled. "Why do you want to do that, Carl?"

"I do not know," he said. "I just want to do it. I think we are of the same family, and I have to build my cabin somewhere. I think that I would like to build it there."

"I think that's rather nice, Carl."

"You do not think it stupid?"

She shook her head. "Not a bit. But how would you find out where Charlie Zlinter lived?"

"I would like to go and have a talk with Billy Slim presently," he said. "But I do not think that he will know, because he was not born at that time, I think it is more likely that I would learn something from Mary Nolan."

She smiled. "One of the naughty girls."

He laughed with her. "Yes, one of the naughty girls. But she will not be naughty now. She must be over seventy years old."

"She's sort of sterilised."

They laughed together. "That is right."

She rolled over and looked at him. "She wouldn't talk about that time, would she?" She hesitated, trying to choose her words. "I mean, Carl, if she was a naughty girl when she knew Charlie Zlinter, she wouldn't want to tell people about it when she's seventy years old."

He stared at her, perplexed. "I had not thought of that. You mean, she might know things about him, but she would not say, because of what they did when she was young?"

She nodded. "I should think you'd have an awful job to get anything out of her. She'd have to know you very well before she'd talk, especially to a man."

He lay staring over the rippling lights of the river running over

173

stones towards a dark pool. "It is not about personal things that I would ask her. Only about any papers that he might have had in his cabin, or about what happened to his papers and his property after he was dead."

She smiled. "If she hadn't been a naughty girl she couldn't know anything about the inside of his cabin," she replied. "She probably does know, quite a lot. She might tell another woman possibly, but she'd never tell you."

He turned to her. "Would you come with me to see her? Perhaps she might talk to you."

She laughed. "I meant another woman of her age, Carl. Not a young one like me. Not unless I was a naughty girl like she was. You'd want another woman of her age."

"You are pretty and young, as she was when she knew Charlie Zlinter," he said simply. "I think she might talk to you when she would not talk to me."

"I don't mind going to see her with you," Jennifer said. It would mean another of these delightful days, if nothing else. "It's just possible she might open up with me, but I don't think it's likely. What exactly is it that you want to know?"

"About any papers that would tell us who he was," he replied. "If there was a passport, or identity document, or letters, or photographs of home—anything that would say who he was. What happened to those things after he was dead. And where the cabin was."

"She'd never be able to tell you that now," she remarked. "The place has changed so much. Billy Slim might be a better bet."

"We will try him presently," he said. "We will go across the river and ask him. But will you come with me to see the old lady, one day soon?" If nothing else, it would mean another one of these lovely days with Jennifer.

"Of course I will, Carl. You mean, to Woods Point?"

He nodded. "That is where she lives."

"How would we get there?"

"Perhaps Jack Dorman would lend the utility again, if I pay for the petrol."

"You'll need all your money to pay the fines if you go driving about the country without a licence."

"I would not mind that, if I could find out the things I want her to tell me."

She considered for a minute. "We'd better go on Saturday," she said. "She's a Catholic, so Sunday might not be a very good day."

He hesitated. "You would not mind to do this for me?" he asked, a little shyly.

She turned to him. "Of course not, Carl. I'd like to go and see her with you."

They got up presently, and went to see Billy Slim. The bridge across the river to his homestead consisted of two steel cables

174

slung across the river with planks lashed to them to form a foot-way; another two cables formed hand-rails with rabbit-wire sides from the hand-rails to the footway. Jennifer paused before going on to it, and turned to Carl. "Do you think this is the same bridge?"

"Very likely," he said. "It is only fifty years."

"I'll have to be careful not to do the same thing."

"He was drunk, and it was dark, and he had a dog in his arms," Zlinter said. "It is a little different."

"It was nice of him to carry the dog," said Jennifer. "He was probably rather a nice man."

"Mary Nolan thought so." She turned and saw a gleam of humour in his eye, and made a face at him.

They found Billy Slim asleep, that hot summer afternoon; there was a stir from the bedroom as they stepped on to the veranda, and presently he looked out at them, clad only in a pair of khaki shorts. "Aw, look," he said. "I won't be more 'n a minute." He came out presently with a shirt on. "Just having a bit of shut-eye," he said. "I saw you, Splinter, earlier on today, going down the river somewhere."

Zlinter said, "This is Miss Jenny, who is staying with Jack Dorman."

"This is the young lady who helped you do those operations at Lamirra?"

"This is the one. How did you get to know about that?"

"Aw, everybody knows about that. I heard about it at the Jig." To Jennifer he said, "How do you do, Miss. I'll just put on the kettle for a pot of tea." He busied himself with a Primus stove.

They sat down at his table. "We have just been to see the grave-stones at the cemetery," Zlinter said. "To see the one that has my name upon it."

Slim paused, teapot in hand. "I went and had a look at it myself the other day. Charlie Zlinter and his dog, just like you said."

"I have found out a little more about Charlie Zlinter. He drove a bullock team." He started in and told the forest ranger most of the information that he had collected from Pat Halloran, omitting the information that Mary Nolan was still alive. "Now I would like to find out where he lived in Howqua," he said at last.

Billy Slim set the cups before them and poured out the tea. "You mean, where the hut he lived in was?"

"That is what I want to know."

"You don't know the street or the number?"

The Czech said, "I do not know anything but that he lived here, in the town of Howqua."

The ranger sat down at the table with them and stirred his tea. "I never saw the town myself," he said. "I come here first as just a little nipper some time in the first war, but that was some years after it was burnt through for the first time. The fire went through here in 1909—or was it 1910? I don't know—one or the other.

There wasn't any town here when I saw the valley first, but there were a lot more stumps of brick chimneys, and iron roofing, and that sort of junk. When I come here, I picked up all the iron there was and used it as walls for sheds, with new iron on the roof; I had a stable built of it, before the second fire came through. The chimney stumps, well, they just went away in time. Fell down."

"Were the houses in streets?" Carl Zlinter asked.

"Oh my word," the forest ranger said, "it was all laid out proper. Jubilee Parade ran round by the river from my dad's hotel by the big tree, and Victoria Avenue crossed it running up towards the path that you came down. Most of the houses were on one of those two streets, but there were several others, I know. I forget their names."

Jennifer said, "I suppose you don't know where Charlie Zlinter lived?"

The ranger shook his head, "I don't. I don't think anyone could tell you that, not at this distance of time. What do you want to know that for?"

Carl Zlinter said, "It was just a fancy. I would like to build a little hut here, a place where I could sleep when I come fishing and not always trouble you. A little place of one room where I could leave fishing rods and blankets, and perhaps a few tins of food. It is better when you live always in the camp to have a little place that is your own, to come away to sometimes."

The forest ranger nodded. "Sure," he said, "you could do that. You'd have to buy an allotment from the Lands Department."

"What is that?"

"The Lands Department, in Melbourne, they own all the land, and they've got it all mapped out as town lots in the valley here. They sell these lots, see? like in any town you buy a vacant lot for a house. Well, if you've got a lot and you don't pay the rates, after a while you lose your allotment, and it goes back to the Lands Department, and they can sell it to someone else." He paused. "That's happened with every one of the township allotments here. They're all back with the Lands Department because everybody's gone away and stopped paying the rates, but the township's still mapped out that way, and if you want a bit of land you'll have to buy a town allotment."

Jennifer asked, "You mean, if you wanted to put up a hut down by the river you'd have to buy a town site?"

"That's right. You'd get so many yards frontage on the street, and so much depth."

They laughed, and the girl said, "Number Twelve, Jubilee Parade?"

"That's right."

Carl Zlinter asked, "How much would that cost?"

"Aw, look," the forest ranger said, "there's not a lot of competition for town sites in Howqua just at the moment. I wouldn't pay more than five quid for it, not unless you picked a corner site. They

176

might make you pay ten quid for that, because of having frontage on both streets and being able to do more trade that way." He grinned.

"How much would the rates be?"

The ranger scratched his head. "I couldn't rightly say. The Council's been running on the cheap the last half century. They might make you pay five bob a year for the allotment."

He could not tell them any more, and presently they left him to his lonely life and went back across the wire bridge to the meadow by the river. It was very still and quiet and beautiful in the valley; the sun was dropping towards the hill, and already the shadows were growing long. "It's a lovely, lovely place," the girl said. "Whether you find out about Charlie Zlinter or not, Carl, it's a lovely place to build a little hut."

"You like it so much, too?" he asked eagerly.

"I do," she said. "I think it's perfectly beautiful."

They turned from the river and walked slowly up the track towards Jock McDougall's paddock and the utility. They talked as they went about Paris mostly; Jennifer had spent a fortnight's holiday in Paris in 1946, and Carl had spent several leaves in Paris in 1943 and 1944, so that though they had seen it under different circumstances it was a bond between them as a place that they both knew and had enjoyed. They came to the utility too soon, and stood for a time looking over the wide forest in the evening sunlight.

At last the girl said, "It's been a wonderful day, Carl. Thank you so much for taking me."

She held out her hand instinctively, as if she were saying good-bye, and it seemed better to say what they had to say here in the solitude and quiet of the forest than at the homestead, where there would be other people. He said, "If I ask Jack Dorman to lend us this Chev again, will you come with me to Woods Point on Saturday?"

"Of course. I'd love to do that, Carl."

"I will ask him when we get back." He looked at her smiling. "It will seem a very long time," he said.

"Not so long as that," she said. "I shall see you tomorrow."

"Tomorrow?"

She laughed up at him. "At the inquest."

"The inquest! I had forgotten all about it!"

"That's what I hoped you'd do," she said, getting into the car. "Don't start thinking about it now."

They drove down the rough track through the woods not talking very much, but very conscious of each other. They came out in the end upon the main road to Lamirra, and then, too soon, they were at Leonora, opening each paddock gate as they passed through.

Jack Dorman met them in the yard, glancing critically at the Chev. "Brought it home all in one piece?"

"I have not hit it against anything," said Zlinter. "It was very, very kind of you to lend it to us."

177

Jennifer left him talking to Jack Dorman by the car, leading up to a suggestion that they should borrow it again on Saturday, and went into the house. She found Jane in the kitchen, ironing.

"There was a telegram for you from England, Jenny," she said. "It came over the telephone; I wrote it down." She passed an old envelope with pencilled words written on the back across to the girl. "Not too good news, I'm afraid."

The girl took the paper from her. It read,

"Think you should know Mummy very ill bronchitis and asthma sends you all her love with mine. Writing air mail.
"DADDY"

Nine

THE telegram jerked Jennifer back into the hard, bleak winter of England, that in the heat and ease and beauty of the Australian summer she had almost forgotten. It was only about seven weeks since she had sailed from Tilbury, but in the short time that she had been in Australia she had become so steeped in the Australian scene that it was difficult for her to visualise the conditions of winter weather in England. With the shirt sticking to her back in the heat, it was difficult for her to think about the freezing fogs of Leicester, and all that they meant to her bronchial and asthmatic mother.

At Jane's suggestion she wrote her mother a telegram that they telephoned through to the post office, a telegram of sympathetic, conventional words of love. She felt as she drafted it that it was totally inadequate and for the first time she felt real regret that she had ventured so far from her home, but there was nothing to be done about that now, and no other words but the hackneyed ones to express what she would have liked to convey to her mother.

Jane said casually, "Of course, you can telephone if you really want to. I believe it costs about two pounds a minute. They say it's very good."

Jennifer had become so used already to the Australian way with money that she considered this seriously for a moment. "I don't think so," she said. "She hasn't got the telephone in her bedroom so she couldn't take the call herself. Unless I could speak to Mummy personally, I don't think it would be worth it."

She sat down and wrote her a long air-mail letter instead, all about everything except Carl Zlinter and the Howqua valley.

She went into Banbury next morning with Jane and Jack Dorman in the Ford utility. The inquest was held in the police court next to the police station, a smallish room uncomfortably furnished with a jury box and a dock and a few wooden benches. The coroner was an elderly grazier, a Mr. Herbert Richardson, who had been a Justice of the Peace in Banbury for many years and took the infrequent inquests that arose, as deputy coroner for the district. Jim Forrest was there with Carl Zlinter, and Dr. Jennings, and a fair number of onlookers. Inquests did not happen very often in Banbury.

Mr. Richardson was rather deaf and unaccustomed to an inquest; he needed a good deal of prompting by the police, but finally he opened the proceedings by inviting Sergeant Russell to tell the story of the death of Albert Hanson, which the police sergeant did with commendable detachment. The deceased, he said, had been the victim of an accident to a bulldozer in the bush above Lamirra; the manager of the Lamirra Timber Company was present in the court. The foot of the deceased had been amputated on the scene of the accident by a man called Zlinter, who was present. Mr. Zlinter was not registered as a practitioner in Victoria. He was assisted in the operation by a Miss Morton, who was present, and who held no qualifications as a nurse. The man Hanson had died some hours later at the camp at Lamirra, and Dr. Jennings, who was present, had seen the body shortly after death. The deceased was known to the police as an alcoholic. The circumstances leading up to the man's death appeared to the police to be irregular, but they had not yet made any charge.

On the suggestion of the police sergeant the coroner called Mr. Forrest to give evidence; he took the oath and started in to tell the story, the coroner laboriously writing down his evidence in long-hand. Presently he asked:

"So you authorised the man Zlinter to take off the foot of the deceased man, did you?"

"Too right," said Mr. Forrest, "I couldn't do anything else. Zlinter said the foot would have to come off anyway, and I could see that for myself."

"Did you know at the time that he had no medical licence to practice in Australia?"

"I knew that."

"But you authorised him to do this operation?"

"Aw, look," the manager said, "what would you have done? We couldn't get a doctor, 'n we couldn't leave him there all night. If we'd tried to shift the sticks and bulldozer quick, we'd have dropped one on top of him, like as not. I reckoned I was lucky to have a doctor of any sort there, even if he was a crook one."

The old man wrote all that down slowly. "I see. And then when you got him to the camp, what happened then?"

The tale went on. "And then some silly bastard went 'n give him a bottle of whisky," the manager said at last. "He got fighting drunk 'n it was all that we could do to keep him in the bed. My word. And then, after an hour or two of that, the doctor give him something, 'n soon after that he died."

"When you say the doctor, you mean Mr. Zlinter?"

"That's right. Mr. Zlinter."

"Who was in charge of this man when he got the whisky?"

There was an awkward pause. "Well, we was all in charge of him, you might say. I'd got the doctor and the nurse there, 'n I was round about myself most of the night."

"By the nurse, you mean Miss Morton?"

"That's right."

180

The coroner whispered for a moment with the police sergeant. "That will do, Mr. Forrest. Call Miss . . ." He peered at a paper before him. "Miss Jennifer Morton."

Jennifer went to the witness stand and took the oath in a low voice. The coroner said, "Are you a registered nurse?"

She shook her head, and said, "No."

"Eh, what's that? What did she say?"

Sergeant Russell said, "She said, no, sir." To Jennifer, "You'll have to speak up a bit."

The old man said, "Were you in charge of the deceased man at the camp, before he died?"

She said, "I—I don't think so."

"But you were acting as a nurse?"

"Yes. I was helping Dr. Zlinter."

The coroner said testily, "Will you please stop talking about Dr. Zlinter. As I understand it, he is not a doctor at all."

The girl flushed, and said nothing. There was a pause. At last the old man said, "Were you supposed to be looking after this man before he died?"

"I don't think so, sir. I couldn't have been. I was helping Mr. Zlinter in the next room with the other operation."

"That was the head injury?"

"Yes. We must have been in that room for over two hours. It was in that time that he must have got the whisky."

"And in that time you were not looking after him?"

"No, sir."

The coroner whispered to Sergeant Russell, who shook his head. "That will do, Miss Morton," and Jennifer went back to her seat tired with the brief strain. The coroner said, "Call Dr. Jennings."

The doctor took the oath. "I understand that you examined this man shortly after death."

"That's right."

"What was the cause of death?"

The doctor said, "Operational shock, aggravated by an excessive amount of alcohol. I understand that the man drank a whole bottle of whisky."

"Yes. You conducted a post-mortem?"

"I did."

"Did you find whisky in the body?"

"I did. I found a very large amount."

"In your opinion, if this man had not taken this unfortunate dose of whisky, would he have recovered from the operation?"

The doctor said carefully, "I think he would have recovered. He had an enlarged liver, somewhat diseased; I have preserved a sample of that. That condition is usually due to habitual excessive drinking. Such a man would not be a good subject for an operation of any sort, and so it is a possibility that he might have died after the operation in any case. But the operation was skilfully and

181

properly performed, and so I should say that he would have had a good chance of recovery—apart from the whisky."

It took some time to write that down. "The operation was properly done?"

"I examined the amputation at the post-mortem," the doctor said. "It was properly done, and I should have expected it to be successful."

"I see." The old man finished writing, thought for a minute, and then said, "I understand that this man Zlinter did another operation on the same evening. Can you tell us anything about that one—how that is going on?"

Dr. Jennings said, "That was a much more difficult operation than the amputation. It involved the removal of a portion of the skull completely, and the lifting of two other pieces. Normally one would not like to tackle such an operation without full hospital facilities, but in this case it was done by Mr. Zlinter in very difficult and improvised conditions, assisted by Miss Morton. That operation also seems to have been very well done, particularly well in the circumstances. The patient is now conscious, and likely to recover."

There was a long pause while this was written down. "I see. Am I to take it that these men received satisfactory medical attention, then?"

The doctor thought deeply for a minute. "So far as the operations are concerned," he said, "I think they were well done. The after-care was not so satisfactory. It was probably impossible to remove the head injury to hospital until the ambulance became available. It would have been possible, perhaps, to take this man Hanson into hospital, and he wouldn't have got the whisky there. But that is being wise after the event, and I don't think one should blame Mr. Zlinter for his decision to keep both men at the camp till I arrived with the ambulance."

The coroner whispered again to Sergeant Russell. Then he said, "Have you ever know the man Zlinter to do an operation before?"

"No sir. I have known him to do dressings and first aid for minor injuries, which have sometimes come to me for treatment later on, at the hospital."

"And you have been quite happy that he should do that sort of work up at Lamirra?"

"Yes, sir. I understand that he is qualified as a medical practitioner in his own country, but not in Australia. He is quite competent to do that sort of first-aid work."

"Do you consider him competent to do the sort of operations that he did on this occasion, Dr. Jennings?"

The doctor said carefully, "As a general rule, sir, I should not regard him as competent to operate until he had complied with the regulations of the Medical Registration Board, which means that he should have to do a further period in a medical school here. In this

182

particular emergency both these men would probably have died but for his care. That was the alternative. The operations that he performed should have saved both lives, but unfortunately one man has died through his own intemperance." He paused. "I should like to make it clear that I have quite a high opinion of Mr. Zlinter's capabilities as a surgeon."

The old man blinked at him. "You have a high opinion of him?"

"Certainly, sir. If he were properly qualified in this country I should be glad to have him as a partner."

A further bout of whispering with the police sergeant.

"That will do, Doctor, thank you. Call Mr. Zlinter."

Carl Zlinter stepped to the witness stand and took the oath.

"What is your nationality, Mr. Zlinter?"

"I am a Czechoslovakian, sir."

"And have you any medical qualifications?"

"I am a licentiate of the University of Pilsen and a Doctor of Medicine, sir." He pulled some papers from the breast pocket of his coat. "I have here my diploma."

He passed it to the police sergeant and the coroner, who looked at it with interest, unable to read one single word. "Very good."

The coroner leaned back in his chair. "You have heard all the evidence, Mr. Zlinter," he said. "I think we have heard enough evidence now to determine the cause of this man's death, and I do not propose to ask you any questions. I have called you because I have some things to say to you."

He paused, and went on slowly and deliberately, "You have heard the evidence, and from the evidence it is fairly clear that in an emergency you performed two operations competently and well, one of which was a very serious and delicate operation. I have to thank you on behalf of the community, and at the same time I have to give you a warning. You are not licensed as a doctor in this State or in Australia at all, and if you should do any further operations, and if they should turn out badly, you would be open to a charge of manslaughter, because in this country you are not a doctor. I do not want to seem ungrateful to you, but that is the law. Before doing any further operations you must get yourself qualified, or you may find yourself in trouble. Do you understand that?"

Carl Zlinter said, "Yes, sir. I have always understood that ver' well."

"Well, you'd better get yourself qualified as soon as you are able to. Thank you, Mr. Zlinter; you can stand down now."

Carl Zlinter went back to his seat, and the coroner whispered again with the police sergeant. At last he raised his head, shuffled his papers, and said,

"This inquest has been called to ascertain the cause of the death of Albert Hanson. The evidence that we have heard shows that the man died of operational shock following upon an accident with a bulldozer, and that the operational shock was aggravated and intensified by a great quantity of alcohol which the man got hold of in some way that cannot be ascertained, and drank. I do not think the fact that the operation was performed by an unregistered surgeon had any particular bearing on the cause of death, but the fact that whisky was supplied to him after the operation was certainly a factor in his death. For this the management of the Lamirra Timber Company were responsible. I cannot close this inquest without expressing my opinion that some negligence occurred on the part of Mr. Forrest in the after-care of these men. It appears that no organisation for the treatment of serious injuries exists at Lamirra. I think that there should be such an organisation, a small hospital or dressing station where such injuries can be properly treated and isolated. If that had existed, the life of this man might have been saved. I find a verdict of accidental death, with a strong recommendation that the company should consider what I have said. I shall not be so lenient with them if this should happen again."

He shuffled his papers together, rose from his seat and went out of the court; the people on the public benches began to stream out of the door. Jack Dorman unostentatiously got out early, and fell into step with Dr. Jennings as he walked towards his car.

"All went off very well, Doctor," he said.

The doctor nodded. "I was sorry Jim Forrest got a rap, but I suppose somebody had to have it. I think there *was* some carelessness. Jim must have known the man was a boozer, and he might have thought some of his mates would try to slip him something."

"Aye," said the grazier, "but I don't suppose Jim'll lose much sleep."

"He should put up a dressing station of some sort."

"Maybe he'll do that." He hesitated. "It was good of you to say what you did about Splinter," he said. "It could have gone crook for him."

The doctor nodded. "I know. He did a good job, as good as anybody could have done in the conditions. I thought it was only fair to make that clear."

"When you said you'd be glad to have him as a partner," Jack Dorman remarked, "I suppose that was just a manner of speaking, for the police and old Bert Richardson?"

The doctor stopped and glanced at him. "I don't know that I meant it to be taken very seriously," he said. "We could do with two more doctors in this district, but we're not likely to get them so long as any young chap just qualified can put his plate up in a suburb of the city and make a go of it. If Zlinter was qualified I wouldn't mind having him; he's probably quite a good doctor. However, he's not qualified, so there's an end of it."

"He might be one day," the grazier said.

"Are you thinking of financing him?"

Jack Dorman laughed. "Not on your life. I was just wondering

184

how you'd feel about it if he ever turned up in this district as a
proper doctor."

"I wouldn't mind a bit," the doctor said. "He certainly did those
two operations very skilfully."

Outside the court-house Jane Dorman stopped Carl Zlinter as
he was about to get into the utility with Mr. Forrest. "Carl," she
said, "what's the best way to get hold of this man Shulkin? What
would be the best time to go and talk to him about pictures?"

"I think the week-end," Zlinter said. "In the week he will be
working always, on the railway somewhere."

Jim Forrest said, "He won't be working today, Mrs. Dorman."
She turned to him. "Why not?"

"The railwaymen are on strike."

"Are they? What's it for this time?"

"It's a twenty-four-hour stoppage," he said. "The wharfies went
to the Arbitration Court for another pound a week for something or
other, and they didn't get it, so they've stopped work for a day to
show their displeasure, and the railwaymen have done that too.
Like what they call a Day of Mourning in India."

"My word," said Jane. "Everybody's making too much money
in this country, that's the trouble."

"Too right," said Mr. Forrest.

"You think I'd find Shulkin at his home?"

"Unless he's in the pub. These twenty-four-hour stoppages, most
of 'em spend the Day of Mourning in the pub."

"I do not think that Shulkin will be in the pub," said Zlinter.
"I think he is a serious man. I think that you will find him in his
garden, or perhaps painting."

Mr. Shulkin was painting, but not in the style that Zlinter had
visualised; Jane and Jennifer found him distempering a bedroom of
the little weatherboard house beside the railway coach. He got down
off a chair to greet them, brush in hand; a little girl about five years
old, smothered in distemper and rather dirty, stared at them, finger
in mouth. Jane said, "Are you Mr. Shulkin?"

He smiled. "I am Stanislaus Shulkin."

"Mr. Zlinter was telling me that you paint pictures."

He beamed at her, pulled forward the chair and dusted it.
"Please—I am so sorry you must find me like this. Carl Zlinter, he
was telling me that there is—there is a lady who was wanting
beautiful picture. So?"

Jane said, "I do want a very, very nice oil painting, Mr. Shulkin.
The trouble is, I don't want just anything. I don't even know what
I do want until I see it."

He smiled. "Also, you do not know if I can paint such a picture,
that you will want."

She laughed with him. "That's right."

"I can paint any kind of picture," he said. "Just like the carpenter, he can make any wood—a chair, a table, a bed, a cupboard. The

185

good carpenter he can make all things, in all woods. So the good artist, he can paint all kinds of picture. But the good carpenter, he makes some things in some woods ver', ver' well, and the others, just like anyone could make. So the good artist. Some things I can do ver', ver' well, and others just as any artist, so-so." He glanced at her. "You understand me?"

"Perfectly."

"So. Now we will go and I shall show you some pictures."

He took Jennifer and Jane to the railway coach and showed them his pictures. For half an hour he pulled canvas after canvas out of untidy piles, set them up upon the easel, and described them. Of the ten or fifteen canvases displayed, Jane set aside three, all landscapes, one of them the Delatite river picture with the wattles that Zlinter had admired.

"These are something like it," she said slowly, "but not just what I want. I'm sure they're good enough in the technique, but they are not *my* picture. Do you understand what I mean?"

He nodded. "I understand ver' well."

She said slowly, "Let me tell you something, Mr. Shulkin. I grew up with pictures, and I never thought about them much. I was born in England and my people were well off, and there were lots of paintings in the house. I think some of them must have been very good, but I never thought about them at the time. It's only now that I'm getting old that I'm beginning to realise what a lot you miss by not having good paintings. When we couldn't have them because we hadn't enough money I never worried about them, or thought about them much. But now we've got a bit more, and I want a good picture almost more than anything."

He nodded slowly. "May I ask a little question, or two?"

"Of course."

"What is it that you do?" he asked. "What interests have you?"

"I don't do anything except the housework," she said. "It's a whole-time job upon a station. You can't get any help."

"Are you interested more in flowers or in people?" he asked.

She smiled. "Cold beef or Thursday." She thought for a moment. "I think, really, I like flowers more than people. They never disappoint you."

"Do you like the high mountains and the rivers better, or the bright lights in shop windows in the coming darkness of a winter night?" he asked.

"I like the high mountains and the rivers better," she said. "I don't really like the city."

He said surprisingly, "This young lady, she is a relation of you?"

"Why, yes. This is Jennifer Morton, Mr. Shulkin—she's a kind of niece. She's only just arrived from England."

"So—she is English." He moved round Jennifer and looked at her in profile, thoughtfully. "Ver' interesting," he said at last. "Now one last question, Mrs. Dorman. Do you like better the picture that is full of colour or that is full of good drawing, with the colour more quiet?"

Jane thought for a long time. "I think the picture that is full of good drawing," she said. "One gets such brilliant colours in this country all day long. Unless it was very unusual colour, it would be a repetition of what you see all the time, and I think one might get tired of that. I think I like quiet colours with good drawing."

"So," he replied. "Now I will say what I can do for you." He looked at her, smiling. "I like to paint," he said, "but I cannot now buy canvases and paints for pictures that nobody will buy. I would like to paint three pictures, of this size," he raised a canvas, "and show the three for you to choose which you like best. If you like one to buy it, you shall pay me seventy pounds. If you do not like any of the pictures, then you shall pay me five pounds for the cost of the canvases and the paints. That is all that I would need, the money that I shall have spent."

"That sounds fair enough," Jane said. "But if I don't like any of the pictures, you'll have done a great deal of work for nothing."

"I like to paint," he said simply, "I will have been able to paint three more pictures because you will have paid for the materials." He paused. "Also," he said, "the work is not alone for me. This young lady will require to work with me."

"Me?" asked Jennifer.

"These pictures are to have quiet colour and good drawing," he said equably. "Your head also has quiet colour and good drawing. One of the pictures is to be a portrait of you, upon some landscape background of this place."

There was a momentary silence. "It's not a bad idea Jenny," Jane said at last. "You've got some lovely colours in your hair, if he could ever get them right."

"I also have notice those," said Mr. Shulkin. "It will be ver' difficult, and I may not do well. But I would like to try the portrait, for one picture."

"I don't mind sitting," said Jennifer. "I've never done it before, though. How many times should I have to come?"

"Three times," said Shulkin. "If it was not possible in three sittings, then it would be impossible, and we should stop and do something different. But I think it will be possible."

They arranged for Jennifer to come down to his cottage in the evenings after tea; he wanted her at the week-end, but she objected to that, having in mind her excursion to Woods Point with Carl Zlinter. She thought of offering to drive herself in to these sittings in Jane's little Morris; she had driven her father's car in England a little and she held an English licence. But she abandoned that idea; Jane was still proud and jealous of her little Morris, and would probably not have taken kindly to the idea, and the Chevrolet was bigger than anything that Jennifer had driven, and she was rather frightened of it. "It won't be any trouble, driving in after tea,

187

just three times," Jane said. "I should come into town more anyway."

The week was an uneasy one for Jennifer. Each day a letter from her father came by air mail; she knew that he must be very troubled to be writing every day. These letters had been written earlier than the cable that she had received, of course, and disclosed a crescendo of her mother's illness, worse with each letter. She got no more cables, which comforted her a little; she wrote to her mother and father every day, long cheerful letters about the Australian scene.

These troubles were half smothered by the beauty and the interest of her life at Merrijig. She went into market one day with Jack Dorman and spent a couple of hours among the pens of sheep and pigs and cattle with the grazier and Tim Archer studying the form and characteristics and the prices of the beasts; they sold one of the homestead cows that had gone dry and bought another one, and she enjoyed every minute of it. She sat twice for Shulkin in the little railway coach, a couple of hours each time till it became too dark to work, while dumpy little Mrs. Shulkin brought her cups of tea and little foreign macaroons and biscuits that she had made herself; conversation with Mrs. Shulkin was difficult because she spoke practically no English. With the artist she got on very well.

Once she asked him, "Are you glad you came to Australia, Mr. Shulkin?"

He did not answer at once, being in the middle of a careful stroke. He finished it, stepped back from the canvas, and then said, "You are just from England, no? Not Australian?"

"I'm not Australian," she laughed. "You can say what you like with me. I'm English."

"So . . . the pose again, please, just for one minute. So . . ." He stepped up to the canvas, worked for a moment, and stepped back again. "I think it was best to come to Australia from the camp in Germany," he said. "When I come first and I was told that my work would be on the railway, I was sad then that it had not been possible to go to the United States. But there also, I think perhaps my work would have been upon the railway, because there also they have their own teachers of fine arts. So, if it is to work upon the railway in Germany or America or Australia——" he stepped up to the easel again and began to work—"then I think Australia is good, because here is more opportunity for my children than even in America."

He stepped back again and looked critically at his work. "One little minute, and then you may relax. . . . Also," he said, "it is now three years that I have worked upon the railway, and it is not bad work. It is happier, I think, to live quietly in the country than to strain always with the mind, to teach art all the day, and to think art all the day, nothing, nothing, nothing' but art. So, I think the mind will soon be sour, like bad milk." He waved his hand towards the untidy stacks of canvases. "I have here pictures that I painted before

188

the war in Kaunas, that I took with me in the war to Germany, and so to the camps, and after here to Banbury, because I thought they were good pictures, ver' good, that would show me the great artist in Australia. But now, these pictures do not please me; they are strained, too much complicated, too much technique, too little to be said. You may rest now . . ."

He stepped back and looked critically at the picture. "Too much art," he said. "Art all the day and night; I think my mind was sour. Perhaps it is better to work on the railway for a living, and come to art for pleasure, not so often." He stood with half-closed eyes staring at the portrait. "This will be a good picture," he said thoughtfully. "This will be better than the paintings that I brought from Germany."

In these sittings Jennifer could sit quietly with her own thoughts, and these were mostly on the Howqua valley and the memory of her day there with Carl Zlinter. The Howqua had a dream-like quality of unreality for her, a place so beautiful and so remote from anything she had encountered in her life before that it fell into the category of a fairy story in her mind, a fairy story with a Prince Charming, moreover. Her life up to that point had been in the somewhat bleak settings of Leicester and the London suburbs. These places were more real to her than Melbourne or Merrijig; she knew what to do with a red London bus, but it was still unreal to her that a horse should be used in this country as a normal means of locomotion. Stranger still was the story of Charlie Zlinter and his dog, whose tombstone she had felt and touched, who had driven his bullock team daily from this town named in the memory of Banbury near Oxford only fifty years ago, and who had drunk and loved in a town called Howqua that had vanished absolutely from the face of the earth, and had left only beauty in the place where it had been. This sort of thing didn't happen in Leicester or Blackheath, and as she sat quiet in the little railway coach, while the Lithuanian platelayer painted her portrait, she wondered which of her two lives was real and which was a dream.

Carl Zlinter rang up from Lamirra on Wednesday evening to ask Jack Dorman if he could borrow the utility on Saturday to go to Woods Point with Jenny. "That'll be right," the grazier said. "She told us you wanted to go over there. Want to speak to her?"

When she came to the telephone she was in a slight flutter of eagerness to speak to him, which annoyed her slightly because the telephone was in the kitchen and everyone was there. She made the arrangements with him about lunch and time of starting with elaborate casualness that deceived nobody. Then he said, "There is one other thing. I have now got a map of the town of Howqua."

"Where on earth did you get that from, Carl?"

"It was in the Shire Hall, at Banbury," he said. "It belongs to the Lands Department. I went in there yesterday to see if perhaps there would be anything, and there I found this map. It is very yellow and torn, and they would not allow me to take it away, and so I went out and bought paper and I made a tracing of it."

"Does it show where the houses were?"

"It shows all the streets and all the town allotments with their numbers," he said. "It does not tell us where Charlie Zlinter lived or anybody else, because there are numbers only on the map, street names and the numbers of the lots. It is ver' interesting."

She said, "Could you tell from it where any particular house was?"

"I think it would be possible," he said. "There are marks on it which a surveyor will understand, but I do not; these I have copied with great care. I will ask Mr. Forrest before Saturday if he can tell me what they mean, and how to find the place where any house was from the map."

"That's fine, Carl. I'm awfully glad."

"What have you been doing all the week?"

"I've been sitting for my portrait—to Mr. Shulkin."

"For your portrait?"

"Yes. He's painting me. I'll tell you about it when we meet."

"I shall want to see this portrait," he said. "I must visit Stanilaus."

She laughed. "You're not to till it's finished—if then. Good-night, Carl."

"Good-night, Jenny. I will not promise anything."

He came to the homestead on Saturday morning with his grill and his steaks in newspaper, having got a lift down from Lamirra on a truck. She was ready for him and the Chev was full of petrol; he made a half-hearted attempt to reckon with Jack Dorman, who said, "Aw, forget it. It all goes on the farm, 'n comes off tax." So they started for Woods Point before the day grew hot.

Jane watched the Chev go off across the paddocks to the road. "Well, there they go again," she said. "I don't know what her father's going to say, or her mother."

"From the looks of it, her mother won't be saying anything before so long," he remarked.

"That's right," she replied. "It doesn't look too good, from the letters she's been getting."

Neither of them had ever met Jennifer's mother, and they could discuss the matter dispassionately. "What'll she do if she dies?" he asked.

"I think she might go back," Jane said. "She's very fond of her father, and he'd be alone."

"She don't want to get too deep with this chap Zlinter, then."

She stood silent for a minute. "It's her business," she said at last. "She's got her head screwed on right. We can't interfere."

As Jennifer got back into the Chev after closing the last gate, and as they started on the road for Banbury and Woods Point, Carl Zlinter said, "Will you mind if I drive over the police sergeant when we go through Banbury?"

"Not specially," said Jennifer. "It might make trouble, though, because you haven't got a licence."

"Does one need a licence to drive over police sergeants in this country?"

"My word," she said. It was easy to fall into the idiom. "You can go to prison if you do that without a licence. Why do you want to drive over the sergeant, anyway?"

"It was not necessary to have that inquest at all," he said. "He knew the answer before he started anything. It was stupid, and it caused me very much worry, so I could not sleep the night before."

"There were a lot of things that could have stopped you sleeping the night before," she observed. "Too much steak, for one thing."

"It was the inquest," he asserted. "I was ver' worried, for that they would send me back to Germany. I could not sleep. If we see that police sergeant we will not run over him, because I have not got a licence, but we will give him a very big fright. Now we will go and see Stanislaus Shulkin on our way to Woods Point and we will see what he has been up to."

She turned to him, "Carl, you're not to go and see that picture. It's not finished, and it's nothing like me, anyway."

"So," he said. "If it is a bad picture of you then I will cut it with my knife so it cannot be finished. If it is good, then I will let him finish it and I will hang it in the house that I shall build in Howqua City."

She burst into laughter. "You *are* a fool. You can't have it; it's for Jane Dorman. He's painting three pictures for her to choose from." She told him what was happening.

"All right," he said. "We will now go and see this picture, and decide what is to be done with it." She could not move him from that, and she did not try very hard.

His mood was different from anything that she had known in him before. Hitherto she had known him as a surgeon faced with a difficult and delicate task in improvised conditions, and as a man with the threat of a manslaughter charge on his mind. She was now seeing a totally different Carl Zlinter, a man on his way out from years of life in camps, a man beginning to enjoy life who was unused to joy, a man laughing clumsily because he was unused to laughter. She did not know quite what to make of him.

Mr. Shulkin was working in his garden; he stopped and came to the gate as the utility drew up. "So," he said, "the model has arrived. You have come to make another sitting?"

"She has not," said Carl Zlinter. "She has come to ride in this utility with me to Woods Point. She has told me that you make a portrait of her, and I have come to see if it is good enough."

Mr. Shulkin said, "I do not think that any portrait will be good enough when you have her with you. A portrait is for when you cannot see the sitter. But you may see if you want. It is not finished."

He led the way into the railway coach and they followed him.

191

The picture stood upon the easel. He had given more space to the background than is usual in modern portraits, using rather a wide canvas and placing the head to one side. For the background he had chosen a part of Leonora station, with the Delatite River, the paddocks, and the wooded slopes behind. He had made it a spring scene when the tips of the gum trees take a tinge of orange-red, so that the colour motif of the Leonora scene repeated the bronze lights in Jennifer's hair.

"It is not a portrait," said Mr. Shulkin, as they looked at it in silence. "It is an order for a beautiful picture with quiet colour and good drawing, that the lady will like to live with. The portrait is nothing, nothing, only a detail of the whole picture—you understand? A bunch of flowers would have done as well, but they would not have had the fine drawing and the delicate colour of the head of this young lady."

"It is a very lovely thing," the Czech said quietly. The artist had painted Jennifer in profile with lips slightly parted and a faint colour in her cheeks as if a blush was just beginning; as he had said, the portrait was subordinated to the colour values of the picture as a whole, and so became the more impressive by a type of understatement.

"It's going to be a very lovely picture," the girl said, "but I don't believe I really look like that a bit."

"I have seen you look like that," the surgeon said. "I have seen you look like that many times. It is very true of you." The girl coloured a little, and looked very like the portrait.

Zlinter turned to the artist. "You must do something else for Mrs. Dorman," he said. "She has not seen this, no? I will buy this one."

Mr. Shulkin smiled broadly. "That is not possible. I have three pictures that I must paint for Mrs. Dorman, and she will choose the one that she will like the best. Already she has paid me for the materials for all the three, so this canvas is her canvas and this paint is her paint. If she will not choose this picture and she wishes to have one of the other two, or none at all, then I will sell you this picture if you can pay enough money. I am ver' expensive. I gain more than ten pounds each week on the railway; I am ver' expensive man." He grinned.

Carl Zlinter said, "You must now paint two more pictures, very, very good, much better than this one, so she will choose one of those. Perhaps you need not show her this one at all."

Jennifer laughed. "She knows all about it, Carl; I told her. You don't want it, anyway. What on earth would you do with it?"

"I would sell it to a manufacturer of soap," he said, "because it is so beautiful." He paused. "Or, I would hang it in the house that I am going to build in the Howqua. I do not know."

"It would be better to sell it to the manufacturer of soap," the artist said, "because then you would have money to build the house.

But I do not think that I shall sell it to you if that is what you are going to do with it."

Jennifer said, "What about me? Don't I have any say in this?"

Carl Zlinter said, "You will get the soap."

"What soap?"

"The soap that the manufacturer will give so you will say it is the best soap in the world, and he can put it underneath the picture."

"Don't sell it to him, Stan," she said. "I don't want it used as a soap advertisement."

"I would not sell it to him in any case," the artist replied. "He is a bad man and not serious, only when he cuts off people's legs and they die. I do not know why you go out with him."

They left him presently, and got going on the road to Jamieson and Woods Point. It ran through pastoral, station country to begin with, an undulating, well-watered country in a bowl of hills, the pastures becoming dried and brown in the hot sun. The road climbed slowly and became more wooded; presently they came upon a considerable river, a wide river running in a series of pools and shallows on a rocky bottom.

Carl Zlinter said, "My word. I did not know that there was such a river here."

He stopped the car by the roadside and they got out and looked at it; it ran completely deserted, winding through the woods and pastures, rippling in white foam at the little falls and rapids, with deep brown pools between. "It must be full of fish, this river," the Czech said.

"What is it, Carl? What's it's name?"

"I do not know. I think that it is perhaps the Goulburn. But I did not know the Goulburn was like this."

The English girl asked, "Can anybody go and fish there, Carl, or is the fishing preserved?"

He shook his head. "It is all free fishing here. There must be very many fish in this river. I will come and fish here one day."

"There doesn't seem to be anybody fishing," the girl said.

"It is not like Europe, this," he replied. "Here, in this country, there are not very many people, and so not many fishermen. It is another reason why I am happy to be here."

She turned to him. "You're very fond of Australia, aren't you, Carl?"

"I have lived here fifteen months," he said, "and I have seen only this little corner of this big country. But now I should be sorry to live anywhere else." He glanced at her. "Are you happy to be here, and not in England?"

"I think so, Carl," she said slowly. "There are so many things, though. I've lived in towns most of my life—one does in England—and all this is strange to me. I like it. I think I'd rather live here than in an English town." She hesitated. "One has so many ties with England, and it's so far away. I've been getting air-mail letters from my father all this week about my mother. She's very ill. I've been wishing I was back in England all this week."

"I am so sorry," he said. "What is it that is the matter with her?"

She told him all about it, standing there with him above the Goulburn River; it was a relief to be able to tell somebody everything she thought. "They've been a very self-contained pair, my father and mother," she said. "I had two brothers, but they were both killed in the war, one in a corvette and one in Bomber Command. Daddy and Mummy had so many interests that they shared, I was always a bit out of it after the war. That's why I didn't mind going away from home to work in London, and why it didn't seem too bad to come out here. But now I wish I was back. I don't know who'll be running the house for Daddy, or how he can be getting on. If Mummy were to die, I think I'd have to go back. I don't know what Daddy would do, all on his own."

"It would be very sad for me, if you went back," he said quietly.

"It would be very sad for me, too," she replied. "I'd rather stay here." She turned to the car. "Perhaps it won't happen. The winter will be getting on now, back in England, and that'll make it better for Mummy."

They drove on through a tiny village and crossed the river, and went on for ten miles or so through the woods along the valley by the river. The sun was hot and the trees made dappled overhung patches of shade upon the road, and the same brilliant parrots with crimson bodies and blue wings flew in the woods ahead of them. They were delighted with the day and with the old car and with each other; twice they stopped to walk down to the river and look at its desolate grandeur, and they hardly stopped talking all the time. They laughed a great deal about silly little things that were not really funny, but they wanted to laugh.

They passed Gaffney's Creek and a small gold mine shut down for the week-end, the first that Jennifer had ever seen. From there the road wound upwards through the woods, till they came out at the summit of a col, the road going down into another valley ahead of them.

"This is Frenchman's Gap, I think," said Carl. "Woods Point will be about five miles further on. Shall we have our lunch here, with the gold grill?"

She laughed again at the little joke. "It's very lovely here." She got out of the car and looked around. "Can we do a grill here, Carl, without setting the whole country grilling too?"

"There is here a fireplace," he said, and he showed her the blackened stones. "I think it will be safe if we shall make it here."

He set to work to grill the steaks while Jennifer laid out the rest of the meal on a clean cloth upon the grass in the shade of a gum tree. "Carl," she said, "tell me a bit more about Mary Nolan. Was she Irish?"

"I think perhaps she was," he said. "There were very many Irish people in this country at that time."

She paused, considering her words. "Did she have a job in Howqua, or how did she come to be there? I mean, a job apart from being a naughty girl?"

He laughed, and she laughed with him. "I do not know if she had another job," he said. "I have thought perhaps that she came to Howqua as a barmaid in the hotel, or perhaps she was to help one of the women with the children. I do not know, and I do not know how she happened to be living on the other side of the river. Perhaps she will tell us today."

"Perhaps she won't," the girl said. "I think we're going to have a job to get anything out of her at all."

They cooked the steaks and ate them hot from the grill, sitting on the warm grass in the shade of the trees, looking out over the blue, misty lines of hills. "It's so different here to anything I've ever known, Carl," she said once. "People with so much money that they don't have to worry, who can afford to be generous if they want to, and all made honestly in farming. In this lovely, empty place. I've always lived where people were hard up, even good, clever people. It's all so different here to England."

He nodded. "I know. I feel like that also. I live in a camp and I must live so for nine months more, but sometimes I wake up early in the morning, and I look around, and I think of all the fine things in this country that I can do in nine months, the things that I could never do in Europe." He looked at her a little shyly. "I have a calendar upon the wall," he said, "and each day when I get up out of bed I cross off one day with a pencil, the day that has gone."

Her eyes moistened a little. "Oh, Carl! Do you do that?"

He nodded. "It is a stupid thing, but that is what I do. In nine months now I shall be out of the camp life, out of it for ever, a free man."

"When were you a free man last, Carl?" she asked. "When did you last live a normal life, with a home?"

"In 1938," he said. "I lived then at my father's house, just after I became a doctor. Then came the Germans, and I joined the army."

"It's a terribly long time," she said softly. And then she looked up at him, and smiled, and said, "Were you ever married?"

He smiled back at her. "No," he said. "I was never married. I was spared that complication."

She said quietly, "You must have been very lonely, all those years."

"I do not think so, not in the war years," he said. "So much was happening, so much of grief and work and pain, I think that one had no time to be lonely. After the war, in the camps, in Germany," he shrugged his shoulders, "perhaps one had got out of the habit of being lonely. Perhaps in Germany, where life was very hard, there was so little happiness in married life that one did not want it. I do

195

not know. It is only in the last year, since I came here to Australia and I have seen men living happily with wives and with their children, and with no war in the country—it is only since the last year I have been a little lonely in the evenings sometimes."

She said, "So then you go out and catch a fish."

He laughed. "Yes, then I go out and catch a fish." He got to his feet and began to put the remains of their lunch together. "Now we must go down to Woods Point and catch Mary Nolan."

They got back into the utility and ran down the long road into the valley before them. Woods Point proved to be a little town of wooden houses at the bottom of a valley, rather a straggling little town that had been wiped out from time to time with forest fires and so was built of fairly modern houses; these houses stood about amongst the trees around two working gold mines. There was not very much of it, a hotel, a bakery, a store or two strung haphazard along the main street; there seemed to be no reason why anyone should live there but for the gold mines.

Carl Zlinter stopped the Chev at the hotel and went in to ask where old Mrs. Williams lived. He came out presently and got back into the car. "It is just a little way," he said. "We must turn round."

Jennifer said, "You've had a beer."

"I have found where Mary Nolan, Mrs. Williams lives," he said. "It is not right for you to say such things."

"It's not fair," she said.

"It is a part of the woman's burden in this country," he remarked, "that they are not allowed in the bar."

They left the utility by the roadside three hundred yards back and walked down a grassy lane, asked at a house, and were directed to the right one. A middle-aged, sandy-haired woman came to the door. Carl Zlinter asked, "Does Mrs. Williams live here, please?"

She looked at him with interest at his accent. "That's right," she said. "Auntie lives here with us."

"Would it be possible if we should have a talk with her a little?" he asked. "My name is Carl Zlinter, and this is Miss Morton."

To Jennifer the woman said, "How d'you do? I'm Elsie Stevens— Mrs. Stevens. What d'you want to talk to Auntie about? She's pretty old, you know, and she don't have to do much talking to get tired."

Jennifer said, "We've come over from Leonora station, out past Banbury. Mr. Zlinter works in the timber at Lamirra. He's trying to find out about a relation of his who was in the Howqua in the old days."

"Leonora?" The woman wrinkled her brows. "Would that be Jack Dorman's place?"

"That's right."

"Oh, I know." With contact established she became more friendly. "Did you say it was about the old days in the Howqua?"

196

"That's right," the Czech said. "There was a man there of the same name as me, who died and was drowned and buried there; I have seen the stone at the grave with his name carved upon it. It is the same name as my own, Charlie Zlinter. I was told that your aunt was living in the Howqua at that time, and I have thought that she could tell me about him, who he was and where he lived."

The woman stood in silence for a minute, "Well, I don't know, I'm sure," she said at last. "Auntie was in the Howqua for a bit before she came here, but she wouldn't remember anything about that now."

Jennifer said, "Could we have a talk with her, do you think? Just for a few minutes? We don't want to tire her."

The woman said slowly, "Well, I don't mind asking her. What did you say the name was?"

"Charlie Zlinter."

The woman stood staring at him for a moment, while the elusive memory of a local jingle scattered through her mind. "I've heard that name before . . ." She paused. "Some rhyme about a dog?"

"That's right," said Jennifer.

"Charlie Zlinter and his heeler hound
Fell into the Howqua and unhappily drowned . . ."

"That's right," the woman said. "We used to say that when we was children, at the Sunday school. Just wait here a minute, and I'll ask Auntie." She turned to Zlinter. "Did you say your name was Charlie Zlinter?"

"That's right."

"Like in the rhyme?"

"That's right. I am called Charlie Zlinter."

"Well, isn't that funny? Just wait here a minute, and I'll tell Auntie."

She went indoors, and they stood in the lane, waiting. Presently she came out again to them. "Auntie wants to see you," she said. She hesitated. "You mustn't mind her if she talks a bit queer. And I wouldn't stay very long."

They went into the living-room of the house. A very old woman was sitting in a chair before the fireplace with a shawl round her shoulders; she wore rather shabby black clothes. Her features were lean and long, and she was wearing steel-rimmed spectacles; her white hair was parted in the middle and done in a bun behind her head; there was still plenty of it. Her niece said to her, "These are the people come to see you, Auntie. This is Charlie Zlinter."

The old woman raised her head and looked at them. "He is not," she said, and there was still a touch of the Irish in her voice. "He's nothing like Charlie Zlinter."

The Czech said, "My name, it is Charlie Zlinter like the man who lived in the Howqua and was drowned there, with his dog." She

197

turned towards him, and fixed him with her eyes. "I do not know if he was a relation of me or not."

She said, "You talk like him. Where do you come from, the same place as he did?"

"That is right," he said. "I come from the same town in Bohemia."

"Who's this?" she asked, indicating Jennifer. "Your wife?"

"No," he said. "Just a friend."

She snorted a little, as if in disbelief. "I wouldn't know anything about Charlie Zlinter, no more than any of the other men," she said. "He got drowned, That's all I know."

Carl Zlinter said, "I am trying to find out if he left any papers or books, or any letters from his family in Pilsen, or anything to tell us who he was. I think you are the only person in this district who was living in the Howqua at that time, and I have wondered if you could tell us anything, if you remember."

The old woman said testily, "I knew nothing about that man, or any other of those men. Why should I know anything about his papers? There was a man there with that name; that's all I know about it."

"Do you remember what happened after he was drowned, perhaps?" the Czech asked. "Do you remember what happened to the things that were in his house? Who took them?"

The old woman made a gesture of irritation. "Sure, how would I be knowing that, after all these years?" she said. "There was many a man went away or died or was away out of it for one reason or another, and there was no keeping track of them all, if a body had wanted to. If a body had wanted to," she repeated.

Carl Zlinter asked, "Can you remember where he lived? Would you know where he had his house?"

"I tell you, I know nothing about the man at all," the old woman said angrily. "He was drunk and he got drowned, that's all I know. How would I be knowing where he lived, or what happened to his gear? I was a decent girl." She stared at them fiercely.

"There, Auntie, there," said her niece. "He didn't mean nothing. He just wants to know if you remember anything about this man."

The old woman sank back into her chair. "I don't know nothing about Charlie Zlinter," she said sullenly.

There was an awkward silence. Jennifer looked up at Carl Zlinter and he nodded slightly; it was developing as they had thought. He said, "I am so sorry—when I heard that you had been in Howqua at that time I thought perhaps you might remember something." He moved towards the door. "I have now to take my utility to the garage before we start back; we have burst a tyre. May I leave Miss Morton here for half an hour till I have had that repaired?"

Mrs. Stevens said, "Oh, that'll be right. I was just going to give Auntie a cup of tea. You'll have a cup of tea with us while you're waiting, Miss?"

"Jenny's the name," the girl said. "I'd love a cup. Can I do anything?" Carl Zlinter slid out of the door behind her.

"Oh, it's nothing." She bent to the old woman. "You'd like a cup of tea, Auntie?" she asked rather loudly. "Jenny's going to have a cup of tea with us—I'm just going to put the kettle on."

"I could drink a cup of tea," the old lady said. Her niece disappeared into the next room, and Jennifer squatted down on a stool before her. "I went over to the Howqua last week," she said. "There's nothing left there now, only the gum trees."

"You went into the Howqua?"

The girl nodded. "We drove the utility up to the top of the ridge, and then walked the last two miles down into the valley."

"Eh, you'd never drive down that track in a motor-car. I heard of one man tried it once, but they had to get a team to pull him out again. Bullocks they used to use when I was there, eight bullocks to a wagon, in and out of Banbury. That was before the days of motor-cars." She peered about her. "What's happened to that man who was here just now, the foreigner?"

"He's gone to take the car to the garage," Jennifer said. "We had a flat tyre coming here; we had to change the wheel. He's gone to get it mended before we start back."

There was a long silence. The old woman sat staring at the paper flowers in the fireplace, in red and silver tinsel. "What did he say his name was?"

"Charlie Zlinter," the girl said. "It's just a coincidence, I think; he's got the same name as a man who used to work in the Howqua."

The old woman shook her head. "He never worked in the Howqua. He was a bullocky; used to drive a bullock team between Banbury and the Howqua." She paused for a while. "He talked like this fellow. Foreign, he was."

There was another long silence; from the next room Jennifer could hear the rattling of cups. "You're a pretty girl," the old woman said at last. "Too pretty for the likes of him. Not getting up to any mischief with him, are you?"

The girl said, "No," and smiled, colouring a little.

"Well, mind you don't. Don't you let him do nothing till he's married you. These bullock drivers, and the miners too, they'll say anything, and then in the end you find they're married already with a wife and three children out behind some place, and you to have a fourth."

Mrs. Stevens came back with the tea and saved Jennifer from the necessity of answering that one. When the old lady was sipping her cup the girl brought her gently back to the subject by asking, "Did the Charlie Zlinter that you knew look like this one?"

"Ah, Charlie Zlinter was a fine, upstanding man," she replied, "twice the man of this one. He was a great strong man with black curly hair, strong enough to break the neck of an ox, and he with his bare hands alone. Broader in the shoulders he was, than this

199

man of yours, and a champion at anything that he'd be setting his hand to. A grand, powerful man." She sat sipping her tea and staring at the tinsel flowers, lost in memories. "There was a slab of stone before the fireplace in his cabin," she said, "the way the ashes would be kept back in the fire. A slab as big as that . . . four hundredweight, he said it weighed. I've seen him lift that slab with his two hands, and carry it away. Sure, there wasn't a man in How-qua could have done the like of that. Anvils, barrels of beer, loads no two men could carry, he'd just lift them down from off the wagon to where they had to be, and he whistling a tune and thinking nothing of it."

"It must have been a terrible loss when he got drowned." the girl said.

"Ah," said the old woman, "it was a sad, sad day, and Howqua was never the same after. The mine closed down, and folks began to drift away, because with the mine shut and the gold finished there was nothing left to stay for. By the time I went out there was every other cabin in the place empty, and folks just walking in and out picking over stuff that had been left behind for that it wasn't worth the charge to take it out to Banbury upon the wagons. It's a sad, desolate thing to see houses left that way, and nobody to live in them. I did hear that the whole of Howqua came to be like that, with nobody to walk along the streets but wallabies and rabbits. That was before the fire came through the valley."

"Which cabin did Charlie Zlinter live in?" the girl asked.

"Number fifteen, Buller Street," the old woman said. "It was just the one room with a fireplace and a bed, and a bench where he'd sit working at the bullock harness, sewing with a palm upon his hand like a sailor. He was a sailor one time, so he told me; that's how he came to be in Australia. He jumped his ship, and came up to the gold-fields, but he found that he could make more money with the wagon."

"Did he make much money?"

"My word, the bullockies made money," the old woman said, "more than the miners or prospectors ever did. Everything that came to Howqua had to pass through their hands, and they charged terrible for bringing it. But they were generous as well, ah, Charlie Zlinter was an openhanded man, a kind, generous man. Many's the thing he used to bring me from the town—a new saucepan from England, or an alarm clock from America, or maybe a length of dress material if it was Christmas—anything he'd see that would take his fancy he'd bring out of town for me, as a surprise, for that I'd never be thinking. Ah, he was a grand kind man."

"You must have been great friends," the girl said.

"Better than we should have been, maybe," Mary Nolan said quietly. "But there, it didn't seem to be no harm at the time, and now it's a long while ago."

There was a silence after she said that. Jennifer sat at her feet hoping that Carl Zlinter wouldn't come back and break the spell; she felt now that she could ask this old woman anything. She said presently, "Did anybody live in Charlie Zlinter's cabin after he died?"

The old head shook. "There was people leaving Howqua every day from that time on. Nobody lived in it before I left. There were houses to spare, the way you'd see doors open all along the street."

"You're sure of that, are you—that no one lived in it?"

"Nobody lived in it before I went," she said. "I would have known about it if they had."

"What happened to all his things? I mean, what *did* happen in the Howqua when a man died like that? Did the police take them?"

Mary Nolan set her cup down. "There was a policeman, Mike Lynch was his name, from County Kerry; he lodged about the middle of Jubilee Parade, but I'm not sure if he was there. I don't think there was anything in the cabin to trouble with. Early in the morning, the day that he was found in the river, I went to his cabin in Buller Street, because he was back from Banbury. I knew that because I heard him in the dark night singing outside the hotel that Peter Slim kept, and I knew that he was having drink taken. And I thought maybe he'd fallen asleep in his clothes or done himself an injury in the cabin, and so I went out and went to his cabin on the far side of the water before it was light, the way the neighbours wouldn't see me go. I had done that before sometimes, and cleaned him up and made him breakfast, and taken his clothes home to wash, very early in the morning, so nobody would know. But Glory be to God, the man was dead already and I crossed the bridge that he had fallen from, and never knew."

Jennifer said, "Did he leave any papers or books in the cabin, Mrs. Williams? Can you remember anything like that?"

"Never a book," she said. "There wouldn't have been many books in Howqua at that time. Charlie was no scholar, but he could read labels and that—not the longer words. He did have papers of some sort with him, although he never showed me. He kept them all locked up in a tin box he called his ditty box, not very big."

The girl asked, "What happened to the box after he was dead? Can you remember that?"

"It wasn't there," said Mary Nolan. "I remember looking for it special when I found he wasn't in the cabin, and his door left open, because I knew he set store by it. Sometimes it stood on a little kind of ledge he'd made in the earth chimney, and other times it wouldn't be there at all. So when I went into the cabin I looked, but the box was away out of it, and then I looked around a little but I didn't see it. I didn't give much heed to it, because it wasn't always there. I wouldn't know what happened to that at all."

"Could he have left it in Banbury?"

"He might. I wouldn't know at all. It could be that he had it with him when he fell into the river."

"He had the dog in his arms," said Jennifer. "He wouldn't have gone to cross the river with the dog *and* the box too, would he?"

"He was a wild, reckless boy when he had drink taken," Mary Nolan said. "But there, he had a way with him and a body could deny him nothing. I would not say anything of what he might have done when he had drink taken."

"What would have happened to the rest of his things?" the girl asked. "Who looked after those?"

"Sure, and there wasn't very much," the old lady said. "He was buried in his Sunday suit, they told me. I never went near, because there had been tongues wagging in the Howqua about him and me, and I knew that if any of the women spoke against me I would have flown out at them, and that I would not do at Charlie's burying. So I stayed in my own cabin all the while, but they told me he was buried in his Sunday clothes. There would have been some working clothes, maybe, but nothing of value, and his wagon and the bullocks. There was a Scots boy worked for him, Jock Robertson; I think he took the wagon and the team. When the working clothes and the harness were gone from the cabin there wouldn't have been much left, and what there was nobody would want, for all the folks were starting to leave about that time." She stared at the tinsel flowers in the grate. "I looked into the cabin once, and the bedclothes were still upon the bed, but a possum or a rat had nested there, and the bucket still half full of water, and a loaf of bread still in the cupboard, all gone green with mould." She shivered a little, and drew the shawl more closely round her. "It's not good to go back afterwards to places where there has been happiness," she said. "It tears at your heart. I never went back again, and soon after that I left the Howqua myself. I'd say the cabin stayed like that until the fire came through."

The girl took one of the old hands and held it in her own. "You must have loved him very much," she said.

"Whisht," said the old woman, "there's a word that you must never use until there's marrying between you, and Charlie Zlinter was a married man already in his own country. He was a kind, gracious man and I looked after him when he would let me; that's all there was between us, child. This foreigner that brought you here today and has the same name, is he a married man?"

"No," said Jennifer. "I asked him that."

"Maybe you'll be luckier than I was," Mary Nolan said. "Maybe he's telling you the truth of it. The other Charlie Zlinter never told me any lies."

They sat in silence for a time. The old woman was tiring, and it was evidently nearly time to go. "One last question," Jennifer said. "Did Charlie Zlinter ever tell you anything about his wife— the wife he had in his own country?"

Mary Nolan shook her head. "He wouldn't be after telling me the like of that."

The girl stayed ten minutes longer for politeness; then she said that she would have to go and see how Zlinter was getting on with the car, or they would be late in getting home. She said good-bye to the old woman; Elsie Stevens stepped outside the door with her.

"She had a nice talk with you," she said. "I haven't seen her so bright for a long time."

"I hope I haven't made her too tired," the girl said.

"Oh, no. I think it does old people good to have a talk about old times, now and then. It comes easy to them. Did she tell you what you wanted to know?"

Jennifer shook her head. "She couldn't tell us anything very much—except where he lived. She did tell us that. But she didn't know anything about him, really."

"Ah, well, it isn't easy after all these years."

She said good-bye to Mrs. Stevens and walked up the lane to the utility; Carl Zlinter was sitting there in it, smoking. "She got talking when you went away, Carl," she said. "She told me a lot of things, but I don't know that any of it's much good to you."

"Shall we drive out of town, and then stop, and you can tell me what she said?"

"Let's do that. Let's go back and stop somewhere by that river, and I'll tell you all I can remember."

They drove back over the col where they had lunched, and down to Gaffney's Creek and to the Goulburn River; presently they parked the car at a place where the river ran near the road, and walked across a strip of pasture to a bend. As they went she told him all about it. "She didn't know much really that you didn't know already, Carl," she said. "There were papers in a box, a tin box, but she doesn't know what happened to that, or what was in it." She told him what she had heard from the old woman. "She did look for it particularly that morning, but it wasn't there."

"She didn't know of any other place he might have put it?"

The girl shook her head. "She thought he might have had it with him when he fell into the river—in that case, it'ld be at the bottom of the Howqua." They walked on for a few steps in silence. "She was so sweet," Jennifer said quietly, "the way she went out very early to the cabin to find where he was and clean him up. She said she often did that."

"She must have been very much in love with him, to do that for a drunken man."

"I think she was," the girl said. "Yes, I think she was."

They came to the rocky edge of the river and sat down on a boulder in the shade to watch the water and to talk. The water made a little lilting noise from the run at the end of the pool, a cockatoo screeched now and then in the distance, and the air was fragrant with the clean scent of the gum trees in the summer sun. "She said he lived at Number Fifteen, Buller Street," Jennifer told him. "Is that enough to tell you where the cabin was?"

He took a folded paper from his breast pocket, and began to spread it out. "What's that?" she asked.

"It is the township plan that I copied in the Shire Hall," he said. He stood up, and spread it on the flat boulder that they had been sitting on; she helped him to hold the corners down. The paper was dazzling in the bright sun. He moved his finger down the plan. "Here is Buller Street," he said. "Here is Fifteen, the number on the block. I think perhaps this was the place."

She bent to look at the faint pencil lines with him, her head very close to his own. Her hair brushed his cheek and he could smell the fragrance of her skin. "This is Fifteen," he said, a little unsteadily. "The cabin must have been on this allotment."

"Could you find the actual place on the ground from this map, Carl? Is there anything left there now to show, that's marked upon this map? She stood up, and moved a little away from him; it was difficult for her, also, to be quite so close.

"I think that we could find the place from this," he said. "Here, this solid marking, this must be the Buller Arms Hotel, and that still shows upon the ground a little. This map is to the scale of two chains to each inch. Perhaps there are other markings left, that Billy Slim will know. I think it will be possible to measure out upon the ground, and find this Block Fifteen in Buller Street."

"When are you going to do that?"

"I would like to do it tomorrow," he said. "Would you come with me once more to the Howqua tomorrow?"

She looked at him with laughing eyes. "I don't know what the Dormans'll think if I keep going out with you like this, Carl."

He smiled back at her. "Does that matter very much? You will be going to Melbourne very soon to start your work, and then we shall not go out any more, and the Dormans will be happy."

"I know." Mary Nolan had told her that the other Charlie Zlinter had a way with him, and a body could deny him nothing. Perhaps these Charlie Zlinters were all the same. "Of course I'll come with you, Charlie," she said, unthinking.

He laughed, and met her eyes, still laughing. "I am not Charlie Zlinter," he said. "I am Carl, and you are not Mary Nolan. That was fifty years ago. We are much more respectable people than that."

She laughed with him, flushing a little. "I don't know why I said that. I've been talking about Charlie Zlinter all the afternoon, I suppose."

"I do not think it is a compliment," he said. "Charlie Zlinter was a very bad, drunken man, and he was a bullock driver."

She looked up and met his eyes, still teasing her a little. "Well, what about you?" she asked. "You're a very bad man, and a lumberman. I don't see much difference."

"I am offended," he announced. "A bullock driver is much lower in the social scale than a lumberman. I would not say that you were like to Mary Nolan. I would not be so rude."

"I hope you wouldn't."

There was a pause; he looked from her across at the little rapids of the river, at the smooth water running to the stones. Then he turned to her again, smiling. "I might have said it," he remarked. "Mary Nolan was kind to a man who was very far from his own home. I might quite well have said that you were like to Mary Nolan."

She did not answer that, but dropped her eyes and picked a little piece of clover in the grass that she was sitting on. "Also," he said, "I think that Charlie Zlinter, although he was not a very good man —he was in love with Mary Nolan. I think perhaps that is another likeness."

"Lonely people often think that they're in love, when they aren't really," she said quietly. "It must take a long time to be sure you're properly in love with anybody, and not just lonely."

"Of course." He reached out and took her hand and held it in his own hard brown one. "Will we be going to the Howqua to-morrow?" he asked.

She smiled at him. "If you want to, Carl." More and more like Mary Nolan, she thought, but she could deny him nothing. "If you're quite sure that it's safe for a girl so like to Mary Nolan to go back into the Howqua."

"It is very safe," he told her. "There is no Charlie here, only a Carl. No bullock driver, only an unregistered doctor full of inhibitions and repressions."

She laughed, and withdrew her hand. "I wouldn't put much trust in those," she replied. She got to her feet. "I'd love to come with you tomorrow, Carl," she said. "We'll make it all right with the Dormans, one way or another."

They began to walk back across the paddock to the car, very near to each other but not touching; to ease the tension she began to question him about the house that he wanted to build in the Howqua valley, how big it was to be, what would it be built of, and how would he get the materials in there. He told her that it would be very small and simple, no more than twelve feet long by ten feet wide; he could afford sawn timber for a house of that description and he thought that he could get everything he needed from the sawmill at Lamirra and get a lorry driver to take it up to Jock McDougall's paddock on a Saturday; from there Billy Slim could probably get it down for him on a sledge, or he would borrow a horse and a sledge from Billy and shift it himself. He would roof it with tarred felt sheeting of some sort. He thought that he could build it in the week-ends before winter. It would be very simple inside, with just one built-in bunk and a fireplace and a table. "It is all I need," he said. "Just somewhere to be at the week-ends and to leave fishing rods."

She said, "And you're going to build it on the site of Charlie Zlinter's house?"

"I think so. I do not really think that Charlie Zlinter was related to me, Jenny. There are many Zlinters in Pilsen. It would be pleasant if he was, but anyway, I do not think that we shall ever know. But since there was a man of my name there, if his house was in a pretty place I will build mine where he built his, because we came from the same town. I think it will be pretty; from the map Buller Street ran up the hill not far from the river, and not far from the track that leads down to the crossing now. Perhaps the track itself was Buller Street; perhaps Billy Slim will know. But if it is a pretty place, I will build there."

Jennifer said, "It sounds as if the house you want to build will be just about the same size as Charlie Zlinter's house."

He nodded. "We are very much alike, both living as single men, both working with our hands, not rich men either of us. My needs will be no more than his needs were. I think it may be very like his house."

She thought of Charlie Zlinter's house as Mary Nolan had described it to her when she saw it last, the swinging open door, the pail half full of water, the loaf gone green with mould, and the bedclothes that a possum or a rat had made a nest in. She shivered a little. "I'm not sure that I like the thought of building there," she said. "Perhaps it's an unlucky place."

He felt for her hand, and took it in his own as they walked along together. "We will go and see it tomorrow," he said. "We shall know as soon as we are there if it is a lucky or an unlucky place. I think perhaps it knew great happiness, that place, and if that is true it cannot be unlucky."

They walked up to the road in silence, hand in hand.

At the old Chevrolet they stopped, unwilling to get into it and drive away. The sun was dropping down towards the tops of the hills; it was time that they were making their way home to Leonora. They lingered by the car a little without speaking, and now he was holding both her hands. "It is here that we should say good-bye," he said at last. "I will not stay tonight long at the Dormans." He hesitated. "It is very impertinent and very wrong," he said, "but may I kiss you?"

She smiled up at him, colouring a little. "If you want to, Carl," she said.

He put an arm round her shoulders and they stood locked together by the car for a few minutes. Presently she drew back a little, still standing in his arms, and said softly, "I don't want you to go away with the idea that I'm in love with you, Carl."

He stroked her cheek, and said smiling, "What are we doing this for, then?"

She said, "Because I don't suppose you get a chance to do this very often in the camp. How long is it since you did this to a girl, Carl?"

206

He thought back over his life, holding her in his arms and caressing the soft hair behind her neck. "In 1943—eight years."

"Poor Carl." She drew closer, and kissed him on the lips. "Eight years is a long time."

Presently he released her, and they got into the car and drove back, sitting very close together in the sunset light, through Jamieson and Banbury to Leonora station.

Ten

JACK and Jane Dorman stood on the veranda of their homestead next morning, watching the old utility as Carl Zlinter drove it to the road across the paddocks, with Jennifer beside him. The grazier made a little grimace, and turned away. "She's going to tell him, I suppose," he said.

His wife nodded. "She didn't want to tell him here, with all of us about."

He glanced at her. "You think she's really serious?"

"She's serious, all right," Jane replied. "I must say, I think a lot of her for this. There was never a doubt in her mind about what she ought to do."

Jack Dorman kicked the leg of a deck-chair. "He couldn't have married her," he said. "Anyway, not for years. He's got another nine months to do in the camp for a start, and then another three years as a student if he wants to be a doctor. It's probably all for the best."

Jane went to the door of the kitchen. "Well, there's nothing we can do about it. She's not known him very long—she may forget about him. She'll have a bad time, though."

Jennifer sat quiet by Carl Zlinter as he drove the Chev from the Lamirra road up through the paddocks on the way to Howqua, getting out at each fence to open the gate for him to drive through. She was tired and rather pale, but she had worked with Jane to get a nice lunch ready for him; whatever might have happened, it seemed to her important not to spoil his day. It was the same fine, cloudless summer January weather that they had had all the time that she had been at Leonora, the same thin wisp of smoke curled up from behind the Buller range, the same flocks of white cockatoos shrieked and wheeled in shining clouds from gum tree to gum tree in the paddocks that they drove across.

As they passed from the paddocks into the woods she roused herself, and asked him, "How are you going to find out where the cabin was, Carl?"

He smiled down at her. "I have a surveyor's tape and little wires with coloured marking rags on them," he said. "They are in the back. I have asked Jim Forrest if I might borrow these things for today."

"Those are what you use for measuring out, are they?"

He nodded. "I think we can measure and find where the cabin was. If Billy Slim is there, he will help us."

They drove on up the track to Jock McDougall's paddock, and the crimson and blue parrots flew ahead of them through the woods as they had before, and a wallaby loped off among the trees till it was lost in the dappled sun and shadows of the aisles. Presently they came up to the meadow at the top of the ridge, and parked the car in the shade, and got out. Jennifer stood looking out over the wide view, at the line after line of blue, forest-covered hills merging into the distance in the bright sunlight.

"This must be one of the loveliest places in the world," she said. "This is where I should want a cabin, if I lived in this country."

He smiled at her. "It would be wet and windy and cold up here in the winter," he said, "with deep snow sometimes. It would be more comfortable down in the valley, by the river."

She did not answer, but stood looking out over the blue ripples of the forests, storing her memory. He glanced at her and noticed for the first time that she was pale and drawn, almost haggard. "You are looking tired," he said. "Shall I see if we can drive the Chev down to the river?"

She forced a smile; she must not spoil his day. "I'm all right," she said. "I didn't sleep very well last night, that's all. A walk'll do me good. We'd better not risk getting the Chev stuck, or we might not be allowed to have it again."

They turned to the utility and took their lunch, and the grill, and the surveyor's gear out of the back. He would not let her carry anything. "It is quite all right," he said. "If there is any more argument, I will carry you too."

She laughed. "I'd like to see you try," she said incautiously.

He dropped everything and caught her round the waist and lifted her quickly off the ground. For a moment she rested in his arms, feeling secure for the first time that day; then she put on the mask of flippancy again, and laughed down into his eyes. "All right, you big brute," she said. "Now put me down again. I knew I wasn't going to be safe here with a Charlie Zlinter, in these woods." He put her down, kissed her on the cheek, and released her, flushing and laughing, and bent to pick up the various packages and baskets.

She stood by him, confused. "I wouldn't like to think that this kissing business was developing into a habit," she said.

"It is the usual thing," he assured her. "In my country we kiss everybody good-morning."

"I don't believe that's true," she replied. "And anyway, this is Australia. If you go round kissing every girl you meet good-morning, you'll find yourself in trouble."

"I would not want to kiss every girl I meet good-morning," he said. "Only one." She made a face at him, and they set off together down the track into the Howqua, all care momentarily put aside.

When they got down on to the river flat where the house had been, they left the baskets and parcels at the end of the wire bridge, and crossed to Billy Slim's house on the other side. They found him chopping wood in the shade; he straightened up and greeted them. "Morning, Jenny. Morning, Carl. Come fishing?"

"We have not come to fish," the Czech said. "You remember when last we came here we talked about the town of Howqua, and where Charlie Zlinter lived?"

"That's right. You was talking of buying an allotment."

The Czech said, "I have found out now where Charlie Zlinter lived."

"Where's that?"

"Number Fifteen Buller Street."

The forest ranger scratched his head. "Buller Street," he said. "Somebody once told me where that used to be. . . . Was it up the hill, off Victoria Avenue?"

"I have here a map," said Zlinter. "I found one in the Shire Hall at Banbury, and I have made this copy."

They went into the living-room of the house and spread it out upon the table. "My word," the ranger said. "All the years I've been here, this is the first time I've seen a map of Howqua. That's right, there's Buller Street, there's Victoria Avenue, and there's the river." He studied the map for a minute. "Aw, look," he said. "It must have led up the hill just a little way upstream from the track. Looks like it was the old track down into the town."

Jennifer said, "Perhaps that's why he lived there, because it was on the track out of the town."

"Too right," the ranger said. "That's where a bullocky would want to live."

Carl Zlinter said, "Do you know anything left on the ground from which we could measure, to find where he lived? I have a tape."

"Shouldn't be too difficult," the ranger said. "Let's get across the river and see. I'd like to have a copy of that map some time."

"I will make you one."

Two hours later, two hours that had been spent in measurement and argument over the dim lines on the land and the pencil tracings on the map, they reached agreement. They were standing on the slope of the hill fifty feet or so above the river overlooking the meadow where the town had been. Here there was a small space of flat land, about half the size of a tennis court, in the middle of the woods.

"This must be it," the ranger said. "This'll be where Charlie Zlinter lived."

Jennifer said, "It must have been a much larger house than I thought. Mary Nolan said that it was just a little cabin, of one room."

"Aw, look," the ranger said, "this wouldn't all have been the house. He'd have to have had a place to put the wagon, and maybe a store for hay and that. The house would only be on just a little bit of this flat. If you wanted the exact place, you'd have to dig around a bit. You'd find stumps in the ground, maybe, or else the fireplace."

"I would like to do that," Zlinter said. "If I come over to your place, may I borrow a pick and spade?"

"Sure," said the forest ranger. "Borrow anything you like."

Jennifer walked with them to the bridge. Carl went across with the ranger to the homestead to get pick and spade, and she picked up the lunch basket and carried it back to the forest flat where Charlie Zlinter had lived. She dropped down upon the grass in the thin shade of the gum trees and sat waiting for him to come back with the tools. She was tired, very tired with sorrow and joy too closely mixed, glad for him that he had found so beautiful a place in which to build his fishing hut, sad for herself that she was never going to see it.

He came back to her presently and found that she had laid a cloth upon the grass and put the food out on it. "We'd better not make a fire here, had we, Carl?" she asked. "I wouldn't like to see you start off by setting the forest on fire, and we've got masses of cold meat here that Jane gave us, without the steaks."

He looked around. "I would like to find Charlie Zlinter's fireplace and cook a steak on it, for ceremony," he said.

She smiled. "We'll dig around a bit after lunch, and cook a ceremonial steak."

They ate together on the grassy patch of ground, examining it as they sat and speculating where the cabin had been. Presently Zlinter got up, sandwich in hand, and drove the spade into the vertical hill face, at the end of the plateau furthest from the river. The earth was blackened with soot.

"Here is the chimney," he said quietly. "By making the house so, against the bank, it was more easy for him; the earth bank itself would make the back of the fire, and the heat would keep it solid. What was above could easily be made of wood. In this way he would need no bricks at all."

They discussed this as they sat eating; it seemed reasonable enough. "Will you make your cabin like that, Carl?" she asked.

He thought about it for a minute. "I do not know," he said. "In the winter, when there is no fishing, my cabin may be empty for several months, and then the earth will be wet, and there will be no fire to keep it dry. It might fall in upon the fireplace. I think it will be better if I arrange my cabin differently, and have a brick chimney away from the earth bank, perhaps on that side, over there. I do not think it would be good to build my cabin right against the earth bank, as he did. It would be better to build it here, where we are sitting now, and not use the bank at all. The water might run down and into the cabin when I am away."

She nodded. "Put the wall about three or four feet from the bank," she said. "You don't want to get the other wall too near the outer edge, though. The earth might slide there, mightn't it, with the weight of the walls?"

He measured it with his eye. "It is to be only a little place, no more than twelve feet long," he said. "I have not got enough money for a palace." She laughed. "I think there will be plenty of room. But you are right; the inner wall should be three or four feet from the earth bank, and then there will be room outside the river wall to make a veranda and a bench to sit on and look out over the river, or perhaps a deck-chair."

She smiled. "You've got it all planned out, haven't you?"

He laughed, a little embarrassed. "It is important to me, this, to have a little place that is my own."

"I know," she said. "You must have that, Carl, and you've picked a lovely place for it."

They sat smoking together after they had finished eating, discussing the cabin, where the door was to be, where the fireplace, the window and the bed. Presently they stubbed their cigarettes out carefully and packed away the lunch; they got up and began to investigate the place more closely. Zlinter took the spade and cleared the briars and the undergrowth from the vertical earth face. The sooty, blackened earth extended over about three feet of the face, showing clearly that the fireplace had been there and about centrally disposed upon the end of the flat.

He stood looking at it critically. "The side walls, they would run outwards from the face," he said, "at right angles. Perhaps one was somewhere here." He set to work and began slicing the turf and leaf-mould from the level ground; in a few minutes he was rewarded by a charred stump of rotten wood sticking up out of the soil. They examined it together.

"Here was a wall," he said. He threw off his thin jacket and went on working in shirt and trousers only, and gradually uncovered the remnants of the charred walls, shown mostly by blackened streaks in the top soil. In half an hour he had laid bare two rectangles of blackened soil and charred stumps, and rested, wiping the sweat from his neck and arms.

"It's fascinating, Carl," the girl said. "It's like digging up Pompeii or something. What would this one have been?" She indicated the outer rectangle.

He shrugged his shoulders. "Perhaps a hay-shed, or a stable. No, he could not have put eight bullocks in there. For hay, I think, and harness."

They rested together, looking at what he had uncovered. Presently she asked, "Where will your cabin go now, Carl?"

"I must make a drawing," he said. "I will do that this week, and give an order to Mr. Forrest for the timber and the planking. I think it would be best to have the chimney there, and the door here, opposite."

She shook her head. "It's going to be very draughty. You

won't have a warm corner in the place, if the door's opposite the chimney."

He nodded. "That is true. I want to keep the outer wall for a window, to see the height of the river when I shall get out of bed, to see if I will fish or stay in bed." She laughed. "The door should be on this side, but we will put the chimney here, on the side of the earth bank but four feet away."

"That's like Charlie Zlinter had it, but moved out a bit."

"That is right."

He measured four feet with his eye from the blackened chimney marks on the earth face, and said, "Here will be the new fireplace." He drove his shovel down into the ground, to mark the place for her.

It hit with a metallic clang on stone. "There is rock here," he said in surprise; till then he had encountered nothing but soft earth. He sliced away the leaves and top soil and uncovered a smooth face of rock, level with the surface of the ground.

Jennifer cried, "It's Mary Nolan's stone, Carl!"

"Mary Nolan's stone?"

"She said there was a slab of stone in front of the fireplace in his cabin, to keep the ashes back in the fire. She said it weighed four hundredweight, and he used to lift it up and carry it about to show her how strong he was. This must be it."

He glanced at her. "If it weighs four hundredweight, I do not think that I will pick it up and carry it about to show you how strong I am. I think we will do that another day."

She laughed. "You're no man!"

"That is true," he said. "Nor are you Mary Nolan." He went on clearing away the soil and revealed at last an irregularly-shaped slab of stone about four square feet in area, practically level on the top. A thrust of the spade showed a white residue of ash between it and the earth face. "There was the fire," he said. "It is as she said it was."

"That settles it, anyway," the girl said. "This is Charlie Zlinter's cabin."

He nodded. "This is the cabin. I suppose they used to put saucepans and kettles on that, to keep them warm before the fire."

She wrinkled her brows. "Would there have been a wooden floor?"

"I think so," he said. "I think they would have had a wooden floor, and not just earth. This stone was to prevent the fire from coming forward to burn the floor. I think that is a good idea."

"If you're going to use it again, you'll have to shift it," the girl said. "It's right in the middle of where your fire is to be, now. You'll have to do what Charlie Zlinter did, Carl—pick it up and carry it about."

He nodded. "It will have to be moved." He stood studying it for a moment, and then smiled at her. "I will pick it up and carry it about in my two hands one day when you are not here," he said. "Then you can come and see it in the new place."

She looked up at him. "I shan't be able to do that, Carl," she said quietly.

He glanced at her. "Why not?"

"I'm going away."

"But you will be coming back again in your holidays, to stay with the Dormans?"

She shook her head. "I won't be coming here again, Carl. I'm going home—to England."

He stared at her in consternation. "To England?"

She nodded. "I wanted to have this last day in the Howqua and tell you about it here, not at Leonora with other people about. I've got to go back to England, Carl—at once. I'm going by air on Tuesday, on the Qantas Constellation from Sydney. I've got to leave Leonora tomorrow."

He dropped the shovel, and crossed to her and took her hand. "What is it that has happened, Jenny?" he asked quietly. "Is it something very bad?"

She looked up at him, blinking. "We got a cable last night," she said, "soon after you'd gone. It was from Daddy. My mother died yesterday, Carl—yesterday or the day before—the times are all so muddling." She hesitated. "It means that Daddy's all alone there now. I've got to go." A tear escaped and trickled down her cheek.

He put an arm around her shoulders. "Come and sit down," he said, "and tell me."

He led her to the bank and they sat down together. She was crying in earnest now with the relief from keeping up the strain of a pretence with him. He pulled out his handkerchief and glanced at it doubtfully. "You have a handkerchief, Jenny?" he asked. "This one is a little sweaty." She smiled through her tears and took it; he held her with one arm round her shoulders and wiped her eyes. "I've got one of my own somewhere," she said, but made no effort to find it. "I'm sorry to be such a fool, Carl. I didn't get much sleep last night."

"I would never think you were a fool," he said. "Would you like to tell me what has happened, or would you rather not?"

She took his hand that held the dirty handkerchief, and held it in her own. "I've told you most of it," she said miserably. "Mummy had bronchitis and asthma, and she died."

A flicker of technical interest lightened his concern for her. "Was she ill when you came away from England?"

"She was always ill in the winter," the girl said. "Not very ill, you know, but not too good. She didn't go out much in the worst winter months. I never thought that she was in any danger, or I wouldn't have come away."

He nodded, thinking of cases he had known in the camps of

214

Germany; a small additional strain or an infection, and the heart would give out, somewhat unexpectedly. "The paper says that it has been a very bad winter in Europe."

She said listlessly, "I suppose that's it."

They sat in silence for a minute or two. Carl Zlinter sat staring through the trees down at the river, sparkling in the afternoon sunlight, thinking of the blank space that would be coming in his life when she had gone. "Tell me, Jenny," he said at last, "have you got any brothers and sisters?"

She knew what was in his mind, and she shook her head. "I'm the only child. I've got to go home, Carl. I spoke to Daddy last night on the telephone and told him I was coming right away. I never should have come out here at all."

"It was a very good thing for me that you did," he said quietly. There was a pause, and then he asked her, "Did you really speak to your father, to England, from Leonora station?"

She nodded. "Mr. Dorman said it could be done, and he arranged it all. The call came through at about four in the morning, six in the evening at home; I could hear Daddy quite well. It only cost three pounds . . ." She paused. "The Dormans have been awfully kind, Carl. I hadn't got quite enough money left to go home by air, and it would have taken months to get a passage home by sea. They wouldn't hear of me going any other way. They're driving me to a place called Albury tomorrow to get the train for Sydney, and Jane's coming with me to Sydney to see me off in the aeroplane. They couldn't have been kinder."

He looked down into her face. "Are you quite sure that it is the best thing for you to go back?" he asked. "Could not your father come here from England, to join you?"

She shook her head. "I thought of that, of course," she said, "and I tried to see it that way, but it wouldn't work. Daddy's been in practice in Leicester all his life. He doesn't like the new Health Service, but he'd never leave Leicester at a time like this. You haven't met my father, Carl. He and my mother were so wrapped up in each other, he'll be absolutely lost, for a time, anyway. But in Leicester he's got all his interests, and his friends in the Rotary Club, and the Conservative Club, and the Masons, and the British Medical Association, and all the other things he does. He'll be all right there once he's got over the first shock, if I'm there to look after him and run the house. He couldn't leave all his friends on top of this, and come out here to a strange place where he knows nobody. It wouldn't be fair to ask him."

"But you," he said. "Would you rather live in England, or live here?"

"I'd rather live here, of course," she said. "There's no comparison. It's a pity I ever came out here and saw this country, since I've got to go back."

"It was a very good thing for me," he said again.

She pressed his hand. "I'm sorry, Carl. It's just one of those things."

They sat together in silence for a time; she had told him everything now, and he had to have time to digest what he had heard. Presently he asked her, "Do you think you will ever come back to Australia?"

"I shall try," she said thoughtfully. "That's all I can say, Carl, I shall try. There may be a war and we may all get atom-bombed in England, or there may not be enough money for me to get back here." She paused. "If the Health Service keeps on getting worse for doctors it might be possible to get Daddy to think about trying it out here, but he's nearly sixty, and that's awfully old to uproot and leave everything and everyone you know. I don't believe I'll ever be satisfied again with England, after seeing this. I shall keep trying to get back here, Carl. I can't say if I'll ever manage it."

His hand caressed her shoulder. "Do you know what would have happened if you had stayed here for another year?"

She looked up at him. "What?"

He said, "I should have got a job as soon as I was free from the camp, and then I should have asked if you would marry me."

She sat motionless in his arms, not looking at him, staring down towards the river. "What sort of job, Carl?"

He shrugged his shoulders. "I do not know. In a business office, perhaps. Any sort of job that would give enough money to be married on." He paused, and then asked gently, "What would you have said?"

"I don't know, Carl." She looked up at him, unsmiling. "One doesn't always do the right thing. I suppose I'd have said yes. I'd like to think that I'd have had the guts to say no."

"Why do you say that, Jenny?"

She saw pain in his eyes. "Maybe it's a good thing that I'm going back to England, after all," she said wearily. "I'd hate to think of you taking any sort of job, just so that you could get married. I'd hate to be the girl that did that to you." She freed herself a little from his arm and turned to face him. "You ought to be a doctor again, Carl. I know it means another three years in a medical school, and I know you haven't got the money. Maybe you haven't tried very hard yet. But if you gave up medicine and just took any sort of job to marry me—well, I wouldn't like myself very much. With your ability, you ought to be a doctor or a surgeon."

"It is not possible," he said quietly. "I have thought of this many times. For me to be a doctor means three years' training in a medical school again. It would cost at least fifteen hundred pounds, and I have not got one tenth part of that money. It would mean that I would be nearly forty years old before I could work in Australia as a doctor. I know it is a waste of my experience, but wars bring much waste in the world, and this is part of it. I shall never be a doctor again."

"I think you will," she said. "I don't believe you'd be happy in any other sort of job, starting at your age."

They sat in silence for a time. At last he asked quietly, "Shall I ever see you again, Jenny?"

She did not answer, but sat looking at the ground, and watching her he saw another tear escape and trickle down her cheek. He put his arm around her shoulders again and drew her close to him, and wiped it away with the sweaty handkerchief. "I am sorry," he said. "I should not have asked that question."

She raised her face. "That's all right," she said. "It was right to ask it, Carl—one's got to face up to things. I'm going back where I belong, twelve thousand miles away upon the other side of the world, and it may be years before I manage to get back to Australia again. You've got another nine months to do in the camp, and after that you'll have no money and nothing to bring you to England."

"I would come to England, somehow, if I thought that you would want to see me there," he said.

"I'd always want to see you," she said simply. "We've not known each other very long, Carl. We don't know each other very well. If everything had gone right for us and you had wanted to marry me in a year's time, I'd probably have been a very happy person. But things haven't gone right for us, and maybe it's just as well. While you're on your own, living as a single man, you'll have a chance, somehow, somewhere, to get to be a doctor again. With a wife and perhaps a baby on your hands, you wouldn't have a hope. You'd have to take just any sort of job that offered, whether it suited you or not. I don't believe that you'd be happy. I don't believe that I'd be happy if I married you upon those terms."

He looked down at her, smiling gently. "I thought that I knew what you were like, what sort of a person you are," he said. "I now find that I know nothing about you, nothing at all."

"That's what I said," she replied. "But that doesn't alter the fact that we might have been very happy if we'd married."

He sat staring down at the river, rippling in the sun over the white stones, holding her in his arms. "I would like to think that we shall meet again before we are too old," he said. "I know that what you have said is true, and that you are now to go twelve thousand miles away to the other side of the world. Perhaps it is not very likely that we shall see each other again. But I am older than you, Jenny, and I have learned this; that if you want something very badly you can sometimes make it happen. I want very badly to find you again, before we have both forgotten the Howqua valley and each other. May I write to you sometimes?"

She said, "If you do, Carl, I shall be nagging at you all the time about becoming a doctor again."

"You may do that," he said quietly. "A doctor in this country could save enough money to get to England."

They sat almost motionless after that for a long, long time, perhaps a quarter of an hour; they had said all that there was to say. At last she stirred in his arms and sat up, and said,

"You'll go on building your cabin here just the same, Carl, won't you?"

He was doubtful. "I am not now sure. It will cost some money even if I get the timber very cheap from Mr. Forrest, and I may need all the money I can save."

She said, "I think you ought to go on with it, Carl. You've got another nine months in the camp, and after that it will be somewhere cheap for you to come for a holiday. Write and tell me how you're getting on with it, and what it's like."

"If I go on with it," he said, " I shall always hold the memory of you, and of this day when first we found this place of Charlie Zlinter's."

She smiled faintly. "Go on with it, then. I wouldn't like you to forget about me too quickly."

Presently he asked her, "Before I take you back to Leonora, will you tell me some things about your home, Jenny? So that I can imagine where you are when I shall write to you?"

"Of course, Carl," she said. "What sort of things?"

"This Leicester," he said. "You told me once that it was rather ugly. Is it damaged by the war?"

"It didn't get bombed very much," she said. "Not like some places. Nobody could call it beautiful, though. It's an industrial city, mostly boots and shoes. It's rather ugly, I suppose. I don't think anyone would choose to live there if they hadn't got associations, or a job."

"Is there beautiful country outside the city?" he asked.

She shook her head. "It's all just farming country, as flat as a pancake, rather grey and foggy in the winter."

"Do you live in the city, or outside it?"

She said, "We live in a house about a mile and a half from the centre of the city," she said, "in a fairly good part, near the university. It's a suburban street of houses in a row, all rather like the one next-door. It's not far from the shops. I shall have nothing very interesting to tell you in my letters, Carl, because very interesting things don't happen to women who keep house in Leicester. But I'll do my best."

"One other thing," he said. "There is so much I ought to know about you, that I do not know. When is your birthday?"

She said laughing, "Oh, Carl! It's in August, the twenty-fifth. And I'm twenty-four years old, in case you want to know. When is yours?"

"On June the seventeenth," he said, "and I am thirty-six years old. I am too old for you, Jenny."

"That's nonsense," she said quietly. "We've got enough difficulties without that one." She paused. "There's so much we ought to know about each other, and so little time to find it out. I can't even think of all the things that I shall want to know."

"It will be something to put into the letters from Leicester," he said. "All the things you want to know about me."

He stood up, and drew her to her feet. "I am going to take you home now, Jenny," he said, "back to Leonora. We have said everything there is to say, and you are very tired. Tomorrow you must start and travel for six days across the world. Before we say goodbye, will you promise me two things?"

"If I can," she said. "What are they?"

"I want you to go straight to bed when you get back to Leonora station and sleep."

She pressed his hand. "Dear Carl. I've got some packing to do, but I think there'll be time in the morning. Yes, I'll go to bed. What's the other one?"

"I want you to remember that I love you very much," he said.

"I'll always do that, Carl."

He left her then, and took the spade and the pick down the hill to return them to Billy Slim; she watched his lean form striding down the hill. She was so tired that she could think of nothing clearly; she only knew that she loved him, and that he was much too thin. She sank down on the grass again and sat there in the dappled sunlight under the great trees, in a stupor of misery and weariness.

When he came back to her he was calm and matter-of-fact; he picked up the basket and the grill, and raised her to her feet. "I am going to take you home now, Jenny," he said. "You have long travelling ahead of you, and I have very much work. We shall neither of us help ourselves or help each other by mourning over our bad luck."

She smiled weakly. "Too right, Carl." And then she said, "I've only been three weeks in this country, but I'm getting to speak like an Australian already."

"We are both of us Australians by our choice," he said. "Some day we shall be truly Australians, and live here together."

They walked up the steep rutted track through the woods slowly, hand in hand, not speaking very much; his calm assurance comforted her, and now the years before her did not seem so bleak. They walked steadily, not hurrying, not pausing; at the end of an hour they came to the old Chevrolet utility parked in Jock McDougall's paddock.

He put the basket in the back of the utility, and turned to her, and took her in his arms. "This is where we have to say good-bye for a little time," he said. "Perhaps it will not be for very long. We are both young and healthy, and for people as we are twelve thousand miles may not be quite enough to keep us apart. We will not stay here long, because we have said everything now to each other, and you are very tired. Other things we can say by letters to each other."

She stood in his arms while they kissed for a minute or two; then he released her, and with no more spoken he put her into the utility, and got in beside her, and drove down the track towards the highway and Leonora station.

They came to the station half an hour later; she got out and opened the three gates; at the end they drove into the yard by the homestead. He stopped the car by the kitchen door. "We will make this very short now," he said in a low tone. "Good-bye, Jenny."

She said, "Good-bye, Carl," and got out of the car, and forced a smile at him, and went into the house. He turned back to the car, expressionless, and took the basket and put it on the edge of the veranda, and got into the car again and drove it into the shed where it belonged. He hesitated for a moment, wondering whether he should go into the house to see the Dormans, and decided against it; he would come in one evening in a few days' time to thank them for the use of the car, after Jennifer had gone. He took his grill and the measuring tape and the wire pegs from the back of the utility and made for the yard gate. He turned the corner of the house, and Jack Dorman was there, sitting on the edge of the veranda, waiting for him.

He paused, and said, "I have put the Chev back in the shed, Mr. Dorman. It was very kind of you to lend it. I do not think that we shall need to borrow it again."

"Jenny told you she was going back to England?" The grazier held out his packet of cigarettes; the Czech took one and lit it. "She has told me that," he said.

"Too bad she's got to go back after such a short stay in Australia," Jack Dorman said.

"It is bad luck," Carl Zlinter said, "but she is doing the right thing, and it is like her to decide the way she has."

"That's right," the grazier agreed.

They smoked in silence for a minute. "What are you going to do yourself," Jack Dorman asked at last. "Got another nine months in the woods, haven't you?"

The other nodded. "After that, I will try to be a doctor again. I will go and see Dr. Jennings very soon, I think, and talk to him, and find if it is possible. If I may not be a doctor here, I will try other countries. In Pakistan I could be a doctor now, at once, but I do not want to live in Pakistan. I want to live here."

"It'ld be quite a good thing to start off with Dr. Jennings," the grazier said thoughtfully. "He thinks a lot of what you did with those two operations."

"He was very friendly to me at the inquest," the Czech said. "I will go and talk to him, for a start."

The grazier got slowly to his feet. "Come along and see us now and then, and let's know how you're going on," he said. "If you need a car to get around in, there's the Chev any time."

Carl Zlinter said, "It is very kind of you, but I would not like to use your car."

"We've got three cars on the station now," the grazier said, "and I'm getting a fourth, a Land Rover. We shan't miss the Chev if you take it. If you're going to be running in and out of town on this doctoring business, you don't want to be stuck for a car."

"It would be a great help, certainly."

"You'd better get yourself a licence," said Jack Dorman. "There's no sense in running foul of the police. You can come and take the Chev when you want it."

Next day, in the afternoon, he drove a white-faced rather silent Jennifer with his wife to Albury to catch the Sydney express, a matter of a hundred miles or so. He said good-bye gruffly to Jennifer at the station and turned his Ford for home. He got back to Banbury by five o'clock, hot and thirsty, and ready for a few beers; he parked under the trees and went into the saloon bar of the Queen's Head Hotel.

It was full of his grazier neighbours, and old Pat Halloran, and Dr. Jennings. He crossed to the doctor and drank a beer or two with him, slaking the dust from his dry throat. Presently he said, "I had a talk with Splinter yesterday, Seems like he wants to be a doctor again after his time's up."

"He came to see me today," the doctor said. "I told him that I'd write to the secretary of the B.M.A. in Melbourne about him, but I don't know that I'll do much good. The Medical Registration Board have made these rules, and that's all about it."

"It's a pity," said the grazier. "He tells me that he's going to leave Australia if he can't be a doctor here. Seems like he can practise in Pakistan on the degrees he got in his own place."

"I wouldn't be surprised," the doctor said drily. He paused, looking at his glass of beer, in thought. "He didn't tell me that," he said. "I could put that in my letter, perhaps."

"How's the chap with the fractured skull going on?"

"He's getting on fine. Zlinter took the most appalling risks with him, operating under those conditions. I suppose he couldn't do anything else. Anyway, the patient's going on all right. He's been conscious for some days now, and he seems to be completely normal mentally. I'm going to put that in my letter, of course."

"We should have a job for a bloke like that," the grazier said. "It seems all wrong that he should have to go to Pakistan."

"Well, yes—with reservations," Jennings said. "He's probably a very gifted surgeon. That sort of skill seems to be born in people—either you can do it or you can't, and if you can't you'd better leave it alone. At the same time, there may be very

221

big gaps in his knowledge and experience that we don't know about. There's only one place to check up on that, and that's in a teaching hospital."

"It needn't take three years, though," said the grazier.

"Well, perhaps not. I don't know much about it, Jack. Maybe they make exceptions in a case like this; maybe they don't. I'm going down to Melbourne in a fortnight's time, and I'll look in and see the secretary."

"I'd like to know how it goes on," the grazier said. He paused, and took a drink of beer. "There's another thing," he said, "and that's that he hasn't got any money. I wouldn't mind helping a bit if that was the only thing."

The doctor glanced up. "That's very generous of you."

"Aw, look," Jack Dorman said, "you know how it is with wool these days. The wife likes him, and Jenny likes him; he's right. If everything else was set, I wouldn't want to see the thing go crook because of the money. Keep that under your hat, though; I haven't told him, and I don't intend to for a while."

"You wouldn't mind if I told the secretary, though?" the doctor said. "It all helps to build a case up, if one can say that local people are prepared to put up money. It's another thing."

"You can tell him that," the grazier said. "I'll drop in and talk to him myself if they want any kind of sponsor. But don't let Zlinter know, so long as you can help it. Much better let him manage it his own way, if he can."

On Saturday evening, five days later, the doctor posted his letter to the secretary of the British Medical Association. In his overworked routine he had little time for correspondence, and he had little practice in setting out a careful, reasoned letter. He finished a draft on Wednesday; he rewrote it on Friday, and copied it out and posted it on Saturday, feeling that if he worked upon it any longer he would make it worse.

On Saturday evening, Carl Zlinter slept at Billy Slim's house in the Howqua valley, tired with a day of strenuous work. He had driven out that morning in a truck belonging to the timber company to deposit his load of sawn lumber and a hundred bricks in Jock McDougall's paddock. From there he had walked down to the forest ranger's house to borrow a horse and sledge, and he had trudged up and down the hill all day transporting his building materials down to the flat where Charlie Zlinter's house had been. He had driven himself hard for ten hours, haunted by the memory of Jennifer at each turn of the road, giving himself little time for grief. By nightfall he had got all his stuff down to the site, and he was glad to pack up, and go and grill his steak upon the forest ranger's fire, and chat with him for a short time before the sleep of sheer exhaustion.

On that same Saturday evening, Jennifer Morton drove in the coach from London Airport to the airways termini at Victoria, dazed and unhappy in the London scene. A thin February drizzle was falling, and the air was damp and raw after the hot Australian summer. She had bought a copy of the *Evening Standard* at the airport and had glanced at the headlines, after which the paper lay unheeded in her lap. The meat ration was down to matchbox size, and was to be increased in price, the Minister for War had made a foolish speech, and the Minister for Health an inflammatory one, full of class prejudice. She knew it all so well, and she was so tired of these people, tired, tired, tired of everything that she had come back to. It was a terrible mistake, she felt, to go out of England if you had to come back. It was far better to stay quietly at home and do the daily round, and not know what went on in other, happier countries.

She was too tired to go on to Leicester that night although she could have done so, too miserable to face her father in his grief till she had mastered her own troubles and grown more accustomed to the English way of life. She took a taxi from the airways terminal to St. Pancras station and got a room for the night at the St. Pancras Hotel, a clean, bare impersonal hotel room, but warm, and with a comfortable bed. Her head was still swimming with the vista of the countries she had flashed through, her stomach still upset with irregular meals served at strange hours and in strange places. She could not eat anything; she threw off her clothes and had a bath and went to bed, and lay for a long time listening to the clamour of the London traffic, crying a little, mourning for the brown foreigner she loved and for the clear, bright sunlight of the Howqua valley.

On Sunday morning Carl Zlinter got up at dawn and went up early to the flat among the gum trees, and stood for a few minutes planning his work. He decided that it was not practical to place his house exactly where the other one had been; he would move it laterally about a foot to clear the charred stumps of the old posts. He came to the conclusion that he would build the brick chimney first and make the wooden house to suit the chimney; for an inexperienced builder it would be easier that way. He marked out the foundations for the chimney with thrusts of his spade and considered the stone slab, reputed to weigh four hundredweight. It now lay more or less where the fire was to be; it would have to be moved back about three feet, and to one side. He went back to the forest ranger's house to borrow his crowbar, resolved to work all day and exorcise his troubles with fatigue again.

On Sunday morning Jennifer Morton came by train to Leicester station and left her two suitcases in the cloak-room for her father to pick up in the car, and walked in a fine, misty rain up the grey length of London Road to her home by Victoria Park. She pushed the familiar front door open and walked into the narrow hall; it now seemed small and rather mean to her. She opened the drawing-room door and caught her father just getting up out of his chair at the sound of her step, and realised that he had been asleep. He looked older than when she had gone away about ten weeks before, and the room was dirty, and the tiny fire of coal was smoking.

His face lit up when he saw her. "Jenny!" he cried. "I was waiting by the telephone, because I thought you'd ring from London."

She crossed to him and kissed him. "Poor old Daddy," she said softly. "I'm back now, anyhow. I wish to God I'd never gone away."

Eleven

JENNIFER soon found that she had a full-time job ahead of her in Leicester. In the last fortnight of her mother's life the house had been in complete confusion, with a nurse living in; because of the extra work the domestic who came in each morning had given notice and left, and it had proved impossible to replace her. The hospital nurse, as nurses will in an emergency, had done cleaning and house-keeping for her patient, jobs which were no part of her duties; since she had left, little had been done within the house. Jennifer's father had been greatly overworked in that grey winter season, and in the crisis he had taken all of his meals out after the funeral and the house had been let go; it was dirty and uncared for, and her mother's bedroom was still full of all her clothes and personal belongings. On top of that her father was working fourteen hours a day and requiring meals at irregular hours, and every day at surgery hours Jennifer had to monitor innumerable patients who came for a prescription of a few tablets of aspirin on the Health Service, or a certificate from her father exempting them from work. Until she came to do the job herself, Jennifer had not realised how great a burden can be thrown upon a doctor's wife in the English system of State medicine without staff and buildings adapted for the crowds of patients.

As she had realised, the loss of his wife had made an enormous gap in her father's life. She found him distracted and morose, and with a morbid interest in her mother's grave, and the choice of the tombstone, and the text to go on it. At first she fell in with these interests because they seemed to be the only ones he had, but presently she came to feel that the continual walks up to the cemetery were not good for him, and started to try to get him interested in other things. They dined several times at a hotel and went to the pictures, but neither of them enjoyed these evenings very much. Edward Morton wasn't greatly excited by the cinema, and both of them disliked the poorly-cooked and standardised meals at the hotel.

Presently she found that when her father managed to get free from patients to go to his club for a game of bridge before dinner he came back relaxed and cheerful from good company and whisky, and she began managing the patients to contrive that he should get at least two of these evenings a week. She came to look with some resentment at the surgery patients with their trivial requirements for free medicine and their endless papers to be signed. The bottom was reached, for her, when a man came for medicine and a certificate exempting him from work because he couldn't wake up in the morning.

Presently she extended these activities, and by disciplining the patients with a sarcastic tongue she managed to free her father for lunches of the Rotary Club, for dinners of the organisations he belonged to, and even for an occasional game of bowls as summer came on. Patients began to shun this cynical, bad-tempered, red-haired girl who thought so little of their rights to free aperients and said rude things about the forms that they brought to be signed by the doctor, and they began to transfer their allegiance and their capitation fees to more accommodating practitioners, which Jennifer thought was a very good thing. With the closer insight that she now had into her father's finances she was coming to the conclusion that he could do a good deal less work and still be comfortably solvent. She was distressed to find how much he had been saving for her mother in case he had died first, and how restricted his own life had been in consequence. She was staggered to find how much her mother's illnesses had cost, how much her father had been paying out in life insurance premiums for her security.

She got him to surrender two of the policies in June.

She had no close friends in Leicester, having worked in London for some years. The two or three girls with whom she had been intimate at school had married and gone away, and though she had a number of school acquaintances in the district she did not bother much with them. She felt herself to be a transient in her own home town, and though she had only been in Australia for about a month, she felt herself to be far more Australian than English in her outlook. Controls that she had once accepted as the normal way of life now irritated her; it infuriated her when she neglected to order coal before the given date and so lost two months' ration of the precious stuff. Studying to make meals more interesting for her father, she thought longingly of the claret that Jack Dorman bought in five-gallon stone jars for seven shillings a gallon, and of unlimited cream; the ration books perplexed her, and meat was a continual, bad-tempered joke.

She did her best to conceal these feelings from her father; she had not come home to England to distress him by whining about a better country on the other side of the world. All his friends and all his interests were in Leicester, and her job was to make the best of it. She was not entirely successful in her efforts; Edward Morton was no fool, and as the grief at his wife's death abated he began to take more interest in his daughter. The frequent air-mail letters that she never discussed with him showed that her interests were very far away, and the fact that most of them were in a continental hand-writing intrigued him; he was quite shrewd enough to realise that in the few weeks she had spent out there a man had come into her life. He set himself to draw her out one evening, sitting by the fire when they had done the washing-up.

"What's it really like out in Australia, Jenny?" he enquired. "Is it very different from this? I don't mean physical things, like food and drink. What's it really *like?*"

She sat staring down at the socks that she was darning.

"It's very like England in most ways," she said. "The people out there think of everything in terms of England. I believe they think more of the King and Queen than we do. England seems to mean an awful lot to them. I don't know how to tell you what it's really like. It's like England, only better."

He sat digesting this for a minute or two. "Is it like Ethel Tre-hearn thought that it would be, like England was half a century ago?"

"Not really," she said slowly. "There aren't the servants and the social life that she was thinking of. All that's quite different. But out there you feel perhaps it may be rather like the England she was thinking of, essentially. If you do a good job you get a good life." She raised her eyes. "It's all so very *English,*" she said. "When they make some money, they spend it in the sort of way we'd spend it, if we were allowed to make any and if we were allowed to spend it."

"You didn't feel as if you were a stranger there?"

She shook her head. "I never felt as if I was a stranger."

He filled and lit his pipe. "Meet any doctors out there?"

"I met one," she said.

"They don't have any Health Service there, do they?"

"I don't think so," she said. "There's no panel even, like we used to have. I think there may be some sort of a voluntary insurance scheme, but I'm really not very sure, Daddy."

"Are there enough doctors to go round? Too many, or too few?"

"Far too few, I think. That's in the country, where the Dormans live. I don't know about the towns."

He sat in silence for a minute, thinking it over. "This doctor that you met—do you know what he charged a visit?"

"I don't know—he wasn't in practice." There was no harm in telling him, and it might make things easier between them than if she were to keep up an unnecessary concealment. "He was a D.P., a Czech doctor who's not on the register. He's the one who keeps writing to me."

"Oh. I wasn't trying to be nosey, Jenny."

"I know you weren't. I don't mind telling you about him."

"What's his name?"

"Carl Zlinter," she said. "They call him Splinter in the lumber camp. All D.P.s have to work where they're directed for two years when they first come to Australia; he works at cutting down trees. He graduated at Prague, and then he was a surgeon in the German Army in the war."

He opened his eyes; this daughter of his had certainly wandered far from Leicester. "How did you meet him, Jenny?"

"There was an accident with a bulldozer in the forest," she said. "I was with Jack Dorman; we came along just after it had happened." She could smell the aromatic odours of the gum tree forest, and feel the hot sunshine in her memory. She stared into the fire, too small for coal economy to warm the room. "Two men were hurt very badly, one with a foot trapped under the bulldozer that had to be taken off upon the spot, and one with a fractured skull. There was nobody to do anything about it but Carl, and no woman to act as nurse but me, so he asked me to help him with the amputation and the trephine. He did both of them beautifully, but then the man with the amputation got hold of a bottle of whisky and got fighting drunk, and died. There was a fearful row about it, because Carl wasn't on the register, of course."

Her father was deeply interested; in all his medical experience such a situation had never arisen in Leicester. He asked a number of questions about the operations and the treatment but refrained from more personal enquiries, and Jennifer did not take the story further than the medical side. Her father had enough information to digest without telling him about the lost township of Howqua, and Charlie Zlinter and his dog. All she said was, "Working with him like that kind of broke the ice. He writes to me still."

Her father smiled. "I imagine that you couldn't be too distant after getting yourselves into a scrape like that." Jennifer's mother had been a nurse; his mind went back to the day when he had met her first, at St. Thomas's, when he was a medical student; he had stepped back suddenly and made her drop a thermometer, which broke, and then he had to pacify the sister and explain that it was his fault. Medicine was strong in Jennifer's family, but it was a pity that she had got mixed up with a foreigner who wasn't on the register.

Jennifer kept up a correspondence with Jane Dorman, largely about Angela's coming visit to England; with some reluctance the Dormans had decided to let her go and take a job in the old country provided that she had a job lined up to go to before leaving Australia, and they had booked a passage for her for the following January. Jennifer and her father went to some trouble over this, and finally got the promise of a job for her at St. Mary's Hospital in Paddington and put her down for a room in a hostel for young women in Marylebone; they were rewarded by an ecstatic letter from Angela and a steady flow of food parcels from Jane. Tim Archer wrote rather a depressed letter about all this to Jennifer, who told him in reply that he had nothing much to worry about; in her opinion Paddington would probably cure Angela of her obsession in about two years, and what he had to do was to get himself a grazing property within that time.

From Jane she heard about her oil painting. Stanislaus Shulkin had painted a picture of the main street of Banbury in glowing sunset light, which Jane liked for its glorious colours and Jack Dorman liked for its exactitude and because it showed the Queen's Head Hotel. It now hung in the kitchen of Leonora homestead, and in planning the new house Jane Dorman was making a special place for it where she could see it as she sat before the fire. It had been much admired in the neighbourhood, and Mr. Shulkin had got commissions from two of their station neighbours who had come to the conclusion that a thing like that was rather nice to have about the house.

"I don't know what he's done with the portrait he was doing of you," Jane wrote. "He told me that he couldn't finish it because you'd gone away, and anyway, he said it wasn't any good. I asked him once if I could see it because I never saw it at all, but he turned all arty and said that he never showed unfinished work to anyone. My own belief is that Splinter's got it, but I don't know that; perhaps you do."

Of Carl Zlinter she said, "We see him about once a month; he came here to tea on Sunday. Dr. Jennings wrote to the British Medical Association about getting him on the register in less than three years, and Carl has been to Melbourne twice for interviews. He thinks he'll probably get some concession, and he seems very anxious now to get on to the register and be allowed to practise in Victoria, but I don't know where the money's coming from to keep him while he studies. Jack told me to see if I could find out how he stood for money, and I tried to without asking the direct question, but he wasn't a bit receptive; apparently he thinks he can manage his affairs himself and of course it's much better if he can, but where the money's coming from I can't tell you. However, there it is, and he seems quite certain that he's going to be a doctor again; the only thing that seems to worry him is that it's going to be a long job, and that he'll be so old before he's able to set up a home."

Jennifer heard from Carl Zlinter at odd intervals, usually four or five times in a month. He wrote to her irregularly, and when the mood was on him; on one occasion she got three letters in a week, and then nothing for a fortnight. His letters contained few protestations of love; they were mostly factual accounts of what he had been doing, sometimes with touches of sly humour. As Jane had supposed, Jennifer knew all about her picture.

"I have your portrait hanging in my hut in the Howqua," he wrote, "and because I go there regularly even in this bad weather I see you every week-end. Last Saturday there were three inches of snow in Jock McDougall's paddock where we parked the Chev and I got my feet wet, but I had plenty of dry wood in the hut and we soon had a big fire going. Harry Peters was with me, the driver of the bulldozer who had the head injury that we operated upon. He is quite recovered now and is back on the job driving a truck, but I do not think he will be able to drive a bulldozer again safely. He does not want to; he wants to go to Melbourne and study metallurgy and get a job in a steel works, and I think he will be doing this before very long. In the meantime he comes out with me each week to Howqua."

Jennifer wondered what on earth they found to do in the Howqua valley in the snow; he had told her in a previous letter that the fishing season was over. Perhaps they worked upon the furnishings and details of the hut. . . .

"I had a great deal of trouble with Stan Shulkin over your picture because he did not want to give it to me; he said it was too good to give to Mrs. Dorman and he was going to keep it and put in an exhibition. I told him that you would certainly bring him to court if he did that without asking your permission, and I should go at once to the Police Sergeant Russell and tell him, and then he said that I could have it if I paid him for it. I told him that he was a very greedy man because Mrs. Dorman had paid him for three pictures, and then he said this was an extra that he had not shown to Mrs. Dorman. However, I got it from him in the end by promising to pay him when I became qualified as a doctor, and now it hangs in the hut at the Howqua, and I look forward all the week to going there to see it again."

He told her very little about his negotiations with the Medical Registration Board; throughout his letters there was a calm assurance that he would be a doctor again, but he had no definite ideas on how long it would take. He said once, "I am going to Melbourne again next week to see the M.R.B. and I think it may be easier to get into a hospital in England than in Melbourne because the Melbourne hospitals are very full of Australian students. I am thinking of booking a passage to England because it may take a long time to get a passage, and they will give back the money if you do not go."

Apparently he was not short of money, and this puzzled Jennifer a good deal. She asked in her next letter if he had really booked a passage to England, but he did not answer, nor did he answer when she asked a second time. She stopped asking after that; if he did not want to tell her things he need not; they were of different nationalities and from different backgrounds, and she knew that it would be a long time, if they ever married, before she understood him thoroughly. His letters were a great pleasure to her, and his calm assurance that all would be well was comforting.

In September she got a letter that thrilled her, and informed her at the same time. "It has been arranged for me here that I can study for the English medical degree at Guy's Hospital in London because there is no room in the Melbourne hospitals. I do not know how long it will be necessary for me to study and I do not think that they will tell me till I get there. I have passed two examinations in Melbourne since you left for England and these results are good in London; you see, I have been working very hard in the evenings at

Lamirra and at Howqua learning again in English all the text-book medicine I learned and forgot when I was a young man. So now they say that if I can get to England I may go to Guy's Hospital. I do not know how long I must work there before I become qualified, perhaps not more than a year and in any case I do not think longer than two years.

"So now I must come to England. There is a ship called the *Achilles* that is now loading sugar at Townsville in Queensland and I may be able to take a job on her as steward or on some other ship because this is the season when the sugar is sent to England. I may have to pay for the passage and if that is needed I will pay, but I have not got very much money so if I can work I would like it.

"I am leaving Lamirra at the end of this week to go by train to Townsville which I think will take three days. I am sorry to leave this place; it has been good for me after so many years in Camps in Europe to work for a time in the woods. I like this country very much, and when I am qualified to work as a doctor I would like much to come back to Banbury and work with Dr. Jennings if he has still no other doctor to help him.

"I am bringing your picture with me in a packing-case. I have asked Billy Slim to look after my hut at Howqua, and I have left him a little money for repairs, and if a window blows in or a sheet of iron on the roof comes loose he will mend it for me, so it will be there for me to have when I can come back to this country. And there for you also, I hope.

"I do not think that it will be possible for you to write to me again because I do not know what ship I shall go on, or when it will start or when I shall come to England. I will write to you to tell you these things as quickly as I know them, and I will come to Leicester to see you very soon."

She read this letter over and over again in the privacy of her bedroom. The sheer tragedy of her return to England was working out in comedy; Carl Zlinter was on his way to England and she would see him again. A picture came into her mind of the dynamic energy and competence of this dark, lean man that had produced this result and in so short a time. In a barrack hut at Lamirra, a hut similar to the one that he had operated in with her, smelling of washing and whisky and raw, unpainted wood, he had studied every night at medical text-books; he had then gone down to Melbourne and sat for two examinations in a language foreign to him in a strange place with strange people, and had passed them. Over and above this academic effort he had somehow or other financed himself, and he had negotiated and corresponded till he had secured himself a place in a hospital in England, twelve thousand miles away, a country that he had never been to, and an alien, enemy country. This man was shouldering his way through all these difficulties and brushing each of them aside in turn, because he wanted to practise as a doctor in the country of his choice, and because he wanted to marry her.

She could not possibly keep this news to herself. At dinner that night she said as casually as she could manage, "Carl Zlinter's coming to England, Daddy. He's going to re-qualify at Guy's."

He noted her shining eyes and her faint colour, and he was glad for this daughter of his, whatever changes there might be in store for him. "That's interesting," he said, equally casually. "How did he manage that?"

She told him, if not all about it, as much as she thought good for him to know. They discussed the matter for a quarter of an hour; in the end he asked:

"What's he going to do when he's qualified? Practise in England, in the Health Service?"

She shook her head. "I shouldn't think so. He wants to go back to Australia and practise at Banbury. There's a doctor there, Dr. Jennings—I told you about him. He's very overworked. Carl thinks Dr. Jennings might take him as an assistant if he can get qualified before anyone else gets in."

He was about to ask her if she would like to go back to Australia herself, but he stopped and said nothing; no sense in asking her a thing like that. He knew very well that if she were free of her responsibilities to himself she would never have come back to England; if this chap Zlinter were to ask her to marry him and go back with him to Australia, he could not possibly stand in her way.

For the first time the thought of going to Australia came into his mind as a serious possibility. Leicester without his wife was not the place it once had been for him. If Jennifer were to marry and go back to Australia he might have to choose between going with them and attempting to carry on alone in Leicester, where he had worked all his life and where all his friends were. It was not a thing to be decided lightly. He would hardly make many new friends at his age in Australia, but he would be desperately lonely if he tried to live alone at home in Leicester. In Australia he might do a little work, perhaps, and earn a little money, and so be able to come back to England every year or two to see his friends. . . .

Jennifer heard from Carl a week later that the *Achilles* had sailed without him and he was coming home upon a ship called the *Innis-fail*, probably sailing in about three days' time. "They will not take me as steward," he wrote, "and I shall have to pay for the journey, which is a very bad thing, but I shall have time to work; I have brought many medical books with me to read upon the journey. If I was qualified as doctor I could work as ship's doctor on the journey because they have difficulty in getting doctors now at Townsville, but although I have showed my Prague degree they will not acccept it because English ships must have an English doctor. When I am an English doctor I shall be able to practise anywhere in the world, I think."

She heard nothing more until she got an air-mail letter from Port Said nearly a month later. His ship had called for fuel at Colombo. "We do not go very fast," he said, "and although we have gone steadily all the time it has taken us thirty-four days to get to this place. I think we shall arrive in London in about another fortnight, and I must then find a place cheap to live near to the hospital. As soon as it is possible I will come to Leicester, but I cannot say what day that will be on."

He came to her on a Friday evening at the end of November. She had walked down to the chemist to pick up a parcel for her father; it was a fine, starry night with a cold wind that made her walk quickly. She was fighting her way back head-down against a freezing wind in the suburban street. She raised her head as she got near the house and saw a man peering at the houses in the half light of the street lamps, trying to read the numbers, perhaps looking for the doctor's plate upon the door. He was a tall man, rather thin, dressed in a foreign soft felt hat and in a shabby raincoat.

She cried, "Carl!" and ran to meet him. He turned, and said "Jenny!" and took both her hands. She dropped the parcel and something in it cracked as it fell; it lay unheeded at their feet as he kissed her. She said presently, "Oh, Carl! When did you get to England?"

He held her close, "We arrived on Tuesday," he said, "to the London Docks. I have found a room to live in, in Coram Street, in Bloomsbury, and I have been to the hospital yesterday, and I am to start working on Monday. I do not know how long it is that I shall have to work, but I think that it will be for one and a half years. I do not think it will be longer than that."

She said, "Oh, Carl—that's splendid! What are you doing now? Have you come for the week-end?"

He said, a little diffidently, "I did not know if it would be convenient if I should stay. I have brought a bag, but I have left it at the station in the cloak-room. Perhaps I could take a room at the hotel, and see you again tomorrow."

"Of course not, Carl. We've got a spare room here—I'll make up the bed. That's where we live," she said, nodding at the house. "Daddy's in there now—he wants to meet you." She stood in his arms, thinking, for a moment. "We've got such a lot to talk about," she said. "Daddy's got a meeting of the committee of the Bowls Club in our house tonight; he's the chairman or the president or something. Don't let's get mixed up in that. Would you mind if we go out and have a meal, some place where we can talk? They finish about nine o'clock generally. We can come back then, and you can meet Daddy."

He smiled down at her. "Of course," he said. "Whatever you will say is good for me."

"Wait here just a minute," she said. "I'll go in and put this parcel down, and tell Daddy what we're doing." She vanished into the house and he stood waiting for her on the pavement. In the dining-room her father was laying out the table with paper and pencils before each chair for the Bowls Club meeting; when this happened they had their evening meal at the kitchen table.

She came to him in her overcoat, flushed and bright-eyed. "Daddy," she said. "I got this parcel, and I dropped it and heard it crack; I believe I've bust whatever's in it. Carl Zlinter's here, and I'm going to make up the spare room for him. I'm going out to dinner with him now, and we'll be back when this committee meeting's over. Could you get your own meal, do you think? It's sausages; they're in the frig, and there's half of that jam tart we had for lunch the day before yesterday on a plate in the larder."

He smiled at her excitement, his concern over the parcel half forgotten. "That's all right," he said. "What have you done with him?"

"He's outside waiting for me."

"Well, bring him in, and let's say how-do-you-do to him."

"Not now," she said. "I'll bring him in when your committee's over, when you've got time to meet him properly. We'll be back about half-past nine or ten."

She whisked out of the room, and the front door slammed behind her. She left her father unpacking the parcel and smiling thoughtfully; changes were coming to him again, whether he liked it or not. Jennifer joined Zlinter underneath the street lamp. "I know a little place where we can get a meal," she said. "Not like we'd have got in Australia, of course, but good for here. It's quiet there, and we can talk."

She took his arm and they went off together down the street, walking very close to each other. She took him to a café near the station, a frowsy place undecorated for some fifteen years, but reasonably warm inside, and cheap: she knew that he was short of money and she knew that he would never let her pay for her own meal. There was no meat on the menu, so they ordered fish pie and cabbage, with apple tart and custard to follow. And then they settled down, and talked, and talked, and talked.

They sat so long over their meal that the bored waitress began turning out the lights; they woke up to the fact that it was eight o'clock and the place was closing. Jennifer said, "We'll have to go, Carl."

He paid the bill, and helped her into her coat. He said, "Shall we go back to the station and get my bag, and take it to your house?"

"It's too early," she objected. "That blasted meeting won't be over yet, and there's no fire in the drawing-room . . . ." She thought for a moment. "There's a little picture theatre, Carl," she said. "It's a bit of a bug-house. It's showing one of those pictures the Americans make for South America, all gigolos and black-haired beauties dancing with tambourines—a perfect stinker. The house'll be half empty. If we go in there we can talk quietly, at the back of the circle."

They went there, and the flick was as she had described it, a noisy picture with plenty of orchestra and raucous singing. In the warmth of the circle, seated very close together, they gave no attention whatsoever to the screen. "Tell me one thing, Carl," she said when they were settled down, "what are you doing about money? You told me once that you wouldn't be able to get to be a doctor again because you'd never have enough money. Are things very difficult?"

He pressed her hand between his own. "I must be very careful," he said. "I have now about one thousand one hundred pounds, and on that I must live till I am qualified. Then I shall ask if you will marry me, and by that time I shall be quite broke."

"We'll manage somehow, Carl."

"I have not asked you yet," he observed. "I am only warning."

"And I'm warning you that if you don't look out, I might say, yes."

He leaned a little from her and undid his overcoat; he fished in an inside pocket and pulled out a little object. He put it in her hand. "It is for you," he said, "one day. Perhaps not yet."

She held it up to the reflected light from the Technicolor scene; it was a ring formed heavily of reddish gold with curious, cable-like markings around it. "Oh, Carl!" she said, "is this a wedding ring?"

He took it from her, "You go too quickly," he said. "It is an engagement ring, but it is not for you just yet. Not till I have met your father and he has said that he agrees."

"Well, let me see it, anyway. I promise I won't put it on."

He gave it back to her. "It's just like a wedding ring," she said. "It's gold, isn't it?"

"I know that an engagement ring, it should have precious stones," he said. "I could not afford to buy precious stones to put in it, Jenny. But this is solid gold, gold from the Howqua." He smiled down at her. "I know that it is very pure gold, because I made it myself."

She stared at him in the dim light from the screen. "You made it?"

"I made it," he replied. "Harry Peters showed me how to make a ring like this, or a bracelet of gold, or a pendant. He is the man who had the broken head, on who we did trephine. It is very lucky that we managed to save his life, or he could not have taught me how to do these things."

"But, Carl, where did you get the gold from?"

"It is Charlie Zlinter's gold," he told her quietly. "It would not be good for you to talk about this, perhaps, even here in England and on the other side of the world."

In the stuffy half light of the Midland cinema she stared up at him. "I won't say a word, Carl. Charlie Zlinter's gold?"

"There was a box," he said. "The box that Mary Nolan told you she had seen, a tin box that he called his ditty box. In this box he kept his valuables."

"That's right," said Jennifer. "When she went back to the cabin the morning he was drowned, the door was open, and she looked for the box to put it away for him, and she couldn't find it."

He nodded. "Charlie Zlinter had put it away before. He was not too drunk to look after his money."

"What do you mean?" she asked. "Where did he put it?"

He smiled at her. "He had a very simple place for his box, a place that would be safe from forest fires and thieves and anything. Perhaps only a very simple man, a sailor and a bullock driver, would have thought of such a simple place to keep his box, and yet that was so safe."

"Where was that, Carl?"

"Under the stone," he said. "The stone that weighed four hundredweight, that only he could lift. You remember the big stone we found together, on our last day in the Howqua?"

She could remember every detail of that day, and the sheer grief of it, and the sunshine, and the clean scent of the eucalypts, and the flashing reflections from the river down below, and the brilliance of the parrots in the woods. "Of course I do," she said. "Was the box under that?"

"It was under the stone," he said. "I found it only one week after you were gone to England, but I did not dare to say that in a letter. I think if it was known I had found gold it would be taken by the police, perhaps in England also, so you must not talk about it. I think that it is better that I use it to become a doctor."

"I won't say a word, Carl. How much gold was there?"

"There were fifty-two coins of one pound," he told her. "Sovereigns, they are called. Also, there was just over five pounds in weight of washed river gold, the gold dust that they find in the river beds, Billy Slim has told me that in Howqua this gold dust was used for money. The hotel would take it for payment, and they had little scales in the bar to weigh the gold with, how much it was worth. I think also the bullock driver, he took gold for payment, too, because in the box were little brass scales also. His gold dust was in two leather bags, one large bag and one small bag."

"Was he a relation of yours, Carl? Were there any papers to say who he was?"

He shook his head. "I do not know. The water had been lying in the hole beneath the stone, and the box was eaten away with rust. There had been papers once, but nothing was left, nothing that I could read. There was only the rusted sides and bottom of the box, and the two leather bags, rotten and with the gold spilling out from them, and the fifty-two gold coins lying in the rust, and the little scales." He paused. "I do not think that we shall ever know who Charlie Zlinter was."

"What a shame!" She sat thinking about it for a time, absently watching the coloured mime upon the screen. Presently she turned to him again. "You must have had a job lifting that stone, Carl," she said. "Did you have anyone to help you?"

He shook his head. "I was quite alone." He hesitated. "I might have had Billy Slim to help," he said. "It was lucky. It was the first time that I had been there since we said good-bye, and I was sad, and I went there to work very hard and to be quite alone, because it is good to work very hard when everything seems bad." She pressed his hand. "I had the timber for the house, and I borrowed Billy's crowbar, and I levered up each corner of the stone and put underneath a wedge of wood. It took nearly all the day to move it four feet back and make the new place for it, and then when it was moved away from the old hole I saw the box."

She asked him, "What did you do when you saw it, Carl? Were you terribly excited?"

He said quietly, "I was very sad that we had not found it together. I stood looking at the rusty pieces and the things in the hole, and I thought, 'That must be the box that Mary Nolan talked about,' and I was not at all excited. I was very sad that you had had to go away, and that you were not there to share the discovery with me."

She put her face up impulsively, and he leaned forward in the half light and kissed her. Presently she said, "What do you do with gold dust when you've got it, Carl? If you can't tell anybody about it?"

He smiled down at her. "There are several things that you can do with gold dust," he told her, "but they are all very wicked and if you are discovered you will go to prison. One way is that you can take out a licence to be a prospector for gold. Then you go camping up the river in deserted places, washing the gravel in a little pan to try to find gold. Presently you find it, and come back with it, and sell it to the bank."

She laughed. "Did you do that?"

"No," he said. "I thought that it would become complicated if they ask where I had found it."

"It might," she agreed. "Well, what did you do?"

"Another way," he said imperturbably, "is to build a little hut in the middle of the woods where nobody would ever think to go."

"Like the Howqua," she laughed softly.

"It could be like the Howqua," he agreed. "And you must have a friend, a good friend who thinks he has a debt to you, who understands metallurgy and how metals can be melted."

"Like Harry Peters," she observed. "I wondered why on earth you took him to the Howqua."

"It could be like Harry Peters," he agreed. "And there in the hut you make a little furnace with a cylinder of gas to heat a little crucible, and these things have to be hidden very carefully from Billy Slim."

"Oh, Carl!"

"And then," he said, "you bring many candles and you melt the wax, and you carve a bracelet out of candle-wax, or it could be a ring like this ring. And you put the wax bracelet in a pan of soft plaster of Paris and you let the plaster set till it is hard. And then you heat the plaster and the wax melts and runs out of a small hole you make, and so you have a mould in the middle of the plaster where the wax bracelet was. Then you pour in the melted gold and let it cool, and break the plaster away, and there is your bracelet or your ring, made of solid gold."

She looked up, laughing. "Is that how my ring was made, Carl?"

He pressed her hand. "I made that ring and a hundred and five bracelets, all in four week-ends."

"A hundred and five bracelets! What on earth did you do with them?"

"It is very tedious," he said. "You must take one bracelet and go to a jeweller in Melbourne, and to him you say that your Aunt Catherine has died who lived in the goldfields fifty years ago, and you have found this bracelet in her jewel box. And then you ask if he will buy it for the weight of the gold. The proper price is fifteen pounds for each ounce of the weight, but he will only give nine or ten pounds." He paused. "It is very slow and difficult, because it is not safe to go to more than two or three jewellers in each town. There is a better way, that I discovered very soon."

"What's that, Carl?"

He said, "This third way is very simple and very easy. You must wait till a ship from India, with an Indian captain, comes to Melbourne, and you wait until the captain comes on shore. You go then to the captain in the hotel and you say, Can I sell you my gold? In Bombay he can get thirty pounds for each ounce, but he must smuggle it out of Australia and into India."

"How much did he give you, Carl?"

"Eighteen pounds an ounce."

"And that's where the eleven hundred pounds came from?"

He nodded. "I think that it was worth the risk," he said, "because I wanted to come to England to see you, Jenny, and to be a doctor again."

"It was worth it, Carl," she said softly. "We'd better forget all about it now, and never talk of it again. We don't want anybody else to get to know about that gold."

They sat talking together in low tones till half-past nine, not paying the slightest attention to the picture. Then Jennifer stirred and looked at the clock by the screen, and she said, "Let's go home, Carl. That meeting must be over now, and Daddy will be waiting for us. We'll go round by the station and pick up your bag. Is it heavy to carry?"

He shook his head. "It is only for the night. I have not many clothes in any case. I must now buy some, but they must be cheap."

They went out of the theatre; in the vestibule they stopped to do up their coats. She took his arm and they went out into the street; in the darkness the freezing wind hit them with a blast. She felt his sleeve, and said, "Is this the thickest coat you've got, Carl?"

"I must get a thicker one," he said. "I had not thought that England would be cold like this. It is as cold as Germany."

They bent against the wind and walked quickly, arm in arm, to the London Road station. "Will you tell me one thing truthfully, Carl?"

"If I know the answer, Jenny," he said.

"Did you really have to come to England, Carl, to do your medical training? Couldn't you have done it in Australia, possibly?"

He looked down at her, smiling. "What questions you do ask!"

"You said you'd tell me."

"I could have done it in Australia," he said. "They grew so tired of seeing me in the office that at last they would have given me whatever I should want. I came to England because I wanted to find you again."

They turned into the bleak, shabby, covered cabway of the railway station, dimly lit for gas economy. "That's what I thought," she said. "It was very sweet of you to do that, Carl. To give up everything Australia has to offer and come back to Europe—after getting away once." She paused, and looked around her at the stained and dirty brickwork, at the antiquated building, at the wet streets in the blustering, windy night.

He laughed at her gently. "Australia is cold and wet in the winter," he said, "and there are dirty railway stations in Australia, too, and dirty streets."

They walked to the cloak-room and he handed in the ticket; they stood waiting while the porter went to fetch his bag. "Carl," she said. "Your hut up in the Howqua—that'll be all right, will it?" She looked up at him half fearful. "You don't think it's like the other Charlie Zlinter's hut, with a door swinging open and a green loaf in the cupboard, and a possum or a rat nesting in the bed?"

He pressed her arm. "I also thought of that," he said. "I left everything there very clean, with no bedclothes or cloths at all, and with insect powder sprinkled all over. Billy Slim is to go there once each week and light a fire and open all the windows, and he has money for repairs, also. It will be there clean and waiting for us when we can get back to it, when we can get away from Europe for a second time."

"We'll get back to it, all right," she said. "Some day, somehow, we'll get back there again."

THE END

239

www.vintage-classics.info